Susannah Morrow

Susannah Morrow

Megan Chance

WARNER BOOKS

An AOL Time Warner Company

Copyright © 2002 by Megan Chance
All rights reserved.

Warner Books, Inc., 1271 Avenue of the Americas, New York, NY 10020

Visit our Web site at www.twbookmark.com

 An AOL Time Warner Company

Printed in the United States of America

First Printing: October 2002
10 9 8 7 6 5 4 3 2 1

Library of Congress Cataloging-in-Publication Data
Chance, Megan.
    Susannah Morrow / Megan Chance.
       p. cm.
    ISBN 0-446-52953-2
    1. Salem (Mass.)—History—Colonial period, ca. 1600–1775—Fiction.   2. Trials
(Witchcraft)—Fiction.   3. Teenage girls—Fiction.   I. Title.

PS3553.H2663 F38 2002
813'.54—dc21   2001056874

To Kany, Maggie, and Cleo
Without you, there is no story

ACKNOWLEDGMENTS

I'd like to thank my family for their encouragement and support—both financial and emotional; the ever-wise Kristin Hannah, for her unswerving faith in me; Marcy Posner, who believed in this book from the first moment she saw it; Jamie Raab, whose editing and enthusiasm have restored my faith in the publishing business; and Frances Jalet-Miller, for her incisive and enlightening comments. Also deserving of thanks are Jill Barnett, whose generosity is unwavering—I owe her a huge debt; Liz Osborne and Jena McPherson, who traipsed the countryside and haunted bookstores for me, among other things; and Elizabeth DeMatteo, Melinda McRae, and Sharon Thomas, who restored my spirit more often than they know.

And finally, I'd like to thank Patricia Krueger, a truly inspiring teacher who went far above and beyond the call of duty, and Barbara Dolliver, who took the time every other Thursday to teach a fledgling writer her craft—to these two women, my thanks are long overdue.

From her side the fatal key,
Sad instrument of all our woe, [Sin] took;
. . . then in the keyhole turns
Th' intricate wards, and every bolt and bar
Of massy iron or solid rock with ease
Unfastens. . . .

She opened, but to shut
Excelled her power; [hell's] gates wide open stood . . .

—John Milton
Paradise Lost

Not to believe in witchcraft is
the greatest of heresies.

—Heinrich Kramer & James Sprenger
The Malleus Maleficium

PART ONE

CHARITY

—Delusion—

We walked in clouds, and could not see our way.

—John Hale
A Modest Enquiry into the Nature of Witchcraft

Chapter 1

———— ❧ ————

Salem Village, Massachusetts—October 22, 1691

I DREAMED THE BABY DIED.

The vision was still with me when I woke, sweating and uneasy, into a night gripped by a shrieking nor'easter. I told myself there was nothing to fear as I lay listening to the pine shakes on the roof clattering and creaking. The boughs of the great oak outside our front door crashed in the wind.

The room was cold, too dark even for shadows. In the trundle bed, my little sister Jude slept on, untroubled. But then, Jude was not like me; she did not hear souls screaming in the wind. She was only six, too young to know the horror a nor'easter could bring: animals lost and shattered houses, men drowned at sea. At fifteen, I knew all these things, and so the storm gave power to my dream.

I did not ignore premonitions. No one I knew did. God sent us signs all the time; 'twas a sin to scorn them. The wheat blight of a few years ago, the scourge of smallpox that raced through our town, a bird not nesting as it should . . . These were marks of His displeasure, and I was a good Puritan girl who knew to pay attention. But I did not know what to do about this one. I crept from bed, shivering as I worked my way by feel and memory toward the bedroom door. I was trying to decide whether to wake my mother, when I saw light come through the seams of the floorboards.

'Twas too early for anyone to be awake.

The floorboards were thin—a single layer only, with cracks between that gave a clear view of downstairs. I knelt at the widest of them, pressing my eye close to the floor to see. I saw my mother bending to the fire, and my father sitting at the nearby tableboard, pulling on his boots with hurried motions.

The wind howled, and before I knew it, I was out of the bedroom and hurrying downstairs.

I stopped on the bottom step and stayed in the shadows. My mother's back was to me as she laid a fire in the huge hearth, and my father was not looking in my direction as he protested in a quiet voice, ". . . I don't have time for that now, I'd best go if I'm to make it back today."

"'Tis not dawn yet," my mother said. "We've hours ahead of us." The flames leaped; she straightened and backed away, her huge belly outlined now in the light. She was not in labor, not yet. I sagged against the wall in relief. The baby was not due for another month, and everything was fine. It had only been a bad dream, no premonition.

Then she gasped. One hand went to her belly, the other clutched the mantel. I could not keep from crying out. Horrified, I put my hand over my mouth to stifle the sound. Too late. My parents both looked toward where I stood in the shadows of the stairs.

"Charity?" my mother asked softly. "Is that you, child?"

I hurried toward her. "Oh, tell me 'tis not the babe coming already."

My mother smiled. I knew she meant to be reassuring, but I saw her strain. I saw her hope and her fear. "Aye." She reached out and held me close enough that I felt the movement of the child through her skirt. Her hand rested lightly on my hair, and I closed my eyes, comforted at the feel of it, at her familiar smell—fire smoke and the mint and sugar she burned on the hearth to scent the room. She nodded to my father, who still sat at the table. "Your father's going to town."

I pulled away in confusion. "To town?"

"To fetch your aunt," Mama said gently. "The *Sunfish* came in yesterday. She's waiting."

I turned to my father. "W-what about the storm? Who's to fetch Goody Way? And the others?"

"You needn't worry about the storm," Father said. "You help your mother."

I felt panicked. "But I had a dream. . . ."

"Hush, hush," Mama said, reaching for me again. When I pulled away, she sighed. " 'Tis only the storm that has you so upset, child. There's no need to worry. Your father will wake Prudence Way before he goes. She'll bring the others. 'Twill all work out. 'Tis good you're awake. You can help with the groaning cake."

I looked to my father. "Can't Aunt Susannah wait another day? At least till the babe's born and the storm's passed?"

Father gave me a look I knew too well, the one that made me flush and stutter and wish I'd kept quiet in spite of my worry. 'Twas not my place to question him, and I looked away again, wanting still to protest, holding back my words.

My mother made a hiss of pain.

"Mama," I said, "you should sit down."

"Standing makes the child come faster," she said when she could breathe again, and then she smiled, but she glanced over at my father, and told him, "You'd best tell Prudence to come quickly."

He stopped. "Perhaps 'tis better if I stay, Judith. Your sister will wait another day."

"No, no," Mama said quickly. "Eighteen years have already passed. I'd not have another needless hour between us."

I held my breath, waiting for my father to remember Mama's other labors, the terrible small graves dotting the thick, wild grass of the burying ground. *He will refuse to go.* The storm was bad, and

Mama's labors were always so hard, and the babe was too early besides. I willed him to stay with all my strength.

"I'll do my best to hurry." He paused at the door, staring out the window as he grabbed his cloak and his hat. " 'Tis as if God put His hand over the sun," he murmured. Then, in a swirl of movement, he was out into the night, and my mother and I were left alone with the fire and the sizzle of rain falling down the wide chimney, while little drafts of wind sent the thin coarse linen of my chemise shivering against my legs.

"Get dressed, Charity," my mother said. "The storm will be over soon, and we've the baking to do."

As the hours passed into morning, and then into early afternoon, neither the storm nor my dread eased. Even when Goody Way showed with the other women from the village—windblown and shivering, soaked through to the skin—I was not reassured.

The women gathered around, eating groaning cake and drinking beer from the pewter tankards we'd set on the table, joking and exclaiming over how tall Jude had grown, but for me, a laying-in had long ago ceased to be a celebration, and I wanted them to go home. All I really wanted was for my father to come through that door again.

He should not have gone. We had not been expecting this aunt I'd never met for another two weeks at least; the *Sunfish* had made the journey from Dover more quickly than we'd imagined, especially for the time of year. It would not have hurt to make her wait.

My mother's pains grew slowly worse; I watched her carefully, waiting for the first sign that something had gone wrong. Experience had taught me that there was always a moment when everything turned, when things went bad, but even as the hours passed—nearly an entire day now, already suppertime again—and my mother's labor grew harder, and we moved into the parlor where the big bed she shared with my father loomed in the corner, that moment had not yet come. Goody Way had not yet started the slow, worried shaking of her head that had grown as familiar to me as the beating of my heart.

It grew late again, and I put little Jude to bed; she was a heavy sleeper, and Mama's screams would not wake her. The storm had begun to ease, and the women drifted away, one by one, fetched by their children or their husbands. Goody Way let them go, because Mama's labor was dragging on and on, and they could do no more good here. Without them hovering around, shooing me out of the way as if I were a small child instead of a woman nearly grown, I could come close to my mother again. I sat down beside the bed, holding her hand. She gripped my fingers tightly.

"The babe is fighting me," Mama said, smiling weakly at me. "It must know the sorrow of the world already."

"It sounds like a good strong boy," I said, hoping it was true. "I should like a brother, I think."

Mama started to smile, and then the pain gripped her, and instead she groaned; she squeezed my hand so hard it seemed my bones would pop beneath her grip. Sweat dripped down her face; her hair was wet and coarse with it.

"Can you walk again, Judith?" Goody Way asked from where she sat at the end of the bed, between my mother's spread legs. " 'Twould help."

Mama nodded and grabbed my arm, but the moment she was out of bed, her knees buckled, and I saw the sudden blot of blood color her chemise. I saw her belly ripple and misshape with the strain, and I knew. . . . This was the moment I'd feared. I glanced up and caught Goody Way's gaze, and there it was—the slow shake of her head—and I knew my dream was coming true. The babe was dying. I felt sick for the hope Mama had had for it. I did not know if she had the strength to bury another infant.

I helped my mother back into the bed, and tried to smile. I watched the window and saw only darkness beyond it, and prayed for the shape of my father's shadow. He did not come, and the hours kept passing, quiet save for the rain and my mother's groans.

Goody Way leaned down between my mother's legs, placing her hands hard on Mama's belly. "Try once more, Judith," she said, her voice hoarse with the effort of repeating it. My mother tried, but weakly. Her moan was nearly soundless.

"Please, Mama," I whispered.

Goody Way murmured a prayer before she sat back again, wiping her bloody hands on the towel lying at the end of the bed.

I stroked back the hair from Mama's face. "'Twill be all right, Mama." I had already said those words a dozen times. I looked up at the midwife. "Is there nothing more to do?"

"Anything else lies beyond my power, child," Goody Way said softly.

"What could be keeping Father? He's only gone to Salem Town."

Goody Way shrugged. "'Tis a black night. The roads'll be mud to the knee. And he's carrying another person. . . . 'Twill be slow going for his horse."

"He said he would hurry."

"Five miles to town and back again. Won't be much hurrying now, I'll warrant. Your aunt picked a fine time to arrive." Goody Way shook her head. Loose gray curls fell from her cap to shiver against her jaw. "Your papa can ill afford to be gone just now."

Mama groaned again. Her belly rippled—this time faintly, as though the babe inside were growing tired of the fight. Mama opened her eyes. "Is your father . . . ?" Her voice was so quiet it was like a breath.

I leaned close. "Hush, Mama, hush. He'll be here soon. Save your strength."

"No . . . 'tis too late for that. Is Jude . . . Is she abed already?"

"Aye."

"Don't wake her. Just . . . tell her . . ." Mama closed her eyes.

"Tell her what, Mama? Tell Jude what?"

"I fear . . . the babe and I . . . We are . . . both for God." I felt the pressure of my mother's fingers on mine, and I tightened my hold, suddenly afraid to let go. I had known the babe could die, but I had never thought to lose my mother.

"No, Mama. No—"

"Tell Jude . . . be good for your . . . father," she said. "You take . . . care of . . . her."

I tried to keep back my tears, but I felt them now on my cheeks, and my vision blurred. Blurred now, when I wanted so badly to see her clearly. "This is silly, Mama," I said. " 'Tis only a few hard hours. Father's coming. Any moment. He'll have Aunt Susannah with him—"

"He . . . loves you, Charity. You . . . remember that. And God . . . God loves you too. You must . . . cleave . . . to Him. 'If Christ hath . . .' "

If Christ hath no possession of thee, thou art possessed by the Devil. I heard the words that she was too weak to say. I knew them already without prompting. She had said them to me nearly every day these last months. I twisted her fingers in mine and said furiously, "Father will be here soon. He'll be here soon, Mama. Please."

My mother's groan sent the tendons in her throat into stark relief. Had she the power to release it, it would have been a scream. I looked desperately at the midwife.

Goody Way sighed. She heaved herself from the stool, leaving my mother's legs flung apart and straining. She crossed the room to the front window.

"What are you doing?" I cried. "Come back here."

" 'Tis in God's hands now. . . ." She bent to peer more closely out the glass. "Oh, thank the Lord—here they be." She threw the bloody towel to the floor and rushed to the door.

Relief made me light-headed. Father was back; nothing bad could happen now. He would not let Mama die.

"They're here, Mama," I whispered. "At last, they're here."

Goody Way flung the door open so hard it banged against the wall. "You'd best hurry, Lucas!" she called out, and the wind whipped her voice right back into the room, along with the rain and a scattering of fallen leaves.

Through the front window, I saw nothing but rain. I heard my father's footsteps pounding on the ground outside the house, and another pair too, and then two people were pushing past Goody Way into the room. Outlined in the doorway, against the gray sky, they were shadows clad in dripping clothing that smelled of wet sheep and horse, mud and sweat. I heard the midwife's quick whispers, and I knew what she was telling them—that my mother would die.

"Father," I said, rising to my feet, " 'tis not so bad. I—"

He brushed past me; I doubted he even saw I was there. He was soaking wet, his Monmouth hat sending streams of water onto his face, his cloak dripping pools on the floor at Mama's bedside. His gloves were black with rain, but he didn't bother to take one off as he reached for Mama's hand—the one I'd dropped when he came rushing over. "Judith," he said, "I'm sorry to be so late."

Mama's eyes fluttered open. I thought I saw the ghost of a smile on her lips. "Lucas," she said. "My . . . dear. I am . . . not afraid."

My father motioned to the doorway, sending water drops scattering across Mama's bedcovers, and there was a desperation in his gesture that matched my fear. "I've brought your sister."

Mama tried to turn her head. Her face was shiny with sweat, her gaze dull. "W-where? Sus . . . annah?"

"I'm here, Judith." The voice was low and soft. For the first time, I looked at the woman who had come inside with my father. My aunt Susannah.

In the candlelight, she was only a bundle of clothing: a dark woolen cloak with a hood that covered her head and hid her face, sodden russet skirts that dripped as she moved. She left wet footprints as she came toward us. I could tell nothing about her. She was only shadows and the glisten of candlelight where it hit here and there on her face—a cheekbone, a nose.

She smelled of fish and lemons, molding leaves and rain, and those smells seemed to make the blood scent of my mother stronger. She came up between my father and me, and he backed into the bed curtains to give her room, gave her my mother's hand. Her own were gloved in black so that it seemed Mama's pale fingers floated in the darkness. "Judith," she said. "Judith, I've come all this way. I forbid you to leave me now." She said it lightly, as if nothing were wrong, and I wanted to scream at her, *She's dying, can you not see?*

But then, my mother smiled, and it was not a feeble smile like the ones she'd given me or my father. It was the first real smile I'd seen on her face since this labor had begun, and with it came a light in her eyes that stunned me, that raised a blinding hope in my own soul. "Oh, Sister," she said, "I have longed so to see you . . . again."

I glanced at Susannah then, to see what it was about this aunt I'd never met that could make my mother smile this way, but the hood still shielded her face. My father gestured to Goody Way, and the midwife scurried over, settling again between my mother's legs, looking doubtful.

"I hear you've a babe waiting to be born," Susannah said. "What think you, Judith? Shall we try again?"

An hour ago, my mother had barely been able to move. Ten minutes before, she had said she and the babe were for God. But now she tried to sit up. My father lifted her, helping her to settle against the bolster. She dug her elbows into the feather bed, and her face contorted, her whole body went stiff. She screamed. I pushed in to help her.

"Charity," my father said harshly. "Go on. 'Tis no place for a child."

"But, Father, she needs me—"

"Your mother has Susannah now. Go on."

I could not make myself go. I could not leave my mother. Hope had settled into me now, but I knew it was a fragile thing. Everything could change in a moment, and I was afraid to walk away.

"Once more, Judith," Susannah was saying softly.

I reached out to touch my mother's bared leg; her skin was wet with sweat.

"Leave us, Charity," Father warned.

Goody Way looked at Susannah. "You'd best make her hurry, or we'll lose the child—if we haven't already."

Susannah leaned close to my mother's face, whispering something, and I could no longer see Mama, only the back of my aunt's head, the water-soaked dark of her hood. I stepped back toward Goody Way because I had to—Susannah was filling up all the space—and the gathered bed curtains draped over my shoulders and against my arm. I thought if I stayed there, I would be half hidden, my father would forget me, but when I looked up, it was into his angry eyes.

"Please don't make me leave her, Father," I said, but just then Mama cried out, and if there had been any relenting in his gaze, it was gone. I stepped away from the bed.

"Again!" Goody Way shouted.

Mama's groan sounded like death. I jerked around, ready to run back to her side, but her scream stopped me. Then there was the sound of a baby's cry, thin and breathless, so quiet it was unearthly. The baby was born; 'twas a miracle. A miracle that Mama had lived, that the babe I'd been sure would die was crying in this dark, close room. For a moment, I was dumbfounded. I saw Goody Way lift the child, the jerking of its arms and legs, and praise for the Lord's kindness spilled from my heart in such a rush I could scarce control it. *Thank you, Lord. Bless you, Lord . . .*

Then I heard the silence. My prayers fell away. I glanced at my father, who wasn't looking at the babe at all, but only at my mother.

Mama raised her hand. I was relieved until I saw how weakly she did it, how it seemed the motion took everything she had. In the quiet, her whispered "Susannah" was unbelievably loud. My father turned away. My aunt leaned close to hear my mother's faint words, and suddenly I went numb.

My mother was dying. Everything in the room pointed to it,

every little sign and movement. I heard a rush of air—the hush of her spirit passing—and I knew: God had taken her to punish me.

It was all I could do to keep from shouting *No!* when my aunt raised her head.

"She's gone," Susannah said.

My father went still; he closed his eyes and I saw his lips move: *Dear Lord, bless my poor Judith.*

"No," I whispered.

"I'm sorry, Charity—"

I shook my head, stumbling across the room. They stood back for me, but I would have gone through them to get to her. I fell into the bedstead, my eyes too blurred with tears to see anything but shadows, and then I sank to my knees beside the bed. "Mama," I said, choking through my sobs. I fumbled for her hand, and when I found it, I clutched it hard; I held it so she could not leave me. "Mama."

It seemed I cried for only a few moments when I felt my father's hand on my shoulder, when I heard his quiet voice. " 'Tis enough, Charity," he said. "She was a righteous woman. There was no sin in her. She is with God now."

No sin in her.

My body went cold. God had taken her, but the sin was mine. *The sin is mine.* All she had done was to keep it secret to protect me.

I squeezed Mama's too-thin fingers and pulled them to my lips, tasting the salt of my own tears on her fingertips. Then I laid her hand gently on the bed rug and backed away, my tears for my mother still blurring my vision. I heard her last words to me ringing in my ears—*God loves you*—and I knew it wasn't true. She was dead, and it was my fault. God did not love me, because if He had, He would have left my mother to prove He could forgive such a stupid, sinful girl. . . .

"She is at last relieved of the misery of this world, Charity," my father said quietly. "Would you cry for such a blessing?"

'Twas all the grieving I was allowed for my mother, and I tried to pretend it was enough. I wanted to fall to my knees and sob my sorrow and desperation against her cheek—but I was too old for such grief now. My father's hand did not leave my shoulder, and I felt his pride at my reserve and reveled in those few moments of his approval even as I thought I would be sick.

Then my father reached over and folded my mother's hands upon her chest. When he knelt at her bedside, I moved into place beside him. Goody Way handed the babe to Susannah before she joined us, and together we stayed while Father's prayer filled the parlor. "Dear Lord, we have been but lambs in the wilderness, led by this good woman. She has ever been Thy servant in word and deed, and we celebrate her return to Thy bosom and pray that Thou wilt lend Thy servants remaining here on earth guidance. . . ."

I noticed that my aunt was not kneeling beside us, that she had stepped back toward the fire. She was not even listening to my father's prayer. Instead, she was bouncing the baby and fumbling with the blanket Goody Way had wrapped around it, making little clucking noises. Suddenly she threw back the cowl of her cloak, and I saw my aunt for the first time.

I could not look away, even as my father's prayer droned on. Susannah's hair was not covered by a cap, but pinned in a great heaviness at the back of her head. Some of it fell over her shoulders like sooty shadows.

She was beautiful.

It startled me. I had expected her to be old—after all, I thought of my mother as old, with her tired eyes and her hair nearly as gray as it was brown—but Aunt Susannah did not seem old. She was so beautiful that for a moment I fancied 'twas not the fire's gold she was reflecting but some light that came from inside her, something so bright that I suddenly knew where my mother had found the will to birth that baby. She had caught some of that spirit in Susannah Morrow's face. I wondered that it had not been enough to keep her alive.

As if my aunt sensed I was looking at her, she glanced over at me. For a moment, our gazes held, and she smiled. It was tender and sad and familiar. It was my mother's smile.

It struck me so hard I had to turn away. In the last months, I had seen that expression whenever Mama looked at me—that terrible, sad smile that only reminded me of how close I had come to damnation, of how all the prayers in the world might yet not bring God's forgiveness.

Chapter 2

⚜

MY FATHER AND I SAT SILENT VIGIL AT MY MOTHER'S SIDE. I'D BEEN praying for strength, listening to the soft slough of water and the mewling of the baby as Goody Way washed her by the fire. Jude had awakened, though it was the middle of the night, and now she sat quietly huddled on the settle, clutching one of my mother's chemises tight in her little hands.

"Mama has gone to God, Charity? 'Tis true?" Jude's small face looked wan and thin, too pale in the candlelight except where the tracks of her tears shone golden against her skin.

My father made a sound—I could not tell what it was—and when I looked at him, his face was unreadable. I reached for Jude and said quietly, "'Tis true, Jude. Mama is with God."

"Will He take our sister too? Like He did baby Isaac?"

Isaac was our brother who had died two years ago—only a few days after he'd been born. In that time, he'd never stopped squalling. Sometimes I still heard his cries in my dreams, along with Mama's constant *Hush, child. Hush-a-bye, now.* I did not know what to say to Jude. There had been too many babies lost since my own birth. I remembered how, when Jude was delivered, I had refused to hold her for the longest time, sure that God would take her too.

"God will do as He sees fit," Father said. He sounded strained.

Susannah knelt beside Jude. My aunt's kind smile set a glow

upon her countenance that was too beautiful to ignore. "You must believe that she will stay with us, Jude," she said. "We can only hope that God—"

"God will do as He sees fit," Father repeated, this time sternly. "You must have faith, child. The Lord's wisdom is not for us to understand."

Jude nodded, wide-eyed, and I envied her; how easily she accepted his scold. But Jude was quiet and easy; she bore chastisements with unflinching attention and then put them aside. I had never seen in her the same hunger I felt, the yearning for a kind word from our father.

Susannah nodded toward Goody Way and my new sister. "The babe will need a name."

Father drew in a breath slowly. "Will she live?"

"It seems so."

"Mama liked the name Deliverance," I said quickly.

"Deliverance?" Father asked.

Jude said, "Can I call her Livvy, Father? Goody Hobbs is Deliverance too, and that's what Goody Abbott calls her."

Father shook his head. "We shall call her Faith." Then he murmured, "Faith" again, as if trying the word on his tongue and finding it a pleasant taste. "Aye. To remind us of what we could use more of in this household."

"You'd best find a wet nurse for this one, Lucas, or won't be enough faith in the world to keep her alive," Goody Way said from the fireplace.

"A wet nurse?" Father frowned, and then he leaned his head back on the bedpost as if Goody Way had exhausted him. In only those few moments, he'd gone from us again, already distant. "God help me, I cannot think of that now."

I nearly jumped from the bed in my eagerness to help him. "There's milk in the cellar. Shall I get it?"

He nodded, and I hurried from the parlor to the narrow stairs just inside the front door. I grabbed the nearest betty lamp. The light gamboled from my hand, sending my own shadow swinging before me. As always, the cellar was dark and filled with smells: the yeast of brewing beer and the tang of cider, pungent onions, dusty dried apples hanging from strings, the moldy sharpness of aging cheese, and the faint sourness of milk.

It was my chore each morning and evening to milk Buttercup and to pour off the milk into shallow pans for the cream to rise, and so even in the dim light, this task did not take long. I heard the talk upstairs, low voices that were only muffled rumblings through the floor, and I hurried, determined to show my father how quick I could be. 'Twas the most useful I'd felt since Mama's labor had begun.

I had just set the milk pan back on the shelf when I heard something.

'Twas a soft sound, like a sigh, but loud enough to hear above the spitting sing of the fermenting cider. I paused, listening, and then felt . . . something . . . the brush of air against my cheek, the faint rise of the hairs on the back of my neck. There was a presence here, and yet I was not afraid as I turned slowly toward the barrels of small beer lined against the far wall.

There stood my mother.

I gasped, afraid to believe what I saw, more afraid not to. "Mama?" I whispered.

She tried to say something, but I couldn't hear her words. I reached out to her . . . and she was gone.

My hands shook on the pail handle; I felt my tears on my cheeks. I stared at the dirt wall, willing her to return. "Come back, Mama," I pleaded. "Come back."

'Twas then I heard little Faith upstairs, starting to cry, a high-pitched wailing that did not sound healthy to me, as if she could not get enough air into her lungs. I heard my father call, "Charity? What keeps you?" and with a final look back at the place my mother's spirit had been, I took the milk upstairs.

When I reached the hall, Goody Way stared at me oddly. "What ails you, child? You look pale."

"She's just lost her mother. I'd think 'twould be reason enough for paleness, don't you?" Susannah asked.

I tried to gather my wits. "I'm well enough," I said hastily, another lie to add to my sins. "Truly I am."

"Well then, bring the milk over," Goody Way told me. "Have you a rag? A clean one, mind you."

I ran to get that too, and when I brought it back, the midwife sat on the settle and pulled the pail of milk close. I watched as she twisted the rag and dipped the end into the milk and tried to dribble it into the babe's mouth. Most of it trickled over Faith's red little cheeks. Her screaming grew louder.

"You'd best start thinking now, Lucas," Goody Way said. "Even if she takes to this, she won't survive on it. She needs mother's milk to thrive."

I so rarely saw my father look helpless. I looked up at him, standing next to the bed he'd shared with my mother, her body only a shadow beyond the curtains that looked gray in the darkness. I thought I saw hesitation and uncertainty in his eyes. And fear. Fear in my fearless father, in the man who I knew was afraid of nothing but God.

He looked so bereft, I longed to comfort him, to be comforted. *Perhaps he feels the same way.* The thought came to me suddenly. I looked at him—yes, he needed me now that Mama was gone. Perhaps he would need me so much that he would love me at last. . . .

"Is there no one who's had a babe lately?" Susannah asked.

"Hannah Penney," I said. "Her Johnnie's but a month old."

My father started. His dark brows came together. "No child of mine will be in that home."

I had displeased him again.

Susannah asked, "Who is Hannah Penney?"

"A neighbor," my father answered.

"Charity is right, Lucas," Goody Way said. Her voice was mild, and it reminded me of the way my mother talked to him, that easy voice that always calmed him and made him listen. The voice I had never been able to copy, and would never have dared to use, in any case. "Hannah's loyalty is to her husband now."

"George Penney is involved enough with Tom Putnam for the both of them," Father said. "And Hannah's father has too much invested in Putnam to let his son-in-law make his own decisions. Who do you think was behind George's purchase of those three acres next to Putnam's land? 'Twas John Tyler. He's got his nose into everything George does."

Goody Way sighed. "Lucas—"

"George and Sam Nurse were arguing over a boundary just last week. 'Tis sure that Tom Putnam's involved in all that too. There's bad blood enough between him and Sam."

"That's all in the past," Goody Way protested.

"Aye. But 'twill cause trouble in the Village Committee, and there's enough argument there as it is. I won't have my daughter exposed to it."

I wished I had kept quiet.

Goody Way only shrugged as if she'd heard these things too often to care. "Will you be the one trying to feed this child, Lucas? She'll be safe enough with Hannah, and you only a few hundred yards away. Thomas Putnam won't be involving any infants in this, and well you know it. You send this babe over to Hannah, Lucas— 'twill be the best thing all around."

My father didn't answer. I saw him look to Mama's body again, and then he glanced at me and rubbed the small beard on his chin, sighing as if I troubled him, and I wanted to creep into the darkest corner of the room. But then he turned to Goody Way and said reluctantly, "Very well. We'll deliver her to Hannah when I take you home again. But 'twill have to be after the storm passes. The babe will drown in this weather before we can get half a mile."

Goody Way nodded. "'Tis the best thing, Lucas."

"'Twill give the child a better chance," Susannah said softly. Her voice was low, like my mother's, and there was a cadence to it that matched Mama's rhythm; so for just a moment, I was confused. I found myself searching again for the spirit—'twas my mother I heard, and Susannah I saw, and I could not reconcile the two.

My father turned back to the darkness, to my mother. He had already forgotten us—me and Jude and even my new sister, Faith. I knew because of the way he stood, that familiar stance. I felt as I had when I was thirteen and he'd come home one day to tell me that he'd made arrangements to send me out to the Andrewses' home in Salem Town. I was past old enough to leave home, and they needed a servant. I had cried and begged him not to do it. I had run to him, throwing my arms around his knees to make him listen, and for just a moment, I had thought I'd changed his mind. I felt him soften, felt his hand on my hair. But then he'd pushed me away and gone outside, closing the door softly behind him.

I remember turning to my silent mother, crying that he cared nothing for me, for any of us, and she admonished me in a soft voice that stung even more, and said, "He loves you, Charity. More than you know." Then she had gone after him. I never knew what she said or what she did, but I didn't go to the Andrewses', and he never threatened to send me out again.

Those things came back to me now, as real as if they'd just happened, and suddenly I felt the dearth of my mother's presence like an icy chill in the damp, smoky air of the hall. Even baby Faith seemed to feel the cold, because she quieted, so that when Father spoke again, his voice sounded too loud. "I'll make the coffin myself. There's a goodly amount of white pine in the barn."

Mama had always loved the smell of pine and the feel of it when my father had planed and shaped it. She had exclaimed over a corner cupboard he'd made only a few days before—the memory came back to me sweetly, and I felt again like crying. When I met my father's eyes, he nodded as if he remembered it too, and the shared memory became, for just a moment, something like a kiss between us, a tenderness that made me long for more, and then it was gone.

"She'll need to be laid out," he said.

I blinked away my tears. "I'll dress her in the green—"

My father looked startled. "'Tis no job for a child."

"I am not a child. I am nearly sixteen." I stepped to where Father stood and reached for the blanket covering my mother. My voice trembled with the need to make him understand. "I can do this, Father. You'll see. I—"

He gave me a long sad look that took my voice. He lifted his hand—he was going to hold me at last. I let my mother's blanket fall and turned. . . . His hand dropped to his side, and his voice was a little rough when he said, "You're still a child. Let your aunt take care of it."

My tears came; I could not stop them. I had misjudged him once again. I could not be the good, righteous girl he wanted, no matter how hard I tried, and my lack settled into me like a stain only the two of us could see.

"You could help me, Charity," my aunt said, but I shook my head—the gift was too scant. It was not what I wanted.

"No, Father's right," I said bitterly. "I am just a child."

"Charity," Father warned, and I could not stand it any longer. I could not bear my own longing for his comfort. I ran from the room, racing for the freezing bedroom I shared with Jude, angry that my father still thought me the smallest of children, that he would not allow me to do the things that were my right. . . . But more than that, I was angry at my mother for dying, for leaving me alone here without allies or friends. Hell was not fire, as Master Parris said. Hell was cold as ice and barren as winter, and it was a place I knew too well. Hell was the distance in my father's eyes whenever he looked at me.

The next day, the storm was gone, taking with it the clouds and the wind, leaving behind bitter cold under clear skies. In those first moments after waking, it felt like any other morning, but then I remembered Susannah, and Jude was out of the trundle and curled

like a hard little ball into my side, and I remembered that the world
had changed overnight.

Mama was gone.

I remembered the cellar and the sad way her specter had looked
at me, and now, with the fresh eyes of a night's rest, I recognized
that it had been a waking dream, and the realization brought a terrible sadness. I could not imagine a world without her.

I got out of bed and fell to my knees in prayer, desperate for the
balm of God's presence, but I felt no reassurance, and 'twas with a
sore heart that I woke Jude and we dressed to go downstairs.

My father had already left, and Goody Way too, along with the
new baby. Susannah was readying to lay out my mother. As we
watched, she poured water into a tub and hefted it. At the parlor
doorway, Susannah stopped and looked over her shoulder at me.
"Are you coming?"

She expected me to watch, and since I could not do the tasks
that were mine to do, I consoled myself with the thought that I
could make sure my aunt made no mistakes. So I followed her into
the parlor. No fire had been laid to corrupt Mama's body, so the
room was dark and cold. I lit a candle and saw that the bed was
mussed, as if someone had lain beside her, and I wondered then
where my father had slept last night, if he had spent the hours
cradling her lifeless body, praying for her soul. I could not imagine
it.

My aunt set the tub next to the bed. In the dim light, Mama
looked as if she could be sleeping. I felt the tears come to my eyes
again, and I blinked them away. The time for crying had passed.
Jude had come in behind me; she stood there looking heartbroken.
I could not look at her. Instead, I turned my gaze to my aunt and
settled myself to watch.

Susannah did nothing at first. She looked down at my mother,
and I heard her murmuring something; a prayer, I thought. Then
she turned to me. "You'd best get started," she said. "You'll want to
be done before your father returns."

I stared at her, unsure how to answer.

She motioned toward the bed. "I don't think you've much time, Charity."

"But I—Father said I—"

"'Tis your right, as you said. She was your mother."

"He told me not to. He said I was a child."

"Well, you're not, are you?"

She smiled, and it startled me. I had not expected this gift, and did not know how to accept with grace. I did not even know that I should accept. My father had been uncompromising: I was to leave the laying out to my aunt.

But I wanted it badly—this last thing I could do for the mother who had loved me and guarded my weakness so well. 'Twas not her fault I had found ways to fall.

"Aye. Take it, Charity," Susannah said, smiling. Then she looked past me to Jude. "And you—you shall not tell your father. It would not do to have him angry over such a little thing as this."

Jude nodded.

I struggled with my conscience. It was wrong, disobeying him this way. He would be angry if he found out. But this was my privilege, and when Susannah nodded at me to go ahead, it felt right, somehow.

There was a comfort in my aunt that reminded me of Mama, and I clung to it greedily, feeling suddenly less alone. This was what Mama's spirit had been trying to tell me: Susannah was to be my new guide. I yearned so to believe it that I forgot my father and his disapproval and how I should obey him. I moved to the side of the bed and looked down into my mother's sleeping face and said, "The green was her best dress."

Susannah stood back, watching as I lifted my mother's arms and undressed her. I had not imagined how hard it would be to touch skin that held no warmth, to move arms and legs without resistance. I had loved this body, and I reverenced it now as I washed her and combed her hair. I felt my aunt beside me, not too close, there to guide me if I needed it. I saw the tears shimmering on her cheeks and knew that she had loved Mama too. I felt the strength of that love, and it bound me to Susannah.

Together we dressed my mother in the worsted that usually saw only Sabbath meetings. When we were finished, Susannah said, "She looks beautiful. You've done well."

I stood back and looked at my mother. I could never tell my father about this, but I longed for his approval enough that I would seek it even through Susannah. "Do you think he'll think so?"

She nodded. "Aye. He'll thank me well for it."

She smiled again, and I smiled with her. I felt my spirit reach out to her—she understood me as Mama had. 'Twas such a relief that I let the control I'd held throughout these last hours slip away. My tears fell again. Father was not here to see, and Susannah's warmth filled the spaces around me, so I did not try to stop. My aunt looked at me with a gentleness that only made me cry harder, and she took me in her arms and pressed me hard against her body, and though she didn't smell like my mother, she felt like her, and her hands went to the right spot just below my shoulder blades as if they knew already where to go, and rubbed with my mother's smooth and even comfort.

" 'Tis all right, Charity," she murmured. " 'Tis good to cry."

But it was not; I knew that. I shook my head against her and pulled away so she had to let me go. Then I wiped my eyes with the edge of my skirt. "She's with God," I said. "I know she is happier now than she could have ever been with us."

"Oh, child—"

" 'Tis just that I miss her. And I . . . I don't know what to do without her. She was so strong. And I . . ."

Susannah seemed to hear what I hadn't the courage to say aloud. "You are strong," she said. "You must believe that."

I shook my heard. "No. It isn't true. Mama always said—"

"Charity, I've a story to tell you."

I wiped at my eyes. "I'm too old for stories."

"Not for this one. 'Tis about a girl just your age. A silly girl who was forever getting into trouble of all kinds, to the despair of the whole village. She had a reputation for being impulsive and disobedient, and she was. She was a weak girl, without any sense at all. But this girl had a sister, and that sister was kind and good and strong. Without her, the girl would have been lost."

I looked up at her. Susannah said, "That girl was me. And the sister was your mother."

"But you—you're not weak at all."

She smiled. "There's weakness in everyone, don't you think? 'Tis just that some are better at resisting it than others. When your mama left me, I did not know how I would survive. But I did, Charity. Just as you will. Your mama taught you well. You remember that. You remember how strong she taught you to be. It's there inside you; I know it."

She fascinated me. I looked into her face and saw the light shining there, and I took strength from it the way my mother had. Susannah was like a gift from God, and it seemed she lifted the staff my mother had left behind, so 'twas as if we'd known each other years instead of only hours. She gave me hope. If my aunt Susannah could survive herself, then surely I could. It was as she'd said: She was just like me.

Chapter 3

———— ❧ ————

IT WAS LATE THAT EVENING BEFORE MY FATHER RETURNED, LOOKING worn and tired.

Together Jude and I watched him as he hung his cloak and came across the room to sit heavily at the scarred tableboard. There was still some pottage in the kettle, and I quickly ladled some into a wooden trencher and sliced some bread, but when I set it before him, he shook his head and pushed it away.

"Where's your aunt?" he asked.

"Here." Susannah stood in the doorway between the two rooms, a folded bed rug in her arms. "You look tired, Brother. You should rest."

I thought how kind she was to him, how like Mama, to be concerned for his health. Father only shrugged and looked away. "Time enough for that later. I've talked to the pastor and put up the notices. We'll bury Judith on Saturday."

He seemed so alone sitting there at that table, as if there were a wall around him that no one could see—it was a gift of my father's, that he could seem alone in a room of people without it being pride that kept him that way. Now it only made him look lonely, and I wished I could go up to him and wrap my arms around his shoulders. I had a vision of the four of us sitting on that bench together, taking comfort from one another, but when I blinked my eyes, it was gone, and we were as we were—a room full of people with distance between us, and my father keeping it that way.

"Faith will be baptized on Sunday," he said.

Susannah frowned. "So soon?"

"'Tis the first Sunday after her birth," he explained.

"A funeral one day, a baptism the next? 'Twould hardly be a crime to wait another week."

"Satan finds his way into children too easily as it is. Shall we give him so much opportunity?"

"She's a babe. She hardly seems bait for the Devil."

My father scowled. "Children have no will to resist him. An infant particularly. Why, she's still wet from Adam's sin—"

"Wet from nursing, more like," Susannah said. "I can't think that my sister—"

"Your sister was a good wife," Father said shortly. "A wife who knew to obey her husband."

I knew to bow to that voice, and I waited for Susannah to hear it too—my mother would have nodded and gone silent.

Susannah said, "Unfortunately, I was given too little time with my sister to know if that is indeed true. But I will tell you that the woman I knew—"

"Is gone," Father finished. "It has been many years since you shared that little house in Lancashire; and to hear Judith tell it, you were too . . . occupied . . . then to know her well. Where have you been since?"

My aunt stiffened. "I loved my sister, sir."

"No doubt you did." Father took a deep breath. He looked down at the table. "And she loved you. But this is not England, and my wife is dead. I will have deference from those in my protection."

"Which includes me?"

"Unless you prefer the woods, madam."

My aunt stood straight for a moment, and then she nodded and turned back to the parlor where my mother lay. There was silence in the hall, except for the crackling of the fire. I felt Jude creep up behind me and slip her fingers into my waistband.

I stared at the doorway. I could not bear for him to be angry at my aunt now, not after what she'd done for me. That feeling, along with my nervousness, conspired against me, so I blurted, "You should see Mama, Father. She looks so peaceful . . ." I trailed off when I heard how loud my voice was, how silly.

But Father only sighed and rose. "Let me see her, then." He went to the parlor, and I followed, anxious to see what he thought, to hear the praise I knew must come. I'd done a good job with Mama—Susannah had said it, and I knew it was true.

The parlor smelled of tallow smoke and the faint sweetness of bodily corruption. When we came in, my aunt was bending over Mama, straightening a fold of skirt. She did not see us right away, and I heard her say, "I never imagined this, Judith. To see you this way after so long. . . . Ah, 'tis not how I wanted it."

My father cleared his throat. She started, then looked up. Without a word, she backed away, easing between the candles lighting my mother's body.

My father stepped past me to the edge of the bed and stood there with his hands resting lightly on the thin scarlet bed rug, looking into Mama's face. I watched the way his gaze moved over her, her dress, her quiet hands, the face I had washed lingeringly and long—she had no cause to fear bathing or exposure to ill-humored air now. He leaned back his head; the candle near him flickered at his sigh.

"She does look peaceful," he said to Susannah.

She nodded, but her gaze went past him to me. And when she said, "Thank you, Brother," I felt the praise in her words too, and I smiled at her, unable to help myself, because he had praised me—even if he had not known it—and she had led him to it. I was grateful and happy that for once I had done something so right. I would bask in the words he'd said to my aunt for a long time.

It was that solace I clung to when my father left the parlor without another word. I was so thankful for my aunt that later, much later that night, when I lay awake listening to the wind whistling through the crack in the windowsill and the barred owl's *Hoo-who cooks for you? Who cooks for you all?* in the oak outside, I reached out in the bed for her hand. I was afraid I would not find it, afraid that I had fallen asleep and she had somehow fled in the night. When I touched her fingers, she murmured something and curled them around mine in a warm and reassuring grasp.

I did not let her go. When I woke, I still gripped her hand. The faint pink light of dawn was easing through the windowpanes, and I pulled away from her, relieved and a little embarrassed, not wanting her to see what I had done, not wanting her questions. I did not know how to explain that I had wanted to keep her with me, that I could not bear the thought that she would sneak away and leave me the way my mother had done, that I would have to find my way to my father without her.

The day of my mother's funeral was cold and bright, the wind biting as we followed the bier with her coffin to the burying ground.

I walked behind, holding Jude's hand, with my aunt Susannah and Pastor Parris a little ways away. It seemed everyone in the village was there; my mother had been well liked. In spite of the things my father had said—and no doubt because baby Faith was now in Hannah Penney's care—Goodman Penney held one of the corners of the heavy purple pall that lay over the coffin. Joseph Putnam was another pallbearer. He and my father had been friends for many years. Joseph was the favorite son of old man Putnam, who'd died and made Joseph one of the richest men in the village before he was eighteen. Since the moment Joseph had been born—the first son of a new wife—old man Putnam had doted upon him. 'Twas like the biblical Joseph all over again, complete with a coat of many colors in the form of a rich estate, and older brothers who despised him. All the village knew of the animosity between Joseph and Thomas

Putnam, who was the oldest son, and the one who should have inherited.

I saw Thomas Putnam now, walking with his wife and their children, keeping their distance. He and Joseph hardly talked to each other, not since Joseph had made things worse by marrying a Porter girl. No one ever said it out loud, and you would never know it to hear them talk to each other at meeting, but the Porters and Putnams had been quietly feuding for a long time. Joseph had shown where his allegiances were.

It had not exactly been a scandal. We did not have scandals in Salem Village. We had *history.* I'd grown up with such stories. I could not even remember how I knew them, but I could look at anyone here and tell you whom they were angry with and how far back that bitterness ran. It was hard to avoid conflict in this village. We lived too closely; we needed each other for too many things.

I heard the pastor talking to Susannah—she was nodding her head and seeming to listen, though I wondered if she really heard him, or if she was thinking of her home in London. I prayed it wasn't so. She had no real reason to stay now that Mama was gone—except that I needed her. I watched her now and wondered what I could say to keep her. I was so caught up in trying to imagine the words that when Jude jerked hard on my hand, I jumped in surprise.

I looked down, thinking she'd tripped on the rocky ground, but she only pointed to a place near the edge of the crowd. "Look, Charity," she said. "There's Mary."

I forgot about my aunt Susannah. I should have been prepared to see Mary Walcott, but I was not. She was walking beside Elizabeth Hubbard, who was everything I was not—plump and sweet and seventeen. They were talking as if the two of them were the oldest of friends.

I should have known the moment I saw Thomas Putnam and his wife that Mary would be here too. She was Sergeant Putnam's niece, and she'd lived in their home as a servant since her stepfather had put her out for lack of room. It had been months since I'd spoken to her. Not since Mama had taken to her bed. Now I heard my mother's voice: *When you open the door to the Devil, child, he doesn't fail to come in.*

I wished there were some way I could disappear. Even as I had the thought, I saw Mary whisper something to Elizabeth and look at me. Her glance was sideways and sly, and I looked away. I focused on my mother's coffin, but it was just an expanse of blurred purple broadcloth before my eyes, and I quickened my step until Jude protested.

Nothing so easy ever kept Mary away. I was not surprised when I felt her come up behind me. She yanked at my cloak, hard enough that my hood fell down around my shoulders. I wrenched it back and kept my gaze straight ahead. As evenly as I could, I said, "Mary, 'tis good to see you. I'm grateful that you came."

"My aunt was a great friend of your mother's." Mary came full up beside me so I could see her smile. "She is grieving so, you see."

I glanced back to Sergeant Putnam's wife, walking huddled beside her husband while their eldest daughter, Annie, herded the rest of the children behind. Mistress Putnam did look pale and wan, but she always looked that way. Mama had often said Ann Putnam was as like to be sick as well.

Mary leaned close. "But the truth is, I think she wanted to meet this mysterious aunt of yours. The whole village is talking about her, you know. 'Tis said she was an actress in London. Tell me, is it true?"

I jerked to look at her. "They say she's a *what?*"

"An actress." Mary smiled again. She put me in mind of a cat, with her satisfied smile and slanted eyes and that little tongue that flicked constantly at her lips. With the gray of her hood pulled tight around her face, the image was even more pronounced. "You know, a mime, a player upon the stage, a—"

"I know what it is," I snapped.

"Well, is she?" Mary glanced over at my aunt. Susannah's heavy hair was covered by her hood, but it was impossible to miss the fine beauty of her face. In the light, her cloak was a deep, true blue, unlike the muted colors I saw every day. She stood out among my neighbors as a cock pheasant among drab hens.

"Of course she's not."

"You sound so sure."

"I am sure," I said. "It cannot be. Why, I've talked with her. She is a godly woman—"

"Is she? Has she been praying with you, then?"

Unbidden, the images sneaked into my mind. Susannah standing at the fire, refusing to come listen to my father's nightly sermon; then again, stepping away, murmuring to little Faith as we knelt by my mother's bed and sent her to God.

"She's a godly woman," I said again, as forcefully as I could.

It was not a lie, but it was not an answer, and I saw that Mary heard it. I saw that faint triumph in her eyes.

"Why, 'twould be terrible if she is. Can you imagine? Look at the pastor talking to her now. He looks truly lovesick, don't you think? Ah, I should like to see his face when he finds out the truth about her. An actress! In Salem Village!"

"Hush, Mary," I said. "'Tis not true, not that I know. How much worse it would be if you were caught telling lies about her."

"You don't know it isn't true, do you, Charity? You don't know for certain."

"I do know. I've talked to her—"

"She's an actress. Perhaps she's dissembling."

"No." I shook my head. "I know her. And even if I didn't, my father would never allow it."

"Perhaps he doesn't know," Mary said.

"Of course he would know."

"Why? Do you think your father cannot be fooled?"

The question was unexpected. I could not answer, and I was dismayed to see that Mary saw it.

"Perhaps she's fooled him. Perhaps she's lying." The slyness was in her eyes again.

I told myself to ignore her. Mary had shown her colors to me already. She had been my closest friend once. That was over, but I knew how she could turn the most innocent things wicked. I knew how easily she could sway me. I struggled to turn from her the way my mother had urged me to.

She could plant doubt in me only if I allowed her, and I would not. I knew what my father said about actors, what the preachers said. The theater was Hell on earth, and stage players were the Devil's minions. Certainly my father would never permit an actress in his own home.

I turned to Mary, meaning to tell her so, confident in my conviction, when a puzzle came into my head—a small piece, but it was disturbing. Then there came another image, and another: the way my father snapped at Susannah as if just the sight of her made him angry, the way she spoke to him, without deference or respect, as if she were afraid of nothing. My mother had not seen her sister for eighteen years—why was that?

I glanced to where my aunt walked with Master Parris, suddenly desperate to see her face, to have her smile reassure me. Her back was to me, and the preacher was talking to her, and doubt crept like a hard little seed into my heart.

"You could find out, couldn't you?" Mary gave me a conspiratorial smile, the one I'd once treasured because it included me. "You could ask her."

"No," I said. How faint my voice was. "I'll do no such thing."

"No, of course you would not."

"What do you mean by that?"

Mary shrugged. "You would never believe your aunt was something so terrible as an actress, would you? Why, no, of course not. You *are* such an innocent."

I did not know what to say. I watched her, trying to find her sarcasm, waiting for her blow, but she only smiled and said, "Betty's calling to me, so I'd best run back." She took a step away, and then she stopped and said, "Oh, Charity, I've been meaning to ask you for weeks now—'tis so odd the way Sammy just disappeared. So suddenlike. 'Twas as if the Devil himself were after him, don't you think? Or maybe . . . Maybe 'twas something else altogether. But I imagine you would know that better than me."

She laughed then and twirled away. I was so stunned I stopped short, and Jude bumped hard into me. Just a word from her, and the images I'd tried so hard to forget flooded my mind as if they'd been waiting for the chance. Sammy bending close, his hands on my body, the warmth of his breath . . .

"Go on, Charity," Jude complained. "Why are you stopping?"

Tears came to my eyes, and I dashed them away with the back of my hand and held the rest back by sheer force of will. I pretended Mary had not shaken me with her rumors and insinuations, or with the name that I wanted desperately to mean nothing to me. But I felt weak and afraid as I followed the bier over that stony road. I would have given the world to have my mother beside me again— or even just her specter, if that was all to be allowed me. *Oh, Mama,* I thought. *Why have you left me?*

It seemed forever before we came to the grave site. The hole was deep and wet from the storm, with mud pooling at the bottom, and the idea that we were putting my mother into it was horrible. I would have looked away except for the fact that my father came over beside Jude and me at that moment. He put his hand on my shoulder.

"Come along," he said quietly, leading us to the very edge of the grave. "Gaze down and mark it well. 'Tis what waits for all of us. Remember how it feels to stand here now and face mortality. Never forget how your mother died. You should pray for God's blessing, that you may have as joyful a death as she."

Jude's little fingers tightened on mine.

Master Parris came forward and rested his hand on the pall over Mama's coffin. His dark hair fell forward, and the wind blew it back again from his sharp cheekbones, his angular face. "My beloved flock," he began. "In life, Judith Fowler was holy and prudent, a woman of sincerity and humility, a woman of great patience and public spiritedness. Who among us ever suffered an unkind word from her? Who among us has ever gone to her for help and found her lacking? Judith was truly a visible saint, and a faithful one. She revealed to me often how uncertain she was of her salvation—would that the rest of us be so uncertain and yet practice such faith and charity! As Jesus Christ to our Lord . . ."

He went on, but I was caught by the sight of my aunt on the other side of the open grave, standing behind the pastor. She was not listening to him. She was looking at my mother's coffin, mouthing words—a prayer, but one I did not recognize—and her hands were held tight, palm to palm before her chest. I caught sight of Mary Walcott. She and Elizabeth were staring at my aunt, whispering to each other, and I felt my skin grow hot and had to look away. All I could think was *an actress.* It could not be. Of course it could not be. My good mother would never have brought Susannah here had it been true. To be an actress . . . 'twas such a sinful thing. She knew my father would never accept it.

Perhaps my secret was not the only one Mama had kept. The thought shook me.

Master Parris finished, and the underbearers moved forward to pull away the pall and tilt my mother's coffin into the grave. I did not think to step back until it nearly grazed my toes. They pushed the casket in, and it landed with a creak of wood and a muffled splash. Droplets of mud covered the fine white pine, and the coffin settled in crookedly, but no one seemed to care about that. They were spading the dirt over, so quickly that before I knew it they were done, and my father was standing before me, sweating in the cold wind. He took off his hat and swiped his arm across his forehead. His curly hair was pressed flat and straight to his head.

" 'Tis time to go back," he said to Jude and me. "The two of you go on, help your aunt and the other women prepare for the crowd."

I did not move. I felt frozen there.

My father frowned at me. "What is it, Charity?"

I hardly knew what to say. My thoughts were torturous, and I had nowhere else to turn. "Do you think there was sin in her?" I whispered.

My father stared at me. I saw his concern for me, and I took a desperate hope from it. I wanted his reassurance so badly I was half afraid to say the words. "If she kept . . . secrets . . . that is not much a sin, is it? Is it?"

His expression changed; I could not read it. He did not take his gaze from me when he said, "If 'twas wickedness she hid, then indeed she sinned. God shuns any weakness—'tis no difference between the big and the small."

Tears of disappointment came to my eyes.

I turned and nearly fell into my aunt. Susannah was standing behind us, the blue of her cloak shining in the cold sunlight, her fine straight nose pink from the cold. She was gazing at my father, two spots of red high on her cheeks. She put her hand on my shoulder. "Come," she said in a hard voice. "Your neighbors are already on their way to the house."

We'd hardly taken a step before the parson was there, smiling at Susannah before he said distractedly to Jude and me, "If ever there was a woman chosen by God, 'twould be your mother."

He went past us without waiting for an answer. To my father, he said in a quiet voice, "Ah, Lucas, I know 'tis merely that you've forgotten . . ."

I looked over my shoulder at them. My father was frowning as he reached into his pocket and took something out, something wrapped in a small cloth, and handed it to the minister. I watched Master Parris open it with quick, greedy hands, and I saw the shine of the sun on gold and knew it was a funeral ring—a gift for the words said at Mama's graveside, and for the sermon the pastor would deliver on Sunday.

My father's face was tight, his eyes cold. I heard the pastor say, "The ministers in Boston are receiving gloves now as well—"

"I haven't the money to spend on frivolities," my father said brusquely. "Gloves are for those richer than I and more important than she was. I've paid you enough for the prayers, Parson, and I thank you for them, but do not expect this means anything has changed between us."

I could not see the parson's face. He bowed, and then he turned away with a quiet word I couldn't quite hear.

I was so busy listening to them that when my aunt touched me again and said, "Come then, shall we go?" I jumped. She looked past me to my father as if she were trying to see what I'd been watching. When she glanced back to me, there was curiosity in her eyes.

"Your minister is an interesting man," she said mildly.

"Father doesn't like him," Jude said.

Susannah smiled. "Oh? Why is that?"

"He says he has no taste for the pastor's preaching."

"I imagine your father has many opinions on that score," Susannah said.

'Twas an insult, I realized. It startled me; I could not believe she'd said it. I said, "My father has a great reverence for the word of God."

Susannah touched my cheek, just a brush of her soft skin. "Of course he does. I meant nothing by it, Charity." She smiled, so I forgot what it was that disturbed me so. "We should go. They'll be home before us otherwise."

It did not take us long to get home—or at least, it seemed that way to me, because my thoughts were so full. 'Twas a lucky thing that we had laid out the food and the barrels of beer and cider before we'd left, because when we got to the house, neighbors had already congregated, ready to drink and eat to my mother's memory. Unexpectedly, I thought how only a few days before I'd been helping Mama bake groaning cakes. Now we were here, feasting on funeral cake and bread and meat, while she was gone forever, so far from me that I would never again feel the soft touch of her hand on my hair or hear her quiet "Hand me the eggs, Charity, my dear" as together we made dinner.

I was so sad suddenly that I could not take another step. My aunt hurried past to greet those just arriving. I let go of Jude's hand, and she ran up the path to the house, calling out to some friend she saw hovering near the door while I stood there feeling weak beneath the weight of my sorrow.

The dark woods beyond the house looked suddenly inviting, but I knew the darkness would come too soon, the shadows on the narrow pathways would lengthen until they took the shapes of demons and savages. Night was an evil thing, and dangerous besides. Lately there'd been much talk of Indian raids not so far from here.

No, I would not run. I trudged up to the house. The door was open, and when I stepped inside, I was surprised to see more people than I'd thought. In the corner, passing a tankard of beer to Jude and her little friend Polly Martin, was Elizabeth Hubbard. I did not have to look far to see Mary Walcott standing just beyond. I backed up a little, hoping to disappear into the shadows before she caught sight of me.

I hit my hip hard on something—a corner, a cupboard that hadn't been there before. In confusion, I turned around. It was no cupboard. There, just inside the door, were two large chests, each heavily carved, brightly painted. On top of one was the thing I'd bumped into, something small and rectangular, covered with canvas.

Slowly I reached out. I pulled back the canvas to reveal keys glowing with the fine polish of ivory—an instrument. It was a virginal, and I knew who it belonged to, just as I knew these trunks held clothes brought all the way from London—more clothing than I, or anyone in my family, had ever had.

I looked up, right into the mean gaze of Mary Walcott, who made a little prancing curtsy like a stage player, and I heard her voice again in my head. *They say she's an actress,* and those words seized and took hold—all these clothes, music, an instrument . . .

Suddenly I was afraid. I did not know how I should feel or what I should do. I turned to the door and saw my father come in, and I waited for him to see these things. He glanced at me. "Are you well, child?"

When I nodded dumbly, he looked beyond me to the chests, to the virginal keys glistening in the candlelight. I held my breath. He looked away again, as if the sight did not distress him—or as if he hadn't even seen those things sitting there, though there was no way to avoid them. He crossed the room to where our neighbor Samuel Nurse stood drinking from the bowl of beer, and clapped a welcoming hand on the man's shoulder as if nothing was amiss.

I looked again behind me, thinking I'd been mistaken, that perhaps I was seeing things. But the virginal was there. I touched one of the keys, unable to help myself. The ivory was smooth and warm, as if it had just been played, when it should have been cold, and that was so disconcerting I drew back. 'Twas an evil thing, I knew, but my father seemed unmoved by it, and that was so strange I did not know how to reconcile it. Mama had once told me that my father could spot wickedness in any man, and I believed that. I knew he saw it in me. Why else did he spend every night drilling prayers into my head, girding me against the Devil? If he saw it in me, why could he not see it in Susannah?

Because it wasn't there. 'Twas the only answer. My aunt Susannah was no actress; Mary had been passing on vile rumors without truth. Gossip spread so easily in this village. Were Susannah a stage player, even my mother's pleas could not have brought her here.

I looked toward my aunt, who was taking a joint of beef off the fire, reminding me of Mama with every movement, and I was relieved. Mary was wrong; there was nothing to fear. The only wickedness in this house was my own.

Chapter 4

—⚬—

'TWAS LATE WHEN EVERYONE BEGAN TO LEAVE, BUT THE LEAVING had nothing to do with the hour. I had known most of these people my whole life; tonight their voices had been loud in the corners, snatches of arguments I'd heard often these last months falling here and there through the house—rumors that Increase Mather had failed in getting the new charter from the king and queen in England, worries about land titles revoked and taxes going ever upward because of the war with the Indians and the French—things I cared nothing for. My neighbors could debate long into twilight; they had done so many times before, 'twas a favored way to pass the time.

So it was odd the way those conversations stopped when the pastor arrived—so late I'd thought he would not be coming. My father sat at the table with the other four members of the Village Committee. When Parris came through the door with his family, they stared at him, their talk dying uncomfortably. The parson seemed unaffected by the deliberate silence. He stood there smiling until my father had to rise to greet him. After that, my mother's funeral feast broke up quickly. The sun had set; the shadows of the woods crowded the pathway, so the threat of Indian attack seemed more real than ever; and the men began to talk of walking back in groups together, their muskets at the ready, their fingers poised at their powder horns.

Jude and the few other remaining children reeled through the hall, dizzy from too much beer, tumbling into the spinning wheels and the barrels of salt meat filling the corners, squealing with laughter as they dodged around the churn and the washtubs. The girls, whom I'd once called my friends, lingered, their smiles wide as they cast their eyes in the direction of the village boys. I watched them with too many memories of the days when I'd done the same. When the last bowl of beer had emptied but for the dregs, and the cakes we'd baked were nothing more than crumbs scattered on the table, they finally left. I was glad when they were gone. My father stood at the door, listening as our neighbors filled his ears with good-byes and murmured assurances of Mama's election. The parson and his family were the last to go.

"'Tis no time for sadness, Brother Fowler," Master Parris said, clutching my father's arm. "Our good sister is embraced now in God's glory."

Father nodded, but his farewell was low and strained. When the pastor took his wife's arm and called for his niece Abigail to lead away his three other children, my father looked relieved. He closed the door too quickly behind them, shutting out the cold wind, leaving us in a quiet that seemed strange after the noise of the day.

"'Tis getting late," he said. "You children go to bed. Tomorrow is the Sabbath, and the babe's baptism." He looked past me to where Susannah tended the fire. "'Twould be best if you took yourself up as well, Sister. You've a long day to look forward to."

She looked up with a little smile. "Aye. Longer still if 'tis your minister giving the service."

There was no answering humor in Father's eyes. "The word of God is welcome in any wilderness."

"I have not said it wasn't, Brother."

He looked ready to say something sharp, but then he only started to the parlor. "As you wish, but I'll say my good-nights. 'Twas a trying day."

I saw my aunt hesitate. Then she straightened from the fire and called out, "Brother—"

My father turned.

"I may have lost my sister, but I know you buried a wife today, and perhaps . . . Well, 'twas no easy thing, I know. I bid you . . . a peaceful rest."

It seemed my father relaxed at her words, though I don't know why I thought it, because his posture did not change. But perhaps the softening I saw in his face was real and not caused by the dimness of flickering candles. It reassured me; I had been right to cast my doubts about Susannah aside. "Aye," he said, and then he saw me standing there. "Charity, Jude, 'tis late."

I knew that tone. So did Jude. I saw her get up from the settle without question, rolling drunkenly into her step as she went to the stairs. I followed her, leaving my aunt alone to rake up the fire for the night.

Our room was cold. The nor'easter had left winter in its wake. The chill wind whistled through a crack in the window's casement, and I remembered how frigid this room had been last winter, how the ice inside the windows had barely melted the whole day through. I went to the window, finding the bits of rag I'd stuffed there rotting now, disintegrating to dust at my touch. Jude was undressing to her chemise and crawling between the homespun sheets of the trundle bed.

"'Tis cold, Charity," she complained. "My toes are freezing."

I shoved the rag as best I could back into the crack and told myself to remember to find a new one tomorrow. Then I leaned close and peered out the window. The moon was rising, full and bright, and the night sky was clear. Against the clapboards of the house, the oak branches scratched and tapped. "'Twill be a freeze tonight, I'll warrant."

Jude was sniffling into the pillow bear now. Soft, muffled cries that it hurt to hear.

"'Tis all right, Jude," I said quietly. "Everything will be fine."

"I miss Mama."

"I know. Me too."

"She never let my bed be cold."

I winced. The hole my mother had left seemed suddenly far too big to fill. "I'm sorry. I should have remembered to get the bed warmer. I won't forget tomorrow."

Jude's sniffling broke into little hiccuping sobs. "I don't want you to remember. I want Mama to do it."

"She's with God now, Jude. You know that."

"Aye, she is."

I spun around in surprised disbelief. I had thought 'twas the spirit again, talking to me in my mother's sweet voice, but it was my aunt standing there. I took a deep breath to calm myself, and then I saw she held the long-handled bed warmer, and I felt glad that she would remember such a thing, that she would know of my mother's habit, and sorrow that I had so easily forgotten.

She came inside with hardly a sound and went over to the trundle. "But your mama hasn't really left you, Jude. You must remember that."

Jude wiped her eyes, nodding silently. Susannah gestured her away from the bed, and Jude scurried back, hugging herself and shivering as our aunt took down the covers and ran the bed warmer over the sheets, letting it rest for a moment at the foot.

Then Susannah drew back. "Hurry now," she said. "Get in before the chill hits again."

Jude did it without a word. She huddled into the blankets, burrowing down so far that all I could see of her was the length of her braid trailing over the pillow like a mouse's tail.

Quickly Susannah slid the bed warmer between the covers of the feather bed she and I would share. Then she knelt again beside Jude, patting the small, rounded hump of my sister. From beneath the covers came those sniffling sounds again.

"Sssshhh, sssshhh," Susannah said. "'Tis all right to cry, Jude. 'Tis all right."

"Father says it's not," came Jude's muffled voice.

"Remember what your father said? About being happy because your mama was with God?"

The lump beneath the covers went still. Then I saw the jerk of Jude's braid as she nodded.

"I think that's true. I think your mama's happy now. But I know you miss her, and 'tis no bad thing sometimes to cry over it."

The covers came down. Jude's little pinched face showed again, her red-rimmed eyes and pink nose, and I watched the way Susannah smoothed back my sister's light brown hair, gently pulling the loose strands from where they stuck to the tears on her face. If I narrowed my vision to just her hand, I could pretend it was my mother sitting there, soothing my sister the way she'd done so often. The only thing different was that Mama would never have told Jude it was all right to cry.

"Jude must learn to control her tears," I said, correcting my aunt gently. "They will only make Father angry."

Susannah stopped her stroking and looked up at me, and there was a pity in her eyes that confused me. "Ah, yes," she murmured, "'tis best not to make him angry."

Her answer unsettled me. It sounded again as if she was insulting my father, though I could not decide exactly how that could be, because her words did not. I found myself wanting to defend him. I went to the shelf beside the bed that held the candle and grabbed up my Bible. "This is where we must look for reassurance. Come, Jude."

"I don't want to get out of bed, Charity," my sister whined. "Father's gone to sleep already without making us—"

I pointed to the floor beside my bed.

Jude sighed, then dragged herself from her warm covers. I felt a moment of regret that I was making her do it, that I was not huddled beneath warm bed rugs and toasting my feet in the warmth of the gathered coals, but I knew what Father expected from us. When Jude was kneeling at the side of the bed, I went down beside her.

The floor was cold and hard beneath my knees. I opened the Bible, letting the leaves fall where they would, and then I began to read. " 'But we are all as an unclean thing, and all our righteousness are as filthy rags; and we all do fade as a leaf; and our iniquities, like the wind, have taken us away—' "

"Oh, Charity," Susannah said quietly, "can you not find comfort from the Lord instead of punishment? Your mother was buried today. Allow yourself to grieve."

I stumbled over the next words, and then the text blurred; I could not read. I saw Jude turn to me, but her face was blurry too, and I had to look away. "I *am* finding comfort in the Lord," I said, and though I meant the words to be convincing, they rang soft and muffled by my tears.

"Shall we leave off the prayers tonight?" Susannah said. "Your father will never know if we don't tell him. Shall I sing you to sleep?"

I looked at her in dumb surprise. *Your father will never know.* I thought of yesterday and how she'd led me into laying my mother out, her words to Jude—*You shall not tell your father*—and something settled uncomfortable and false inside me.

"Sing?" Jude asked. "You mean . . . a psalm? Like at meeting?"

"If that's what you wish," Susannah said. "You would like that, would you not?" Susannah patted the trundle bed. "Come along, Jude. Into bed."

Jude leaped toward that welcoming hand, leaving me kneeling alone by the bed, my limbs numb from the knees down, the cold working into my hands so my fingers were stiff and unpliable, skeleton fingers clutching my Bible.

Susannah tucked Jude beneath the covers, and my sister shivered and smiled gratefully back at my aunt, already forgetting her tears. Susannah put her hand to my sister's hair, and then, without a word to me, she began to sing.

Her voice was soft and sweet. She sang as one used to singing, nothing like the way we stumbled over the psalms in meeting, each singer imagining a different tune, and none of them well. Susannah's words were clear and true. I could almost hear the virginal lending accompaniment. "'Under the greenwood tree, who loves to lie with me and turn his merry note unto the sweet bird's throat. . . .'"

I could not take my eyes away from her, from how prettily she did it—a tilt of her head, a fluttering hand. As if she were acting out the song, performing it for our pleasure. I tried not to think it. But the more I tried not to think it, the more it came into my head.

"'Come hither, come hither, come hither: Here shall he see no enemy but winter and rough weather.'"

I could imagine her on a wooden stage, singing as she played the virginal, smiling at the audience below.

I heard the Devil in her voice. "Stop," I said, but my words came too soft, and she kept singing until I nearly yelled, "Stop it."

She looked up then and put her fingers to her lips to quiet me, gesturing toward Jude, who was asleep already. Then she finished the song, the final words trailing off in a lilt. "'Here shall he see no enemy but winter and rough weather.'

"What is it, Charity?" she asked, rising from Jude's side and making her way to sit on the bed. "Did you not like the song?"

I was afraid. When I looked at her now, I saw wickedness. I had been seduced again—just as Mama had predicted I would be. In my grief, I had taken the easy path that Susannah put before me—lies to my father, secrets kept. The Devil was leading her, and he had known my desires before and answered them. She was what I'd thought—an actress who could lie at will. She was not my mother. I prayed for the strength to push her away, but my hands were trembling. *If Christ hath no possession of thee, then thou art possessed of the Devil.* I tried to say the words, but 'twas as if I'd forgotten their sounds.

"I worry about you, Charity," she said quietly. "'Tis not right to keep yourself from grieving this way. Your mama would not want you to be so brave."

Those brown eyes of hers looked soft and soulful in the dimness, but this time, I knew her for what she was. The knowledge gave me strength. 'Twas easier to fight the Devil now, when I knew what he looked like. I would not be deceived so easily again. "How could you know what she would want from me? I heard what Father said—you'd not seen her for years."

She winced. "I admit we had not seen each other for a long time. But she wrote me every month. I knew my sister well enough."

"My mother."

"Aye. Your mother." Susannah sighed. "I would have done anything for her, had she asked it. 'Tis why I'm here now. She called me, and I came."

That surprised me. "She asked you to come?"

Susannah nodded.

"Why?"

My aunt hesitated. "She longed to see me, I think. As much as I wanted to see her."

"She never mentioned you. I don't think she missed you at all. Why ask you to come after so many years?"

Susannah looked thoughtful in a way that made me nervous, and I wished I had not been so cruel. She did not take her eyes from my face when she said, "I think she was afraid."

"Afraid? Of what?"

"I don't know. Perhaps . . . Perhaps you have the answer to that. I heard what you asked your father today. Tell me, Charity, what secrets do you think your mother was keeping? What could she have been afraid of?"

The question rattled me. I could not help it; I remembered the day I had told Mama about Samuel. I remembered the smell of the white hellebore we had gathered, and the wet, moldy scent of the deep shadows of the forest, the stink of the skunk cabbage in the swamp beyond. I knew I would never forget the look in my mother's eyes, that terrible fear that had made me cry when she whispered at me harshly to shush, that I was courting the Devil, and

I must never mention such a thing again. Not to her, not to myself, not to anyone. . . .

I met my aunt's gaze as calmly as I could. "I don't know what she was afraid of," I said. "Nothing that I knew."

She saw I was lying. She watched me for a moment more, and then she sighed and got to her feet. "Well, there's tomorrow still to find out. And the next day. I've more than enough time."

"You're staying, then."

"Aye. Your mother asked for my help. I've come all this way to give it. And I"—she smiled bitterly—"I won't be returning to London. My life there . . . 'tis best left behind."

Only two hours before, I would have rejoiced at such news. Now I was in agony over it. She was staying—Satan's inroads into my soul had not been enough; now she was here to tempt me still again. I got to my feet, clutching the Bible to my chest like a shield. I wanted no more of her or of this conversation. I was afraid now, again, and worse than before. Only yesterday, I had taken confidence from the things she'd said—I remembered so well thinking she and I were alike; she had given me hope that I could find goodness even with Mama gone.

Now I knew the truth. Susannah *was* just like me. She had not found courage but only weakness when Mama left, and like me, she'd taken the road the Devil offered.

"I'm tired," I said. When I put the Bible down to undress, I felt naked, unarmed, and so I grabbed it up again as I slid between the sheets of the bed, stretching my toes toward the bed warmer below. I kept the Bible hard against my chest, lying there stiffly when Susannah crawled in beside me.

She blew out the candle, and as the room snapped into darkness, I tried to relax into the bed, into the safety of blindness. I closed my eyes and prayed, though the words got lost in my head, and my feelings were a muddle. I stayed awake long after Susannah went limp and quiet beside me, and when her breathing came soft and even, keeping time with Jude's from the trundle bed below, I lay there thinking about the things she'd said, the things she knew. I thought it would be my fear of her that kept me spinning into the night, almost till dawn, but it was not. It was something else instead, the simple question that sparked my memory: *Tell me, Charity, what was your mother afraid of?*

The answer so filled my heart I was afraid she would hear it.

My mother had been afraid of me.

Chapter 5

I WOKE TO THE SOUND OF MY NAME, A QUICK CALL THAT CAME TO me through a dream I could not remember. *Charity. Charity.* I jerked awake to see that it was early still, with dawn breaking in a gray light beyond the windows, the shadows in the room blue and ghostly. Jude was fast asleep, and there were no noises from downstairs; my father was not awake. There was no one calling me, no one near, but I couldn't go back to sleep.

Then I heard it again, not in my head this time, but beside me. I turned in bed, and . . . She was there beside me, facing me, and her expression was sad and loving. I felt her warmth; I felt the weight of her body on the feather bed.

"Mama . . ." I meant to stay still, though I couldn't help myself; I reached out slowly, as if she were a skittish wild bird, and touched her hair, and for that one moment, it was hers—thin and wiry, bouncing beneath my fingertips—

Then she was gone, and it was Susannah I was looking at, Susannah's hair beneath my hand, thick and soft and brown, not gray at all. My aunt's eyes opened, and suddenly she was looking at me in sleepy question, and I could not bear it.

I jerked away, turning my back to her. My disappointment gathered in tears. I thought she would touch me, she would say something, and I waited.

She did nothing. I was so tight and still I thought I could feel even the movement of the air. I heard her sigh, and then she relaxed again into the bed, and before long I heard her soft breathing again in sleep.

It was a long time before I relaxed as well. I saw my mother's face again, and then the quickness of the change—her face on Susannah's body, her spirit in Susannah's heart—but this time I understood what the spirit was trying to tell me. 'Twas a warning. My aunt Susannah was wicked; she would guide me only closer to Satan's arms. *Your heart is an open door, Charity. Do not let the Devil in.*

I pushed aside the blankets and dressed hurriedly, then went downstairs into the darkness. I heard my father moving around in the parlor, up early, as I was. I built up the fire and put breakfast on, and when he finally came into the hall, looking haggard and sleepless, his eyes red-rimmed, he sat beside me at the table and said gently, "Good day, child" while we ate and waited for Susannah and Jude. I thought of telling him what I'd seen, of the things about Susannah that I knew now, but he seemed so distracted and distant I could not bring myself to do it. I kept my thoughts to myself as my sister and aunt came down, and we made our way to meeting.

The meetinghouse stood in the middle of a big clearing, with forest behind it, and Ingersoll's Ordinary next door. The watchhouse loomed across the street, its thick walls manned always by one of the village militia, flintlock at the ready. The meetinghouse was one place I always felt safe. If Salem Village had a heart, this building was it, though there were those—including my father—who said it was the rotten center as well.

It had been many years since the meetinghouse was something to be proud of. The heavy shutters hung at loose angles now, and at least two of the windows were broken out, covered over with boards. It was on the edge of swampland, so throughout the summer, mosquitoes swarmed both inside and out. Now the swamp was still and cold; the few brown leaves remaining on the trees spun to the ground, whipped by a fierce late-autumn wind. Tattered pieces of paper—announcements of wedding banns and sales, new laws and births—fluttered from the nail-pocked wall beside the meeting-house door. The latest announcement, of Mama's death, was ruffled from melting frost, but not torn, not yet. My father's handwriting was still distinct and dark as ever, the iron gall ink unfaded.

My father led us to the door. Behind him went my aunt, who carried two foot warmers, the coals inside glowing meekly through the holes punched into the hardwood. Goody Penney stood just outside, holding baby Faith wrapped tightly in blankets and clasped close to her chest. When my father greeted her, she held the baby out to him, saying something I could not hear. He shook his head and backed away, and so she held the babe to my aunt instead.

Susannah put the foot warmers on the ground and reached for the child. "Ah, how precious she is," she murmured. She cuddled Faith so closely I could not see the baby's face, nothing but the peek of a little gray wool-clad foot. Susannah looked up at Goody Penney, and her face was alight again, as if some sun somewhere resided inside of her, but I knew it now for what it was. I watched her carefully and bitterly. "How does she do, Hannah? Is she a good child?"

"Oh, there's none better," Goody Penney replied. "She's a good eater, that one is. Better than my own babe."

I did not like the way my aunt held her. I did not like how easily she'd taken the child. The Devil was crafty, and Faith was so vulnerable now. I glanced at my father, not believing he could be deceived by her, but his face was carefully expressionless, and I knew she had fooled him.

Susannah handed the babe back to Goody Penney as if she were loath to let go of her, and I saw her eyes lingering on Faith as the goodwife tucked the blanket back around and made little clucking noises to quiet her.

"We'd best go inside," Father said. "The service will be starting." Then he left us, moving through the crowd to his place on the west side, where the men sat.

Anxiously I hurried after, drawing Jude with me and leaving Susannah to follow. Here was a place where God was sure to heed my prayers.

The shadows of the meetinghouse were barely eased by the weak light coming through the windows and the single candle burning in the sconce next to the pulpit. Heavy ceiling beams were indistinct in the gloom, the unmatched clapboards of the walls aging badly and irregularly, so that one looked cast in darkness while another seemed touched with light. Beneath the galleries on either side, the room was so dim 'twas hard to see the faces of the people sitting there.

Some time ago, I had graduated from the back of the gallery where the children sat, and Jude was so quiet and well-behaved that Mama had always kept her with us. Now I did the same. Our family was not rich, but Father had served on the Village Committee many times, and Mama had worked often with the minister for Charitable Causes, so we'd been seated only a few pews from the pulpit. We were in the center, so we did not have the high sides on each end to lean on—though it did not much matter; the tithing-man would not be slow to jab any leaners with his long pole, and he was diligent in his walk up and down the aisles. From where we sat, I could see almost everything in the meetinghouse except the back, where people sat in darkness.

Susannah put the foot warmers on the floor at our feet, but it was so cold already that even through my worn boots I could barely feel them. 'Twas dank and musty, and the smell of damp wood and mildew and wet wool filled my nose. The wind whistled in a high pitch through the boards covering one of the windows, and the candle on the pulpit flickered and smoldered. We settled ourselves in, laying rugs over our legs and sitting up straight on the backless benches, and gradually the voices faded and muffled. When it was quiet, and Deacon Ingersoll stood from his place below the pulpit to call out the psalms for us to sing, I bowed my head and tried to find God's voice through the muffled darkness in my soul.

I sang without listening; I hardly heard Master Parris's sermon, so focused was I in my own search for the Lord. When Master Parris finished the morning service with another prayer, I looked up at the huge hourglass before Deacon Putnam. A little over two hours had passed—it had been a short sermon, and I had not yet found relief or comfort.

Faith's baptism would be in the afternoon service, and now we were left to ourselves for the two hours until it began. As I followed Father into the cold sunshine, I heard people talking about where they would go, what they would do. Those who had come a long distance had their horses stabled in the shelter on the swamp-side pasture. Most would go to Ingersoll's, just as we would, as we always did. Mama had always packed a meal, which we ate in quiet on what passed for a green in front of the tavern, dodging the sheep Lieutenant Ingersoll sometimes kept there. I had not brought any food this day. When I'd tried, Father said we would buy something at the ordinary.

When we stepped through the doors at Ingersoll's, I saw Mary Walcott and Betty Hubbard huddled around a long table, along with skinny, mean-spirited Mercy Lewis, who was also a servant for the Putnams, and Mary Warren, who worked for the Proctors in the tavern they ran off the Ipswich Road. My old friends were laughing together while the church members at the tables around them frowned disapprovingly. When my family came in and Betty caught sight of us, they laughed again, more loudly, and bent to whisper among themselves.

I looked away. My father glanced to them, and then to me. "They are silly girls, Charity. You should count yourself blessed that you are no longer among them."

It warmed me that he had noticed, and it raised that yearning in me again. But when I turned to him, he was already looking away; I was already forgotten.

He led us to a table where many of our neighbors were already gathered: Francis Nurse among them, who was our neighbor

Samuel's father, and who served on the Village Committee with Father. Susannah smiled, catching them effortlessly in her light. Wickedness had such power. Before long, she had the women snared in the telling of her late-autumn sea voyage.

I didn't listen. I could think only of the snickerings that had greeted us when we walked in. Even now, I felt my old friends talking about us in the little prickling of the hairs on the back of my neck. I could not bear that Mary's whispers were true. I remembered my defense of Susannah with embarrassment, and I did not want to have to admit I'd been wrong.

I did not have any intentions of going near them. It was only that I could not sit still any longer and watch my aunt charm my neighbors while knowing the truth about her. I meant only to wander over to the windows overlooking the green—it was not my fault the ordinary was so small, or that the girls sat so near the door. But once I was close, I did not move. In spite of everything, seeing them made me feel lonely, and that loneliness was a curse, I knew— Mama had warned me about it.

I stared out the tiny diamond windows onto the farmlands below, the village spread before me like the wrinkles of God's hand, but I saw nothing. Despite my best intentions, I moved closer to Mary Walcott. It could have been habit, I suppose, but the truth was that I had always felt drawn to her. Mary had a way about her, a disarm, perhaps, or maybe it was just the way she opened up and listened as if you spoke God's pure word and she was thirsting for the sound. It had taken me years to learn that she gathered the things I said close and never forgot them, that she doled out my secrets like treasures to the others, that she led me places I did not want to go simply for the sake of having something to talk about. She had held me tight as Job held his conviction, and when I'd finally realized it, 'twas hard to get loose from her.

Now I gnawed on the hard crust of bread I'd taken from our table and pretended to listen to other conversations, to smile at other people. But when Betty Hubbard looked up and motioned me over, I barely hesitated. I glanced behind me to see my father embroiled in discussion with Francis Nurse, and my aunt listening intently to Goody Sibley. Only Jude was watching me, and I did not worry about her.

I told myself I would stay only a moment, not even long enough to answer their questions, and I went over to the table. Mary Walcott looked up with that sly look, while plain-faced Mary Warren only nodded hello, and Mercy Lewis raised her thin dark brow as if she were surprised to see me here.

"Charity," Betty said as she spread butter thickly on her bread, "tell us what you think. Do you not find it strange that Mistress Parris looks so pale all the time? Why, today I hardly thought she could walk herself down to her pew."

"She's sickly." I shrugged. " 'Tis nothing new."

"My uncle says she's not as sickly as she seems." Betty was Dr. Griggs's niece, and she often went with him on his visits. "He says 'tis something strange going on there."

"She's weakening day by day," Mercy Lewis threw in. She leaned forward so her bony elbow rested on the table, and her dark eyes looked huge in her gaunt face. "Withering away, they say. Perhaps she's being poisoned."

"Poisoned?" I was shocked by the suggestion. "Surely not! Why, she's the preacher's wife."

The others giggled. Mary Walcott hid her smile behind her hand. There was something else here, something they all knew and I did not, and I wondered what it was. But Mary was mischievous, and the rest had nothing better to do than stir up trouble. 'Twould be better for me to be far away from it.

I started to turn away. I heard Mary whisper in that goading way, "Ssshhh! Don't tell her! She'll go running to tell her papa. She doesn't like to keep things from him, do you, Charity?"

Across the room, my aunt laughed. I saw my father look at her, and I saw something in his face, something that was gone so fast I had no time to know what it was, to even guess, though it left behind this little flutter in my stomach that I didn't like, that made me nervous.

I heard myself say in a dull voice, "What secrets do you keep now, Mary?"

"Ooh, she doesn't approve," Betty said.

"I suppose she can't help it." Mercy's tease was mean and low. "Her father's pious as a minister."

"Not any minister I know," Mary Walcott said.

Here, they all laughed as if it were another joke they shared. Their cackling made my skin feel too tender, as if the slightest touch might bruise me. I had grown used to my life without them these last months. I had grown used to spending my days with my mother, catering to her as she ran the household from her bed. It had been like a signal from God, Mama had told me, her needing me just at this time, just when I needed to turn from my friends.

But if God had been watching out for me, then why had He taken my mother? Why allow the Devil to send Susannah to tempt me? It had been hard to leave Mary and the others. If my mother had not taken so ill, I am not sure I would have been able to keep myself from them.

They were all leaning over the table, heads close, still laughing, and God help me, I wanted to be part of it. I had felt so alone in the four days since Mama died.

"What is it?" I asked. "Why do you laugh so?"

"Why, I don't think we can tell you," Mary Warren said—but without the meanness of the others. This Mary was more like me, more a mouse than a leader. She was shy and good-hearted for the most part, so I took her words to mean that she was afraid to tell me, not that she meant to torment me with secrets.

"I won't say a word," I promised.

Mercy shook her head. "I don't think so."

Betty sighed. "It's well known that you can't keep a secret, and with—"

"Wait," Mary Walcott said. Betty stopped, frowning prettily at

her, and Mary's eyes went narrow and considering, as if she were
thinking, but that was an act, I knew her well enough to know.
Mary never said or did anything without first planning it well. She
patted the bench beside her. "Charity's been so good caring for her
mama these last months, 'tis unworthy of us not to welcome her
back into our circle when she most needs us."

I looked at her warily.

She smiled at me. "Come, Charity. Sit with us."

"You aren't going to tell her, are you, Mary?" Mercy whined.

"Well . . . perhaps Charity could help us."

She knew how to draw me in. She knew I would not be able to
walk away from a statement like that. I sat down beside her, and
with that one motion, I was part of them again, so simple, just like
that. I felt their camaraderie tightening in a web around me, holding me there. I was so weak, after all.

How easily I fell.

Chapter 6

"YOU MUST PROMISE NOT TO SAY A WORD, CHARITY," BETTY CAU-
tioned.

Mary Warren looked pale and uneasy. Her gaze darted through
the room as if she feared someone would hear us and come running.
"My master will beat me, should he find out."

"There are worse things than a beating," Mary Walcott said dis-
dainfully.

Mercy nodded. "Aye. Hell would be worse."

"Hell?" I asked. "What are you talking about?"

"'Tis not us who courted the Devil," Betty said. "We're not to
blame."

"Quiet." Mary's whisper was so hard that the others stopped and
stared at her. "Are you mad, Betty? Look around you."

Betty flushed and pushed nervously at a loose blond hair.
"Mercy started it."

Mary didn't yield. "The two of you will get us all a beating if
you're not careful."

I changed my mind. I wanted no part of this, whatever it was.
All this talk of Hell and secrets . . . I had enough sins to answer for
already. I could not afford to add another.

I think Mary saw that on my face, because just then she smiled
and leaned close, patting my hand reassuringly. "Never fear. Betty is

not herself today. Dr. Griggs locked her in the cellar yesterday without dinner, and she has not quite recovered."

" 'Twas an accident," Betty murmured.

"A few hours without food would do you good," Mercy said meanly.

I glanced toward the table where my family sat. My father had not noted my absence, nor I think had my aunt. But Jude was watching me with wide eyes and a little frown. I started to rise. "I should get back. My father will be missing me."

"He's hardly noticed you've been gone," Mercy said, glancing that way.

"Still—"

"Sit, Charity. We did not mean to scare you."

I sat again, knowing they would laugh at me if I walked away. "I'm not frightened."

" 'Tis nothing to be afraid of. Only harmless sport."

They all laughed again, but there was a nervousness to it this time. I told myself there was safety in friends and plunged in. "What's harmless sport?"

They quieted. Mary wrapped her hand around a noggin of cider and pulled it close as if to drink, though she did not taste it. She grew very serious. "If we tell you, you must swear not to repeat a word to anyone."

"So you've said already," I said. "I have not gone away, have I? So I must agree."

Mary looked at me for a moment, those cat's eyes of hers seeming to glimmer and grow sharp in the candlelight. Then she glanced around the table, at mousy Mary Warren, and Mercy's hollow eyes, and finally to Betty. "Very well," she said. "But we cannot tell you here, and not today."

"Why?"

"Not on the Sabbath." She laughed softly. Her voice lowered so I had to strain to hear. " 'Twould be a sin to talk about it. Meet us at the parsonage tomorrow afternoon."

I was confused. "Why the parsonage?"

Mercy snickered into her hand. "You'll see when you get there."

Mary shushed her. "Tell your father you must take something to Mistress Parris. A loaf of bread or a pail of beer. She's ill, you see. The parson will probably be out. He usually is."

"Tomorrow afternoon," I repeated slowly. I saw the hidden message in Mary's gaze, the unspoken *don't disappoint us.* It reminded me of the dares Mary used to throw at me: "You haven't the courage to do it, have you, Charity? Such a mealymouthed girl you are. . . ."

I gave Mary a little nod, and then her mouth tightened and her gaze swept past me and up. When I turned to follow it, I saw my aunt standing behind me, her cloak put aside now that the tavern was warm and stinking from so many bodies; the clothes she wore were startling among the muddied greens and browns and blues of my neighbors—a bodice made of scarlet paragon and heavy skirts green as the richest pine tree. Even in the dimness of the ordinary, those colors were so vibrant and bright they were almost blinding.

"Your father's sent me for you," she said, but when I glanced past her to where my father still talked ardently with Francis Nurse, I knew she lied.

"I haven't heard the drum," I told her. 'Twas insolent of me to speak to her in such a way; even Mercy Lewis looked surprised by it. Mary did not take her gaze from Susannah. She stared at those beautiful colors as if fascinated by them.

My aunt laid her hand on my shoulder, a gentle pressure that was insistent just the same. "You'd best come, Charity."

'Twas a mother's touch, a mother's quiet scold, and I resented it. I jerked my shoulder away, but not violently, just enough so she would feel it and know I did not want her there. She let her hand fall softly back to her skirt, seemingly undisturbed, and smiled at my friends, and I saw how that smile took them, how they were captured by it—so beautiful it was, on that face Satan had smiled upon.

It snared even Mary, though she recovered sooner than the others and gave me a satisfied look that reminded me of the rumors I knew now were true. I bade my friends farewell.

My father looked up as my aunt and I approached the table. "Your mother wished you away from those girls," he told me. "You will follow her desires in this."

Francis Nurse said in his low, gruff voice, "Insolent wenches. Tom Putnam deserves those two he has."

I was saved by the sound of the drum summoning us back to the meetinghouse.

I could think of little else during the afternoon service. Master Parris continued his sermon, and I tried to listen, but my mind kept turning back to Mary. I knew my father was right. I should stay away from my old friends, but today I realized how much I'd missed them, how lonely I'd been.

The light outside was fading when the sermon wrapped to a close, and the list of my neighbors' sins was read, their punishments decided on. The list was a short one this week, only two: an overly gossipy Hannah Dow was suffered to be put in the stocks for an hour for telling tales about her neighbors, and the miller's apprentice sentenced to three hours in pillory for overcharging a buyer and lying to his master about it. Once the prayers over their souls were said, Goody Penney handed baby Faith to my father, and he went up to the front of the church to have the pastor baptize her.

I could not remember how or even if my father had held Jude when she was a baby. My mother loved babies, and she held them close, and so I suppose he never had to. The way he held Faith now showed how unpracticed he was. The babe squirmed in his arms, and his hold was awkward and loose, as if she were a feral cat ready to bite and scratch and he was wary but trying to be gentle.

Father had no sooner reached the front of the church than Faith began to cry. By the time Master Parris began to speak, she was wailing with all the strength of Heaven, so loudly that it was hard to hear the parson's words as he entered her into God's kingdom and welcomed her in Christ's name. The minister raised his voice, and she cried louder, until he was red-faced and stumbling. The water he sprinkled her with only made her howl. In the back gallery, children who had already been squirming began to cry and whimper as well. Father looked confounded. Nothing he did seemed to soothe her; Faith only jumped and wriggled in his arms, and her howls grew into high-pitched screeches.

Goody Penney hurried up the aisle, and my father looked shamefacedly relieved as he handed the babe into her arms. The goodwife pulled Faith closer and bounced her gently, but my baby sister was not to be comforted this day. Not even when Goody Penney undid her bodice and tried to latch the babe to a breast. Faith only turned her little head away and beat her tiny, mottled fists against the air.

I saw Goody Penney mouth the words: *Come now, child, come now*. She jounced and bounced, and Faith screamed, and the minister fumbled with the Bible and tried to find his place.

Had my father done so much as look helplessly at me in that moment, I would have rushed to his aid and held my sister close and hummed to her my mother's lullaby. I know she would have quieted for me. But he did not look at me, and so I sat hot and red-faced on the pew as those around began to look at Jude and me as if we were somehow to blame for our sister's ill behavior.

It was Susannah my father looked to.

When she went hurrying forward, I was stunned. When she took Faith from Goody Penney without a word and held her close, I wanted my sister to scream her protest with all the strength she held in her tiny chest. I imagined how Susannah would be unable to calm her. I imagined my father having no recourse but to turn to me. I would go up there and she would go silent in my arms, and my father would look at me with gratitude and love.

"Scream, Faith," I told my sister in a whisper too soft for anyone to hear. "Keep screaming."

Instead, she quieted. The moment Susannah touched her, Faith went still. Her cries dissolved into soft hiccups, and my aunt bounced her gently against her shoulder, patting her back in soft rhythm as though Faith were just one in a long line of babies that Susannah had comforted. I heard sighs around me, and the tension in the meetinghouse eased into relief. One or two women laughed and whispered together as if to say, *Ah, yes, I remember how it was,* and the men grumbled among themselves and shifted in their seats.

My father's face was soft with gratitude and relief. I was so cold I could not feel my skin. I turned to glance through the congregation, and met a pair of hazel cat eyes, and a thin smile. I knew then that I had a safe place to go, someone to turn to, someone who understood.

Mary was not fooled by my aunt Susannah.

The next day, my father left early in the morning to deliver a spinning wheel. 'Twas almost too easy to make the excuse to my aunt to go to the parsonage. Mama would never have let me go without a hundred questions, and even then she would no doubt have taken the bread to Mistress Parris herself and left me to watch Jude. But Susannah did not question me; she only bade me take a pie to Mistress Parris as well.

The wind itself seemed to lend speed to my feet as I left the house. It was cold, with the sure touch of winter, the clouds leaden and low and the smell of snow and ice in the air. I drew my hood closer about my face and pulled my basket up against my chest to ward off the wind as I cut across the fallow cornfields. 'Twas a little over a mile to the parsonage, which was just beyond Ingersoll's, hidden in the trees. The short path from the road was rocky and closed in by darkness. It gave way after only a few yards to a clearing with the ministry house in the center, and orchards and garden and barn beyond.

The house was a large one, with its four rooms and its lean-to, and I knew many villagers who resented that only eight lived within a house large enough to hold many more. There were those—my father among them—who resented that the deed to the land and house had been given over to Master Parris in spite of the fact that there had been a resolution that it should be forever held by the village. It was one of the reasons I had not been to the parsonage for a very long time, why I would not have been here now had my father been at home.

I went to the heavy front door and took a deep breath before I knocked. I heard no sound from within, and there was no one about, and for a moment I thought perhaps I had the wrong day, or that this meeting had been a lie, an unkind joke. But then I heard a shuffling behind the door, and it opened to reveal the dark face of the Parrises' West Indian slave woman, Tituba.

She was dressed in somber gray, with a stained apron, and the brown skin of her hands was dusted with flour. She did not seem surprised to see me. Her dark eyes flicked over me; there was an impatience there that shook me. "I-I heard the mistress was poorly," I said, stuttering and nervous as if she were Queen Mary instead of just a slave. "I've brought bread, and my aunt sent a pie—"

"They just in there, girl," she said, her voice heavy with an accent that spoke of Barbados.

She stepped back and motioned me inside. Though I felt her eyes on me again, and I didn't like it, I did as she said. Even as gray as the day was, it was brighter outside than in the house. I had to stop for a moment and blink until I could see. Inside the heavy front door were the steps to the cellar. Beyond them was the hall. I could just glimpse the huge hearth within, the fire burning hot and orange, though it was as cold where I stood as outside. The ceiling was low, the big summer beam that ran the length of the house was dark and smoke-stained.

"Go on now," Tituba said. "You letting the heat out."

When I stepped into the hall, I saw them sitting at the long tableboard before the fire: Mary Walcott and Mary Warren, Mercy Lewis and Betty Hubbard, and beside them the Parrises' youngest daughter Betsey, who was just nine, and her cousin Abigail Williams, who was eleven. I'd never had much to do with her. She had the coldest gray eyes I'd ever seen. In the corner, the older Parris girl swept. I didn't see the little Parris boy anywhere.

They were bent over the table, and not one of them said a word. They were staring into something: a bowl, with a lit candle flickering just beside it. The room smelled of smoke and dampness. I hesitated, and the slave smiled. "Go on. Go join them," she said. "They need only one more to find the Devil himself."

"The Devil?" Betsey Parris started then, and looked up with a frown on her peaked little face. She looked worriedly at the slave woman standing beside me. "'Tis not so, Titibee, is it? You said—"

"There be many spirits, child," the woman said. Her voice went soft and warm. "You need fear nothing today."

Tituba crossed the room toward the fire, holding the basket I had not even felt her take from me, and the walls seemed to close in until the room was nothing but darkness and fire with a light glowing in the center, flickering across the faces of my friends.

Mary sat back with a sigh. "The spell's broken now anyway, Betsey. You must learn to be quiet."

"Aye, hush up." Abigail raised her hand as if to strike the child, and Betsey drew back hard. Abigail let her hand fall with a nasty smile. "We've so little time as it is. You cannot go on ruining everything."

"You let that child be," Tituba said from the fire. She had not even turned around. "You got time enough for these spells."

I found my voice again. "Spells? You're casting spells? In the preacher's house?"

" 'Tis as safe a place to hide from the Devil as any," Mercy said with a small laugh.

Mary frowned at her. "Quiet, Mercy." She looked at me. "Oh, Charity, 'tis nothing as bad as all that. Betty wanted to find what her future husband would look like. We're only fortune-telling."

"Spells are for witches," I said slowly. " 'Tis a sin—"

"If you've come to preach at us, you can just go away," Betty said irritably. "I'm sorry you told her to come, Mary. She's spoiling everything."

"No, no, I'm not spoiling it. But I—"

"Come over, Charity," Mary urged. "Don't tell me you don't want to see the future. Why, I'll warrant there are things even you want to know."

It was still day outside, yet I thought I heard the hooting of a screech owl, the high, mournful sound rising and falling in the trees beyond the windows. From the corner of my eye, I saw a movement in the shadows—a trick of the light. Goose bumps skimmed over my skin, and I pulled my cloak tighter about me, reminded suddenly of times long since past, when Mary and I and some of these others had gone berrying in the woods at the far side of the village and after filling our pails, spent the rest of the afternoon in the humid shade of the forest, playing blindman's buff in the shadows. Even in the summer, the woods were dark as twilight—'twas easy to see an Indian in a shadow and run screaming back to the others in excited fear, the hairs on the back of your neck prickling, the blood running hot and tingly into your hands and feet.

The fear I felt now was like that. Prickly and exciting, but there was a danger to it that was different. The Indian had been only make-believe; this was something different, something real. Yet it was . . . compelling.

Mary moved over on the bench, and Betty moved too, though I thought reluctantly. "Last week, Abigail swore she saw a man fashioning a spinning wheel. We think her husband's going to be a carpenter. Come and join us."

Slowly I went over. When I sat on the bench between them, I saw that bowl of water on the table, the candlelight reflecting upon the surface so it looked like a bowl of molten gold. The fire was blazing in the hearth, not far away, and though I felt its warmth against my back, I was cold.

Mercy Lewis leaned forward and closed her eyes, so her bony

face went almost soft, and the girls around the table went still and quiet.

"Show me my husband," she said in a hushed voice. "Show me my love."

That was how it all began.

Chapter 7

AFTER THAT DAY AT THE PARSONAGE, THE WORLD FELT DIFFERENT, as if everything had shivered and gone still, waiting for something. It was turning colder day by day; winter had decided to settle in. The hoarfrost in the mornings was thick and hard; in the lee were spots that often stood frozen the whole day through. Trees were bare and black against skies the color of lead. Even when the sun dared to break the clouds away, there was no warmth in its rays, and people were beginning to talk in soft dread about long winters and signs of cold—heavy stripes on caterpillars, beaver dams walled thick.

I reassured myself that was all it was, though there was a part of me that knew the day at the parsonage had changed things. But it wasn't until Pope's Night that I understood. It wasn't until then that I knew to be afraid.

When we came home from the Thursday lecture, the cannon booms from Salem Town echoed like faraway thunder, the faint glow of the bonfires lit the horizon in a soft golden sunset. We did not attend the celebration in town; we never had, though I'd heard tales of the revelries. Most of the villagers agreed with my father that Pope's Night was frivolous; there was too much work to be done. 'Twas in the bigger towns like Boston, and now Salem Town, that sailors and strangers gathered to burn the effigies of Guy Fawkes and the pope and the Devil on the shores near the wharves, and fired the cannons that echoed into the night.

I would have liked to go. Betty had once attended with her uncle when he went to pay a call in town, and she'd told us all about it. But I had to be content with watching the bonfires' distant glow. When Father sent me to fetch the cow from her foraging in the clearing behind the house, I went eagerly, anxious for the chance to spend a few minutes on my own, imagining that I would somehow be able to see something more of the celebration if I stared long enough at the horizon.

I hurried around the corner of the house, already straining to see past the clearing. Our land was on a small rise, and I knew if I stood on a stump at the crest of the hill and leaned out a little, I could just see the expanse of the Crane River stretching nearly to the North-fields of Salem Town. The river was quiet now, with a gray glow like buffed pewter. I could not see much beyond its banks; even as barren as the trees were, the woods were too dense for that. But my imagination leaped to the muddy streets of Salem Town lit by bonfires and torches, the smell of fire and burning straw, the dodging shadows of dancers. Things a godly girl should not be dreaming of. I remembered last year, how I had watched from my bedroom window as Sammy streaked across the darkness, sneaking out to dance at the bonfires, and how I had longed to go with him.

Behind me, Buttercup snapped a twig, and I turned to see her disappearing already in shadow—the colors had faded, and the world was blue and black and gray. I heard the early hoot of a screech owl—not the barred owl that lived in our oak, but another bird, one I did not know, and the air changed the way it had that day at the parsonage, as if it were gathering in force, too heavy to bear, swirling with expectation.

There was someone behind me. I felt the presence as surely as if I'd been on a street in the middle of town. It was Father, I thought, come to fetch me back, but I knew even before I turned around that it was not. I knew it before I raised my eyes.

She was there again, my mother's specter, trailing her winding sheets, pale as mist. She held out her hands to me imploringly, and I froze, alarmed at the pure agony in her face. I did not see her speak, but her voice was loud in my head. *I cannot go. I cannot go. Beware. . . .*

I had never heard my mother so anguished, and it frightened me. I stared at her in horror, unable to look away or to move. 'Twas as if she held me fast. "I-I don't understand," I managed. "Mama, I don't understand."

Beware, she said again, so loud I put my hands to my ears, though I could not mute the sound. Then, before my eyes, she vanished into the trees, into shadow. But I felt her all around me, touching me; I heard her crying in my head. With an overwhelming grief, I longed for her to come back. I had wanted so badly to see her again, to know her, to hear her advice, and now here she was. But she was in a pain that was unbearable, a pain I knew instinctively I could ease if she would only explain to me, tell me. . . . I heard a moan—my own sound. "Mama, come back. Come back. . . ."

Then I heard Buttercup lowing, and suddenly the safe twilight sounds were back: the scatter of a squirrel across a tree branch, the pound of my father's hammer from behind the barn, the gurgle of the creek just beyond.

The pasture was empty, the specter gone. There was nothing to remind me of it, yet the terrible anguish of my mother's specter lingered, her warning. Suddenly I understood. 'Twas as if a veil had been lifted from my eyes, and I knew what she was trying to tell me. My mother's spirit would not rest until Susannah was gone—and I must be the one to banish her.

I was the only one who understood what she was. I must protect my family. That was my mother's warning. But 'twas a task so big I did not know how to manage it. As I led Buttercup into the barn, I was shaking.

When she was settled, I hurried back to the house. Susannah

was at the hearth, and Jude was working with her hornbook, and neither of them looked up as I went inside. My aunt was putting the pottage for supper back on the crane to heat. As she did it, I heard the muffled *boom* from a cannon, and her feet did a little step— something I couldn't quite explain, a shifting of toe to heel, the twist of her hips—so her bright russet skirts twirled about her ankles, barely missing a tongue of flame shooting from the fire.

'Twas as if the other things in the room simply faded away. I saw only her, and the fire in the hearth became a fire shooting sparks and cracking branches, roaring before me. She was a shadow dancing before it, her dark hair loose and falling over her shoulders, twisting and laughing while her skirts tripped over her legs, and she held out her hands to a man dancing beside her. A man so black and shadowed no light touched him.

When the fancy left me, I felt weak, and my mouth was dry. It had only been my imagination, but it lingered in the firelight reflecting off the kettle and the pewter tankards on the table. I backed away, moving to the window, drawn to it, though I could not have said why.

I saw my father coming from behind the barn. I watched him take off the long canvas frock he wore over his clothing and shake the sawdust from it. He glanced up, frowning when I met his gaze through the thick, greenish glass of the window. I resolved then to say something to him about Susannah. The thought made me so nervous I was twisting my skirt in my hands before Father even reached the door.

"Is supper ready?" he asked as he came inside.

Susannah barely turned from the fire. " 'Twill be a minute more. I've just put the kettle on."

He went to the tableboard to pour a noggin of beer. He swilled it in three or four gulps and then poured another, sitting on the bench with a heavy sigh. At the end of the table, Jude kept her nose buried in her hornbook, and I waited in the shadows. I think I might have waited all night had he not looked over his shoulder at me and said, "What ails you, child? Is there nothing you can do to help your aunt?"

"She's fine as she is," Susannah said. "The lights from the celebrations are a rare entertainment. She should watch them if she can."

I winced. My father wiped his mouth with the back of his hand and frowned with his thunderous brows. "Charity."

I stumbled in my haste to come away from the window. "I-I wasn't watching the bonfires. I wasn't."

He ignored me. He looked at Susannah. "God designates days of thanksgiving and humiliation. Any other holidays are only excuses for wasteful frivolity."

"Even God cannot expect a man to eschew sport completely, Brother," she said, and I did not miss the slight smile on her lips, as if she were teasing or playing a joke.

"We've the Sabbath for that," Father said.

"Aye, 'tis a restful day, indeed." Susannah turned back to the fire, and her words lingered a little. Again I searched to find ridicule in her meaning, but I could not find it. My father did not look away from her, and in the dim light his expression was hard to read, but I told myself he'd heard it too, the tacit criticism, the words that didn't mean quite what they said.

This was the moment, I thought. He was suspicious of her, I was sure of it. I should touch his shoulder, I should say that I had something to tell him. I went up behind him and reached out my hand—

"Have you a head for numbers, Sister?" he asked my aunt.

The question seemed to come from nowhere. He was intent on her and had not seen me at all. I let my hand fall back to my side— the moment was gone already, so fast. I realized he had missed the criticism I'd heard in her voice, and I could not believe it. I was unsure suddenly, and so I stepped away from him to watch his face.

Susannah looked at him over her shoulder. She wore no cap,

and the darkness of her hair glimmered red in the firelight. "Some. Judith had the genius of it, I'm afraid."

My father nodded and sighed. "Aye. I left it to her, and she was too good at it to change. But now . . . I can barely read her hand."

"I'll take a look at the account books if you like. I've been reading my sister's letters for eighteen years. I'll be able to decipher it, at least."

My father looked into his beer, and for a moment, he looked so sad that my own heart sagged with him. "I would be grateful."

Susannah turned fully from the fire. "I don't want your gratitude, Brother. If I am to stay here, I expect to do my share. I'll earn my keep."

Father looked up again. There was something in his eyes then, though he was not looking at me directly, and it occurred to me that this was a conversation the two of them had had before, though I could not imagine when. " 'Tis not an easy life here. This is not London."

She laughed; it was not a happy sound. "I've no wish for London."

"There are no niceties here."

"My sister lived without them for years. 'Twill not be a hardship for me."

"You should think well on this," my father said. "Judith would not have required you make such a sacrifice."

My aunt looked oddly wistful, an expression that confused me until I remembered how tricky the Devil could be. "I've had months to think on it," she said. "This is what I want. Do not tell me you could not use some help with the children."

"But I'm here for that," I said before I thought. They both looked at me in surprise, and I braved on. "I'm not a child. You needn't stay for me. I'm old enough to care for Jude and Faith."

"Charity, quiet," Father said. "Your mother hasn't been gone a fortnight. Do you think she would countenance such impertinence?"

"N-no, sir." I dipped my head, my fingers trembling. "I-I'm sorry, F-father. I . . . I didn't think—"

"Aye, you don't think, Charity. That is the problem."

Tears blurred my eyes, and I dared not look at him. My tears would only make him angrier, I knew, and I could not explain them away. I could not say to him that Susannah was dangerous, that she fed the disobedience in my nature, that we should send her away. He would not believe me. I had to somehow tear away his blindness; I had to make him see.

"Apologize to your aunt," he said.

I swallowed. "I'm sorry."

"Charity."

I did what he wanted. I looked up at her, into her face, so I could speak with the sincerity he expected, and suddenly my tears were gone and there was a coldness in my soul. She was watching me with a careful look that was as clear to me as the gentle eddies of Crane Brook where it bent past our farm. In her eyes, I saw her heart, and there it was: the Devil's smile.

She was dangerous. I knew to resist the pull of her and yet I felt it still. I knew what she was and yet I wanted her comfort. Satan knew me too well; he knew the things I craved, the things I longed for.

I prayed for God to take Susannah away; I cared not how.

"Forgive me," I managed to say. "I am sorry for speaking to you that way."

"I am no monster," she said to me. "I did not come into your life to take it over, Charity. I expect you to tell me how you feel. Only then can we respect each other."

I felt my father's silence, and I felt the temptation in her words. I had never seen an actress, but I imagined she must be one of the best. Had I not known what she was, I would have believed the things she said completely; I would have trusted her with my soul the way I'd trusted my mother with it. She knew just what to say to bring my cooperation, and I had no choice now but to smile and pretend to give it.

So that is what I did. "I will do better, I promise." It was a small lie, mostly for my father's benefit, because I could see that I was not the actress Susannah was, that she did not quite believe me.

But she nodded and turned back to adjust the crane with our supper hanging from it, and I glanced over to my father.

He was watching her, and there was an intensity in his gaze. His hand was clenched around his tankard so tightly that even in the candlelight I could see the whiteness of his knuckles. I felt as if I'd intruded on a moment so private not even he knew it existed, and I looked away quickly, ashamed and disturbed, though I had no idea why. For no reason that I could say, I thought of Sammy, of his large and loving hands. I felt a longing for him.

The window to my soul was opening ever wider, and now I feared for my father as well. The Devil was called "the prince of the air," and I knew why. I felt him in every breath of wind.

The next day, I woke to an anxiety I could not lose. The memory of yesterday stayed with me. I could not look at Susannah without seeing my own damnation in her sly smile; I felt lost. My father had gone early that morning, but I knew that even had he been here, I would not have found the courage to approach him. Instead, my thoughts turned to Mary and the others. They would listen to me; they would understand. As the morning hours passed, I grew to believe it more and more, until the urge to go to Mary was so strong I would have made up any excuse to see her.

As it turned out, I did not have to lie. I'd just finished trimming the last of the wicks when Susannah asked me to run into the village. Mary Walcott's stepmother had a length of cotton for baby clouts that she'd never used, and she'd offered to trade it for a new wooden pail. Within minutes, I was out the door, dragging Jude behind me before Susannah had time to notice and protest. The pail my father had made for Mistress Walcott was sitting by the barn door, and I made Jude grab it up, and together we hurried into town.

I walked fast to put the miles past us, so that Jude had to stumble and run to keep up. She huddled into her cloak and complained the whole way, but I barely heard her. The two miles beyond the Walcotts' to the Putnams' were not such a great distance. My spirits rose; it was almost as if I'd found Mary already.

Captain Walcott and his family lived only yards from the parsonage. Once we were there, I hesitated, wondering if I should go on to the Putnams' and stop back here on the way home, or stop now. In the end, the decision was made for me, and that, too, was fortuitous, because I'd been leaning toward going on. But Mistress Walcott saw us coming up the hill and waved to us from the garden, where she was clearing away the last of the dead vines.

"Come along," I said to Jude with a sigh. "We may as well go up. She's seen us."

Jude's face scrunched in a puzzled frown. "Isn't this where we're going anyway?"

I didn't bother to answer her. Jude was not good at keeping secrets—I would not have brought her at all except that I did not want her around Susannah. I'd been planning to keep her quiet with my best dire threats, but now there was no need of it. Because as we went up the hill, Mary came out from the house. I stopped in surprise, catching my breath and then nearly falling to my knees to praise God for making it all so easy. 'Twas as if He were pointing my direction. "Charity!" Mary called out, raising her hand in greeting, and I hurried the few yards to where she stood. I was breathless when I reached her.

There must have been something in my expression, for her smile faded, and her hazel eyes darkened. "Why, what is it?"

"I've been looking for you," I said in a low voice.

"I've been up at the sergeant's. You knew that."

"'Tis hard for me to get there."

"And hard for me to leave." She glanced toward her stepmother, who was straightening and wiping her dirty hands on her apron. "Mother asked me over today to help with the preserving."

There was an edge in her voice when she said this, a slight resentment, and I knew it was because Mary disliked her stepmother. I don't think she had ever forgiven the woman for sending her out to the Putnams', though 'twas a natural choice, because Mary's own mother was long dead and her stepfather had no reason to want the child of his first wife around. Mistress Walcott's brother was Thomas Putnam, who had many children and a sickly wife. He needed the help, while Mistress Walcott did not—she had Mary's four half siblings there to help with her own infants.

Mistress Walcott called out, "Thank goodness you're here already, Charity. I've needed that pail for days now."

"Father just finished it this morning," I called back. Then I nudged Jude and told her, "Don't just stand there. Take it over to her."

I waited until Jude had gone out of earshot, and then I turned to Mary. "Can you talk a moment?"

She sent a glance to her stepmother, then nodded. "Come inside. I've jelly ready to boil." She called out, "Mother! Charity's asked for some cider!"

"She's come a long way. Set some out for this little one too!" Mistress Walcott called back.

I followed Mary into the house. The hall was sweaty and warm, with the tang of cranberries and sugar making my mouth water as I stepped inside. The kettle was hissing over the fire, and Mary hurried over to it with a sound of distress, and then calmed when she saw it was not boiling. She took a long-handled spoon and stirred it, and the steam rose into her face and sent the fine hairs peeking from beneath her cap twining into little curls. I had the small, envious thought that she was so pretty that even the damp flush on her face was sweet.

Sweetness was a word that did not keep when it came to Mary. My thought vanished the moment she turned to me with her assessing, slanty eyes and her thin-lipped frown. "All right, then, we've only a few minutes. What do you want? This isn't about the other day, is it? What have you done, Charity? Gone and told someone?"

"No. No, of course not. I gave my word."

"It wouldn't be the first time you've broken it."

I was stung by her scorn. "Not this time."

"Then what?"

"It—it's about my aunt."

"Your aunt?" She looked surprised. "What have I to do with her?"

"You were right about her," I said breathlessly, glancing toward the door to make sure no one came in. "I think she is an actress."

"Really?" Mary drew herself up with a smug, triumphant little smile. "I knew it. Does your father know too, then?"

"I don't think so. 'Tis what worries me."

"Why, I'm amazed. I wouldn't have thought he would miss such a thing." She paused, and then she laughed in great amusement. "But then, he didn't even know his own daughter was playing the trull with his apprentice—"

"Mary!" Mary was rarely so coarse.

"I'm only complimenting you, Charity. When you feel like keeping a secret, 'tis true you keep it well."

"It . . . I never meant for that to be a secret."

"No, of course not. Did you not wonder, Charity, why Sammy wanted you to keep it so? I would have thought he would court you openly instead of stealing your virtue in a barn."

I wanted to sink through the floor at the loudness of her voice, at the things she was saying. I said in a hoarse whisper, "Not so loud, Mary. What if someone should hear?"

She shrugged. "No one is near enough to hear us."

"If they should come through the door—"

"Tell me, Charity—" Mary leaned as close to me as she could while still stirring the jelly. "Those things that Sammy wanted you to do . . . Did you do them? Did he like it?" She lifted her fine brows suggestively.

I wanted to squirm away from her; I was sorry I'd come. The things she said brought memories so clearly into my head that the sharpness of them hurt. I was sure she must be able to see in my eyes the things Sammy and I had done, the things she knew he had urged me to do, because I had gone to her for counsel. Mary had gleefully encouraged me to give in to him. *If you love him, Charity, you'll do whatever he asks. Do you want to lose him to someone who can satisfy him that way when you will not?*

I made myself turn away, and Mary laughed and said, "It's just that I'm jealous, Charity. We all are. Why, except for Mercy, you're the only one of us who's felt a man's touch."

"I would not have done it had you not advised me to," I said. My voice was so thin it seemed to disappear into the hiss of steam from the pot.

"But you were glad of it, weren't you? You would do it again if you could."

"No." I shook my head violently. "No, I wouldn't."

"If Sammy came back into town—"

"He won't be back."

"He won't?" She paused. I felt her looking at me with that thoughtful stare, though I did not dare look back to her. "How do you know that?"

"I-I don't . . . really," I lied.

"You mean . . . one morning you woke up, and he was gone. He just . . . disappeared into the night. Is that the truth of it, then?"

"That's the truth of it," I told her.

I don't know if Mary saw that lie too. I don't know what she saw. All I know is that she left the long-handled wooden spoon spinning in the jelly, and stepped over to me, putting her steam-hot hand on my arm so it nearly burned my cold skin. The empathy in her face was such that I forgot the meanness of the other things she'd said to me.

"Oh, my poor Charity," she said. "What sorrow his leaving must have brought you. No wonder you did not want anyone to know—why, he used you and left you, and what else is there for you to do but wonder how you displeased him?"

"Aye," I managed to choke out, because in a way that was true enough. It had not taken much to make Sammy go. Not nearly as much as I'd hoped it would.

"Well, I won't say a word," she whispered. "It will be our little secret. But you must promise to do something for me."

I drew back, wary again. "What?"

"That red paragon bodice your aunt was wearing at meeting. Can you get it for me?"

"What?"

"Can you get me the bodice?"

"You . . . you don't mean . . . steal it?"

"No, you silly widgeon. I don't want you to steal it. Just . . . Could you borrow it? For a night, 'tis all. There's a man—"

" 'Tis not mine to lend you, Mary."

"Oh, don't be so pious. It's not as if you wouldn't borrow it yourself if you had the chance. If Sammy were still here . . . why, you'd take it in a minute. Think how pretty you would look in it."

"I wouldn't take it."

Mary's eyes flared. "You know, Charity, sometimes you make me forget why I even like you. Mercy would do this. Betty borrowed a lace cap just last week. But you . . . You think you're so much better than the rest of us—"

"I don't," I protested. "I don't think that."

"Then prove it."

"Mary, this isn't fair."

"It's not as if I'm asking you to do something so terrible. Just borrow it for a night. I'll return it to you the next day. I promise it. She doesn't even have to know."

" 'Twould be a sin to take it that way."

"What's one more to add to so many?" Mary smiled, but I saw the deliberation of it, and I knew I was losing her allegiance.

"I don't want to borrow it," I said desperately. "I don't even want to touch it. She's a wicked thing. Did you not hear me before? She's an actress, I know it. And the way she looks at me—why, 'tis as if the Devil in her is waiting to trap me. Yesterday, I even saw—I think I saw . . . Mary . . . I . . ."

The kettle spat and bubbled up. Mary spun to look at it. With a small cry, she hurried over, grabbing up the spoon. The tendons in her arm bulged and went taut as she tried to stir the boiling jelly down.

"Mary." Mistress Walcott's voice came from the doorway. I jumped at the sound, startled, and turned to see her. She smiled at me and bustled inside, bringing Jude in with her. The wooden pail my father had made was filled with withered roots and vines. "Don't tell me you've left poor Charity standing all this time without her cider?" She set down her cuttings and went to the tableboard to pour Jude and me a tankard.

She passed it to me first. I wasn't thirsty—my stomach was in such knots I wasn't sure I could drink it without vomiting, but I managed a few gulps before I handed it to my little sister. Mistress Walcott helped Mary lug the kettle off the fire. When Mary spilled jelly as she tried to pour it into the crocks assembled on the table, her stepmother grabbed the ladle from her hand.

"You graceless girl," she scolded. "Do something useful now— go upstairs and bring that cloth I'd saved to give to Charity's mother. Go on now."

Mary's face was sullen, but she hurried to do as her stepmother bade her. When she came downstairs again bearing a square of folded cloth tied with twine, I took it from her without catching her eye and bade farewell to Mistress Walcott.

"Mary will show you out," she said. "Thank your father for the fine pail. He's to be praised for such work."

I did not want Mary to show us to the door. I knew she would

ask again about the bodice, and I did not know what to do. I felt
the favor hovering between us, and I knew it for the test it was. I
could not think of a way to escape it. When we got to the door, Jude
went ahead, and I tried to say my good-byes hastily. Mary grabbed
my elbow and pulled me back before I could, and whispered, "Remember what I said. Bring it to me next Monday."

"Mary, I can't—"

She smiled. "Charity," she said slowly, "think how Mercy will
tease you if she finds out what a frightened little rabbit you are.
Why, she might just insist that you not come to our meetings anymore. If we can't trust you—"

"Of course you can trust me," I said, and there was a part of me
that was ashamed of how anxiously I spoke, how I nearly cowered
to keep her good opinion of me. "You can trust me."

"Well, I believe you, of course," Mary said. "But the others
might not. They might want some kind of proof—"

"A red paragon bodice," I said dully.

She smiled again. "We're meeting at the parsonage on Monday
afternoon. Don't be late."

Chapter 8

———— ❧ ————

I NEARLY RAN HOME, PULLING POOR LITTLE JUDE BEHIND ME. THE sky was gray and the wind had come up again, heavy with the scent of fire smoke, littered with chimney ash that fell against my cheeks like soft dry snow, and all I could think was that it was the fires of Hell that fed it.

Mama had always said I could not tell the difference between good and evil, that I was too easily misled. Mary made everything sound so simple—everyone else did such things all the time; 'twas not such an immoral thing to borrow a bodice. It would be returned the next day, and no one would be the wiser. . . . But I knew it was wrong to take the bodice, even for an hour, just as it had been wrong to take Mary's advice when it came to Sammy.

I hurried faster, my breath coming hard and raspy. Jude was carrying the fabric Mistress Walcott had given us, and she dropped it twice trying to stay up with me. I could not make myself slow, though she asked me to again and again. When we finally got to our house, I stopped outside. I had nearly run to get here, and now I could not make myself go in.

Jude looked at me as if I were mad as she went past me to the door. "Are you going to stand there all night, Charity? I thought you wanted to be home again."

"Aye. I'll be in shortly."

She gave me an exasperated sigh. "'Tis too cold for me."

She opened the door and disappeared into the house, and I stayed there in the cold and felt the bite of the wind on my cheeks and through my cloak.

I heard a noise then, the thud of hooves, the rattle of wheels. I jumped, remembering yesterday, the spirit's visit. When I saw a shadow moving through the woods beyond our house, I froze—in that moment, I was sure 'twas Mama's specter coming for me. It felt as if my belly had dropped to my toes. But then the horse appeared from the woods, and I saw my father following alongside.

On any other day, I would not have waited for him, but when he came from the woods—no spirit woman, just my father, my savior—it felt as if God were pointing the way for me after all. I could almost hear the Lord's voice thundering in my head: *Talk to him. Now he will believe you.*

Led by that voice, I hurried toward my father, my stomach twisting and churning. I nearly lost my courage when I saw the way he halted Saul and stood staring at me as if I'd lost my wits. I felt in that moment that maybe I had, that he would not believe me and 'twas foolish to even try.

"What is it, Charity?" he asked me as I came before him. "Why are you not inside? 'Tis growing dark."

"A word with you, Father, if you please," I said. At first, I was not sure he heard me, because he said nothing. But then he looked at me, and I had a quick vision—of waking to find him watching me as I slept, his face soft and tender—and I suddenly found myself mute. It was unbearable that I did not know if it were real or not, that I could not remember.

The expression left his face then; I wondered if I'd truly seen it, or if 'twas only a trick of my desperation. He sighed. "Come now, Daughter. 'Tis cold."

"Oh, Father," I whispered. "Father, I-I am afraid we have been cruelly deceived."

"Deceived? How so?"

I saw how intently he was listening to me, and I . . . 'Twas an amazing thing, to hold his interest this way. "She's the Devil, Father." The words came spilling out of me so fast I could not stop them. He was listening to me, and I trusted him. He was so much wiser than I; he would know what to do. "She's trying to make us all believe she cares for us, but she's lying. She hopes to bend us to Satan's ways. . . . She's an actress, Father. She's an actress."

He looked confused. "What are you prattling about?"

"I didn't know how to tell you. I saw the spirit, and I've been so afraid—"

"Charity." He said my name slowly, and I quieted. He took my elbow and gave me a little shake. "Slow down. Tell me clearly. Who is an actress? Whom do you accuse?"

The things I'd wanted to tell him faded in the strength of one thought. He was touching me. He was touching me, and even though his fingers hurt, I had longed for this so often and so many times that I could not bear the thought of him letting go. I stood there in stunned silence, unable to say the words that would let him release me.

He made a sound of impatience. "Now, Charity."

"Susannah," I said. Her name left my lips like an exhaled breath. I felt weak for having said it, as if the name itself had lent strength to my bones, and now that it was said, the strength was gone with it.

"Susannah?" My father dropped my elbow, and I swayed into him, falling against his chest so I could smell the scents of sweat and wood shavings on his rough wool cloak, so I felt his warmth against my cheek. I closed my eyes to drink in the feel of him, and he let me stay there. For one minute, I believed he wanted me there. I believed in the truth of his tenderness. I felt the steady rise and fall of his breathing, the faint brush of his hand. But I took it too far; I went to put my arms around him, and that was when he pushed me away. I could only stand there like a weak reed blown hither by the wind.

"Your aunt is not an actress, Charity," he said gently.

I wanted to believe him, but his quiet voice was like the breeze before a storm; I heard undercurrents in it that made me look at him carefully. What I saw in his eyes sent my hopes scattering. He was not trying to reassure me—it was just that he did not believe me.

"Father," I said desperately, "she has you fooled. She's fooled us all—"

"She's not fooling anyone. She's no actress."

"'Tis what she wants you to believe."

"Do you think I cannot discover truth for myself? That I cannot see wickedness beneath my very nose?" There was such disdain in his voice, and I thought of the things I'd done, my own wickedness, and I was afraid again. I knew he could be fooled. I stood in front of him so he could not move while the horse blew soft, foggy breaths into the air and pawed the ground as if he were impatient to be back in the barn. I said carefully, "The Devil wears many pleasing faces."

He made a sound, a short laugh, and shook his head. "Aye. And I've seen enough of them to last a lifetime." He took my arm again, this time to pull me out of the way, and clicked at the horse to walk.

"Father!" I called after him. "Please!"

He stopped and turned to look at me while the horse walked slowly on. "Enough, Charity," he said wearily. "Go inside."

He did not believe me. I closed my eyes and tried not to cry, and the images came to me: my mother's spirit stretching out her hands, Susannah singing Jude to sleep, Mary's slant-eyed gaze, and the candle flame flickering in a bowl of water . . .

And Tituba. Tituba. *Those girls need only one more to find the Devil himself.*

My eyes snapped open. I watched my father lead Saul into the barn. Darkness came upon me, and in it, I heard again my mother's voice. *Beware.*

*   *   *

'Twas that moment that took away my doubt about borrowing the bodice. I hadn't changed my mind about not wanting to touch it, nor about how wrong it was to take it. But now I thought of it as a way to curry Mary's favor—I would bring her the bodice, and she would have no choice but to help me with Susannah.

It became a matter then of when to take it, and how. I did not want my aunt to miss it, and so I could not keep it for very long. I planned for Saturday night, but I did not get the chance, and though I didn't like to do something so dishonest on the Sabbath, it seemed I had no choice. But Susannah went to bed soon after we returned from meeting—I imagined a day of trying to seem pious was exhausting for her. She certainly looked pale and tired, and when Father suggested that she stay with us for the evening prayers, she snapped at him that she would be served better by rest, and disappeared up the stairs.

Except for the virginal, which stayed in the hall, tucked away in the corner behind the wool wheel, Susannah's things had all been moved into our already crowded bedroom. Her trunks were large; the room was so full now, 'twas hard to walk through it. She kept most of her clothes in the chest shoved against the foot of the bed, and I did not dare try to go through them when she was in there, even as soundly as she slept.

Sunday night, I did not sleep well. My nerves were strung tight. The threat of Monday afternoon loomed large before me. I lay in bed beside my aunt and berated myself for waiting too long, and as the hours crept into deepest night, I was so desperate I nearly rose from bed to sneak into her trunk. Then she stirred, and I sank hopelessly again into the mattress.

When morning came, I tried to outstay her. I dallied over my dress; I fumbled with my hair and my cap. But she didn't leave, and I knew she would not let me stay when she said, "Hurry along, Charity. We've plenty to do today. There's the churning, and your father brought the malt from town yesterday for the beer."

My heart sank. We would be brewing small beer today; I would be lucky to find a spare moment before afternoon, and even then, 'twould be nearly impossible to get to the parsonage. I suppose that thought should have brought relief; after all, if I could not get to the parsonage, I could hardly give Mary the bodice I hadn't "borrowed." But I knew she would suspect that I was avoiding her deliberately, and I knew her well enough to know the things she would tell the others. More than that, I could not bear the thought of delaying things any longer. My talk with my father had convinced me of that. I needed a shield against Satan. I had no choice but to find a way to get to the parsonage, bodice or no.

Jude hurried along after us as we left the bedroom. On the stairs, she pushed past me to Susannah. "Will you show me another stitch for my sampler today, Auntie?" she asked, tugging at Susannah's sleeve.

I stumbled so that I had to put a hand on the wall to keep from falling. *Auntie.* I'd never heard Jude call her that before, and the look on my little sister's face was bright and smiling as she looked up into Susannah's eyes. Jude had always hated working on her sampler; it had taken all of Mama's admonitions to keep my sister seated and quiet. I remembered that just the week before Mama died, Jude had murmured "Damnation!" while she was sewing, and for punishment, Mama made her sew for another hour. Jude had bit her lip until it bled, trying to unknot a terrible stitch.

"Aye, we'll try one later," Susannah said to my sister. She reached down, laying a gentle hand on Jude's light brown hair. There was a possessiveness to the gesture that terrified me. "Perhaps you should try to work on the other one I showed you for a while."

I stammered out, "B-but, Jude. You hate your sampler."

"I love to sew now," she said to me. "Since Auntie told me a song to sing while I do it. Do you want to hear it? It goes—"

"No," I said quickly. "No, I don't want to hear a song. And you'd better not let Father hear you sing it, either."

Susannah threw me a quick glance over her shoulder, and I was sure I saw triumph in her gaze. I despaired; I had tried not to leave Jude alone with Susannah—there had only been the few times, not many. . . . But the Devil was strong, and, as my father had once said, children had so little defense against him. It made my task harder and more urgent. I would have to find a way to the parsonage. I would have to find a way to get hold of that bodice.

When we got downstairs, Father was already there, pulling on his boots. He stood by the door, as if he could hardly wait to go outside, though the frost was heavy on the windows, and the hall was so cold our breaths froze.

"Good morning, Brother," Susannah said in her soft voice.

He jerked as if she'd frightened him, though we had been talking all the way down the stairs, and he had to have heard. He barely looked over his shoulder at us. "Good morning," he said. He put on his hat but not his cape, and I knew then that he was only going to the barn. It was strange that he would go like that before he ate breakfast.

I hurried past my aunt to the samp mill above the mantel, and pulled it down. "I'll make breakfast quickly—"

He shook his head and waved me away. "I've eaten," he said abruptly, and then I saw the half-empty tankard of cider on the table, the crumbs left from a hurried meal of bread—without butter, because we had still to churn some. Then, before we could protest, he opened the door and stepped out, and I had the fleeting impression of ice-washed trees and frost-gilded ground—the whole world in translucent white—before the door closed again and he was gone.

I stood frozen with my hand on the samp mill. Since I'd told him my suspicions about Susannah, he had dismissed every task I'd tried to do for him, as if my presence troubled him. He would not even look at me now. I poured corn into the samp mill and turned the crank, grinding my despair with every turn so vigorously that I saw my aunt look over at me in surprise as she skinned eels for our dinner.

I made my plans as we ate. As I sped through my other chores, I watched Susannah as she stirred the steeping malt for the beer. It was a careful task, one Mama had never let me have the care of. If the malt got too hot, the beer would sour; not hot enough, and there would be no flavor. Susannah went about it with her usual competence, and I resented her for that too, that she should be so good at everything. 'Twas as if she'd been born to this life. Before long, the hall was filled with stinking steam that sent my fine hair straggling from my cap and raised a sheen of sweat on Jude's cheeks as she rocked the dasher of the churn. Susannah never looked anything less than fresh and beautiful, and as I saw the way the curls of her hair escaped the hidden pins to dangle against her cheek, just so, impossibly beautiful, my resentment grew into a hatred so powerful I was nauseated with it. It seemed she sensed that too, and that she enjoyed the power she held over me, because she smiled when she gave me another task, and then another, as if she knew my plans and hoped to thwart them: Get the canary wine and the hops from the cellar, fetch a pumpkin and slice it up to boil for dinner, scoop some yeast from the old beer barrel, and get enough for the eels too. . . .

I was sweating and trembling from sheer anxiety as I put the last of the pumpkin into a kettle of water, and my mind was racing. My father would be in soon for dinner; perhaps I could appeal to him, perhaps there was some chore he could give me that would take me into town—

"The butter won't come," Jude complained. "I've been churning for hours."

"'Tis cold," my aunt said. "It may take a while today."

"Not this long. My arms are tired."

Susannah looked over her shoulder. "Try this, Jude. 'Twill make the time go faster. Sing: 'Come, butter, come. Come, butter, come. Peter stands at the gate, waiting for a buttered cake. Come, butter, come.' 'Tis a bit of magic, you'll see."

Jude sighed. "'Come, butter, come—'"

"Jude!" I jerked away from the kettle. "You can't say such a thing. Why, 'tis a spell!"

I knew at once that I'd given myself away. Susannah turned to me, and that turn was quiet and slow, as if she knew I would wait all day for her to look at me. Her expression was kind, but I saw past the surface to the lie.

"There's no harm in it, Charity," she said. "Let her be."

"I won't!" I said. "You've given her a spell!"

"'Tis a rhyme, nothing more—"

"It's come!" Jude shouted. "Look, Auntie, it worked! The butter's come!"

I spun from the fire in horror. "You see!" I cried. "It *is* a spell!"

"Charity," Susannah said. "Charity, don't be such a fool."

I saw that she was going to tell me another lie—one to reassure me, to silence me, and I knew then that I could not stay. I left the pumpkin boiling, and I ran upstairs to our bedroom, ignoring her calls to come back. I slammed the door shut behind me and waited to hear her footsteps on the stairs, trembling in terror lest I hear the sound.

Susannah did not come after me. I hardly knew what to make of that, but I didn't hesitate. I went to her trunk and threw open the lid, listening for any noise on the stair. Her clothes were neatly folded inside, and for a moment, I stared, stunned by the colors I saw, the sheer brilliance and richness of the fabrics. But then, I didn't tarry. I rifled through the trunk until I found the red paragon bodice, and I pulled it out and laid the other clothes on the top and hoped she would not be able to tell. Then I shoved the bodice beneath the bed and closed her trunk, and I sat there, waiting, and heard . . . nothing.

Finally, when my heart had calmed, I went to the crack in the floorboards and knelt beside it, leaning down to see through. I saw Jude and Susannah at the tableboard, and Susannah was kneading the butter in a bowl of clear water, speaking slowly and patiently to Jude. I wondered how I could leave them together, how long it took the Devil before he could claim a child's soul, and knew I had no choice but to leave things like this today.

It seemed I waited a long time, but finally Susannah patted the butter into a firkin and wiped her hands on her apron. Then she said something to Jude, and I saw her move toward the cellar door. I heard the creak of it opening, and then its close.

It was my chance. I reached under the bed and grabbed the bodice, shoving it beneath my skirt, and then I went as fast as I could. The stairs creaked as I came down them, and Jude looked up from the table and said, "What ails you, Char—"

"Sssshh!" I hissed. "Quiet!"

"But—"

I came close to her, a mere inch from her face. Jude started to back away, but I grabbed her and held her firm. "I'm leaving," I said, catching her glance and holding it. "If you say a word about this to anyone, I'll beat you within an inch of your life when I get back."

"But, Charity—"

"I mean it," I said. "Especially, don't tell *her.*"

I wanted to wait until I saw assent in Jude's eyes, but I didn't dare. I had no choice but to trust that she would keep quiet. I gave her my most threatening stare, and then I hurried to the front door and crept out, staying in the shadows for a moment until I was sure Father was not coming from the barn. Then, as quickly as I could, I ran down the pathway to the road beyond, clutching the bodice beneath my skirt, breathing easy at last.

Chapter 9

———— ❧ ————

THEY WERE ALREADY GATHERED AT THE PARSONAGE WHEN I ARrived, but Tituba was nowhere to be seen. 'Twas Abigail who opened the door when I knocked, who looked me over with cold gray eyes before she motioned me inside. "We've not much time, and you must be very quiet," she told me. "My uncle's gone only to visit Sergeant Putnam's, and my aunt is sick upstairs."

I glanced toward the darkness of the stairs. " 'Tis just as well. No one knows I'm here."

"Did you sneak out, then, Charity?" Mercy Lewis spoke from where she stood at the entryway of the hall, a clever look on her thin and bony face.

"Aye." I let her think what she would about it. At this moment, I cared for little but the task at hand. "Where's Mary?"

Mercy stepped back, and I went past her into the hall and saw them all huddled around the table again, but this time there was no bowl of water on it, and Mary and Betty and Mary Warren were whispering and laughing quietly among themselves. Young Betsey Parris sat at the end of the long bench, looking pinch-faced with worry, her blue eyes huge. The little Parris boy played with a wooden spoon near the fire. He banged it in an indifferent rhythm, on the settle, and then the floor, and then on an upturned trencher, and the different sounds rang hollowly in the room: *bang bing bong,* over and over again.

I glanced back at Abigail. "Where's your servant?"

She shrugged. Her pale eyes looked eerie in the dimness of the room. "You mean Tituba? She's somewhere."

"Oh, there you are, Charity!" Mary called out from the table, and there was a false heartiness in her greeting, and then a faint needling when she said, "I wondered if you would be here today."

"I said I would, didn't I?" I went farther into the room, the bodice heavy against my legs, seeming to burn my skin where it was crumpled beneath my skirt. "Did you really think I would not?"

"I wasn't sure." She came over to me. Her gaze went to my skirt. "Why, Charity, what are you hiding at your belly? At least, I hope you're hiding something, and there's not some other reason for there to be a lump there."

Mercy laughed. I flushed and reached under my skirt to pull out the bodice. "Here," I said, holding it out to her. To my dismay, my hands were trembling. "Take it."

Mary smiled. She took my aunt's bodice into her hands with a gentleness I'd never seen in her before; she caressed the double camlet with special care, turning it so the silk and wool weave shimmered softly in the candlelight. "Ah, 'tis as beautiful as I remember," she said quietly. "Where do you suppose she ever got such a thing?"

"In London," I said. "She has more clothes than I've ever seen." I stepped close to her and lowered my voice so none of the others could hear. "Mary, now I'd ask a favor—"

"Ah, how beautiful that is." Mary Warren had come from the table to look over Mary's shoulder.

Mary held the bodice to her breasts and twirled around. "What do you think?"

"It makes your eyes look brown," Mercy said.

Betty nodded. "The red is perfect for your skin."

"Do you think he'll notice me in this?" Mary asked.

"If he does not, he's blind," Betty assured her.

"Mary," I said, "if I could have a word—"

"Who is blind?" Abigail pushed past me. "Who are you talking about?"

"Mary's enamored with Robert Proctor," Mercy teased. "Such an old man as that!"

Mary blushed. "He's hardly old. Why, he's just thirty."

"And set in his ways. I don't think he's even looking for a wife."

"He may not be looking, but I expect to show him what can be found." Mary made a little prancing step, and laughed with a low, delightful chuckle that reminded me how pretty she was, how I'd once been jealous of the way Sammy looked at her, and that made me think of everything that had led me here, and I was desperate to get her attention. But she was paying me no mind. She was laughing with the others while Mary Warren said thoughtfully, "'Tis true, Master Robert's handsome enough. And he's not so old. He doesn't get along well with his father, though. I think 'twould be hard to have John Proctor as a father-in-law."

"No, you'd rather have him for a husband," Mercy joked, and Mary Warren flushed.

"Well, Robert's the eldest son," Mary said, smoothing the bodice again—'twas as if she could not stop touching it. "And . . . Goodman Proctor *is* nearly sixty."

Betty laughed. "Aye. You'd have him in the grave tomorrow. I can see you've already set your sights on all that property in Ipswich."

"'Twould get me out of this tiny village," Mary snorted. "Don't tell me the rest of you don't want the same."

"I wouldn't marry an old man for it," Abigail said. "Can you imagine him touching you with those dry hands—"

"I imagine you'd learn to tolerate anything for the right to be called 'Mistress.'"

"Anything but that." Abigail shuddered.

"You're young yet," Mary told her. She glanced at me, and her smile was knowing and clever. "There will be a time when it won't seem so bad. It might even be fun. Isn't that right, Charity?"

I could not give her an answering smile. "'Tis what I've heard," I managed. I wished she would stop talking, that the others would go back to their fortune-telling and leave me the chance to have a word with her. I wished she would put the bodice away. It only reminded me of the urgency of my task and the risk I'd taken in getting it for her. It didn't help that whenever I looked at it, the bodice seemed to shiver and gleam as if it had a life of its own. I could not help thinking of my aunt Susannah standing at the table in Ingersoll's Ordinary, her face glowing with her special light. I imagined 'twas the same light I saw now on that bodice, and I shivered at the thought that there was something of her here, watching me, haunting me.

Mary looked at Mary Warren. "You're sure Robert's at the tavern today? He did come down last night from Ipswich?"

Mary Warren nodded. "He's there. You should have heard the row he had with his father last night. I thought he would return today for certain. But I heard him say he would stay until tomorrow."

"Then it must be tonight," Mary said.

"What must be tonight?" I asked.

Mary tilted her head at me. "Why, a visit to the Proctors' tavern."

"You wouldn't dare."

"Aye, I would." She laughed, and I heard the excitement in her voice and knew she would do it. She would walk the miles to Ipswich Road in that red bodice just to catch Robert Proctor's eye, even knowing that her master would cane her for sure if she was caught, even knowing that Proctors' Ordinary was a haven for outsiders. He was licensed to sell only to travelers on the Ipswich Road, and not the village, and no one we knew ever went there.

She was so fearless. I admired her for it; I longed for some of her courage and cleverness now.

"What will the sergeant say when he finds you're gone?" I asked.

"He won't know," Mary said. "I've told him I've gone to Papa's house today."

"What if he sends for you?"

"He won't. Mistress Putnam's had a falling-out with my stepmother. They're not speaking just now. She told me good riddance when I asked for permission to visit." Mary folded the bodice over her arm and motioned us over to the table. "Now let us see my fortune before I go."

We all went over; I was the slowest to go. My stomach knotted—I thought I would see that bowl of water after all, and I did not want to look into it. I was nervous enough already—I did not want to give my vague foreboding a chance to blossom. I was relieved when I got close enough to see there was no bowl. Just a pair of shears and a sieve strung on a piece of string.

Carefully Mary laid the bodice on the bench and picked up the shears. "Now, who shall hold the other end?" she asked. Her hazel gaze moved over us, and I wished this would all be done. All I needed was a minute with Mary alone, just long enough to ask for her help.

"Oh, I shall hold it," Abigail said. She came forward and reached for the shears, and Mary jerked them back from her grasp and shook her head slowly, a small smile on her face.

"I don't think so." She looked at me. "Charity, I think. Charity shall hold the other side. For this, I want someone with experience."

Again I heard the implication in her voice. I'd never before done anything like this divination, and so it wasn't that experience she meant. I looked at the others, and I saw that most of them understood that too.

I could not keep the heat from flooding my cheeks. I reached for the shears, taking one handle. After Mary told Abigail to tie the sieve so it was hanging suspended between the points of the shears, I leaned close and whispered against her ear, "I must talk to you."

She threw me a quick glance, a little frown, and then she

mouthed, *Why?* I shook my head slightly to show I meant it to be a secret.

"Quiet!" Abigail said to the boy still drumming before the fire. His noise stopped. He cowered as if he expected her blow, but she had forgotten him already. "'Tis ready," she said to Mary. She stepped back from the sieve.

"Charity, you hold your side as still as you can, and I'll do the same. If the sieve moves toward you, the answer will be no. If it moves to me, then yes! Now the question." Mary took a deep breath and closed her eyes. When she spoke again, it was with a strong, steady voice. "Will my love notice me tonight?"

She opened her eyes. The room went still; no one shifted; there was not a single hushed sound. I felt us all leaning toward the sieve, the force of our stares crowded the air. At first it was like that, just smoke, harmless tension, and then the air changed. I felt it moving closer, growing heavier, until it seemed so heavy I could not fill my lungs with it. I knew this feel—I was suddenly afraid. But this time, no spirit appeared to me. Instead, though there was not a breeze or a movement in the room, not even a breath, the sieve began slowly to swing. First toward me, then toward Mary again; then it hovered in the middle. I kept my side of the shears still, I swear I did—I have no idea what propelled it—but I watched in disbelief as that sieve moved slowly toward me.

Little Betsey Parris gasped; she had been so quiet that I had forgotten she was there. When I looked at her, she was staring at the sieve, and her little bowed lips were trembling as if she'd just seen the Devil himself. I knew she felt the air too; I knew she understood, as I did, what a dangerous game this was—

Mary jerked the shears from my hand and threw them on the floor. They skidded to a stop near the settle, dragging the sieve behind until it caught on an uneven board and stayed there, the string stretching taut between the open scissors and the sieve. It looked like a Y there on the floor, until I saw the shadow it made. A shadow like a cross. We all stared at it for a moment, silent. Then Mary said, "I hate this game. 'Tis nonsense."

"The sieve never works," Betty assured her. "We should have used the bowl of water."

Little Betsey shook her head. "I don't like the water. It makes me more afraid."

"No one cares what you think," Abigail said.

"Perhaps we should try something else," Mercy put in. "We could ask questions with the Bible—"

"About true love?" Mary scoffed. "I think not. This is silly, anyway. How could it be true? How could he not notice me in that bodice?"

Betty nodded. "Perhaps it was only saying that he would not notice you without it. We phrased the question all wrong. Ask again."

Mary's voice was thoughtful and a little hesitant when she said, "No, I think not tonight." She stared at the sieve for a moment, and I wondered what she was thinking, what schemes were turning in her head. She grabbed up the bodice from the bench. "There's only one real way to find out."

Quickly she undid the laces of the plain brown bodice she wore and pulled it off, letting it fall in a heap to the floor. She stood in her skirt and her shift, fingering the rich red fabric of Susannah's bodice; then, with almost reverent fingers, she drew it on.

It was too large for her—Susannah had a more womanly shape—but not so much that it was noticeable once the laces were tightened and the virago sleeves were tied into the armholes, the wings in place over her shoulders. Betty and Mercy helped her put it on. I stood back; I'd had enough of touching it. When they were finished, I had to admit that Mary had been right about it. It did make her eyes seem browner and darker, and the red brought color into her skin. She fairly sparkled in it—now I understood why the village women never wore anything but muted colors, why they left such rich and vibrant fabrics to those who had not made their covenant with God. "The pride of apparel was evidence of a proud

heart"—I had heard the admonition many times. Now I understood why. Mary looked worldly and seductive, made for sin. She
was what the women in the village had warned us against since we
were old enough to talk.

"Why, it looks beautiful on you," Betty said.

Mary smiled. She smoothed it with flat palms, as if she could
not get enough of touching the fabric, and her smile was dreamy
and fascinating. "Two slashes," she said, turning her arm to see the
way her chemise showed through the cuts. "'Tis perfect."

"Are you sure you want to do this, Mary?" I asked her. "Remember, it won't be just Robert Proctor seeing you there. What will
everyone think?"

Mary frowned. "I don't plan to spend my life wasting away
here—what do I care for what they will say?"

"Still, I—"

"What a prig you are, Charity. As if you've a right to be. Why,
the whole village knows what you were doing with Samuel Trask."

"Mary—"

"What was she doing with Sammy?" Mercy looked at me with
her avaricious eyes, as if she could swallow me whole. "What? So it's
true, then? Is it true?"

"Don't be a widgeon," I replied hotly. I stared at Mary and
begged her silently not to say anything more. "Tell them, Mary.
'Twas only that I fancied myself in love with him. Tell them."

Our gazes met for a moment—it seemed an eternity—and then
she sighed and said in a stiff voice, "I was only teasing."

I heard only insincerity, but it seemed the others didn't notice.
They said nothing more. I breathed a sigh of relief that lasted only
until Mary said, "Well, I'd best be gone. If I don't get to the Proctors' before Robert leaves, I may have to keep this bodice a few more
days—maybe even a week, until he comes back."

"You can't," I said in a panic.

Betty laughed. "Poor Charity's in a fit, Mary. You shouldn't tease
so. You go off. I'm for home. 'Tis nearly time for dinner."

"Aye. You don't want to miss that," Mercy teased.

Betty flushed, crossing her arms over her heavy breasts as if she could disguise them. "If I don't get back to cook it, the doctor will whip me for sure."

"Very well," Mary said. "Here I go. Wish me luck."

She was leaving already. She was leaving without my having a chance to talk to her, and I could not go another day without her advice, without her help. I lurched forward and grabbed her arm, and she looked at me in startled surprise. "No, you can't go already. I . . . Remember, I—"

"Oh, yes, you need to talk to me. Can't it wait until tomorrow?"

"No."

"Talk to her about what?" Mercy asked. "Why can't we all hear?"

"'Tis nothing," I said. "I need her advice about . . . about a . . . a skirt. She's the only one who's seen it."

Mary looked at me oddly. "A skirt? Really, Charity, I haven't time to waste."

I held her gaze and spoke as quietly and intently as I could. "You owe me this. Without me, you'd have nothing to impress your Robert with tonight."

Mary hesitated. "Very well, then. Come along."

"Come along?"

"If you want to talk to me, come with me to Ipswich Road."

"I can't. It's so far."

"You said you sneaked out anyway. If your father doesn't know you've gone, how will he know how long?"

I thought of Jude and wondered how long she could keep silent. How long would it be before they checked the bedroom or she confessed that she'd seen me run out? After dinner? Before? No doubt they knew already that I was gone. I had to go back.

But I needed to talk to Mary now. I could not afford to think of how angry my father would be, or how he would punish me. Instead, I thought of the delusion I'd seen in his eyes. *Your aunt is not an actress.*

"Very well," I said to Mary.

The others went home; for a moment, I worried that Mary Warren would walk with us. After all, she was a maidservant in the Proctors' house, and 'twas where she would be returning. But she had another errand to do first, and so Mary and I started out to Ipswich Road.

"Oh, Charity, I cannot believe it!" Mary said. "I am sure that Robert will notice me at last."

"The red becomes you," I told her.

"Aye, it does."

"Just don't soil it."

Mary made a face. "Ah, poor Charity. Will your aunt punish you much for this, do you think?"

My aunt. I was so relieved that she'd mentioned Susannah. "That's what I wanted to talk to you about."

"I won't soil it, Charity, I promise. I would hardly ruin my chances to ever borrow it again."

"No, no, that doesn't matter. It's . . . Mary . . . I'm afraid. I don't know what to do about her."

Mary smiled. "Don't worry. Together we should be able to think of what to tell her. If she finds you with the bodice—"

"Listen to me," I hissed. "That's not what I'm talking about at all. She's an actress. It's as you said. Everything you said . . . is true."

"So you told me. Why, it's scandalous, don't you think? What will those old gossips think when your father throws her out?" She fingered the edge of the bodice longingly. "'Twould almost be a pity—"

"I don't think he's going to throw her out."

There was a little frown between Mary's eyes. "What do you mean?"

"I told him that she was an actress, and he doesn't believe it. You . . . You should have seen his face, Mary. I could tell . . . He won't listen to a word against her. She's deluded him somehow, I know it. 'Tis what the Devil does. He can tempt even the best of us—"

"Are you sure she's so wicked, Charity? She seems too . . . well, beautiful. 'Tis obvious God has favored her."

"She's an *actress*," I said. "Can you doubt her debauchery? And it's as Master Parris is always telling us: The Devil wears many pleasing faces."

Mary hesitated. "Aye, but . . . but . . . Perhaps it's not what it seems, Charity. She does not seem bad. Would it hurt to . . . I mean, think of the stories she has to tell. An actress, here in Salem Village! How interesting it would be to hear about the world instead of this little mud-filled village."

I should have turned around then. We weren't far, only just past the village. 'Twould have been an easy matter for me to leave Mary to herself and go home. It was clear she didn't understand. We thought so differently—I should have remembered that. But I did not want to go back home and face my father's wrath. I would have taken punishment gladly had I achieved what I meant to, but now the thought of bearing a daylong sermon in addition to my disappointment . . . I could not bear it. The thought of looking at Susannah in the face and knowing that she had beaten me . . . I could not do that, either. So I kept walking with Mary; I listened to her speculation that my aunt must know a great deal about satisfying a man—"Perhaps you should ask her about that, Charity"—and watched as the storm clouds rolled in and thought, *Perhaps it will rain and I'll get soaking wet and die of a fever.* It seemed a better fate than the one that wended ahead of me now.

But the weather held, and Mary was shivering with excitement by the time we reached the ordinary. It was just off the Ipswich Road, and there were horses hitched out front and two carts. I recognized none of them, but I would have been surprised if I had. 'Twould only be strangers here, and worse than that—strangers from Salem Town and Ipswich. Both Mary's stepfather and her uncle would have been horrified to find her here, and as for my father . . . well, that was a matter best not thought about.

None of this seemed to bother Mary. As we walked up to the door, and I heard talk from within, the shadow of the house seemed to block out the sky, and I shivered, feeling even more strongly that 'twas a bad idea to be here. But Mary was already inside. There was nothing left for me to do but follow.

The smell of beer and sweat filled my nostrils, heavy and thick after the cool air of outdoors. There was a long table in the middle of the room, and when we walked in, the men sitting there turned to look at us. At the far end of the room, Elizabeth Proctor was pouring a tankard of beer. She was John Proctor's third wife, only thirty or so to his sixty, and pretty in a worn sort of way. She was usually pleasant, but today she frowned when she saw us. She brought the tankard to one of the men at the table and wiped her hands on her apron as she came over to us.

"I had not thought to see you here," she said. "Is there—has someone sent you for something?"

"No," Mary said. "We've come for beer." She tossed her head and unbuttoned her cape to show the bright red of the bodice.

I saw the startlement in Elizabeth Proctor's eyes, and then the speculation. "Does your uncle know you're here, Mary?"

To her credit, Mary flushed. "He cares little for what I do," she said, and there was challenge there, in her words and her voice; she stared right into Goody Proctor's face as if daring the woman to throw us out.

It did not seem to faze the goodwife. She looked at me. "And what of you, Miss Charity? Does your papa know you're out here on the Ipswich Road?"

I hardly knew how to answer her. It turned out I did not have to. One of the men from the table stood up and came sauntering over. I did not recognize him at first, but when I saw his eyes, and the angle of his jaw, I knew him for his father's son. Robert Proctor.

"Is there a problem, Elizabeth?" he asked quietly.

His stepmother's mouth tightened. She gave a quick little shake of her head.

Beside me, Mary smiled. "Why, Goodman Proctor," she said. "'Tis a long time since you've entertained us with your presence. What brings you from Ipswich today?"

He glanced at her, and his glance stayed. His eyes were full of that red bodice—he could not look away from it . . . or her. It was like a charm holding him hostage. "Forgive me. Do I . . . ?"

"Mary Walcott," she said with a bob. "And 'tis us you must forgive. 'Twas a long walk, and my friend and I only meant to appease our thirst. Had I known there would be so many important men here, we would have walked on without disturbing you."

"And they'll be walking on again, as soon as the beer is drunk," Elizabeth Proctor said.

Mary gave her a truly venomous glare.

"'Tis a pity," Robert Proctor said. "A pity."

He went back to his table then, but slowly, and once he sat down, he kept looking at Mary, who preened in that red bodice like a robin in the springtime. Together we sat on a bench against the wall, and Elizabeth Proctor served us the beer and leaned close to whisper, "Quickly now. I won't be flayed alive by your parents for keeping you here. Drink up and be gone."

I was ready to do as she said. In spite of the long walk and my dry throat, I was not thirsty at all. I could barely swallow. But I forced myself to gulp that beer until it was half gone, and I was dizzy and warm from it. When I looked over at Mary, she was sipping slow and easy, and when a bit of the thin, bitter foam caught on her lip, she licked it off with that pointed, delicate cat's tongue of hers. Her eyes never left Robert Proctor's. When I glanced over at him, I saw he was staring at her with that hungry look I knew too well— I'd seen it in Sammy's eyes, and I knew what it meant. In spite of the fact that it was not directed at me, my belly warmed, and heat came into my cheeks.

"Let's go, Mary," I whispered to her. "We should not have come here."

Mary did not even look at me. "Goody Proctor will have to throw me out herself before I go. Do you see how he's looking at me?"

I looked down into my beer. Outside, I heard the low and not so distant rumble of thunder. "It's going to storm. If we don't leave now—"

"Go then, if you want. But I'm staying." Mary rose abruptly. I stared after her as she walked to the table where Robert Proctor sat with men I did not know. She leaned down to whisper something to him. He laughed, and told the other men to move down on the benches, and they did, making room for her to sit there beside the man she wanted. From the hearth, Elizabeth Proctor scowled.

I felt the storm coming closer; I heard the thunder in my head. All I wanted was to disappear into the wall, to quietly leave and turn back the hours so I had never set foot into this place where I should not be. I prayed that Goody Proctor would not see fit to tell my father.

I heard Mary laugh, and then another man, a younger one, rose from the table. I thought he was leaving, because he was moving toward the door, but then I realized I was sitting on the bench near the door and he was coming over to me. I froze, my tankard halfway to my mouth, and stared up at him while he smiled down at me.

"Your friend doesn't want you to be alone," he said. "Come, sit with us."

I swallowed hard. They were men sitting at that table, not the village boys we were used to, all of them older than Sammy had been, and at twenty he'd moved far too fast for me. Each step of the way with him, I'd been drowning, and I did not want to think of what Mary was doing now, of the danger she was in. Robert Proctor was thirty years old—the things he must know that Mary did not. How afraid Mary should have been. As afraid as I was when I looked at this man standing before me.

"I don't think so," I said, ashamed at how weak my voice was, just a whisper with no force to it.

"Come along now, girl, of course you shall." He reached for my arm. I felt his fingers close around it, warm, strong fingers, and I had a flash of Sammy's hand closing around me just that way, pushing me to my knees—

I jerked away so hard the beer splashed from my tankard and onto his breeches. His smile went thin. "Now, look what you've done," he said. "I've a mind to—"

I saw his mouth move, but a rumble of close thunder filled the room, taking over his voice. I felt a rush of wind that chilled me to the bone, but I was inside—there was no wind here—and in confusion, I turned to see the door opening, and someone coming in, a woman—

My aunt Susannah.

Chapter 10

⸙

THE ORDINARY WAS EERILY SILENT; THE ONLY SOUND WAS THE WHIP-ping howl of the wind. Susannah shut the door, and the moment she did, I heard the rain come crashing down, almost as if it had waited only for her to find her way to shelter. It seemed the clouds had been too heavy to contain it another moment and had let it all fall at once.

My aunt seemed not to notice—not the rain nor the silence. Her face was serene and calm, not a single hair out of place as she lifted the hood of that startlingly blue cape. She smiled, and that smile released me. I drew back into the shadows of the corner and prayed she would not find me there. If she went to Goody Proctor, I could be out the door before she saw me.

The man who had been standing before me moved. For a moment, I thought I was doomed to disaster. Susannah began to turn toward him. I held my breath as if it would somehow make me invisible, but then Robert Proctor rose. She glanced at him, and 'twas all I could do to keep from crying in sheer relief. She hadn't seen me. Not yet. If I had my way, she never would. If she would just turn her back completely to me for a single moment, I could make the door. . . .

Then I saw her stiffen. I saw what I had forgotten, and why

there would be no escape, not today. Susannah was staring at Mary, at that glowing red bodice.

Robert Proctor grinned at my aunt. "It seems you just missed the rain. Would you care to sit with us? We've a spare seat at our table."

Susannah's eyes flickered from Mary; she smiled at Robert Proctor as if she hadn't a care, and shook her head. "Thank you, no. I won't be staying."

Goodman Proctor pressed his hand to his heart. "Ah. I am disappointed. Is there nothing I can say to convince you not to hurry away?"

"I'm afraid not." She nodded toward Mary. "But it seems you've someone there already to ease your disappointment."

Robert Proctor glanced at Mary and said, "You misunderstand. She's only sharing a tankard with us."

"Why, I'm glad to hear it. 'Tis good to know a man of your experience is not dallying with someone of such tender years." The words were delivered with a honeyed tone, but Robert Proctor flushed. At the table, I heard Mary gasp, and when I looked over at her, she was nearly as red as that bodice.

Slowly Susannah walked over to the table. She looked right at Mary. "I shall be home tomorrow afternoon. Will I see you then?"

I had never seen Mary so ill at ease. My aunt only smiled and said again, "Tomorrow?"

"Aye," Mary said sullenly. It had been many years since I'd seen her so angry, not since, as children, her stepmother had chastised her in front of a young and handsome Joseph Putnam for spilling a bucket of berries. She had paid her stepmother back the next day by setting the cow loose to trample through the garden, and I wondered now how she would take revenge for this—whether it would be my aunt Susannah or me who would have to pay.

Susannah straightened. She said, "Charity, 'tis time to come home," without turning around, and again I was not surprised. 'Twould have taken a miracle for her not to have seen me, and I suspected now that she had known I was here even before she opened the door. I had the uneasy sense that somehow the bodice had given us away, that it had led her here, though I could not explain how. God made miracles all the time, and as for Satan—what powers could he give those who had joined in covenant with him?

I put down my beer and rose to follow her, not daring to look at Mary as I left. Susannah did not even turn to see if I was behind her as she put up her hood again and went to the door.

She pulled it open, and the rain stopped, just that sudden. A ray of sun burst through the gray clouds overhead to cast its weak light on the sodden ground, and then was gone again, leaving only the dark sky and the wicked wind that billowed her cloak—the only spot of color in the whole horizon. Outside waited Jack, saddled and pillioned, and I stared at the mule in shock—it was so seldom we rode, if ever. We walked everywhere because the mule and the horse were needed for work. The sight of him now told me that my father knew I had disappeared, and though I'd never doubted otherwise, I could not keep the tears from coming to my eyes.

"Is Father very angry with me, then?" I asked.

Susannah shut the door behind us and looked at me. "He thinks I've gone to pull flax, and that's what I intend to let him believe."

I stared at her in stunned surprise. "What?"

She mounted Jack and held out her hand to help me onto the pillion. "Come. We've not much time."

I looked at her outstretched hand, and I was afraid. I did not understand why my father did not know I was gone, why she had not told him. My suspicion that it had somehow been the bodice that led her grew so strong I could not make myself disbelieve it.

Susannah sighed impatiently. "Come, Charity. Unless you'd prefer your father discover you've gone missing."

"How did you find me?" I asked stubbornly.

"Jude was worried for you. When I called you for dinner and you did not come, she told me you'd gone."

"She did not know I was coming here."

"No. But while I was searching for you, I ran into your friend Mary Warren." Susannah smiled slightly. "She is very bad at telling lies, and it seemed 'twas a relief for her to tell someone where you'd gone."

Mary Warren. Running errands. I remembered the way she'd looked at Mary when we talked about Robert Proctor, as if she did not quite approve.

It all made sense. But still . . .

"It was not the bodice?" I asked.

Susannah's smile faded. "Ah, the bodice. 'Tis true that bodice and I have found each other time and time again. But in this case . . . 'twas Mary Warren, Charity. Now, come, before it starts to rain again."

I did not let Susannah's explanations soothe my fears or my suspicions. I knew already how clever she was. So I was wary as I took her hand and mounted behind her on the lumpy pillion.

She set Jack to a faster trot, and so 'twas impossible to talk as we rode, and that was fine with me, though I was burning with questions and misgivings.

The road veered off through the trees, into darkness made worse by the heavy overcast sky. I waited for Susannah to set Jack to a faster pace, to race through the woods, with its shadows and demons, as I did, not slowing until there was nothing but barren fields and a road clean of shadows behind. But she slowed the mule, and said over her shoulder, "Now, Charity, why don't you tell me what happened?"

Her words struck terror into me. "I owe you no explanations. I'll leave the story for my father."

"Ah. Is that what you want to do then? Tell him?"

"I was disobedient. 'Twould be best for me to take my punishment and pray for forgiveness."

She was quiet for a moment. "Your punishment," she said thoughtfully. "Does your father punish you often, then?"

I heard that criticism again in her voice, and I said hotly, "'Tis necessary sometimes."

"Oh?"

"Children have an evil nature—"

"I see. But you are not a child, Charity—or so you've said."

I was suddenly confused. I was not sure what she wanted. Warily I said, "There is no one truly good among any of us. We all must fight our debased natures however we can. We carry Adam's sin—"

"I know the text, Charity," she said. "What I don't know is what you believe your sins are, or why they frighten you so that you think you deserve a beating for them."

I went cold.

"Or perhaps," she went on thoughtfully, "it's not a beating you feel you deserve, but damnation itself."

"That isn't true."

"Those girls—your friends—do they care about you, Charity? Or is it just that they want someone who will do whatever they ask? Today, 'tis not much—a stolen bodice. Tomorrow, what will it be?"

"Mary didn't want me to steal it. I was only borrowing it for the night."

"Aye. This time. What shall it be the next time? Two nights? A week? Shall I open my trunk one day to find half my clothes gone?"

"I would never do that."

"Maybe not. Or maybe you would. Do you even know that yourself?"

I thought of Mary saying, *Perhaps I'll need it another few days, or a week,* and *I would hardly ruin my chances to ever borrow it again.* My hands were sweating now where I gripped Susannah about the waist, and I had to fight the urge to push away from her and jump down and run. I felt the woods closing in around me, crowding my head with wiry branches that pulled and tore so that I could barely think. My fingers began to tremble. I tightened my grasp to hold them still.

Susannah did not seem to notice. "For your own sake, Charity, you should do as your father asked and stay away from those girls. I know your mama felt so too."

It did not take much longer to reach my father's fields and the road leading past our house. As we reached the footpath that cut through the trees to the clearing, Susannah pulled Jack to a stop. She turned in the saddle to look at me.

"I'll say nothing of this to your father," she said to me, "and you should not, either. There's no need for a beating, not today. He thinks you're feeling unwell, and Jude has promised to keep quiet." There was an intensity in her dark eyes that seared me. "This is what I want you to do: Stay here until I get to the house. I'll call him to the barn to help with the mule, and you run inside. Go upstairs and stay there until I call you down for supper."

It was a lie she wanted me to tell. A terrible lie. But the darkness was crowding my head, and I could not think, and her eyes held me. She had to peel my fingers from around her waist because I could not let go, and she had to help me down. Even then I stood so help-lessly that she grabbed my arm and gave it a little shake. "Do you hear me, Charity?"

"Aye," I said.

And so I waited. I hid behind a tree and waited while I listened to the dull thud of Jack's hooves going up the path, the snap of branches as they caught on Susannah's skirt. I heard her call, "Brother! I'm having trouble with the bridle. Can you help me?" and the thud of the door as it opened and closed. Next came my fa-ther's voice. "You're dry. Did you find shelter, then, during the storm?" She said, "Why, the storm missed the flax field completely," and then their voices trailed off as they went into the barn, and I ran. I ran up the path and into the house, and though I saw Jude sitting at the table, and saw how she looked up at me when I came in, I said nothing to her. I ran up the stairs and into our bedroom, where I went to the window and looked out on the woods, barren and shadowed. The trees seemed alive to me, bending as they were in the wind, their branches wicked and stretching, and within them was a movement, a shadow. I caught my breath and meant to step away, to turn my gaze, but I couldn't. Before my eyes, the shadow became a presence; it grew weight.

Mama's specter.

She gestured to me, and I saw her speaking, though I heard no words, and as I tried harder and harder to listen, the spirit grew more desperate. 'Twas as if she were trying to reach me, but could not. The trees were crowding ever closer, penning her in, curling wicked hands about her.

I watched the spirit struggle, and I knew: 'Twas because of me. 'Twas my sin giving strength to those branches. My sin holding her here. The power of my lie, the way I'd given in to Susannah once again . . .

I heard my own sobs like a faraway moaning, and long after the vision disappeared, and I heard my father and Susannah come in again from the barn, I could not take my eyes from the place where I'd seen the spirit. The trees were like a living darkness in my head.

Chapter 11

❦

'TWAS MY GREATEST SIN THAT, EVEN AFTER THE THINGS I'D SEEN, the warnings I'd had, I was too weak and afraid to defy Susannah. When she called me down that night, I pretended I had been ill. My stomach was in such knots that I did not have to feign a lack of appetite. When my father sat us down to prayers and lessons that night, my guilt was so great, I thought I truly would be ill. I felt guiltier still when he dismissed me after a few minutes, saying, "You'd best go up to bed, Charity. You look as pale as death."

The truth was, in spite of my guilt, I was grateful for his reprieve. I could not sit there and listen to him and know that he knew nothing of what I'd done this afternoon. His prayers of damnation would have been better. I wished Susannah had never found me, that I did not have to look at her quiet face and see my own secrets hiding in her eyes.

The very air in the house had changed—I felt the evil in it. The next morning, I woke to the first snow, powdering the barren trees and dusting the ground. The worst cold of winter had begun, but it was nothing compared to the cold I felt in my bones.

When I finally dressed and went downstairs to see Susannah bent over the samp kettle and Jude already working on her sampler, I paused there on the step and wished I did not have to go down.

When Father came from the parlor, 'twas all I could do to say good morning to him.

He started at my voice, as if his mind had been in some far distant place. "I trust you're well today," he said. "You look better."

There was concern in his eyes, a warmth that in my guilt I could not bear. I twisted my hands into my skirt when they began again to tremble. "Aye," I whispered.

Susannah pulled the samp kettle off the fire. She brought it to the table and set it down with a thud, and then ladled the mush into trenchers. My father went to the window, and I felt his restlessness as he stared out at the falling snow.

"Charity, come to the board," Susannah said. "Jude, put away the sampler and eat. Hurry now before it gets cold."

Mama had never had to urge Jude twice to set down her sewing. But now Jude sighed and lingered over the linen before she finally laid it on the table. I saw the knots and frayed threads of the upper portion, the first few letters of the saying Mama had designed for her, messy and uneven, torn out and redone ten times or more: *Judith Fowler is my name/England is my nation/Salem is my dwelling place/and Christ is my salvation,* and I saw with surprise that the letters beyond those first few were perfectly done. Not a single knot, the stitches careful and even, and I felt a terrible hopelessness at the sight. How could I fight this? How could I fight Jude's obvious pride in her work now or Susannah's patience with her? What could I say—'twas the Devil's art that made Jude's fingers so nimble now, that Susannah's soft and patient instruction was not mentored by God?

I came to the table, and Susannah pushed my trencher toward me. When I looked up to take it, our eyes met, and I saw her satisfaction at the knowledge that I was in her power at last, and my hands trembled so I could barely pick up my spoon to eat.

At the window, my father said, "'Tis a light snow. It should stop soon."

Susannah glanced up. "Then you'll be going to the village after all?"

"Aye. There's another committee meeting."

Village politics again. No doubt it was that distracting him this morning.

"Perhaps you should take Charity with you," Susannah said.

I looked up in surprise. I did not know whether to be grateful or disturbed at such a plan. My guilt was so huge, another hour with my father would be misery. But then again, I longed for the reassurance of him—to feel his quiet presence leading me safely through the trees, to try to tell him again how dangerous Susannah was.

"Charity has chores to do. There's no reason for her to go into town."

"She can pick something up for me," Susannah said. "I took my bodice in to have Mary Sibley sew on a piece of lace. It should be finished by now."

My father shook his head. "Send her to get it when there are other errands to run. 'Tis a waste to walk in only for that, and the meeting could take a few hours."

"I really do need the bodice," Susannah said.

My father looked at her, and I felt something move in the air between then, disturbing and strange, a struggle I did not understand. But I recognized the clash of wills, and though I did not know what Susannah's purpose was, I felt a terrible dread—and I knew that if she changed my father's mind, I would be very, very afraid.

My father's voice was firm and unyielding. "Not today."

I was greatly relieved when he refused her. She had not influenced him yet; his will still belonged to God. Susannah looked at him as if debating whether to push him, and then it seemed her decision was made; she let it lie, and I was so glad I thought everyone must see. I looked down into my trencher to hide my smile.

She changed the subject. "I've made some headway with the account books."

I took a bite of samp and let the meal linger on my tongue.

"That's good news," my father said.

" 'Tis not so difficult to decipher as I thought. There are a few names written that I cannot attach significance to yet. Israel Porter, for one."

"For wood," my father said. "He owns the sawmill."

"Ah. I knew there was a reason. Sibley?"

"We traded him half a hog for some corn last fall."

"There's one more"—Susannah reached into her bulging pocket and pulled out a scrap of paper torn from Mama's almanac—"ah, here 'tis. Samuel Trask. Who is he? I've not heard of him."

I choked. My father looked at me in quick concern and then away again when I grabbed my cider to help me swallow.

"Sam?" he asked, his brow furrowed in puzzlement. "Why would he be in the accounts?"

Susannah shrugged. "I don't know. Who is he?"

"My apprentice. He ran off a few months ago."

"Well, this was"—Susannah checked the scrap of paper again—"Judith paid him five pounds in September. She has it listed as the eighth. When did he leave?"

"The ninth," my father said. "He disappeared on the ninth."

I stared down at my trencher, and a memory pushed into my head—not of Sammy, but of my mother. My mother on the day I'd told her that I loved him, that I wanted to marry him. *But you're just fifteen, Charity,* she'd said. *What can you know of love?* I told her I had given myself to him, thinking the truth would force her to find a way for Sammy and me to be together. There would be no other choice. What we had done was a sin—it could only be undone with marriage.

Now I saw again the anger on her face that startled me. And though her voice had been calm, her words had hurt. *My dear child, don't you understand what you have done? Remember what I've told you? Satan has found an open window in you—you have gone and let him in! This is a mistake. You cannot marry Sam; you must understand that.*

That was all, no reasons, nothing more, no matter how I cried. I had thought she would change her mind—how could she not, after what I'd told her? But there had been no opportunity. The next morning, Sam was gone, and Mama had dried my eyes with soothing touches and calming words. *'Tis better this way, Charity. You will come to understand it when you're older. He was not the man for you—if he loved you as you say, 'twould have taken more than five pounds to send him on his way.*

She had promised to keep everything secret, and I was heartbroken at both Sam's leaving and how easily I'd mistaken him. The depth of my own wickedness horrified me, and I had been grateful to her for saving me from sin, and for keeping safe my father's opinion of me.

And now, it seemed, it was all come to naught, and I had Susannah to thank for that too. Feeling numb, I glanced up at her, at my father. I waited for him to see the truth in my eyes at last.

Susannah said, "Five pounds. 'Tis a lot to give an apprentice."

"Aye," he said grimly. "What could she have been thinking?"

"Could the boy have stolen it?"

" 'Twas not like him to do such a thing."

"But you say he disappeared. Was that like him, then?"

Father shook his head.

"Then perhaps stealing was a new skill as well."

"Judith would have told me if he'd stolen it. We had no secrets from each other."

'Twas all I could do to keep my face expressionless. Susannah looked at me, and I had again the sense that she somehow knew my thoughts. "Do you know something of this, Charity?"

"What would she know?" my father asked. "She's a child."

"So you say." Susannah's expression was pensive.

"Who knows what the coin was for? Judith was a compassionate soul; perhaps she saw him leaving and gave it to him to buy some bread. She's in the grave now, so we shall never know." My father said it with finality, and I thought with relief that it was done. But Susannah did not take her gaze from me, and I knew she saw something that my father did not.

I could not eat after that. My father finished his breakfast and left to go into the village. I turned then to face my enemy. The table was cleared, and Jude was bent again over that sampler. Susannah sat beside her, nodding as Jude showed her some stitch, but my aunt was watching me.

"Go to the cellar and fetch some onions, would you, Jude?" she asked my sister.

"But I want to show you—"

"Show me later." Susannah laid her hand gently on Jude's. "If I don't start dinner soon, we'll have to eat samp again."

Jude was oddly obedient. When she was gone to the cellar, Susannah turned back to me.

"It seems strange that your mother would give five pounds to an apprentice, does it not?"

"Perhaps he told her he was going to market, and she asked him to bring her something."

"Aye." She nodded slowly. "But he never returned with it, did he? And your father says he was not a thief."

I said nothing.

"What do you know of this, Charity?"

"You claim to know my heart so well—read it for yourself." I threw out the words, but then I was strung tight waiting for her answer, afraid that she would say the truth and show me for certain what a friend of the Devil she was. I wondered what I would say if she did, what I would do.

She gave me a long, strange look, and said quietly, "I see. I think I begin to understand this trouble your mama wrote me of."

I did not understand what she meant, and I didn't like how unsettled I felt when she said it. I twisted my shaking hands into my skirt, and tried to blink away the trees crowding again into my mind, the vision of Mama's specter struggling within them.

The knock on the door startled us both. Susannah jumped a little on the bench before she gave me a questioning look and rose. "Who could be out in this weather?" she asked. When she went to the door and pulled it open, there was Mary Walcott standing outside, shivering in her dark gray cloak, her eyes burning.

Susannah bade her come in, and Mary did, though I saw how reluctant she was. Her gaze went to me, and I nodded back in acknowledgment.

"Would you take some cider?" Susannah asked. "Or something warm? 'Tis a long way to come, and cold."

"No, thank you, ma'am," Mary said. Her voice was polite but frosty. She pulled the bodice from the folds of her cloak and laid it on the table. It was bundled and wrapped far more neatly than when I'd brought it to her crumpled into a ball. "I've come to return this."

"Ah, yes, the bodice," Susannah said, as if she'd forgotten all about it. She lifted it and unfolded it onto the table, and I was startled at how lifeless and ordinary it looked in her hands—as plain as the sad-colored one I wore now. There was no light dancing across the silky fabric, no shine to its nap. In the candlelight, the red looked dull and dark—there was nothing special about it at all.

I glanced at Mary and wondered if she was thinking what I was: It had cost us far more than it was worth. Her expression was sullen; I saw the way she watched Susannah spread out the sleeves and finger the cloth, looking for damage or soil.

"I didn't hurt it. I was as careful as if it were mine," Mary said.

"But it was not yours, was it?" Susannah folded the bodice again and left it there.

"No, ma'am. 'Twas wrong to take it."

"And wrong to involve Charity as well."

Mary glanced at me. I said, "I took it of my own free will. 'Twas my choice."

Susannah ignored me. She kept her gaze on Mary. "I've decided there's no harm done this time. The bodice seems in good condition; 'twas gone less than a day. But I trust this will not happen again."

"No, ma'am," Mary said, but insolently this time. Susannah stared at my friend with that thoughtful gaze.

"You're a pretty girl, Mary," she said. "What makes you think you need a bodice such as this to catch a boy's attention?" She smiled after she said it, and her tone was close and friendly, the kind that made one want to share secrets.

But Mary was not me. Mary was not so easily tricked. I saw her jaw clench. "I was foolish, 'twas all."

Susannah nodded. "Aye. Well, a word of advice, Mary, from one who knows. The next time, try your wiles on the village boys, not grown men. You might be more successful."

"I was successful enough until you happened by. You could have any man in the village. Why must you choose the one I want?"

"The one you want?" Susannah laughed. "Child, you mistake me."

Mary's eyes narrowed. "Do I? Do I really?"

"Where's your mother, that she's not helping you choose a proper suitor?"

"She's dead."

"Well, if she were here, she would tell you as I do: Tend your business close to your home, and you won't be disappointed."

Mary snapped her mouth shut. I felt sorry for the next person she met on her way home. She fairly glowered at Susannah. "May I go now?"

My aunt hesitated; then she sighed and waved Mary away. "Aye. Go on. Show your friend to the door, Charity, won't you? You've something to say to her anyway, I think."

I knew what she meant; she wanted me to tell Mary I could not see her anymore. I had no intention of doing any such thing, but I hurried after Mary, who stalked to the door without waiting. When she slipped outside, I followed after, shutting the door carefully behind me.

It was freezing. I had on nothing but my dress, and the wind cut through to my skin and blew the wet snow into my face. Quickly I backed again into the mean shelter of the doorway and rubbed my hands up and down my arms to keep warm.

Mary turned so quickly to face me that her cloak flew out around her legs like wings, scattering snowflakes. Her eyes were like sparks.

"I see what you mean about her, Charity," she said. "She's a demon."

"I told you."

"Did you hear what she said to me? As if I were a child! 'Tend your business close to your home,'" she mocked. "Who does she think she is to say such things to me? What makes her so righteous?"

"'Tis what I've been saying."

"Did you see the way Robert looked at her yesterday? His eyes nearly popped from his head! Once she left, he hadn't a single glance to spare for me. Not one! Before she came, he'd been looking at me as if I were a tankard of beer and he was like to die of thirst."

"I saw it," I said, freezing, rubbing my arms harder.

"You cannot tell me she doesn't want him too. He's the most eligible man in the village." Mary paced, stamping down the thin layer of snow to the frozen dirt beneath. "She plans to steal him from me!"

"How can you be sure of that, Mary?"

"She does!" she spat at me. "And even if she didn't, she humiliated me in front of him! She'll pay for that, I promise it."

"She's clever, Mary. You won't be able to take your revenge by setting loose a cow in a garden."

Mary had been moving in circles like a crazed thing, but now she stopped, and there was a bitter smile on her face. It froze me colder than the snow or the wind. It seemed to cut right through me.

I stopped my rubbing. "What? What is it?"

"The spells," she said.

"What spells?"

"The ones we've been doing at the parsonage."

"What about them?"

"Tituba calls them our English tricks. 'English tricks,' she says. 'You won't get no spirits with them.'"

Such talk made me nervous. "So?"

"So Betsey told us the other day that Tituba could see the future. That sometimes, when she stared into a bowl of water, the things she saw came true."

"You mean she's a cunning woman?"

"More than a cunning woman, I should think." Mary came close to me, close enough that I could see the golden flecks in her hazel eyes. "Abigail says she knows things. Real spells."

"Tricks."

"No. Spells, Charity. Like how to bring animals ailing, or to curse—"

"No." I recoiled. "'Tis asking the Devil for help against himself."

"Don't be absurd. 'Tis nothing of the kind."

The snow was swirling beyond her, flakes falling onto her shoulders, into my face. I said, "There has to be another way."

Mary shook her head. "It took her less than an hour to read my heart and wrench it from me. How long do you think it will be before she reads yours, hmm? Do you think she will hesitate to tell your father about you and Sammy?"

Mary's words hit hard. This morning unfolded before me again, Susannah's questions, that knowledge in her eyes. *What do you know about this, Charity? Who is Samuel Trask?* My own desperation rose with the fury in Mary's eyes. The shadows in my head crowded ever closer.

"What do we do?" I whispered.

Mary smiled. In the pale whiteness of the snow, she was a black shadow. "We ask Tituba."

Chapter 12

MY FATHER HAD BEEN WRONG ABOUT THE SNOW. IT DID NOT LET UP that day, or the next, and the heavy white flakes grew lighter and drier, the weather colder, so there was a thick film of ice on the windows, both inside and out. The heat from the fireplace escaped out the chimney and barely touched the room beyond the first few feet. The only warm place was just before the hearth, but to stand in front of it meant a burning face and a freezing backside, so there was no truly comfortable place to be but in a thick feather bed.

The snow kept us prisoners in our own house; we could not go outside. So I began the spinning. My mother had taught me well; I could spin a thread as fine as most of the matrons in the village. Until this winter, I had never minded the chore. There was something peaceful about spinning, about watching the spindle and the wheel turning round. Last year, my mind had been full of daydreams as I'd worked. The wind howling past the house had been the whisper of Sammy's voice, my steps those of a courting dance. I had no memory of cold air or numb hands—I had been warmed by thoughts of love.

But now I knew those thoughts for what they were: sinful temptations borne by the Devil, and the big wool wheel only reminded me of all the things I'd done. Still, 'twas a task that allowed me to stand in the same room as Susannah, to study her with Jude while pretending to concentrate on the spinning. I set myself to work, and beside me, the window glimmered with the light of winter snow. At first, I did watch Susannah, but 'twas so quiet and so uneventful, that soon I found myself staring blankly at the wheel again, at the spindle and the thin, taut stretch of wool as it quivered into yarn.

When I heard the laughing, I thought at first 'twas only the hum of the wheel. Then it grew louder and louder, and I looked up, startled to see Susannah before me, wearing the red bodice and laughing. She reached out for me, and I tried to back away and could not move; 'twas as if I were frozen there. In desperation, I glanced toward the window, and there I saw my mother, her face pressed against the pane, her eyes wide, and I saw the black man beside her, holding her tight.

I was suffocating, and the trees crowded in my head, blocking out sound and light. I dropped the wool, grabbing at my throat—

Something clattered, loud and hard, and suddenly the Susannah before me melted away like heat vapors on a summer day. My vision cleared; I could breathe again. I realized in a single moment that Susannah had dropped the wooden peel, and that she was standing at the hearth wearing a mossy green bodice and a brown skirt the color of dead leaves. Not red, not that wicked red bodice. She had not moved from that place.

I glanced slowly at the window, afraid of what I might see. If Mama's specter had been there, it was gone now, and there was no sign it had been present. There was no man so black that light could not touch him. Nothing but the white of snow beyond the glass, cut by the diamond panes into wavering patterns.

I stumbled out of the room and hurried upstairs, desperate to be away.

Once I was in the room that we used for storage, I sat on a powdering tub with my back against the corner and stared out at the room, at bushels of oats and rye and peas and a bundle of dried codfish hanging from the wall. I longed to restore the ordinariness of my life. I longed to be just a village girl with a mother and father who loved her.

Instead, I saw again the vision of Susannah, of my mother's torment, and I began to shake. Tears moved into my throat and settled there, and soon they formed into a lump I could not swallow. I put my head in my hands and prayed to God for a way out of this, a way to save myself from the Devil, a way to cast him from my family.

What came to me then were Mary's words. *We ask Tituba.*

I could not go to the parsonage that day nor the next. The snow piled over the pathway and inched up the foundation of the house. The winter world was barren, set in black and white, but I had always found it less frightening than summer, with its leaves filling out the woods in thick lushness, creating darkness and shadows, the mugginess that gave the air solidity and presence. In the summer, it was easy to believe in demons—they, too, liked the warmer air.

Winter was not like that. True, the darkness came early and stayed long, and the nights were bleaker. But there was no temptation to open the windows to let in the cooling vapors—or the night humors that came with them—it was too cold for that. Already chilblains had started to develop on my toes and fingers. I could bear the cold if it meant that there would be snow to take away the shadows and open the world.

But it did not feel so open in the close press of the house, and with all the snow, there was no place to escape. I had offered to help my father in the barn, and he said 'twas no job for a well-bred girl and that Susannah needed my help in the house. So I did as he wished, and with each chore she assigned me, I grew to hate my aunt more; with each moment in her company, I grew more afraid. By the time a week had passed, I found myself longing for the snow to stop. In every shadow, I saw again the vision of her laughing. At every window, I imagined the press of my mother's face, her desperate eyes.

The morning I woke up to find the sky clear and blue, and the white glittering on the ground like starlight, I could barely contain

my relief. I did not know if Mary or the others would be at the parsonage—Mary and Mercy would have to walk nearly two miles in
the snow to get there—but I did not care. Abigail would be there to
take me to Tituba. I prayed the parson would not be home. Surely,
on the first clear day after a snow, he would have some good works
to see to?

It was no easy matter for me to get out. The snow was piled
against the door, tramped down only in a thin path from the house
to the barn so that Father could work in the bitter cold and I could
milk Buttercup. That morning, my father decided 'twould be best
to clear it away completely and spent two hours widening the pathway. It was impossible to get away while he was at the door, and the
morning was too busy for me to attempt it anyway, because Susannah had decided to clean the house while she could get in and out.

It wasn't until after dinner, when we were clearing away the
trenchers, and I was growing desperate trying to find a way to escape, that there was a knock on the door. It was Goody Penney,
bearing Faith, come for a visit—the delight on my aunt's face when
she looked at my little sister made me heartsick. So I lied. Father was
in the barn; I told Susannah that he'd asked me to take something
into the village for him, and she was too distracted by Goody Penney and the baby to question it. I had my cloak on and was out the
door before she had time to remember to ask me anything, and I ran
the first half mile in the stinging cold, slipping and sliding over the
icy road, because I was afraid she would run after me.

It was far colder than I'd thought. The air seared my lungs, and
my breath came in fast, frosty clouds. My cloak was not thick
enough to protect me, and my boots too thin, and I was shivering
and so cold I could not feel my fingers or my toes by the time I
reached the village and the parsonage. I knocked on the door hard.
There was no sound, no movement, and I crumpled in tears on the
doorstep when I thought that perhaps no one was home. But then
I heard footsteps, and the door creaked open to reveal the dark face
of a man—John Indian, Tituba's husband, and another slave to the

Parrises. When he saw me, he smiled, big and broad, flashing white teeth, and said in his heavy Island accent, "Ah, you girls, you watch each other? Be that how you know?"

I stared at him in confusion, and he smiled again and stepped back to let me in.

"They all be here too," he explained. "The first day after a snow, and *bam!* you cannot wait to try out the demon spells."

I looked beyond his big form and saw the others in the hall— Mary and Mercy Lewis, Mary Warren, Betty, Abigail, and little Betsey. And there was someone else there too, a thin blond girl who was too tall for her age. Annie Putnam.

I ignored John Indian and went inside, taking off my cloak as I went. The room was warm because of all the bodies, and the fire was built up high so that flames were shooting up the chimney. The crane, with its hanging pots, had been swung out onto the hearth. In front of it stood Tituba, rubbing her hands over her arms as if she were cold, while the little Parris boy played with a jar of buttons beside her.

Mary looked up as I came inside and gave me a smile that warmed me. "Come over, Charity," she said, motioning to me, and then she gave me a knowing look, and glanced toward Tituba as if to tell me we were together in this. 'Twas a relief to know I was not in this alone, that I was not Susannah's only enemy.

Annie Putnam was sitting beside Mary. She looked slyly up at me. With her pale blond hair, she had always been a pretty child, but there was a delicacy about her now that was faintly unhealthy. Her skin was too pale; there were dark circles beneath her eyes.

"Mercy brought Annie," Mary told me. "She's threatened to tell her father if we didn't. Isn't that right, you little angel?" She smiled thinly at Annie and pinched her arm so the girl jumped and squealed.

"She's been having bad dreams," Mercy explained. "She thinks she can see the dead."

Mary snorted. "It's her mama who believes that."

"Mama worries about my aunt and her three babies," Annie said to me with the greatest solemnity. "They torment her at night."

The whole village knew the story. Annie's aunt had died soon after moving to Salem Village, with each of her three children dying quickly after. My mother used to say that the elder Ann Putnam had never truly recovered from those deaths, and that they tormented her to illness, even though she had six children of her own to help ease her grief.

Mercy went on explaining. "She wants to talk to the dead."

Little Betsey Parris started at this, and her big blue eyes grew wide and frightened. "Talk to the dead? But 'tis a sin! We aren't going to talk to the dead, are we?"

"We don't know how, you silly goose," Abigail said. "We need Tituba for that. You've said she can do it, haven't you, John Indian?"

I had not seen John slinking into the hall, but suddenly there he was, standing beside me, his big bulk smelling of hay and livestock and sweat. "Aye, you little sly one, she can do it."

"You shut your mouth, Mr. John," Tituba called from the fire. "I told these children there won't be no talking to the Devil today."

"But 'tis why I've come!" Annie protested.

"You don't mean it, do you, Titibee?" Betsey asked. She was near tears, she was so frightened. "You can't really talk to the dead?"

Tituba turned from the fire and smiled reassuringly. "Don't you worry, little one. You got nothing to fear."

I noticed that she did not deny it, and I shivered at the thought, but then I caught Mary's gaze and saw the smile on her face. I knew what she was thinking: If Tituba could talk to the dead, she could surely curse the living. I felt suddenly light-headed.

"Please, shall we continue?" Betty asked. She was at the end of the table, kneeling on the bench so she could see better into the bowl of water set there. "I've bought an hour, but then I shall have to be getting back."

Abigail nodded. "Ask the question first."

John Indian laughed and walked away, shaking his head. Tituba said, "You go on, laughing man, there be plenty enough for you to do." He eased by her on his way out the door, setting his big hand against her hip for a moment until she swatted him away.

He made me nervous: He was too big, too loud. Tituba worried me, because I saw the powers in her dark eyes, but John Indian was just a fool, and there was no telling what he would do or say. But I forgot him as Betty laughed and leaned closer to the bowl. She whispered, "What shall my husband be?" so close to the water that it shivered and rippled with her breath. Then she took the little bowl Abigail handed her and tipped it into the water. What was inside shimmered in the candlelight, wiggled, and slipped out. Egg white.

It was so quiet in the room 'twas as if no one even breathed. They watched the bowl of water, and the egg white inside as it shifted and twisted into shapes.

"Why, is that a fish?" Abigail called out. "I do think it's a fish, Betty. Look at the way it moves!"

"It is a fish," Mercy said.

"A fish." Betty's round face broke into a smile. "A fisherman! He's to be a fisherman!"

Mary looked impressed. "Quite a living for a man."

"Perhaps I'm to move to Salem Town, then." Betty sighed. "I shan't be a servant my whole life. I had visions of serving my uncle clear to the day I died!"

They all laughed, but I shivered. I saw the way little Betsey looked too, worried and afraid. Annie Putnam leaned forward with the rest of them. "It's my turn now. It's my turn."

"Your turn? Why, today's the first time you've deigned to come around. You shall have to wait," Mercy said.

Mary Warren sighed. "Oh, let her go."

"Not yet." Mary shook her head. "You ask, Charity. Ask it a question."

"I haven't one to ask."

"Surely you do," Mary urged. "Why not ask it . . . Oh, I don't know. Ask about your future, or—no, wait—ask about your aunt."

"Her aunt?" Betty said. "Who cares about her aunt?"

Mary shrugged. "She's tormenting Charity. I'm just wondering what her future is to be, how long she'll be staying."

"It's not Charity she's tormenting." Betty laughed. "You're just angry because she caught you wearing her bodice at the Proctors'."

Mary's face tightened. "Aye, I'm angry. But not for that. You should have seen the way Robert looked at her."

"He's too old for you anyway," Mary Warren said.

Mary shot her a terrible glance. "She humiliated me in front of him. I won't forgive her that."

" 'Tis no good, wishing her ill that way," Mary Warren offered.

"Quiet. I've no patience with your mealy mouth," Mary said. She looked at me. "Go on, Charity. Find out her future. Ask the 'crystal ball.'"

"You be careful." Tituba's voice was low, but it pulsed in the room like a heartbeat, lingering long after she'd spoken. "The spirits, they be tricksters. They be looking for those who ask questions when they mean ill."

I hesitated, but Mary said, "Go *on,* Charity," and so I went to the table. Abigail emptied the bowl of water and brought another, and Betty cracked an egg and separated out the white. Then she handed the bowl of egg white to me, and there was a wicked gleam in her eyes, as if she were daring me to go on.

I took a deep breath and looked into that bowl of water. I saw nothing, only water and the grain of wood through it. In that moment, it seemed so innocent, like playing. I leaned close to the water and asked, "What will become of my aunt Susannah?" Slowly I poured the egg white in.

I held my breath. The candlelight glistened on the water; the egg white shone like gold as it twirled and shifted, moving apart here, coming together there. I could see nothing in its shape at first, and then it seemed to congeal; it seemed to grow defined, with hard edges and straight lines. Beside me, I heard Betty gasp in shock.

"A coffin!" she said. " 'Tis a coffin!"

"'Tis not," I said; yet I saw the form and knew it too well. I knew Betty was right. It was a coffin. It was unmistakable.

Quickly I plunged my hand into the water. I did it with such force that egg white and water splashed out, pooling on the table, and then I twisted my hand to make sure the rest was dislodged, ruined. On the bench, Betsey began to shake, and when Abigail slapped her arm, the little girl began to cry in earnest. She slipped from the bench and ran to Tituba, who enveloped her in her skirts. After that, there was no sound but that of Betsey crying, while the rest of us stood there looking at each other in shock and fear.

"'Tis only a game," Betty said, but her voice was trembling. "Surely it means nothing."

"It didn't even get Mary's fortune right last time," Mercy said. "Robert Proctor *did* notice her, and it said he would not."

"That was the sieve, you fool," Mary said. "'Twas a different trick altogether."

"Still, it was just a trick," Betty said.

Mary Warren looked tearful. She hugged herself hard. "Are you sure 'twas a coffin?"

Betty nodded. "I saw it. Charity did too. Didn't you, Charity?"

"Aye," I whispered. "'Twas a coffin."

"Maybe it wasn't," Annie Putnam said. "Ask again."

But I shook my head. "I won't ask again. 'Tis too much power to give him."

Mary went still. The others looked at me in confusion.

"Give who?" Mercy asked.

"Satan." I could but whisper the name, but in the wickedness of that room, it seemed a loud sound. Loud enough that Tituba looked up from Betsey and stared at me.

"There is no Devil here, child," she said, "just the spirits of the air and water. They give you what you want, that's all. 'Tis not your black man."

But I knew she was wrong. I knew what Satan felt like, and he was here, filling up this place. I saw him in the eyes of my friends, in the flickering and profane light of the single candle. Betsey Parris stopped weeping, and my friends were silent too, until the parsonage seemed filled with the awful, roaring sound of the air and the distant murmur of a screech owl calling in the middle of the day. We looked at each other, and the fear was palpable in that room, along with the evil. I know they all felt it.

We left quickly after that, each of us whispering excuses and trying not to look afraid. When Betty said, "'Tis only white magic, nothing more," I nodded my agreement and glanced at Mary, who had a soft, satisfied smile on her face.

Betty's words were a rhythm in my head as I fled that house, as I let that heavy wooden door thud shut behind me, and raced down the pathway through the woods and back home.

That night, I slept fitfully, and I was burning even though the room was so cold that both Susannah and Jude had the blankets pulled nearly over their heads. But my dreams were black and disturbing, and Mama's scream was still in my ears when I woke with the dawn. I went to the window and looked out on the white world I loved, but I saw only darkness there. There were shadows on the snow that I had never seen before, shadows that loomed before me, that mocked me with my innocence. And trees that crowded my head so I could see nothing else, nothing but the dream I'd had, and the sight of a plain, white pine coffin being borne through the streets of Salem Village.

PART TWO

LUCAS

—Obsession—

Hell hath no limits, nor is circumscribed
In one self place; for where we are is Hell,
And where Hell is, must we ever be.

—Christopher Marlowe
Doctor Faustus

Chapter 13

———— ❧ ————

I LOVED MY WIFE. I DON'T THINK I EVER SAID THE WORDS TO HER while she lived, but it was the truth. I remember the first time I saw her, standing at the back of a tiny room in some tavern in Lancashire while my master preached. The rest of the congregation was loud and unruly; only Judith listened with a true heart.

She had a way of calming my worst moods; the touch of her hand made me realize the crudeness of my passions and quieted them. Judith was my savior, and I do not say that with blasphemous intent; God understands that if He understands nothing else. She was, in every way, the perfect wife. I never looked at her that my restive emotions did not settle.

When she died, I grieved for my own wretched existence without her. That Judith had been one of God's elect, I did not doubt. She was with God, but I . . . I was alone without her, and I was crippled at my loss. I had a duty to my children—how could I counsel them to celebrate her victory in joining our Lord, when I could not do the same? I held in my tears and my grief, and bade my daughters follow me. Yet once they were asleep, I crawled into bed beside Judith and held her cold, stiff body close as if I could breathe life into her again. Instead, I woke before dawn with a corpse cradled in my arms—a body without my Judith's spirit, and I was repulsed at what I'd done, at the foulness of my soul. I had valued her too highly, above even God.

I vowed then, in the shadows of our bed, with the curtains drawn dark and quiet all around, that I would never forget those last moments we had together, that I should remember her suffering, her dying.

It does me good to think on her last day. I can see again the darkness of the storm outside the window, and the way Judith bustled at the hearth making breakfast as I readied to leave. I remember the worry on Charity's face, and how her pale blue eyes grew large with fear when I made to go. I did not want to disappoint her, but neither could I spoil the child I loved by giving in to her pleas. 'Twas my task to keep her pure of heart and spiritually strong.

And so I stood my ground and let Judith comfort her, and I prayed to the Lord for strength as I left the house and went out into the pouring rain and that hellish darkness. Had I known what I would find when I reached my destination, I would have turned around again and faced my wife's disappointment. I would not have gone—not that day nor any other.

The way to Salem Town had been slow, the path nothing but mud that came a foot up Saul's legs, sucking at his every step, and he was exhausted before we'd gone many yards. I unhitched the cart and left it by the side of the road. As the lightning split the sky and the thunder crashed around me, I cursed the *Sunfish* for making such good time, and I cursed Judith for wanting her sister so badly that I must go out in this storm to fetch her.

By the time I reached Salem Town, it was already late afternoon, and I was worried for my wife and angry that I had left her. I could not keep the thoughts of her other labors from my head: the struggle, her anguish, and then the grief when the child died. My diaries over the years were filled with anger toward God over the deaths of my children; I was such a poor servant, to not trust Him to know what I needed. My life was but a picture on God's wall; He knew it better than I could hope to. It was Judith who faced those losses with stoicism. As always, even in her sorrow, she was the better Christian.

The rain slashed and my horse struggled against the wind as we came into Salem Town, past the closely spaced houses and the muddy, rutted meetinghouse green, with its stocks and whipping post standing black and ugly in the rain, the dogs in the nearby pound yowling with fear at the storm. I smelled boiling soap and the lingering odor of fish left to dry on hundreds of flakes littering the shoreline, the rank tannery fumes that no nor'easter could wash away.

The sea was everywhere in Salem Town, infringing at every point. Inner Harbor slashed through the town, its waters alive with sail and rigging. There were few wharves; at low tide, ships heeled on the mudflats. Now the tide was in, and the ships were bobbing and tilting on the waves.

On the waterfront, empty barrels rolled drunkenly, driven by the wind. The harbor churned with wood and foam and seaweed, debris cast ashore, pummeled into the mud by the rain, and all was gray. Gray sky, gray rain, gray shadows of the ships, their rigging ghostly and black, plunging into the low clouds to disappear until lightning danced about their lines. 'Twas folly to be out in such weather. I would not have been blamed had I stayed home with the wife who needed me. No one would have expected me to come.

No one except my wife's sister. The very thought embittered me so that, as I made my way to the shop owned by the *Sunfish*'s captain, I was ready to throw her back to the sailors if she gave me the slightest reason to do so.

Salt mist and rain nearly blinded me as I approached the run-down little shack. The roads were so bad that I had dismounted, and Saul pulled at the lead rope and followed so reluctantly he nearly wrenched my arm from my shoulder.

I was only a few yards away when a shadow stepped from the door—a woman, I saw, though more than that was impossible; she was only a dark-cloaked shape. She made no move to find shelter from the rain; she merely stood and waited, watching me, and I knew before I reached her that this was the woman I had come to take home.

"Lucas Fowler," she said in a soft, quiet voice. "'Tis you, is it not?"

I stopped, wiping the rain from my eyes, though it still dripped in a steady stream from the corners of my hat. Saul pranced nervously. "Aye," I said. "'Tis me."

She drew back her hood and turned so I could see her face. Judith had told me that Susannah was beautiful, and I'd doubted her, because Susannah was her sister, and sisters often thought better of each other than neighbors did. I knew which of them had the better heart, and in my naïveté had not been able to fathom that God would give a beautiful face to the one whose spirit was lacking.

But as I looked at the woman standing before me, with her hood lowered and rain falling on her face and drenching her hair, I knew Judith had told the truth. I was struck dumb at Susannah Morrow's beauty.

She motioned to the shop. "My trunks—"

"I've no place to put them," I told her, my voice sharper than I'd intended. She looked startled for a moment, and then she glanced at the horse. "'Tis the storm," I explained. "Had I brought the cart, you would be waiting two more days."

"I can send for them, then," she said. "Shall we go?"

"It may be a few days before someone can bring them out. Have you what you need?"

"If I don't, I'm sure Judith will lend me whatever's necessary." She pulled her hood up again and lifted her face to the sky. "How long will it rain, do you think?"

"Until it sees fit to stop. We'd best hurry. My wife is in childbed."

"In childbed? Already?"

I nodded, and the bitterness of the morning came back to me, my own fears. "'Tis a month early."

"Your horse looks exhausted. Will he make it, do you think?"

"God will provide one way or another."

Susannah was slight and easy to boost into the saddle. Saul was too tired to take the both of us, so I led him from the wharf and past the houses and the green with its pillory, out of Salem Town. The mud that had slowed the horse was no better for me; at times it was so thick and viscous that I nearly lost a boot. Other times, puddles that looked shallow turned into small ponds that came to my thighs as I led Saul through, and Susannah drew her feet up with a little cry, pulling her skirts so I saw they were not good working boots she wore, but square-toed shoes made of pale kid, tooled in blue and gold. It seemed she had not changed in the years since Judith had last seen her. I did not dare think on what that might mean.

Night came quickly on a day such as this, and before long, we were plunged in darkness. My fowling piece was slung over my shoulder beneath my cloak, along with a powder horn, but the day was so wet I doubted I could light it, and so I kept my eyes alert, searching the woods about us for signs of Indians or thieves.

The wind and the rain came up again, so we could not talk, and I was glad of it. With every step closer to home, my anxiety grew, until my arm began to ache from pulling on Saul's reins to urge him to a faster pace. I did not know what we would find when we arrived there, and I prayed that we were not too late.

But it was late when the house finally appeared before us, a black shadow with light glowing dim in the windows. I led Saul into the yard.

Just then, the front door flew open, and I saw Prudence Way in the doorway, her skirts blowing around her feet, her apron blotchy with dark stains I knew were blood. I held my hand for my sister-in-law, and she took it and jumped down, stumbling as her feet found purchase. I had no time to tend to the horse, as good as he had been; I only swatted him and regretted that I must leave him foaming and saddled and let him make his own way to the barn. I would care for him later.

I cannot forget the sight that greeted me when I walked through the door, the heavy scent of blood and fire smoke. When I saw Judith twisting weakly on the bed, and my daughter's tear-filled eyes, I knew my wife would die.

Prudence's whisper only confirmed it. "She's not much time left. Nor the babe, either. You'd best do what you can to ease them toward God."

The world narrowed before me. I saw only Judith's pale face as I went to the bed. She grasped my hand. I was so tormented by the thought of her death, by what I would do when she was gone, that I was paralyzed. God help me for that, for thinking only of myself in her suffering. I saw my wife weakening, the pool of blood on the sheets, and I cursed myself for putting her through this misery, for being unable to control the unseemly desire to take satisfaction in her body when it was so clear she could no longer withstand the inevitable result—the labor of childbirth.

Later that night, as the house quieted around us, and I watched my wife's endless sleep and the peace of her features, I tried desperately to be happy that she had found salvation, but all I felt was the overwhelming responsibility her passing had cast upon me. I felt lost without her.

As I crawled into bed with my wife's corpse, and took her into my arms, I murmured into her ear the words I had never been able to say to her in life.

My wife was dead, but I had loved her. Yes, I had loved her.

Judith and I had lived in Salem Village since Charity was born, ten months after our marriage. Judith's parents had been loath to let her leave Lancashire, especially to go so far, where they would never see her again. Susannah had left the year before, at the tender age of fifteen, to run after some yeoman's son who'd decided to seek his fortune in London, and so they had no daughters left to see them into old age. I had never met Susannah; when Judith and I met, her sister had been long gone already. When Judith spoke of her, it was with love mixed with bitterness. Judith told me that she had protected Susannah all her life, and I had never doubted her loyalty to the sister who hardly deserved it; I looked forward to a lifetime of being the beneficiary of that loyalty myself.

So I married her, and I never had cause to doubt the decision, even when it proved that her womb was weak and inhospitable. 'Twas God's will, and I came to accept that, though I had wanted a big family. In the end, I was even grateful for it, because I proved to have as faulty a heart as her womb was rocky. I loved my children from the moment they came bloody and squalling from Judith's body, and I was afraid of how I would have sacrificed anything for their delicate little souls.

Had I indulged them as I wished, there was no doubt they would turn to evil, and so I kept a firm hand and kept my love for them under the strictest rein. I did not even let Judith see how I revered them, because I was ashamed. In that love, there was no room for God, and so I knew it for the blasphemy it was. I knew the basest nature of my soul was that I loved my children more than I loved the Lord.

One night, as I gazed upon their sleep, I looked up in the doorway to see Judith watching me with sorrow in her eyes.

"You must come away, Lucas," she'd whispered to me. "Before God punishes you for such pride."

I had come away without looking again at my daughters, and I hardened my heart when Judith comforted them and smiled upon them. She was their mother, but I . . . I was their spiritual teacher, and it was my responsibility to deliver them safely and reverent to the Lord. I could not take the chance that, in my love, I would not ask enough of them. As time went on, it grew easier, and though I knew the progress of their spiritual development, their physical and emotional growth was like a closed book to me; I knew them as my children, and yet I did not know them.

And so now, Judith's death frightened me, not just because I was afraid of what I would become without her quieting touch, but because I saw the way Charity and Jude looked at me, with fear and grief and hope in their childish expressions. I knew they would turn to me and that, unless I married again shortly, 'twould be my duty to guide them through this time and further, into young womanhood, and I was ill-equipped for the task.

I should have been stronger, but I was afraid. In those first days after Judith's death, when 'twas my task to take my daughters in hand, I left them to Susannah. I should not have, but I could not bear my own grief or that my daughters should see it, even as I counseled them every night to celebrate their mother's passing.

And so, the day that Susannah came to me in the barn, where I spent my hours shaving white pine to a smooth, burnished shine and building a coffin tight as a drum, I was too distraught to do what I should have done: send her back to London.

I was sweating and dusty, and at the sight of her in her bright green bodice and brown skirt, I felt awkward and coarse. I straightened from the plane and dusted off my hands.

"What is it? Is something wrong? Are the children—"

"The children are fine." She came fully into the barn, pausing to look through the dark gloom at the shadows of plows and yokes, the felling ax and pitchforks and saws hanging from hooks set in the wall. There were no windows; the only light came from the open door and the two betty lamps suspended from hooks on the wall, which I had to watch constantly for fear the drippings would overflow the holding plate and start a fire.

"What is it?" I said.

"Judith is gone now," she said. "I've been wondering about your plans."

"My plans?"

"Aye. For the girls."

"I don't understand."

"'Tis simple enough. You're a man alone with two young daughters—"

"Three."

She nodded. "Three. But Faith is at the Penneys' until she's weaned. For her, there's naught to think about yet, but the other two . . . Will you send them out?"

I thought back to the plans I'd had to send Charity to the Andrewses' home, and how she'd cried and screamed. I had not been able to bear the thought of sending her away, but I'd thought 'twould be best for us all—'twas a sin to keep her so close to me, selfish pride. I remembered Judith's soft words. *You have not taught her well enough, perhaps, my husband. 'Tis clear she has not learned reverence or obedience. Will you send her to the Andrews family to show them how lacking her education has been?*

Now I looked at Susannah and shook my head. "No. They are my daughters. They shall stay with me."

"Is that what is best for them, do you think?" There was censure in her voice, and the familiarity of it was intolerable.

I spoke as coldly as I could. "'Tis kind that you came to visit your sister, but, as you've said, she's gone now. There is no reason for you to trouble yourself further over my family."

"They're my nieces—don't forget."

"Though they've not had sight of you till now."

"It was not my choice."

"Then whose?"

She did not answer me. I turned my back to her in hopes that she would take my meaning and walk away.

"When my sister wrote and asked me to come, she spoke of trouble," she said.

"Aye, she had trouble enough," I said. "A fallen womb and a baby she was afraid would die."

"There was that. But I'm speaking of something else."

"There was nothing else."

"Why would she tell me of it, then?"

There were inferences in her tone that I didn't understand, an accusation I couldn't decipher, and it made me angry. I looked at her. "What did she tell you? Come now, Sister, I'm curious to know. What trouble did she describe to you?"

"None. That is what puzzles me."

"Perhaps she told you of nothing because there was nothing. Just her own troubled mind. She had dreams that the baby would die. Did she tell you this? Had she a premonition of her own death?"

"As much as any woman has," Susannah returned, "when childbirth is so troublesome."

I turned back to my work. "Aye. 'Twas all it was, then."

"Even so . . ." She paused for long enough that I looked at her again. She was staring at the board beneath my hands, her expression thoughtful. "Even so, I think I shall stay on a while. Do I have your permission to do so?"

"My permission?"

" 'Tis your household."

"My household is like any other. Family requires no invitation." I needed help with my daughters until I was ready to find a new wife. And Susannah was family; 'twould be a sin to throw her out. "You're welcome, if you choose to stay. But this is not London. 'Tis not the life you're used to. You would do well to think on this before you decide."

"I've thought on it well enough," she said, and I heard her triumph when she left me, as if she felt she had won this battle between us, as if she were girding herself for war.

Chapter 14

THERE WERE THOSE WHO QUESTIONED THAT I LET HER STAY: AFTER all, she was beautiful enough that no one could fail to see it. And after Faith's baptism, when Susannah quieted the child with such skill, there was gossip about her place in my household, despite the fact that she was Judith's sister, and therefore my own. I know this because Samuel Nurse was a good friend and was quick to quell such gossip when he heard it, and then warn me of what was being said. But though Susannah's beauty was a distraction, I was relieved she was there to take responsibility for my children. I had other duties to attend as well: Earlier in the fall, I'd been elected to the Village Committee, and now village politics consumed many of my hours.

Chief among our problems was the pastor, Samuel Parris. In the twenty years since Salem Town had given its permission to build a meetinghouse, the village had wallowed in the controversy surrounding it—chiefly, who was to be the first pastor, and who would make the choice. By the time Judith and I had arrived, the warring had already split the village in two. The situation was hindered by each successive pastor, bad choices all, each himself an agent of dissension. As each failed to bring peace to the village, that division only widened. None was an ordained minister; those who wished to take Communion had to go into Salem Town each Sunday. 'Twas a relief when the village was given permission to form a church, but that relief was marred by the minister the village chose to ordain. I—along with many of my neighbors—believed Samuel Parris was not worthy of the office.

I was not the only one to find Parris an unpleasant man. The negotiations surrounding his hiring had been difficult and adversarial—we should have known then that he would serve our village poorly. But Tom Putnam was his greatest supporter, and a man of some influence, negative though it may be, and we'd had few other choices; Salem Village had a well-deserved reputation for contention. Until Samuel Parris, we had never kept a minister longer than a year or two.

In my less charitable moments, I believed that the village deserved Samuel Parris. We villagers had not been able to reach accord with each other for years. I was as guilty as the rest, though I tried to love my neighbor. In this, again, Judith was my teacher, for she was unfailingly kind to all, and understanding when I could not be. How many times had she said that men like Tom Putnam were their own worst enemies, and that he should be pitied for his bitterness rather than blamed. I tried, but 'twas difficult for me to bear more than a few moments in his company. Tom was a discontented man who wanted the village to sever all ties with Salem Town—something I could not countenance. Much of my business came from the town; I should be destitute if Putnam had his way. So though I attended Salem Village church, I kept my membership in Salem Town, where I took Communion. I could not see Samuel Parris as my conduit to the Lord—such a man as that, so rigid and merciless, who argued unceasingly for a greater salary, who preached bitter and divisive sermons, who demanded gold candlesticks for the altar when the meetinghouse itself seemed ready to fall apart at the slightest breath of wind. . . . This was not a man I felt worthy to lead any congregation.

Judith did not agree with me on this. She did not relish the long trips to Salem Town for Communion, and she was one of the first to join the village church. After my initial attempts to lead her to a better path, I did not attempt to stop her when she told me her desire to transfer her membership from Salem Town. She was my wife, not my slave, and her soul knew already what would serve her best.

But I had to follow my own heart as well. I did not trust Parris or like him. I had refused to pay my taxes for his salary for months, as had many of the other villagers. When I was elected to the Village Committee, along with Francis Nurse, Daniel Andrew, Joseph Putnam, and Joseph Porter—all men with little love for Parris—one of our first decisions was to assess no tax for Parris's salary. This was no hasty decision; we had discussed it for months. We had used more subtle means to urge him toward resignation before now, but all our efforts had either gone unacknowledged or been bitterly contested. Now we'd lost our taste for subtlety.

Judith was angry at me for my part. 'Twas important, she said, that I lead the girls by example, and how was she to say that I took no part in village conflicts when it was clear I was involved? Yet in the end, she bowed to my arguments, though I know she did not agree with me.

Perhaps she was right; I don't know. What I do know is that in those first weeks after her death, I grew more and more troubled by the growing divisiveness in the village, yet my own worries made me step away. I was concerned only with how I was to bring up three girls without a mother's guiding hand. I knew vaguely of what was progressing; I knew that the church elders had requested that the committee levy a tax for Parris's salary. I knew Joseph Porter was adamant in his refusal. I thought 'twould end there. I hoped it would. But a week later, Francis Nurse called for an urgent meeting of the committee.

The day we were to meet, I woke early. But when I came out of the parlor, Susannah was already awake and at the hearth.

She looked over her shoulder, and the firelight came into her face. "Brother, come, sit down. I've breakfast almost ready."

"I'm to the Nurses'."

"Certainly the meeting will wait until you've supped."

I did not expect her attempt to dissuade me, and I had no argument ready. She was right; 'twas early yet. Joseph Putnam would be coming from some distance as well. I had plenty of time.

So I sat. She turned back to the fire. I sought some idle bit of conversation, but nothing came to me. In my life, I had never been so tongue-tied by a woman. Even when I had first been so impressed with Judith, I had never found myself lacking for words. I was ashamed of it.

I pulled the pitcher toward me and took a deep, full breath of bitter hops and malt in an attempt to clear my head.

"Are you well, Brother?" she asked, and I looked up to see her standing at the side of the table, her expression sharp.

"Aye," I said.

She set a trencher of samp before me and sat across from me with her own. I heard her soft chewing, her quiet swallow, and stared down at my own food. When I heard Susannah say, "I've been worried about Charity," the words seemed a foreign tongue, so distracted was I.

"She seems troubled," Susannah went on. "Does she not seem so to you?"

"Troubled?"

"I've awakened several times in the night to see her staring out the window. There is a . . . distraction . . . about her."

"She has always been an imaginative girl."

"And you think that's what this is?"

"She has been sensitive of late. Judith believed 'twas merely growth pangs."

"Growth pangs?" Susannah laughed, but 'twas not an amused sound. " 'Tis something different than that, I'll warrant."

"You should know better than her own mother?"

"I was a girl once. I am not blind."

"Neither was Judith," I said sharply.

Susannah nodded as if in agreement, but she was not finished; I saw her hesitation. "Has Charity a suitor?"

"A suitor? She's but a child."

"Have you looked upon her lately, Brother? She's a young woman already—perhaps more than that. She has a worldly look in her eyes."

"That is absurd."

She only tilted her head at me. "Is it? Look closer, then."

I thought of my daughter, of her pale blue eyes lit with adoration, and I remembered when she was but six, how she used to attend me in the barn until her mother put a quick end to it and started her on needlework. "You've known her less than a month, and yet you think to tell me—who has known her her whole life—about the look in her eyes?"

"I recognize it," Susannah said stubbornly.

"Aye. So you would." My words were deliberately cruel, and when she flushed, I felt both satisfaction and shame.

"How often do you tend to your children, Brother, except to discipline them?"

I stared at her in disbelief. "Do you accuse me of neglect?"

"You would know best if that is true."

"I am with my children nearly every hour. I do not take my duty to their souls lightly."

She waved her hand, a quick dismissal. "That's not what I mean. Did you know that she is seeing those friends of hers again?"

I went blank. *Those friends of hers.* Then I remembered the day of Faith's baptism, Charity sitting with those worthless girls at the table at Ingersoll's, Judith's words ringing in my ears. *We must keep her busy enough that she does not have time to tarry with them.* "I have asked her to stay away from them," I said.

"Well, she has disregarded you in this."

"She's a dutiful girl," I said angrily. "That you accuse her of disobedience—"

"Oh, Lucas, now 'tis you who's blind."

There was contempt in her words. I thought of the stories Judith had told me of her sister, and as I looked at her now, those things were not hard to believe. I pushed aside my trencher and got to my feet. "You'd best watch your words, madam. You have no place to judge me or my daughters."

"You misunderstand. I didn't mean to—"

"When you left your poor parents to chase after that yeoman's son, did you mean to cause them such humiliation? Did you think twice about what they would do without you?"

She blanched. "You know nothing of it," she said in a strained voice.

"Nor do you know anything of this," I told her. "I shall tend to my daughter in my way." I went to the door, grabbing my cloak from its hook and slinging it over my arm, not bothering to fasten it about my throat until I was out of the house, and she was far behind me.

As I led Saul to the path, I tried to forget her words, but they stayed with me. I began to wonder: Had I been neglectful? Was my eldest daughter moving beyond my reach? I decided no; how could she be? I was with my children every evening for prayers and readings. Susannah knew nothing of this household. She was but a temporary visitor.

It seemed a short distance to the Nurses' house, so lost was I in my thoughts. Francis's home was one of the finest in the village. It stood at one of the highest points, and the land was gentle and rolling down to the meadow, its stone walls and rail fences well kept, as were the orchards that reached to the pine and birch forest beyond. The flax patch was full of cut flax rotting away in the wet in preparation for gathering. Francis Nurse was elderly now and his wife frail, but between them they were more industrious than many of my neighbors.

I led the horse to the barn and then made my way up the long, curving path to the house and knocked upon the heavy oak door studded with nail heads. I stared up at the sundial carved into the wall above it until Francis opened the door. "Ah, Lucas, 'tis good you've come. Come in."

He led me into the low-ceilinged hall with its vast fireplace and pristine wooden floors. Already at the tableboard were the others, even Joseph Putnam, whom I'd thought to beat. "So I'm the last," I said.

"Not by much," Joseph assured me. "I've only just arrived. How do you, Lucas?"

"As well as I can," I answered him, coming to the table.

"Ah, well, 'tis a difficult time, I imagine. 'Tis good you've a woman to help you," Daniel Andrew said. I saw him glance to Joseph Porter and the look that passed between them, and I felt my own face burn. So they, too, had been talking of her—my own friends.

"For a time," I told them, taking my seat. Francis handed me a tankard of beer. "Where's Rebecca?"

"She's been feeling poorly of late," Francis said. " 'Tis the wet."

"Aye. 'Twill be a bad year for it too, I fear; I can feel it in my bones," Joseph Porter said, rubbing his graying beard.

" 'Tis a bad year all around," Daniel said glumly. He was a young man still, a lawyer who served as selectman in Salem Town as well—the only one of us who did. He ran his hand through his reddish hair and shook his head. "And this thing with the church looks to grow worse still."

I took a sip of beer. "How so? Tell me, how did the elders take our refusal to assess Parris's salary?"

They each looked at the other—I was the only one who had not been at the last meeting. "What is it?" I asked, alarmed. "What has happened?"

" 'Tis why we've called the meeting," Francis told me. "The church has filed suit against us."

"Against whom?"

"The committee."

"But that's ridiculous."

"So I've told them," Daniel put in. "But they filed the complaint with the County Court last week."

"Who's signed it?" I asked, though I knew already who 'twould be.

"Nate Putnam, Tom Putnam, and Thomas Wilkins," Daniel said.

'Twas the answer I'd expected. "Tom's like a dog with a bone," I said.

" 'Tis enough that we are against the pastor, that my brother should be for him," Joseph Putnam said with a small smile. "Tom would sooner see me dead than agree with me. Uncle Nate's no better."

"It would be easier if you were the only reason," Francis said. "But you were too young to be the start of this dispute."

"What do we do then?" Daniel asked. "I must warn you, 'tis our own pockets at risk here. If the council were to decide in their favor, we could be fined for neglecting our duties."

"What are the chances of that?" I asked.

Daniel looked glum. "I wish I could say they were bad, but the County Council is impatient these days with any who take issue with rules laid by the General Council. And the contests between the town and the village are well known and numerous. I fear our luck cannot be good."

"But the principle—"

"They've no patience with the high-minded," Daniel interrupted sharply. "They'll see only that we've refused to assess the tax for Parris's salary—and that is our main duty as a committee, mandated twenty years ago."

"The man cannot remain," Joseph Porter said angrily. "Demands for firewood, demands for gold at the pulpit, and that just the start. Lucas, you have said that he demanded gloves at dear Judith's grave, and others have said the same. Gloves! As if this were Boston! Parris's biggest concern is for his own comfort. 'Tis obvious he cares little for his congregation. He has already broken his covenant with us."

"They won't see it that way." Daniel sighed. "But I shall do my best to persuade them, you know this."

We all nodded, a few said "aye," but the news Daniel gave was bleak indeed. I was incensed by it, and voted with the others to stay our course—the principles we stood for were worth the threat of any fine.

During the meeting, I had forgotten all about Susannah, about the argument we'd had, but the moment we rose from the table to leave, those thoughts returned.

I did not look forward to going home. I took my time about it, though I had things to do, another spinning wheel yet to finish, and a cupboard for a man in Salem Town. Susannah's worries about Charity nagged at me. Again I felt the full weight of the responsibility Judith had left on my shoulders, and the relief of knowing Susannah was there to help was suddenly no relief at all. My conscience was sore and troubled. I came out of the woods to the path leading up to the house and saw Charity standing there outside our door, staring at me as if she'd seen the Devil in my shadow.

Charity is troubled. There was a moment, something I saw in my daughter's gaze that made me think Susannah was right, but then it passed. I wondered if I'd truly seen it.

Charity said, "Father, a word with you. I'm afraid we have been cruelly deceived."

She had always been an imaginative child, a dramatic child. Now her words were so serious, so grave, and there was an intensity in her expression that I suddenly realized I had not seen for many years, and I wondered why. Had it simply been that she had outgrown the days when a broken go-cart had brought paroxysms of grief, or a dusting of snow exclamations of awe? Or was it something more, something I'd missed?

She was talking again, too quickly to understand until she said, "She's an actress, Father. An actress."

"Charity," I said, in that way I'd used often when she was just a child, trying to calm her through a tantrum or tears. I took her elbow to make her listen. "Who is an actress? Whom do you accuse?"

I had thought she would name one of her friends, or perhaps someone from outside the village or on the Ipswich Road. I did not expect it when she said, "Susannah."

I was stunned. Then I realized the rumors must have followed Susannah already to Salem Village. I wondered how that could be, who could have known.

It was some moments before I realized I was holding Charity. I had not held her this way since she was a baby, and I hoped God would forgive me for keeping her there a moment more. Then, I knew I could not spoil her. 'Twas my duty to keep her strong.

Gently I pushed her away, and told her the truth in the kindest words I could. "Your aunt is no actress, Charity."

She was a child, caught up in a melodrama of her own making. Sensitivity was her flaw. The world would tear her to pieces if I could not give her the strength to fight it, so I made my voice hard and put an end to her accusations and her exaggerations, and then I left her.

But my daughter's wounded expression did not leave me. Her words echoed in my head, along with the image of my neighbors talking among themselves, that glance Joseph Porter and Daniel Andrew had exchanged. The rumors were in the village now, and I knew I must do something to stop them. For my daughters, I told myself. To protect their innocent bodies from insinuations of wickedness. To keep their futures unsullied. For my daughters.

Chapter 15

I WAITED UNTIL AFTER OUR EVENING PRAYERS, UNTIL THE CHILDREN were in bed. 'Twas a dark night, and the house seemed darker still, the encroaching shadows creeping through the windows to crawl across the floor, the firelight an uncertain bulwark against it. I lit a candle, and then another. When Susannah looked at me in surprise, I took up one of Jude's boots and my cobbling kit and made to repair it. "There is not enough light for this," I told her.

"I welcome it," she said as she scrubbed the trenchers. "It seems that here . . . 'tis always so dark. I'm surprised you're not on your way to bed yourself, Brother."

"I've shoes to repair."

She paused a moment, and then said, "Aye," and I thought I heard the knowledge of my lie in her single word. I wondered why I hadn't just said the truth, why I was hesitating. I was here because I had to talk with her; why not discuss this and be done with it the sooner?

"And . . ." I turned Jude's boot over in my hand, noting the wear of it, the stretch of a seam, the way the dark impression of her little foot marked the leather. "And too . . . I wish a word with you."

"Ah. Without the children hearing?"

"Aye."

"How important this must be, then, to spare them the sound."

I looked up to see that she faced me. She held a trencher before her like a shield. It was still wet, and water dripped silently onto the brick hearth; its sound was lost in the crackle of the fire.

"They've been wounded enough by it already," I said.

"Wounded?" She frowned. She set aside the trencher and came toward me, pausing at the end of the table. "I don't understand."

"When I returned today, Charity told me that she'd heard rumors in town."

"Rumors? Of what?"

"Rumors that you tread the boards."

"Oh." She sagged onto the end of the bench; I felt the rock of her weight, the steadying of the bench beneath it. "I cannot believe that would have followed me so far."

"Perhaps you were not so guarded as you thought."

Her look was sharp. "This did not come from me. It has brought me enough trouble. 'Twas long ago, in any case. Scarcely worth mentioning."

"Not for someone."

"Aye." She looked thoughtful. "Aye. 'Tis true enough."

"Then who?"

"Did Charity hear it herself? From Judith? From you?"

I shook my head, startled at the thought. "We hardly mentioned you."

She made a quick little breath. I saw I'd hurt her, and the ache was strange upon her face, an expression I had never thought to see on her. I knew more about Susannah Morrow than she could have believed—Judith did not lightly release old hurts, even when she loved. This I knew: Susannah had a discontented spirit; she had long ago lost her way to God. That it mattered to her what she'd left behind had never occurred to me before that moment, not until I saw the quick downcast of her glance, the careful folding of her hands in her skirt.

"Have you brothers or sisters, Lucas?" she asked quietly.

"Only one brother now. I think."

"You think?"

"It has been many years since I've seen him—"

"Where is he?"

There was an odd insistence in her voice. When I looked at her in puzzlement, she pressed on. "Do you hear from him?"

"No." I shook my head. "Not since coming to New England." Though in truth, it had been much longer than that. I had left home when my only remaining brother was barely five—I would be surprised now to find he even remembered me. I could but hope he lived still, though even that I was not sure of, given my stepfather's brutal nature. My mother, I hoped, had died long since. I wanted a safe and good eternity for her, who had been so beleaguered on earth.

But these things I did not say to Susannah. They were not her concern, and I did not trust her reasons for wanting to know. So I was silent.

"Have you told your daughters of them—of your family?"

"My family is scattered to the winds. What remains of them, I've no wish to rediscover."

"Do I fall into that same sentiment, then?"

I sighed in impatience. "'Tis pointless to—"

"No," she said firmly. "You said that you and Judith did not speak of me to your daughters. Were you so ashamed?"

"Aye. Aye, of course." I gestured to the room. "Look about you. This is a pious family, a God-fearing one. There is no room for wickedness here."

"And I'm wicked."

"Can you say you are not?"

"I was never an actress."

"You *lived* with actors," I accused. "You fornicated with them—"

"With one," she said. "With a single man. His name was Geof-frey."

I laughed disbelievingly. "And then you moved on to another."

"Robert was no actor. He was a cobbler."

"You lived with him."

Her eyes flashed. "Aye. I did. I loved him."

"But you never married him. You never married any of them."

She rose and slapped her hand hard on the table. She leaned close. "I have known men like you, Brother. Always the first to cast stones, always the first to cry out sinner. Then you sneak home to gratify yourself in a dark corner and take out your frustrations on anyone who crosses you. Do you think I don't know what you are? Do you think I don't know that 'twas you Judith wrote me of?"

"Me?" I stared at her, angry now. Without thinking, I grabbed her wrist, holding her away. "I gave Judith no cause to complain. And why she would trust her dearest thoughts to you, when you so easily betrayed her, is a mystery to me."

"It seems most things are mysterious to you."

She made no move to push me away or jerk from my hold. Then the anger left her eyes, and something else came into them, something that startled me.

'Twas as if I'd been blind, and suddenly my gaze cleared. I dropped her wrist. "Forgive me," I whispered. I sank onto the bench, my face buried in my hands. "Forgive me. I should not have said those things."

"Nor I." She sounded shaken.

I did not look at her. I heard her move away. I heard her at the hearth, raking up the fire.

"I shall . . . put these words behind me," she said, her voice so quiet I was not sure at first that I'd heard her. "There is no need for us to be at arms."

"Aye," I agreed. " 'Tis forgotten already."

"Good. Then . . . I'll say good night."

"Good night," I said.

She paused another moment, and then she nodded and went up the stairs, leaving only the sound of her step behind.

I picked up Jude's shoe from where it had fallen on the floor and set it on the table, and then I snuffed the candles and made my way in darkness to the parlor, where the bed I'd shared with Judith was a shadow at one end. I undressed and crawled between sheets cold as the grave, without even a bed warmer to ease my way. I wanted the discomfort; I wanted the reminder of mortality, the chill on my soul. But as I lay there in bed, I burned.

The torment was too much. I rose again and pulled my shirt over my head and went to my desk in the corner. I lit the single, pitted candle and reached for comfort from the stack of books piled on the floor. It opened to the page I knew, a page creased already by the sweat of my fingers: *So soon as we rise in the morning, we go forth to fight with two mighty giants, the world and the Devil; and whom do we take with us but a traitor, this brittle flesh, which is ready to yield up to the enemy at every assault?*

I closed my eyes and thought of Judith: her cold hands, the stiffness of her body beneath mine, the forbearance in her eyes. Gradually the fire inside me died. Gradually I could breathe again. I closed the sermon and blew out the candle, then fumbled my way back to my bed, where I drew the curtains closed. I was tired; it was late. I thought I would drift off into deep sleep, but dreams of Judith haunted me until I woke again with the dawn, exhausted past bearing, feeling as Jonas: *I am cast out of the sight of God.*

The first snow came, and kept falling, until it was piled by the door, and we were housebound but for the barn. Charity especially seemed to suffer from it. She had grown pale and wan these last weeks, and she seemed distracted, staring out the windows in a daydream when she should have been working, watching me with an intensity that disturbed me. Then, one morning, I woke early. I had been unable to sleep, the bed too cold and too empty, my dreams unresolved and vaguely wicked. Susannah was not yet awake. When I heard the step on the stair, I took the last gulp of beer and made to go outside. From the corner of my eye, I saw it was not Susannah but Charity.

When I saw my daughter, I stopped. I found myself staring at her, noticing how unrested she seemed, the shadows beneath her eyes, her skin too pale. Suddenly I thought of a conversation from a few days ago, Susannah's oddly intense question about my old apprentice, Samuel Trask, who disappeared one day without a word. *What do you know of this, Charity?*

I had not been thinking of Sam, nor had I been considering the five pounds he'd taken. But now I felt his presence, and with it, an unsettling connection to my daughter. I remembered Judith standing before me, her mouth moving, the substance if not the words coming to me again, something about Sam, about Charity. "Talk to him, won't you, Lucas?" she'd asked, and I'd agreed to do so, though I was too distracted with the jobs I'd meant to do that day. So I hardly understood what it was Judith wanted me to talk to Sam about, and I forgot my promise moments after. Now the memory lingered as a faint dread.

"Good morning, Charity," I said.

"Good morning." She sat at the tableboard and poured some beer into a noggin with a weariness that bent her spine.

"Are you ill, child?" I asked her.

She looked up as if the very sound of my voice surprised her. For a moment, she looked as if she might say something, but then she shook her head. "No, Father."

I thought I saw her spirit in her eyes, and it seemed broken and hopeless so that it nearly rent my heart. I could not keep from asking, "What troubles you?" Though I was afraid of how she would answer.

She dragged the noggin toward her, though she did not drink. "How does the Devil come?"

I had been expecting her to say something of Samuel, and so I was nonplussed for a moment. I frowned. "In many ways. 'Tis our task to recognize him whenever we see him."

"I remember when our neighbor told Mama she'd seen him. That he sat on her in the night—"

I nodded. "A nightmare. When she prayed, the vision left."

"But what if it didn't go?"

"It did."

"But what if"—she took a deep breath—"what if you prayed and prayed, and he did not leave?"

I should not have been so relieved at her question, but I was. This was nothing to do with Sam after all; 'twas merely my daughter's worries over her own salvation—a natural result of her mother's death. "Charity, you must listen to me. Satan's greatest trick is in making us believe that God is lost to us. Will you give him that power?"

"I don't want to. But I-I'm afraid."

"You must pray for reassurance, child. God has not abandoned you. Think of that when you are afraid."

She nodded, yet hesitated, and I remembered something Susannah had said about the girls Charity had once called her friends. 'Twas now, when her faith was so fragile, that Charity most needed guidance. Those girls, with their mischief, could only confuse her. Carefully I said, "The Devil has many guises, Charity. Be careful who you trust and what you believe."

Her eyes went wide. I saw knowledge in them, a surprise that brought satisfaction. I had been right to say something. 'Twas indeed her friends filling her head with doubts.

"I have heard that you continue to see those girls, despite my admonitions. I have no choice, I'm afraid, but to forbid you to have anything more to do with them."

She looked alarmed. "But, Father—"

"'Tis for the best," I said firmly. "Your mother believed they were leading you astray, and I find that I must agree."

She was silent, but I saw her struggle. "You will find other friends," I said. "Ones who do not court wickedness. Am I understood?"

Her lips pressed tight together, but she nodded.

"Very well. Now go to the hearth and pray. I feel sure God will grant you the reassurances you seek."

I watched as she moved from the bench to the settle, kneeling before a fire that I had only just built up. She bowed her head, and I saw her lips move with prayer. I felt a calm come over my own soul. My child had reminded me of God's grace, and for the first time in weeks, my heart was still and quiet. I would come in early tonight, I vowed. We would spend the evening in prayer and scripture until her fears, and my own, were gone.

As I was turning to go, I saw a movement on the stairs. When I looked up, I saw Susannah there, half hidden in the shadows, watching Charity.

Whatever calm I had managed disappeared. She glanced at me, and for the briefest of moments, our eyes held. Then I turned away and hurried out the door.

I did not pray with Charity that night. I forgot about her fears and my own reassurances. I stayed in the barn until very late, until I could no longer see through the dimness half lit by the faltering lamp, until my fingers were too frozen to move—as if cold could calm my soul.

Chapter 16

For the next several days, I worked until late into the evenings, coming inside only for supper and for evening lessons, then retiring early. I surrounded myself with published sermons and a well-thumbed Bible, pounding God's lessons into my heart.

It had become a routine I took peace from, a measure of sanity and control, and I did not like it disrupted. So when I came in one evening after supper to see Charity sitting pale and tearfully distraught at the table, darting venomous glances toward Susannah, I was irritated. I did not want to be involved in their squabbling. I was not good at such things.

Then I realized that Susannah, who was at the settle with Jude, going over a sampler, seemed unaware of Charity's distress. For a moment I was relieved—there had been no quarrel—then I remembered the last conversation I'd had with Charity. With the memory came a stab of guilt that I'd neglected her since. She needed my guidance still; it had only been two months since Judith's death, and the two of them had been close.

I went over to her. "Have you done your lessons for today, child?"

She wiped quickly at her eyes. "Aye."

"Tell me. Isaiah fifty-five: seven."

She swallowed. " 'Let the wicked forsake His way, and the unrighteous man His thoughts: and let him return unto the Lord, and He will have mercy upon him; and to our God, for He will abundantly pardon. "For My thoughts are not your thoughts, neither are your ways My ways," saith the Lord. "For as the—"'"

I held up my hand to stop her. She had recited the text perfectly, yet there was a distance in her gaze that alarmed me. "What meaning take you from this?"

"'Tis as you said, Father. God will pardon even the most wicked, should he turn to the Lord."

'Twas as I'd taught her. Still . . . "Have you taken comfort in the words?"

"Aye."

"Then why the tears?" I touched her cheek, and she leaned her face into my palm as if she ached for the warmth of my hand. That alarmed me too, such longing, so I drew away again. "There is wool to be spun," I said gently. "Or was it only in my imagination that you and your mother carded every day this fall?"

Charity blanched. "I won't . . . I cannot spin."

"Why is that?"

"Because . . . because I-I hurt my hand."

"Ask your aunt to put some salve on it."

"I would do it myself."

Her dislike of Susannah was hard in her tone. I sighed. "Your mother would not like your distrust of your aunt. 'Twould be better if you could accept things as they are."

My glance fell upon Susannah, who looked up at the same moment. I commanded my daughters to the settle for their nightly lessons. 'Twas all I could do to stumble through the sermon I'd planned out for them.

Finally I could stand it no longer. I said a final prayer and sent my daughters to bed, trying not to feel despairing as I watched how slowly Charity went up the stairs, trailing behind Jude with burdened steps. When they were gone, I went quickly to my own room without a word to Susannah.

In the parlor, my bed was shadowed and cold, the curtains half drawn. A small fire had been lit, but the wood was wet, and it only smoked and smoldered and gave no warmth. I went to the window and looked out at the bare black trees and the snow glowing in the faint light of a crescent moon.

I was confused and afraid. I had lost my way these last weeks since Judith's death. There were currents in my own house that puzzled me; I did not understand the dislike between Charity and Susannah, or why Charity was so inconsolable. My well-ordered household was suddenly foundering, and I could not think of what to do. All I knew was that I could not rid myself of the nagging feeling that Susannah was to blame.

I prayed until the night passed into the small, dark hours, searching for answers, for reassurance. Finally I undressed and went to bed, drawing the green harrateen curtains all around before I crawled between cold sheets. They still smelled of Judith: strong soap and mint, the herbs she'd nestled among our clothes. I stared up at the darkness, at the bunches of horsemint and chamomile she'd hung at the bedposts to softly scent our slumber, and one of her sayings came to me: *God will provide.* In my exhaustion, the words were comforting. Aye, the Lord would show me the way. I had not kept my faith. With that reassurance, and the thought of Judith full upon my heart, I fell asleep.

I'm not sure what it was that woke me; one moment I was deep in dreams, and the next, wide awake, startled and confused, my own breath filling the dark around me.

At the foot of the bed, the curtains opened, pulled aside by an unseen hand. Though there was no light, not a candle, not even the moon shining dimly through the window, I saw her standing there as if it were day, so bright was she.

Susannah.

Her face was luminous, her dark hair down around her shoulders. She wore a red bodice—the same she'd worn the day of Faith's baptism, too bright for common folk, too scarlet for anything but vanity. It seemed to glow as she came toward me, through the curtains that fell shut behind her as she crawled over the headboard, up and up until there was scarlet all around me, the bed rug, her bodice, that terrible glow.

I felt her weight on my feet, my shins, my knees, up to my thighs, where she stopped and settled heavily upon me. I could not speak; 'twas as if my throat had closed. I could barely breathe as she straddled me.

"Wh-what are you doing?" I managed finally, though my voice sounded strangled, hardly there.

She smiled wickedly and leaned slowly forward, until she lay upon me with her full weight, her breasts upon my chest, her pelvis cradled against mine. Her hair spun and caught on my stubbled cheeks. I could not move, speak, or stir, though I tried. The temptation of her dizzied me. *Can you bear to be alive half an hour in fire, and if not, how can you bear to live in Hell for all eternity?*

The words of the sermon came to me like a message from God, and with them, my strength. "No!" I shouted, and I pushed at her shoulders. She sat up easily and laughed as her hands came down around my throat; squeezing, choking, she possessed a most unholy strength, one that held me where I lay. A mere woman, holding me still with only her delicate hands, but there I was: a prisoner.

Her weight grew heavier and heavier. Then, when it seemed I could not bear it another moment, she said to me, "I will have you" in the softest of whispers, a mere tremor of breath.

She was gone.

She left me that suddenly; there and solid one moment, vanished the next; my body my own again, my movements no longer controlled by her. I put my hand to my throat, thinking that I would still feel her there, that the press of her fingers must surely be branded on my skin, but there was nothing. I could breathe again; I could move. There had not even been a shiver of the bed curtains.

I snapped awake, gasping for breath, shaking in terror. 'Twas a dream, only a dream. I tried to reassure myself, but it had been so real I could not tell it from this moment now. I could not stop my-self from pushing aside the curtains, scanning the darkened room for a sign of her. Naked, I padded across the floor in the frigid cold. The window was open—yet it had been latched since the end of summer. The freezing air came inside, blown by a sudden night wind. Dark clouds scudded across the sky, wisping across the frail outline of a thin moon. Snow crystals brushed my face.

I yanked the window shut, hard enough that it thudded and shook against the sill. I latched it with shaking hands, and then latched it again to be sure it was stiff, hammered it into place with my fist. Then I stumbled to my desk, shivering, my fingers stiff with cold as I grabbed the Bible and let it fall open to Psalms, the last marked place. I murmured the words aloud as a talisman against evil. "'There is none upon this earth that I desire beside Thee. My flesh and my heart faileth, but God is the strength of my heart, and my portion forever. . . . I have put my trust in the Lord God, that I may declare all Thy works.'" When I'd said them so often the words ceased to have meaning, I mumbled vague prayers instead: "Dear God, help me, guide me. Protect me from temptation. . . . I am but a poor servant, my Lord. . . ."

When dawn broke, I was still at my desk, cold clear into my bones, shivering. I could no longer feel my hands as they skimmed the pages; my throat and tongue were dry from the feverishness of my prayers. My skin felt touched with ice. Yet I did not move, not until I heard the creak of the crane at the fire, the unmistakable sound of Susannah awake and tending to breakfast.

Hurriedly I went to pull on my clothes, my numb fingers fum-bling with buttons and ties, my feet like cold blocks inside my boots. Last night had been a dream only, a temptation sent by the Devil, no flesh-and-blood woman. My logical mind knew it.

I had only a single thought: I was bowing beneath temptation. Last night had been proof of it. In spite of all my reasoned argu-ments over why she should not go, I no longer had a choice. Soon—

today—I would have to tell my wife's sister that she was no longer welcome in my home.

It wasn't until that night that I found the courage to do it. I came into the house, girding myself for the task, and stopped short at the sound of voices and laughter. The unmistakable laughter of Hannah Penney. It should not have been a surprise. Hannah came over often now, bringing Faith to visit, but I had not expected her so late.

Jude was near the hearth, churning, while Charity scrubbed pewter at the washtable. Hannah was at the tableboard, and Susannah sat across, dandling Faith on her knee.

I stood quiet beside the door.

"Shall we play matrimony?" Susannah asked Hannah. I saw that in her other hand, the one not holding Faith, there were cards.

Hannah shook her head. "George would put me out if he heard I did."

"We won't gamble, then," Susannah urged.

Hannah seemed to hesitate. Then Faith began to fret, and Hannah looked over at her and saw me.

She froze for a moment. Then her eyes grew large in her pale face, and she shook her head vehemently and said, "No, not that. George only allows whist, and we need two more for that."

"Whist?" Susannah said. "Such a boring game—"

Hannah shook her head. "Even your brother cannot disapprove of whist, can you, Lucas?"

I came fully into the room, though I was afraid to come too close. "I cannot approve of cards at all," I said with feigned calm as I took off my gloves.

Susannah set her cards on the table and turned, grabbing Faith close to her chest as if afraid I would take the child from her. "You would disapprove of something Queen Mary does herself?"

"The queen does not dictate morality to me, madam," I told her. "Only God can do that."

"I don't remember God saying anything about cards—or is that in a Bible I'm not familiar with?"

"I cannot say what Bibles you are acquainted with, if any. But 'tis clear He does not countenance gambling."

"Ah." She smiled. "So God gives us whist for our pleasure, but not matrimony."

Hannah chuckled softly at the jibe. Susannah bowed her head in acknowledgment of her cleverness, and more—I had the sense that 'twas me she was mocking.

I reached across Susannah and grabbed the cards lying there, and then I strode across the room and threw them in the fire. The gilded edges curled, and then the flames caught and leaped, too high for such little fodder, high enough that I backed away and Jude jumped a little at the churn. I heard Charity's gasp.

Susannah said, "Those cards came all the way from London."

"There are more to be had there, I'm sure," I said, still angry, not thinking. "When you return, no doubt they'll be waiting."

There was silence. I had not meant to say the words, not that way. I knew what Susannah heard in them, and I expected anger, perhaps, or resignation. I did not expect her stillness, or my sense that she was afraid.

For the first time, it occurred to me that she might have as much reason to want to come here as I had to send her away. I had not bothered to ask why she'd made the journey now, at this time of year. The waters were treacherous; few traveled in the late fall and winter if it could be helped. I knew that Judith had asked her to visit us many times before, but Susannah had never come. Not until now.

"Do you plan to return?" Hannah asked quietly. "I'd thought you meant to stay."

Charity jerked around. In the corner, Jude stopped her churning.

'Twas as if the lack of sound stirred Susannah. "Go on, Jude, don't let it sit. Charity, keep scrubbing."

"You aren't going back, are you, Auntie?" Jude's voice was thin; I heard the fear in it. When I glanced over, her dark blue eyes were wide, her thin hands clutched on the dasher so hard her knuckles were white.

"She must go back sometime." Charity's hopeful expectation was almost uncomfortable in its intensity.

Jude ignored her. She said accusingly to Susannah, "You said you weren't going back."

"You must let her return if she chooses to, Jude," I said, more sharply than I meant to.

"Do I have a choice, Brother?" Susannah asked softly.

Hannah Penney was glaring at me; Jude seemed as if she might cry; Charity's anticipation was painfully sharp. Susannah had pinned me neatly. I knew what she was doing: clearly naming me the villain. If I told her to go, there would be no way to mitigate it, not with Hannah sitting there, listening to every word. She would have it to her husband, who would tell Tom Putnam, and he would then tell Parris. 'Twas an uncharitable thing I meant to do; now the whole village would know it in fact, instead of merely speculating on whether I had told her to go or she went of her own free will.

Yet the memory of last night was still close; it rushed through my consciousness like a fevered delirium. I had no choice. I opened my mouth to tell her so.

Faith began to cry. As if she sensed what I was about to do, she set up a wailing so loud and hard it was impossible to bear. Susannah began rocking the babe against her breast, but I stepped forward. "Give her to me," I said coldly, thinking that I should learn to comfort the babe if I meant to send Susannah away.

Susannah hesitated only a moment. Then she gave me Faith. The child was squirming and beet-faced, squalling in a high-pitched scream that pierced my ears. She was warm and heavy, and her little cotton-capped head fit nearly in the palm of my hand. I felt again as I had in the church during her baptism, overwhelmed and helpless. I jiggled her in my hands, and she threw up her arms and clenched her little fists and commenced to squall harder. "Come, come," I murmured to her, afraid to hold her tightly, afraid not to. I tried tucking her into the crook of my arm, where she did not want to stay.

"Try her against your shoulder, Lucas," Hannah suggested, but instead I looked into my daughter's squinted eyes. Even in the deformity of her anger, she looked to me like Judith, the shape of her face, her determined little jaw. I wrapped her in my arms, trying to hold her still, bouncing her as I had watched Judith do countless times when Charity and Jude were babes.

I turned my back to the others and went to the hearth. I would calm this child of mine if it took me all afternoon. I kept bouncing her, though the movement was not enough. "Come now, Faith," I said again. "Quiet now."

Suddenly I felt Susannah behind me. She leaned around me, and said in a soft voice, "You should talk to her, Brother. 'Twould help, I think."

"I have been talking to her."

She laughed lightly. "She is too young to understand your sermons, and 'tis not what she wants now."

"She cannot know what she wants—or what is good for her."

"Then pray to her," Susannah suggested, giving me a small smile. "But do so quietly."

I looked back into Faith's face. Her howling hurt my ears, and I was desperate to make her quiet, and so I took Susannah's advice, though I did not want to. I leaned close to my daughter's ear and whispered a psalm. At first, they were just words, the poetry of God's song. But then the Windsor tune came to me, and I heard it winding through my voice, a song to God in my voice alone. It had never sounded so fine in the meetinghouse, with all my neighbors joining in. Though I had never thought I had an ear for music, I remembered the tune far better than I'd expected. I sang it for her.

Faith began to quiet. I was amazed she could hear me through her tantrum, but she did. Her little eyes opened, and she stared into my face as if trying to see it for the first time, as if 'twas not clear to her. Her sobs died away, seemingly bewitched by my voice.

She was a beautiful child, apple-cheeked, round-faced, with a fuzz of dark hair peeking from beneath the simple soft cap she wore. She was a satisfying weight in my arms, and I lost myself in her face the way I'd lost myself in all my children, enchanted by the way she stared up at me, by the cooing of her soft little mouth, the fat fingers that reached up, trying to grab the hair on my chin, misjudging the distance. She was no longer crying, but her tears left tracks on her cheeks, still glistening in her tiny lashes.

I forgot the others. For a few moments 'twas only Faith and I who existed in this world, and I felt myself falling in love with her the way I had not allowed myself to do before now, the way I had with Jude before her, and Charity. I felt the emotion grow in my heart until there was room for nothing else. When she made a bubbly, tiny noise at me and reached again for my bearded chin, I smiled at her. I would have sworn I saw her smile in return.

And then . . . Then I felt a shift of movement beside me; I saw a flash of muted color, and I remembered where I was. I glanced up to see Susannah staring at me. She had seen my pride. She had seen my weakness.

"You have a good smile, Brother," she said.

I did not know what to say to her. When she reached out her arms to take Faith away, I hesitated. Susannah smiled, and there was no wickedness in it, but only consolation.

"Come now," she said again, with the slightest nod of her head, a nod that led my eyes inescapably to Hannah, who was frowning as if she thought I was no fit guardian for such a tender soul, and I realized in a slip of strangeness, in an incongruity I could not reconcile, that Susannah was trying to guard me from Hannah's greedy eyes.

I gave Faith into Susannah's hands. I released her as if it meant nothing. But when she was gone, I felt cold; I felt the impression of her solid little body still in a fading warmth against my skin. I looked at Susannah, at the way she held Faith, the way she rocked her. My daughter gripped Susannah's finger, cooing in a happy sound, while Susannah murmured back, their own language, one I did not know or recognize. I knew I could never send Susannah back to London. For better or for worse, she was here now, and part of my family. Whatever temptations the Devil put to me, I would have to battle on my own.

Chapter 17

THE NEXT NIGHT, AS I FINISHED EVENING PRAYERS, I NOTICED AGAIN how reluctantly Charity took herself off to bed. I watched her go, the hesitant shuffle of her feet, the strange, strained submissiveness of her posture, and my worry grew.

I did not realize how long I stood staring after her until Susannah said from the fire, "She grows ever worse."

We were alone. The circumstance surprised me—how had that happened without my realizing it? "She and her mother were close."

"So you've said. I think 'tis more than that."

She was watching the now-empty stairs. I saw only her profile, but she seemed thoughtful; she wore a little frown.

Then she turned to me, and the beauty that lived on her face was muted and soft. She seemed uncertain when she asked me, "How well do you discipline your children?"

I hesitated, uncertain what to tell her. Reluctantly I admitted, "Judith was the better parent when it came to that."

"Did she beat them?"

"She was not so indulgent as I."

"Indulgent?"

"If my children are not submissive enough before God, the fault is mine, not Judith's. She was determined in that."

Susannah looked at me for a moment, and then she began to

laugh. "What a fool," she said, shaking her head, laughing still, mocking me.

I turned into the parlor. "I will not stand here to be insulted."

"No, no, you misunderstand."

She stopped me with a touch, pressuring me to turn again.

"I didn't mean you were a fool, Lucas," she said. "I meant I was. *I* have been a fool."

I was confused. "I . . . don't know what you mean."

"I came here because Judith led me to believe you beat her."

For a moment, her words distracted me from her presence. I thought of my soft wife with her stone-hard core. "Why would she say such a thing?"

"She did not say so—at least not plainly. I'm afraid I assumed 'twas what she meant." Susannah gave me a small smile. "I am relieved to know it was not true. I had thought . . . Well, it doesn't matter."

"You had thought what?"

"She had written to me of trouble, and I had believed . . . Our father used to beat us, you see, and the way she wrote . . . 'Twas how we used to talk when we were maids. In secrets."

"Your father . . ." I frowned at her, trying to comprehend this thing I had not known. Judith had said nothing of it to me. Certainly Susannah was exaggerating. "'Tis the duty of every father to discipline his children."

"Shall he beat them until they're bloody, then? Until they cannot stand? Did you never see the scars on your wife's back and wonder at them?"

"Of course," I said quietly. "She said 'twas a fall from a horse. . . ."

"We were too poor for horses," Susannah said. "Had you looked close enough, you would have seen it."

The images came into my head before I could stop them: Judith lying stiffly on her back, the chemise she refused to remove shoved up to her hips, breasts covered, life closed off while I took my own wretched pleasure.

"What is it? Lucas?"

I blinked. "'Twas nothing," I said brusquely. "I . . . You must know, I never laid an angry hand on her or my children."

She nodded. "I know that now."

We stood there silently and still.

The Bible slipped in my hand, and in catching it, I broke the spell. I backed away. "Good night," I said, and then, without waiting for her reply, I turned into the parlor. I was so distracted that I didn't realize until I'd shut the door that I'd closed it in her face.

I could not seem to stop watching her. I would be coming to the house from the barn, and instead of going in, I would go to the window and try to find her. I could never see her clearly; that was the point of it. She was a figure distorted by thick and rippled glass, cut into planes by the lead panes, diamond shapes of muted color and form shifting as she moved. She was a spirit that had no body and little shape, a figment purely drawn of my own imagination. I didn't understand how she could be so compelling; she who had such a lamentable history.

I could think of only one way to keep from giving in to this temptation of watching her: I took myself off for a few days. The heavy snow of the last week eased and turned to rain and the temperatures rose. The ground heaved and thawed as if 'twas spring already in mid-January. The roads turned to quagmires, mud thick as glue. It was hard to travel, but I made as many deliveries as I could before the ice and snow came again. God had seen fit to give me a respite, a time to strengthen myself, and I took advantage of it gratefully.

I managed to stay away from the house for several days. But to be away from home was wearying, and I was tired and my mind heavy when my errands were done and I came to the village again. 'Twas only luck—or divine interference—that made me take the road past the Proctors' tavern; luck and the wish to lengthen my journey, though I would not admit that. It was how I ran into Daniel Andrew.

"How glad I am to see you, Lucas," he said, walking over at my wave. "I stopped by your house, but your sister said you were out, and that she did not know when you would return."

"I'd errands in town."

"Ah." Daniel made a heavy sigh. "Francis has called another meeting of the Village Committee."

I was surprised. "Has the court decided?"

"No. No. 'Tis just that . . . Parris has been making demands again. 'Tis the lack of firewood, and the cold of this winter . . ."

"What would he have us do?" I asked bitterly. "Find a forest to cut for him?"

Daniel shrugged. "I swear 'tis easier to deal with a horde of contentious selectmen than this one pastor."

"A meeting, then," I agreed. "Where?"

"Rebecca has worsened," Daniel said. "She has requested quiet, so we won't meet there. Putnam's too far—"

"My house," I said quickly. "We can meet at my house."

Daniel didn't hesitate. "Very well. I'll tell the others. Shall we meet this afternoon?"

I agreed, and we parted company. I knew it was absurd, but home was somehow easier to bear knowing that the others would descend on it within hours. The time would pass quickly until then.

When I arrived home, Susannah was on the floor amidst buckets of soapy water and sand, her skirts hiked and tucked. She had Jude carding wool near the fire. When I came in, I saw Susannah's surprise and the self-conscious way she pushed her hair from her eyes.

"Why, Brother," she said, "I did not know when to expect you."

I turned abruptly. "Aye. Well, I am home now. My errands are done, at least for a few days."

"Had I known it, I would have had this done before you came home."

"Had I known when I was coming, I would have told you." I glanced around the room, nodding a greeting to Jude. "Where's Charity?"

There was silence, and Jude dipped her head and rocked the carding combs as if her election depended on the cleanliness of the wool. I looked back to Susannah, who said, "She went to take bread to the parson's wife."

"The parson's wife?"

Susannah was expressionless. "Mistress Parris is quite ill, I understand. Or so Charity has told me. She has been visiting there a great deal lately."

It was unfathomable. "She is visiting the parsonage?"

"Aye."

I laughed bitterly. "This is a fine thing. . . . The Village Committee is meeting here this afternoon to discuss how best to roust Parris from the village, and yet my own daughter is bringing him food—"

"She tells me Judith went there quite often," Susannah said quietly. "Or is that not true?"

That revelation set me aback as well. I had not known it, though it did not surprise me. I sank onto the bench. "I knew nothing of it. But Charity is no liar."

Susannah said nothing. She bent again to scrub the floor, and though I did not understand why, I had the sense that there was something more here, that there were things unsaid, though I could not imagine what they might be.

"Is there something else?" I asked.

Susannah dipped the brush in the water. She sprinkled sand from the other bucket over the floor before she looked up again. "No, Brother. Should there be?"

I knew she lied. I knew it, though I did not know how or why. She kept my gaze for a moment longer before she bent again to her work, and I stumbled past her to the parlor, where I built up the fire and sat on my bed staring into the flames, listening to the swishing of her brush upon the floor.

My neighbors began arriving shortly after dinner, though Charity stayed away. I was angry with her, and I felt betrayed—not just over the fact that my daughter was caring for the parson's wife, but that Judith had done so as well. It gave a new and bitter meaning to the prayer Parris had uttered at Judith's grave—I had thought his words hypocritical platitudes, but 'twas plain his compliments of my wife were well founded.

'Twas hard for me to concentrate as the committee men arrived, and Susannah took their capes to dry by the fire. I could hardly reply to their talk until the door opened and Charity hurried inside. Her breath came fast, as if she'd run the entire way home, and her eyes went wide when she looked up to see me.

Susannah said, "Charity, 'tis good you're back. Fill the tankards."

My daughter hurried to do the task, but as she went past me, I grabbed her arm and drew her back. She jerked, and I was surprised to find she was trembling beneath my fingers.

"Your aunt says you were at the parsonage," I said quietly, for her ears only. "Is that true?"

She swallowed hard. Her nod was quick.

Susannah called, "Charity, the beer."

"We'll talk of this later," I promised my daughter, releasing her to attend to my neighbors.

The meeting went well enough. The strain of waiting for the court's impending decision over the church elders' lawsuit was palpable, yet we hardly spoke of it. Instead, we talked of Parris's increasing demands for firewood, his chastisements of the Village Committee in last Sunday's meeting, the growing discord set by him and his supporters—especially Thomas Putnam—against the rest of us. Last week, Tom had cornered his brother at the smithy and demanded that he change his vote and do what he could to change ours.

"He used family against me," Joseph said in wonderment. "He threatened to gather the others—as if they aren't all already on his side."

"This cannot go on much longer," Daniel said.

"Parris is a stubborn man," I put in.

"He'll tear the whole village apart rather than walk away," Joseph Porter agreed.

Francis sighed. "He has plenty of support. With the exception of Joseph here, all the Putnams are behind him, not to mention many of the other villagers. I'm afraid Daniel is right. If we don't back down, we could be looking at a war."

"We cannot back down," I said. "Shall we give over to such a man as that simply because he refuses to go? What of Joshua at Jericho? Or David against Goliath?"

The others murmured their agreement.

"I'm ready for a war," Joseph Putnam said with a small smile. "It has been a long time coming."

We talked longer about what course of action to take and who should present our case to the court if they required it, and soon the talk turned to other things: the growth in town; the large and splendid homes being built by those who'd made money in trade there; the French spies who were rumored to have been sent out among us; the steady Indian assaults on outlying settlements. Before I knew it, 'twas truly dusk, and our arguments had changed to laughter and joking. I lost track of how many times Charity refilled the beer pitcher. Susannah lifted a pudding from the fire and split it open before us, so the smell of dried apples and raisins and beef with spices filled the air.

Their admiration for her started slowly, so I was barely aware of it. Daniel Andrew smiled as she leaned over his shoulder to pour a tankard. Joseph Putnam whispered something to her that made her look to the fire and laugh. Joseph Porter watched her as she moved about the hearth.

Only Francis Nurse seemed unmoved by her—which is not to say she didn't charm him too; she did. She had a way with people that was comfortable and kind, a characteristic she shared with her sister. There was not a day that passed that someone did not tell me that while they celebrated Judith's reunion with our Lord, they felt the hole she'd left on earth.

Susannah would leave the same void, I knew. I saw her moving these men who had wives of their own, and I saw that on her, the Morrow charm had a slightly different effect. Judith had never been coveted by another man; not that I knew—and I would have known. There wasn't a man alive who couldn't read the signs.

But I saw those signs now for Susannah. As the evening went on, I found myself resenting that they could request her attention when I was forbidden it. I hovered over my beer, watching them all in silence. I longed for solitude, but they lingered, now well into that false camaraderie that comes with too much drink. When Joseph Porter said, "Was that a virginal I saw when we came in?" I knew what was coming next.

I rose. "It grows late. Perhaps—"

"Lucas, you have not been forthcoming," Joseph chided. "Where did you acquire a virginal? Which girl plays it?"

"'Tis not mine." Charity had been standing by the window. She yanked at the shawl around her shoulders. "I cannot play it."

"Then who?" Joseph asked. "Little Jude?"

"'Tis mine," Susannah said. She turned from the fire and I sank helplessly back onto the bench. "Are you a devotee, sir?"

"Hardly that." Joseph laughed. "It has been a long time since I've heard one. There was a girl out on the Ipswich Road who played upon occasion—"

"Out at Bishop's Tavern," Daniel put in. "I remember her. Was she not one of Edward's daughters?"

Joseph shrugged. "A distant relation, I believe. She'd come out from England and brought the thing with her. She was not very good, in any case. Can you play, Miss Morrow?"

"Aye, play for us," Porter said. "Something to take my mind off these wretched troubles."

I would have forestalled her, but the cry for her to play was too loud, and I would have been accused of churlishness had I tried to stop her, so I said nothing.

She brought the virginal from its place in the corner behind the spinning wheel. It was not large, and not heavy, but she struggled with it. When Daniel jumped up to help her, I envied him.

Daniel set the thing on the end of the table, and with a flourish, pulled off the canvas covering it. I had seen few virginals here in the country; they were expensive and difficult to master, and though it didn't surprise me that she should have one, I wondered how she'd obtained it, where she'd learned to play. Not at home, certainly; her parents had been simple farmers, hardly worth more than a few shillings, and this had obviously cost much more than that. The wood was gleaming and polished, with pretty scrolling carved into the edges and along the bottom. There was a delicate holder for music, though she did not use it. Susannah spread her skirts, and with a little bow, she sat at the instrument. Lightly she ran her fingers across the ivory keys, a run of pretty notes. Then she began to play.

The music was lively and haunting. She played expertly, as one born to the instrument, as if 'twas her voice that came from it, and we were all silent, watching the firelight play across her face, watching her hands move across the keys without effort or strain, the oddest chords easy to hold.

I knew suddenly and without doubt where she'd got the instrument, who had taught her to play it. Judith's words came to me: *She left him for an actor. He was a lead player, I think, and she said he was handsome. He must have been, to turn* her *head.*

Susannah had told me his name. Geoffrey. Geoffrey. I hated the sound of it. I pictured him, fair to my darkness, brawny to my sinew. I pictured him bringing her the instrument, sitting behind her, helping her hands move over the keys, showing her each note while she leaned back into him, laughing, kissing. . . .

I must have made a sound, because suddenly she glanced up at me, catching my gaze. I saw her start—'twas the only misstep she made, a single discord—and then she looked down again.

If Susannah was aware of the currents in the room, she showed no evidence of it. She began another tune, and this time, she sang in a low, clear voice that perfectly matched the instrument. "Under the greenwood tree, who loves to lie with me—"

Charity's gasp was so loud we all turned to look at her, but when the others turned back again, I did not—'twas fear I'd heard in my daughter's sound.

She was still by the window. Her fingers fumbled with the edges of her shawl; she pulled it closer and closer as if she were freezing cold, though it was already wrapped so tightly about her 'twas a wonder she could move within it. She was staring out the window. 'Twas as if she were talking to someone, though there was no one there. She was trembling.

I left the table to go over to her. I leaned close to whisper, "Are you ill, child?"

My daughter glared at me as if she did not know me. Her hands grasped convulsively at her shawl. "Ill? No. No."

"Do you not like the song?"

Her eyes went wild. "I won't listen to it!" She jerked back from me as if I'd touched her, when I had not even lifted a hand. "I won't! I shall not!"

Susannah's hands came down on the keys, discordant and then silent, so that Charity's words lingered there in echoes. Charity reached for my hand, the shawl coming loose to half fall off her shoulders. "You cannot be fooled, Father, can you?" she pleaded. "You cannot be fooled?"

"Fooled by what, Charity? Fooled how?"

She dropped my hand and shook her head, frenzied again, before she burst into tears and ran from the room, past the table and my neighbors, up the stairs, leaving me to stare helplessly after while Jude followed her.

"She hasn't felt well." Susannah's voice was soft in the sudden silence. When I looked at the table, I saw that they were all looking at her, confused, bleary-eyed. The mood had changed. Discomfort, tension . . . Francis Nurse unclenched his hand from his tankard and rose.

"We should be going," he said. "'Tis late, and much to do on the morrow."

"Aye." Joseph nodded. He got to his feet as well, and gave a small bow to Susannah. "You play beautifully. I would be delighted to hear you again some time. For now . . . I thank you for the unaccustomed treat."

They left then, disappearing together into the darkness.

I watched as Susannah covered the virginal again, leaving it there on the end of the table while she collected the tankards and took them to the washtub near the fire.

"What ails her?" I asked.

She was quiet for a moment, as if debating whether or not to speak, and this made me angry. So I said again, "What ails her? I am her father. You're keeping something from me. Tell me."

"I confronted her this morning," she said.

"Confronted her? Over what? You speak in riddles."

Susannah sighed. She turned again to face me, leaning back against the tub, resting her hands on its rim. "I told her that I'd found Samuel Trask."

Chapter 18

"SAMMY?" I ASKED, MUDDLED, NOT UNDERSTANDING. HIS NAME seemed to come from nowhere. "You found Sammy?"

"In Andover," she said. She reached into her pocket and pulled out a creased piece of paper. "I've a letter from his master."

"From his master?" I frowned at her, even more confused. "Why? Why were you searching for him?"

"Have you forgotten the five pounds?" she asked.

"The five pounds?" It came back to me then, the strange entry in the ledger. "Aye. Judith gave him the money. 'Tis all I need to know."

"But why? The reason—"

"The reason is with her, and she is with God," I said. " 'Tis enough that she had one."

Susannah put the letter again into her pocket. She stepped toward me. "You are not an ignorant man. Why do you close your eyes to this?"

I watched her warily. "I don't understand you."

"There was something between Samuel and Charity. I know it."

"She's a child."

"Did she seem a child to you tonight?"

"Aye. One in the midst of a nightmare."

"A nightmare about what, Lucas?" Susannah came closer still.

"Do you not wonder why she is so afraid? This trouble Judith wrote me of . . . I thought 'twas you. I know now 'tis not, but I wonder . . ."

"You think she wrote of Charity?"

"What else could it be?"

"A hundred things," I said.

She made a sound of exasperation. "I don't understand why you refuse to consider this. Is there something else I don't know? Some secret?"

"Secrets." I threw up my hands. "There are no secrets in this house."

"I tell you there are."

The conviction in her voice stopped me cold.

"I tell you there are," she said again, quietly. "I have been thinking perhaps 'twould be best to . . . send her out. There is something here that frightens her, something . . ." She shook her head in puzzlement. "I don't know what. But I think . . . I think 'twould be good for her to be in another place for a while, perhaps in town. . . . She needs a place to heal, Lucas."

Her words were startling in their bluntness. I hardly knew how to answer her. "To heal? From what?"

"From her mother's death, if nothing else."

"Where better than here? With her family?"

"She's troubled here. I don't think . . . Ah, Lucas, you do not help her. I think . . . I think you may even make things worse."

I felt as if I stood outside a darkened window, trying to see the figures within, sensing movement and light, feeling only danger. "Why?" I whispered.

"Because I think Charity is sick with guilt."

"What possible reason could she have—"

"I think she was in love with Samuel," Susannah said. "I think she may have been . . . intimate . . . with him."

I was stunned. Charity was only a child, and a godly one. Samuel had been nearly twenty, too worldly to take notice of a young girl. He had to know I would never allow it. Yet . . . there had been Judith's warnings too. . . .

I refused to think of it. Angrily, I moved toward Susannah, advancing as she backed away. "I don't want to hear such lies about my daughter again. I will not have it. Not in this village, nor in my house."

She lifted her face to me, and there was anger in her expression now too. " 'Tis a pity you cannot control me the way you control yourself, isn't it, Lucas? Did you control my sister as well?"

"I did not need to. She was a good mother and a godly woman."

"And she was lying to you. She knew about Charity and Samuel. 'Tis the only explanation for the money. She gave him five pounds to run away."

"Quiet!"

"Your daughter is not a child. She's nearly a woman grown—"

"I won't hear it."

"You had better hear it. 'Twill be disaster if you do not." She was against the wall now, unable to back any farther away. "She needs guidance, Lucas, not—"

"Enough!" I raised my fist, meaning to hit the wall, and she jerked away, closing her eyes and turning her head so violently I heard the thud of her skull against the wall.

I realized in a moment what she'd thought: I was about to hit her. That knowledge stole my anger in shock and sick dismay; of its own accord, my fist opened, my palm slapped uselessly against the planks just above her head.

Her eyes opened. She glanced at me, and then looked at my hand, my fingers curling against the wall.

We stood so close her hair caught on my sleeve, fanning like a spiderweb between us.

"My God," I whispered, my own voice, yet not my own. It seemed to come from a dream. "My God, do not tempt me this way."

She looked up at me, a look so candid it caught my breath—

and I knew: She felt what I did. I did not mistake it. Perhaps it was that frankness that cut through the binds of feeling. I only know that when I saw her expression, I thought of Geoffrey and Robert. I thought of the yeoman's son. They stood between us, a queue of men who had trod this land before me, and each smiled and mocked: *Go ahead. She wants you to take her. Go ahead,* and I was suddenly sickened. At her. At myself.

"You have me trapped, Brother," she said quietly, moving her head so her hair loosened from its catch on my sleeve.

I let my arm fall; I backed away. When she eased quickly past me, I bowed my head. "Forgive me," I murmured, words for myself more than her, low enough that I did not think she could hear.

But I heard her stop. When I looked up, it was into her pitied expression. "'Tis your daughter who needs it, not I."

The next morning, I waited at the table until Charity came downstairs.

She stopped when she saw me, and she had the strangest look on her face, as if she were relieved to see me, yet horrified as well. She looked ill; there were red chilblains on her chin that I had not noticed yesterday, bright against her pale, gray skin. It seemed her hands must always be cold, because she wrapped them convulsively in her skirt.

"I've been waiting for you," I told her. "Come and sit."

She hesitated, then sat silently across from me at the board.

"Susannah tells me you've been often to the parsonage."

She said something, a bare sound I could not understand.

"You must know how I would feel about such a thing," I said. "What is there that you have such need of? If 'tis spiritual guidance, then 'tis better found in town. Let me take you there. Nicholas Noyes is a far better pastor—"

"No," she said.

"Why?"

"'Tis not . . . 'tis not that. I . . . I have been . . . seeing to . . .

She's ill. . . ." Charity let the words sink into silence. Her shoulders shook from the movements of her hands in her skirt. Her brow was wrinkled in worry; her thin upper lip disappeared into the fullness of the lower; her chin was set.

She was not telling me the truth, I realized with a shock. She was dissembling. There was something more here. But then she looked up at me, and more startling even than her lie was the expression in her pale eyes. I saw fear there—if not fear of me, fear of something.

I frowned at her, trying to understand the mysteries of her face, and in that moment, it seemed to coalesce before me. Every separate feature was pressed with the faint likeness of her mother, though finer—it put me in recollection of my own mother, and I realized in surprise that I had never seen that in her before. More than that, I realized 'twas a woman's face I was looking at. A woman's face. *She's not a child. She's a woman grown.*

Ridiculous. It could not be. She was still a little girl, with plump hands and fine hair. . . . No, her hands were slender; her fingers were long and tapered. Her hair was thick and straight. . . . No, no. There had not been enough years, not nearly enough—*Sammy and Charity . . . She gave him five pounds to go.* . . . The thoughts jangled in my head, hard to set straight, incongruous—

There was a knock on the door.

I leaped to my feet. Charity started to rise.

"Stay there," I ordered. "We have not finished." I went to the door and swung it open. When I saw 'twas Samuel Nurse standing there—in the midst of heavily falling snow—holding his fowling piece tight in his fist instead of slinging it over his shoulder as was usual, I felt a quick and sudden dread. His nine-year-old son, George, stood behind him, holding at the ready a gun too large for his childish hands, scanning the woods and fields beyond the house as if he expected someone to appear at any moment.

"Sam?" I asked, frowning in bewilderment.

"A word with you, Lucas," he said.

"Of course." I stood back to let him in, and George too, who came quickly, glancing over his shoulder. I closed the door and motioned to the table, where Charity sat. I saw Jude and Susannah coming down the stairs. "Have you supped? Can I get you something?"

"No, no," Sam said. "We can stay but a moment." He nodded a greeting to Susannah.

She stepped forward, a worried look on her face. "What brings you out on a morning like this, Sam? It cannot be good news."

"I'm afraid 'tis not." Then Sam said to me, "There was an Indian attack on Wells a few days ago. One on York too. 'Twas bad, Lucas, from what we've heard. Over a hundred captured. 'Tis said that York . . ." He paused and glanced at my listening family. " 'Tis bad."

Wells was less than eighty miles away; York was only a little farther. Already we lived in constant terror of Indian attacks or of raiding parties made up of the French woodsmen called *Coureurs de Bois.* Retaliations, counterretaliations . . . One attack often led to another, to another, to another. Salem Village was scattered over fields and hills that were undefendable—we were vulnerable to any attack. I thought of the stories I'd heard over the years: the torture of young men, children taken captive and left orphaned. There was not a person in the village who had not been touched in some way. Many villagers had come here from Maine and New Hampshire, where the war was at its worst, and memories of a two-year-old attack on Lancaster—forty miles from here—still retained their power. Seventy of Salem's best men had been lost there.

I was suddenly light-headed. "Is there to be a training day?"

"We're prepared enough," Sam said. "Captain Putnam has assigned a double watch for the time being. You and I have been given the evening hours."

"We're to leave our own families unprotected?"

"They can gather together at my father's house. They'll be safe enough there—"

"Look at the snow," Susannah broke in. "Surely no Indian will attack today. We'll be safe enough here—"

"You'll go to Francis's," I said tersely. "I'll fetch you from there on my return."

"But, Lucas—"

I gave her a quick glance, meant to silence her, but still it surprised me when she quieted, when she nodded her allegiance.

"Every man in the village is to bring what extra powder he has to the parsonage. We'll take it from there to the watchhouse, as it seems the parson has his hands full."

"With what?" I asked meanly, unable to help myself. "Cutting his own firewood?"

"One of his children has suddenly taken ill—"

"She's barking, sir," George cut in. The boy was obviously unable to keep silent; the news was so remarkable.

"Barking?"

Sam shrugged. "'Tis what I've heard. Or mewing. When Father went over there to tell the parson the news about Wells, the child began climbing under chairs and galloping about on her hands and knees."

"Like a dog," George said. "Mam says they can't understand her. She's talking gibberish and such."

"Son," Sam warned. Then he looked at me. "It's been going on a few days, I hear. Some little fit. The child's always seemed delicate to me; no doubt she's overtaxed."

"Which one?" The words were low, hardly spoken. It was Charity. She was standing now at the table, her fingers clenching the edge as if she might fall without its support. All color had gone from her face. When we all turned to look at her, she said, "You said 'she.' Master Parris has two daughters. Which one do you mean?"

Sam looked confused, but George said, "'Tis Betsey. Betsey's barking like a dog."

Charity sank hard onto the bench. She went so pale I feared she would swoon. "What is it?" I asked. "Charity?"

She did not answer me. Instead, she put her hands to her face, and her thin shoulders shook as if she were crying. I glanced at Susannah, who looked distressed as she went hurrying over. She put her hands on Charity's shoulders. "Charity, perhaps you—"

My daughter wrenched away. "Don't touch me," she said. The words came in a low, furious sound. "I know what you are—I know!" She seemed transformed—not my quiet, sweet daughter, but someone else entirely, her face so contorted with anger and fear it did not seem to be her own. She was shaking visibly as she rushed past Susannah to the stairs. We heard her footsteps, the slam of the door.

Susannah looked as shaken as I felt. "She's been troubled of late," she said, and I realized with a start that she was talking to Sam. What must he think of that display, when I myself did not understand it? "And she has been spending much time at the parsonage."

"Aye. Well, I wish you luck with her, then," Sam said. "We'll come by here this afternoon and walk up to my father's together. Then, Lucas, you and I can go on to the watchhouse."

I nodded my agreement, and Sam and George left, back into the cold, into the snow that had not stopped but only seemed to grow heavier in the time they'd been here. I shut the door behind them; thoughts of Indian attacks faded quickly in my worry for my daughter.

Susannah sat near Jude, whose eyes were wide and watchful, and put her arm around the child's shoulders. "You look afraid, Jude," she said. "What frightens you?"

"Indians," Jude said in a whisper. "Charity."

Susannah glanced up at me. "Your father and the other men will protect us from the Indians," she said to Jude in a reassuring tone. "You've nothing to fear from them now."

"Are you sure?"

"As sure as I can be. But . . . what of Charity? What is it that frightens you about your sister?"

Jude shook her head. She had her mother's eyes, wide and blue, with the same expressiveness that Judith had possessed—'twas possible to read her every emotion in her eyes. Now, with her cap covering her light brown hair, tied neatly beneath her chin, accenting the soft oval of her face, she seemed so small, so fragile. Such a little thing in such a dangerous world. I found myself offering up a prayer to God—*Protect her, Lord. Keep her safe*—before I asked, "Is Charity ill, Jude? Has she confided in you?"

Jude dropped her gaze. "She . . . She would be angry if I said."

"Charity is not your master. 'Tis only me you must answer to, and God. Your sister cannot command you."

"Not so loud, Brother," Susannah said. "You'll frighten her."

"I want an answer."

She gave me a look that silenced me. "And you shall have it." Then she turned again to Jude. "If Charity is in trouble, you cannot help her by remaining silent."

Tears welled in Jude's eyes. With a swift glance at me, she brushed them quickly away. "She's . . . scared."

"Why?"

"I don't . . . know. 'Tis Mary Walcott. . . ."

"Mary Walcott?" I asked. "What has she to do with Charity now?"

"Charity sees her most every week."

I glanced at Susannah. I saw the guilt in her eyes. "Did you know this?" I demanded.

"I have told her she should stay away from those girls," she said.

"Aye, she should. I have forbidden her to see them. Weeks ago, I forbade it." I could not keep the anger from my voice.

Susannah's arm tightened around Jude's shoulders. "Quiet," she said to me; then she turned again to Jude. "How does she meet these girls, Jude?"

"At the Parris house," Jude said in her meek little voice, and suddenly I understood the lie I'd seen earlier in Charity's eyes. I knew what she had been keeping from me.

I saw the warning in Susannah's expression, and I reined in my temper before asking, "At the parsonage? What mischief can they do there?"

I did not expect an answer. But Jude's tears began to fall in earnest. "I think . . . I don't know. But Charity is afraid, and so am I. Please . . . Will you please make her stop?"

Susannah gathered Jude to her breast, stroking my daughter's back, and my anger died away. Charity was in trouble; Susannah had been right. And I . . . I had been blind too long.

Chapter 19

———— ✥ ————

I COULD NOT THINK OF WHAT TO DO, ONLY THAT I MUST DO SOME-
thing. My daughter had disobeyed me, she had met in secret with
girls I had forbidden her to see, and she had lied to me about it.
Charity had never done such a thing before.

I waited until I felt I could contain my temper, and then I went
to her bedroom. I did not give her time to find a way to avoid me.
I opened the door.

She was standing at the window, hugging herself, fingering the
edges of her shawl. She looked alone, strangely forlorn. I had to steel
myself to discipline her.

"You have been seeing those girls, despite my commands not
to," I said.

She turned to me in surprise, and opened her mouth. I held up
my hand to stop her.

"Don't lie to me again, Charity. I know you have been meeting
with them at the parsonage."

"Mis-Mistress Parris has been ill."

"And who better to comfort her than a group of gossiping girls?"
I shook my head. "'Twill not do, Charity. I will not tolerate lies. I
will not tolerate such disobedience."

She pressed her lips together, looking as if she might cry, and I
hardened my heart against it. "I wonder at you. What is it about

them that compels you enough to disobey me? You know better than this. Are the lessons I've taught you meaningless?"

"No, Father. 'Tis just . . . Do not . . . Do not ask me not to see them. Please."

"Your mother disliked them. Even were I to set aside her feelings, I have my own experience to consider. You were never a liar before now."

She bent her head and quietly sobbed.

I did not waver. "'Tis a sin, and one I do not take lightly. Nor should you. You will keep yourself home for the next two weeks and study the text I will give you. We will pray that God forgives you. You are not to see those girls again."

I had expected more tears, pleas to rend my heart, but 'twas as if I'd said some spell, some word that miraculously calmed her. Her sobbing stopped. Slowly she lifted her head, and I found myself staring into eyes still wet but amazingly composed. Again I had the sense of my daughter full grown. This was not a child standing before me now.

"As you wish, Father," she said. "Forgive me. 'Tis Mama's death. . . . I have felt alone, or I would not have turned to them."

She stole my self-righteous anger, my need to discipline. "Aye. Well . . . you are not alone, Charity. God has given you a family who loves you, and His grace is bountiful, should you submit to His will."

Charity nodded. Her glance slid to the window, as if something caught her attention there.

"There is one other thing," I told her. "It disturbs me to see the way you disrespect your aunt. She is here to help you. Now that your mother is gone—" I broke off, disturbed by the sudden fear on Charity's face. "Charity. Child, is something wrong?"

She swallowed. "Nothing, Father. I understand."

"Very well," I said. "I will give you the text tonight."

She was quiet as I left her. I told myself all was well—I had disciplined her; she had asked for forgiveness. She was my child again.

Yet later, as I wrote for her the Bible text I meant for her to study, I could not rid myself of the sense that I had not soothed her at all.

For several days, there was little talk of anything but the recent Indian attacks. Men were on edge, jumping at every unexpected noise, and we moved about in groups, guns always at the ready. But as the nights passed without incident, and the snow kept falling, whitening the hills, making movement across fields easy to spot even from far away, the fear and the dread became only a vague and pervasive apprehension. 'Tis the nature of man to lose interest in a threat that does not soon materialize, so the talk of Indians faded, replaced with gossip about little Betsey Parris and her strange illness.

Whatever malady afflicted her, it had not grown better. Instead, the child had retreated into a world where she was impossible to reach. She spoke in gibberish; she scrambled around as a dog or a monkey, hiding beneath chairs and in darkened corners, screaming out when anyone approached her. These were all things I heard, because I did not see the child myself. Though I dismissed much of it as gossip, her illness worried me, especially given the fact that Charity had visited the parsonage often these last months.

As with the other men in the village militia, I'd taken my turn at the watchhouse in the past. Now, in spite of the fact that the villagers' fears over Indian attacks had eased, we continued with the doubled watch, and so my turn came more frequently. I was glad of it. I had been happy twice to draw the evening watch and leave the care of my household to Sam and some of the others. It kept me away from the house when I was at my most vulnerable. I had found myself touching Susannah more and more often, finding excuses to brush by her in a doorway, to lean back slightly as she served me just to feel the slight brush of her skirt against my back. 'Twas the kind of touching that is inevitable in close quarters—yet I could have avoided it. I wanted to, but my body would not obey my mind in this. The knowledge of what I'd seen in her eyes, the hint of reciprocated desire . . .

The blockhouse was low to the ground and thick-walled. We kept the heavy battens open on either end as two of us sat huddled, each stationed at one while the icy winter air and snow blew inside. There was a fire in the hearth, but it was nothing against the cold; it served only to heat bean porridge for a hasty meal.

Daniel Andrew had drawn the evening watch along with me, and we had long since ceased talking. Each of us was too concerned with staying warm and keeping an eye on fields that began to fade into dusk, or shadows that imitated movement as they were blown by the wind.

I could barely feel my hands through my gloves, and my face was cold, my lips dry and chapped. I was numb by the time John Rea and Joseph Hutchinson came to relieve us.

"We've seen nothing to worry you tonight," I told John as Daniel and I readied to leave.

"Seems the only worries to be had lately keep bound to the parsonage," Joseph muttered.

Daniel's expression was grim. "How is the child today?"

"The same." Joseph shook his head. "I will say this: Parris seems honestly concerned about the girl."

"Aye, of course he does," John said. "He would not like it bandied about that 'tis the minister's house the Devil chooses to visit."

The words were lightly said, but I frowned at John. "The Devil? Who has said anything about that?"

"No one yet," John said. "But they will if this thing spreads. Memories are long and unforgiving. There's still those won't go near Sarah Good because of the gossip that she brought the pox all those years ago."

"She's nothing but a helpless beggar," said Daniel. "A bad-tempered woman, to be sure, but there's no evil in that."

"I'm just saying . . . Folks're unsettled. They're frightened enough now over Wells and York—they'll turn on Parris soon enough if it goes beyond his house, especially now that the older girl's ailing. He knows that. I'm guessing 'tis why he's so weepy-eyed."

My alarm heightened. "The older girl's ill as well?"

Joseph nodded. "Aye. Parris's niece. Leaping and yelling and shivering—"

"My wife says 'tis quite a sight," John put in. "Near frightened her to death."

I met Daniel's gaze and saw in his expression what must have been in mine. I was disturbed at this news, and not just because of Charity. John was right about one thing: The people in the village were not only superstitious, they also did not forget or forgive easily. There was enough strain between us all now, especially with the Indian scare. 'Twould behoove us to try to calm the waters.

"I'll pay a visit to the parson myself," I said. "Has he thought to call the doctor?"

Joseph shrugged. "I had the feeling he wanted to keep this quiet."

" 'Tis too late for that, I'm afraid."

Together Daniel and I left the watchhouse. Dusk had fallen, shadowing our faces. Our frosty breaths were like a fog; it made it hard for me to see Daniel's expression as he grabbed my arm, halting me before we had gone more than ten feet down the path.

"It seems strange—does it not—that this has all happened now? The timing is unfortunate, what with the suit before the court. . . ."

". . . and his dwindling supply of firewood. Aye." I nodded. " 'Tis suspect."

"His daughter's but nine. The niece is . . . what? Ten? Twelve?"

I shrugged. I had no idea. I barely remembered what she looked like. Bossy, I thought, and had a sudden vision of her herding the other Parris children from my house the day of Judith's funeral.

"Has he enlisted his children's help, I wonder?" Daniel asked.

"Perhaps we are too suspicious. What possible good can this do him? John is right: Suspicion can be too easily turned in Parris's own direction. To involve his daughter—'tis too uncontrollable." I shook my head. "No. I'm willing to believe this is as he says: a strange illness. Until I'm convinced otherwise."

"Perhaps you're right," Daniel said, though he was doubtful still, and his green eyes were troubled. "I've no daughters of my own as yet; I do not know how biddable a girl might be. . . ."

I was silent at this, though he must have expected a response from me—a man who had only daughters. But I did not know what to say. Two months ago, I would have scoffed at the idea of such dissembling in a well-raised girl. But now . . . Now all I could think of was Charity's pale face and shadowed eyes. Now I knew the answer. *Too biddable.*

I was troubled as I left Daniel and made my way home. My thoughts were so full I was hardly aware of the cold walk. I know only that when I reached my own door, 'twas dark, and I had gone the entire way without thinking once of Indians, with my gun slung casually over my shoulder. When I stepped inside, it was quiet, candles snuffed. Everyone was abed already. 'Twas past bedtime, and I had not known it.

There was a movement in the darkness beyond me, a sound, and I realized I was not alone. I hung my hat and cloak, and then stepped slowly past the jut of the cellar door, fully into the hall, and I saw the single candle burning.

"Susannah."

"Lucas," she said, rising from the table. She seemed nervous. "I thought you might be hungry. And . . . 'tis a cold night. You must be freezing. I thought to . . . to leave a fire for you, and so I could not go to bed."

I stood there like a fool, until I finally gained control. "Thank you. I'm here now . . . to watch it. If you would rather seek your bed—"

"No." She shook her head. "No. I'm not tired. Let me get you something to eat."

I was tired and confused, my heart troubled, so I nodded to her and made my way to the table. When she brought me a steaming trencher, along with a slab of bread and some beer, I motioned for her to sit across from me.

We sat in silence for some moments. Once food was brought before me, I realized I was hungrier than I'd thought, and the pottage was hearty and good. Susannah waited quietly until I paused, and then she said, "What news is there from the village?"

"The Parris girl is not better."

"Ah." She sighed. "I had hoped 'twould be over by now."

"'Tis worse than that. It seems the niece is now afflicted as well."

"Abigail?"

"Is that her name? I'd thought to go over to the parsonage tomorrow."

She nodded and said, "I'll go with you. I've had some practice nursing. Perhaps I can be of help."

"Nursing?" I was surprised. "Judith told me nothing of that."

"Judith did not know everything in my life. Though I'm sure she believed she did." She turned as she said it, as if afraid to show me her face. "A man I knew, a surgeon who studied next door to us, needed help for some months. I was . . . happy . . . to give it."

If she had been anyone else, I should not have thought twice at her explanation. I would have accepted it and gone on, one more puzzle piece neatly in place, one more thing to know about her. But all I heard was: *A man I knew,* and my mind leaped to the biblical meaning of that word.

"Lucas—"

"Go to bed."

"I know something worries you, Lucas. Tell me what it is. I know you would have told Judith—"

"You are not Judith."

"No." She was quiet. So much so, and for so many moments, that I looked up, thinking she had gone. She was not gone. "But perhaps I can help to comfort you. . . ."

I stared at her. "You don't know what you're saying."

"Then tell me." She came around the edge of the table. She was beside me before I could stop her, before I could move. I felt her hand on mine, the smooth, soft slenderness, the pads of her fingers, her warmth. Before I could stop myself, I captured hers and held it tight. And then, driven by an impulse I was beyond controlling, I brought her hand to my mouth. She jerked, but I held her tight.

I kissed the inside of her wrist, lingering until I felt her pulse beat against my lips. I touched my tongue to the sweet salt of her skin. I heard her gasp.

It was not the sound, but the silence after, that moved me. She waited for me, and it was that realization, finally, that stopped me.

I could not release her hand. "You must go now," I told her, "because I cannot."

I felt her slight tug, and I released her. Then I heard her walk away, and I laid my head upon the table, in the cradle of my arms, and felt my life slipping away, past bearing, past redemption—and, most frightening of all, past caring.

The next morning, snow was heavy on the ground and the narrow road was nothing but troughs and ice as I led my family to the parsonage.

We were a strange, silent parade as we made our way to the village. Pale and stiff with cold, we were wrapped in woolen cloaks, with shawls swaddled tight around our heads and shoulders. We wore gloves and thick felt hats with brims turned down so that only our eyes were uncovered. Anyone passing us would not know who we were. 'Twas so cold outside there was no hope of warmth from clothing.

When we reached the parsonage, it seemed both too long and too short a time, and I hesitated, trying to right my unsettled thoughts, trying to shake away my preoccupation before I knocked upon the door. It was opened by the Parrises' slave woman, Tituba—an anomaly in the village, and one of the reasons I believed Parris was not the man of God he fashioned himself to be. To own another human being, even one who was inferior, was anathema to most of us.

The woman's gaze swept over us, and I opened my mouth to tell her why we were here just as I saw her eyes go to Charity. Her gaze rested on my daughter, only a brief moment, but I saw there recognition, and something else—bitterness, perhaps, though I was not sure of that. It startled me enough that I believed I must be wrong.

Tituba stepped back. "Come in," she said in a soft, Barbados-accented voice.

Susannah held up a basket she was carrying. "I've brought bread," she said, "and a portion of fish pie."

"'Tis kind of you, madam," the slave said, taking the basket as we passed. She ushered us all inside and then closed the door. And the room seemed suddenly very dark before us. Parris came out from the hall, running a hand through his long, dark hair, looking distracted and harried, gray-faced, sleepless. He glanced at us, obviously startled, and then quickly composed himself when I took off my scarf and hat and he saw who I was.

"Brother Fowler," he said. I thought he seemed nervous. "You've come to see them, of course. Everyone has. Come in."

"We've not come to make things more difficult for you," Susannah said. "Is your wife home?"

"Upstairs," the preacher said, gesturing vaguely to the steps. "She cannot bring herself to get out of bed. This has been . . . most dreadful for her. Most dreadful."

We followed him into the hall. I heard Jude say, "Charity, you're too slow!" and Susannah's quiet "Come, Charity. Don't tarry so." I focused only on what was before me, and tried not to feel my usual indignation over how Parris had managed the ownership of this house that should have belonged to the village.

A fire was raging in the hearth. Parris's other slave, John Indian, was unloading wood into a pile beside, and I caught Parris's resentful, sideways look to me. "'Tis the last of the firewood," he whined. "I don't know what we'll do. The winter is so cold. . . ."

Then I saw the two girls sitting on the settle, which had been turned away from the fire. The two of them, the little child and the older girl, sat side by side, almost too still.

'Twas then I realized there were others in the room. Four other villagers: John and Nathaniel Putnam, Joseph Porter, and Mary Sibley. They stood back, nearly against the walls, in a state of suspension, as if awaiting the start of a performance they were not sure whether to dread or appreciate. The feeling of apprehension was such that we barely acknowledged each other; Joseph Porter made a light wave. Mary Sibley bustled over to Susannah. I heard her whisper: "Have you come to see it? I've only just got here myself."

I felt Jude come up behind me, close against me, and Charity on my other side. They were both terrified, and I did not blame them; this atmosphere courted terror. The house was in shadows, with the only light coming from the fire and one or two candles and that which came thin and pale through the windows.

Parris went over to John Putnam. The parson had a Bible in his hand now. He said in a low voice: "I've been reading scripture to them, to no avail—"

"No! No!"

There was not one of us who did not jump. 'Twas the little girl, Betsey, who moaned and fell to the floor, where she began to bark—sharp, quick barks like a small dog—as she crawled on all fours around the settle.

I instinctively drew back against the wall, holding my daughters in place behind me.

"Dear Lord," Mary Sibley murmured. "Oh, my dear Lord."

Charity grabbed my arm, her icy fingers squeezing so I felt the press of her short nails into my skin.

I didn't know what to say, how to offer comfort. The little girl was horrifying to behold, but her affliction was nothing compared to the older girl, who began to scream, "You shall not have me! No, I say!"

John Putnam rushed to help her, but she pushed him as if he were no more than a child. He backed away in startled bafflement. The moment he did, she rose from the settle and began to walk around it, half bent, murmuring words I could not understand, some ridiculous language, babble in rhymes.

Nathaniel Putnam approached Abigail Williams warily, but she seemed not to see him. When he tried to bar her way, I thought she would walk over him. He moved back quickly, and turned to us as if we should have the answers. "What is she saying?"

" 'Tis a terrible illness," Parris said.

On the floor, little Betsey whimpered and crawled into the darkened space beneath the settle. Her big blue eyes were wide and frightened, as if she saw something the rest of us did not. Charity's hand tightened on my arm, hurting now. When I glanced down at Jude, she was too still, too watchful, taking it all in the way she did everything, with that almost fatalistic acceptance that worried me no less now than it had at her mother's death.

Abigail twisted, and Charity jumped and screamed, and buried her face in my back. I glanced over to Susannah and saw the way she was watching us—Charity, me, Jude, and not the afflicted girls. I felt Charity's sobs at my back, and I took her hand and pulled her firmly away.

I saw how shaken she was, how she trembled. " 'Tis a passing illness. The doctor will find a way to treat this, I'm sure." I glanced to Parris. "Have you called Griggs?"

The pastor looked startled at my question, and then confused, nervous. "No. No, not yet. I was . . . We were hoping 'twould pass."

"There must be something you can give them."

"Aye, there's something," Mary Sibley said thoughtfully. "Though I doubt the doctor will think of it."

"Quiet, woman," Joseph said—the first time he'd spoken since he'd greeted us. "Watch what you say."

Mary Sibley pressed her thin lips shut and shook her head, and I was glad that Porter had quieted her. I did not want to hear what she thought. There were suspicions growing in my own mind. This was not an illness I'd ever seen before. It looked more like—

I cut off the thought, refusing even to form the word in my head, to consider it. I grasped Charity's hand tightly and murmured a prayer against evil, because I felt it palpably in this room. I caught Susannah's glance and motioned to the door. "We should be leaving now," I said to Parris.

He nodded, distracted still, and said, "Aye. Good day, then," as if we'd simply met on the street and were not sharing this horrifying spectacle.

"I'll go with you," Joseph Porter said. "I can bear this no longer."

No one made a move to show us to the door. Parris was too busy clutching his Bible and looking helpless, John Indian had disappeared out the back door, and Tituba only stood back against the wall and watched us go.

I held my daughter's hand more tightly. I was afraid—for her, for my world, which seemed lately to be changing too fast around me. I thought—absurdly—that if I did not release her hand, she could not grow into this woman I'd begun to see in her face, none of this could affect her.

"'Tis worse than I'd thought," Joseph said from beside me. He adjusted his cape, pulling a scarf more closely about his face.

"What is it, do you think?" Susannah asked quietly.

Joseph ignored her and looked to me. "We'd best be careful. 'Twould be best if the committee did not meet for a while."

"Aye." I understood too well. 'Twould not be a good idea to bring attention to ourselves, not now. I felt a threat in the wind as Joseph trudged off over the icy path, and I led my family home.

Chapter 20

MY INSTINCT TO KEEP TIGHT HOLD OF MY LIFE AND THOSE IN IT only grew as the hours after our visit to the parsonage passed. When we arrived home, Charity was quiet, but there was an energy to her stillness that was unsettling. Her gaze was faraway, but strangely focused, as if she saw something beyond us that no one else could see.

That night, when I sent the girls to bed after quiet prayers and readings from scripture, I lingered over the fire, reluctant to go to my own bed, to twist and turn in the silence of my thoughts.

I put another log on the fire, though it was late already. I took a poker to it, watching the dry bark catch and spark, sending the flames rushing higher until I felt their heat. My mind was full of too many things: Indian attacks and little Betsey Parris twisting her head to bark, my own weaknesses and my daughter's troubled eyes. Judith seemed to stare at me from the fire, her face contorted by the flames, and I imagined I heard her contempt over how badly I'd handled things in her absence.

So lost was I in these thoughts that when Susannah said my name, I jumped, losing hold of the poker; it clattered on the stones of the hearth.

"Forgive me," she said. "I did not mean to . . . You look so . . ."

I bent to pick up the poker, and set it at the hearthside.

"You seem always so alone, Lucas. I have wondered at why that is."

"I am rarely alone," I told her.

"Perhaps that is the lie you tell yourself."

I shrugged. "I have two children, and . . . you . . . in my house. The Village Committee takes up much of my time." I looked away from her, back to the fire, back to my imagining of Judith's condemnation. The worm of conscience twisted in my head. *Above all keepings, keep thy heart*, and yet I had not, could not.

"You are troubled," Susannah said.

"I am amazed you are not."

"What we saw today . . . Do you think it real?"

"Aye, I think 'tis real," I said. "Who would do that willingly? Who could?"

"The mind can conceive of many things, I think."

"They are but children."

"The youngest one, yes," Susannah agreed. "But the elder . . . I think you do not give children their due, Lucas. Did you not invent things when you were a child?"

In my memory, I saw an ill-kept hovel, roof thatch falling through in big, rotting patches, icy rain puddling on the dirt floor. I saw a street filled with ailing chickens and scrawny goats, so thick with sewage that my legs were filthy and dotted with sores that never healed. I saw darkness and close spaces; I felt again the press of my knees drawn up to my chest as I huddled in a corner, hearing my stepfather's footsteps, the crack of a bottle against the door frame. "No," I said.

She said, "I see," as if she suddenly understood something. I wondered what she knew of me, and for a moment I tried to imagine what Judith must have said, what kind of sieve she'd strained me through to give her sister the portrait she thought would most impress. I already suspected that what I knew about Susannah Morrow was only what Judith had wished for me to know. How much was true, how much merely fiction—things she needed to believe for herself, ways of living with whatever had come between them: the yeoman's son, their father, a lifetime of slights and pleasures, of little hates, little loves.

"Wherever I turn in this village, I see fear and trouble," Susannah said.

"'Tis not so hard to understand. This is not London. We are in a wilderness here, with enemies to fight."

"Most of them of your own making. This is what I fear, Lucas: This is all some great lie, some game. Children can be so easily led—"

"Can they?"

Susannah lowered her voice. "I looked at Abigail today, and I saw Charity. Can you deny that what's been happening here is similar?"

She had read my thoughts. "I won't deny it. I've thought of little else all night."

"You must stop it before it becomes worse," she counseled me. "Is there someone you know in Boston? Someone you trust?"

"In Boston? Why?"

"For Charity's sake, I think you should send her away as soon as possible. To a place where no one can fill her head with lies."

I frowned at her. "I don't know. . . ."

"Ah, Lucas!" She took a deep breath, obviously frustrated. "I am afraid. I'm afraid that if you do not send her out, she will destroy herself. She should be with someone who can watch over her soul—"

"That job belongs to her father."

"But you are *here*." She gestured to the room. "You belong to this village, and they hold you. If you sent Charity to a God-fearing family in Boston, perhaps she would heal. Everything here must remind her of Judith. And those girls . . . I do not trust them, Lucas. I'm not saying Charity is a liar. But what if she believes in lies? What then? Please, Lucas. Please. Send the girl out. 'Tis what's best for her."

As much as I wanted to protect my daughter, to lead her to her rightful relationship with God, I knew I had already failed in that. "Aye," I whispered. "'Tis best. I will send her out."

I felt Susannah's relief. "Do it quickly, Lucas."

I looked up at her. She was staring at me, and our gazes met and held—too long a moment, too short—before she turned reluctantly away. "I'll wish you good night," she whispered.

When she was gone, my troubles came back with a suffocating weight, and I wanted her calm certainty and her belief. I wanted her back with a desperation that frightened me.

I resolved to ride to town the next morning to find a place for Charity, but 'twas snowing so hard, such a distance was impossible. I did not like the delay, but it could not be helped. I took comfort in the fact that no one else would be traveling, either. There would be little chance for the illness in the parsonage to spread.

But later that morning, as I chopped wood in the barn, a snow-covered Francis Nurse came to see me. He was red-nosed, haggard, and worn. "What is it, Francis?" I asked sharply. "Is Rebecca . . . ?"

"Still not herself, I fear," he said. "But no, that is not why I came."

"The court? Has there been a decision?"

"Not that, either." Bluntly he said, "Griggs went to look at Parris's girls."

I felt ill. "And?"

"He says 'tis bewitchment."

The word had dimension and weight; 'twas a word I'd feared, a word I had not allowed myself to even think.

"Is he certain?"

"Aye," Francis said. The wind picked up, fluttering the thinning gray hair that his hat did not cover. "He's not told anyone else, Lucas, but the news will soon be out. These things have a way of spreading . . . 'Tis as if the wind itself has a tongue."

"And Parris . . . What does he say?"

"He did not seem surprised."

"I doubt anyone will be," I said. "Is this not what we all suspected?"

Francis nodded. "Aye. Parris spoke of turning to others for prayer and advice. Perhaps John Hale or Noyes. My guess is he'll do that right away."

John Hale and Nicholas Noyes were neighboring ministers, of Beverly and Salem Town respectively. They were both highly respected men, and I knew Noyes well, and admired him—he was pastor of my church in town.

"Of course he will. It cannot be good for him to be seen as a minister who harbors Satan in his house."

Francis looked at me sharply. "This cannot be good for any of us. If the Devil is here, Parris will do what he can to fight him. His position depends on it. He cannot be seen as the cause of this—do you take my meaning? He will not shoulder the blame, and Tom Putnam will support him."

I understood too well. Parris had too much at stake; his position was already too tenuous. To be seen as housing the Devil would turn some villagers against him. His only choice was to turn the blame to someone else.

"One of us should be at that prayer meeting," I said.

"One of us will not be enough," Francis told me. "If this grows . . ."

"Will Parris try to keep us from it?"

Francis shook his head. "He must let us come. 'Tis a terrifying thing; others will want reassurance."

"Then who should go?"

"Not Putnam. His presence will only inflame his brother. And Porter . . . no. There is too much contention already between their families."

I regarded him slowly, with dread. "That leaves only you and me, and Daniel."

"Daniel is a town selectman; 'tis best if he stays clear of this.

Thomas and I have had our disagreements, but there are no linger-ing animosities. And you: You have had no disputes with Parris be-yond the committee ones, and . . . your own daughter has been seen at the parsonage. She's been seen with those other girls—you have an interest in the proceedings."

Your own daughter.

I answered steadily, "Very well. The two of us, then. When shall the prayer meeting be?"

"I don't know yet. I'll talk to Parris." Then Francis sighed. "I had hoped . . . Ah, well, 'tis one of God's trials. I had thought myself too old for this."

"Let us hope it does not get worse."

"Aye," he said. "Aye. And . . . You will be careful, Lucas?"

"Is it possible, Francis? Could it be that Satan has come to the village?"

Francis's look was long. "What else could it be?"

Chapter 21

'Twas nearly a week before the snow stopped, changing overnight to rain, a new thaw that had trees cracking and icicles breaking from the eaves to plunge into softening snow. The cold was of a different kind now, a dampness that eased into the bones.

Now that the roads became passable again, neighbors would meet, women would gossip, and the news of Griggs's pronouncement of bewitchment would be embellished beyond recognition.

Thus it was more urgent than ever that I get Charity from the village. But the morning I planned to go, I came into the hall only to see Charity already at the window—her usual post these last days.

I went behind her, trying to find what absorbed her attention. I saw bare trees and snow-covered ground, a crow, the steady drips from icicles hanging before the window. "What is it you see?"

She jumped as if she hadn't known I was there. Her face went white. "'Tis gone," she said, rubbing viciously at a new chilblain on her jaw.

I reached out and stopped her hand. "I told you to get some salve for that."

"I would not take anything she gave me," she said.

"I have told you that I will not—"

Her gaze leaped beyond me. I glanced over my shoulder to see Susannah come into the room. Charity twisted from my grasp, and then she leaned close. "Do not let her fool you, Father. Please. The Devil wears many pleasing faces. You know this, do you not? You know this?"

"Of course I know it." I reached for her hand again. She looked startled at my touch, and then afraid. She snatched her hand back and ran from me.

"Charity!" I called, but she hurried up the stairs, slamming her bedroom door.

Susannah said in a soft voice, "You must get her from this place soon."

I sat heavily on the bench. "The snow has let up. I'm going today to make arrangements."

"She barely eats. 'Tis as if she thinks I will poison her."

"She doesn't trust you, though I have tried hard enough to reassure her."

Susannah said nothing. She busied herself at the fire, but I felt her tension. I saw her unspoken words in the rigidity of her movements.

"What is it?" I asked her. "Have I offended you?"

" 'Tis nothing—"

"Tell me."

She paused, and hung a kettle onto the crane before she turned to face me. "How well do you really know your child?"

"Well enough."

"Lucas . . . Do you know that she hangs on your every word? That you wound her nearly every day with your uninterest and inattention? Do you know that she is frightened nearly to illness of your sermons and your God-fearing prayers, but she listens because 'tis you who speaks?"

"I am not inattentive—"

"Do you know," she went on, stepping across the room toward me, "that she knows enough of life to understand what is between you and me? She senses you may have reasons to lie to her when you speak of me. Perhaps you have not said to her that I mean you ill, but she cannot help but see that you think it. The way you avoid me, the anger in your voice when you speak to me—"

"Enough," I said. "You have said enough."

"I have not said nearly enough." Color defined the angles of her cheeks. "Tell me, Lucas, because I do not know what to believe. . . . Tell me: Have you castigated yourself so much for the desire between us that you've convinced yourself I'm the villain Charity believes me to be?"

The words, the words . . . I did not want to hear them. "We . . . must not . . . discuss this. It cannot . . . be."

"I did not wish it so," she said. "But you're wrong to think we must not discuss it. We have no choice but to do so."

I sank my head into my hands. She said nothing for a moment, then bent close to me. "Shall we admit what we want of each other, Lucas? Or deny it still?"

I looked at her. "I will deny it to my last breath," I said violently. My vehement reaction seemed to surprise her.

"We cannot live with each other this way."

The world spun out of my reach, and I hated her for taking my well-ordered life from me. I jerked to my feet, and the bench crashed to the ground. "What would you have me do?" I asked angrily. "Shall I bed you and damn us both? Is that what you want?"

She did not flinch. "Aye. Perhaps then, this thing would die. But you keep it close; how can it help but grow?"

"Do . . . not . . . torment me."

"You torment yourself," she said bitterly. "And me, because you will do nothing."

She left me. She went to the cellar door and disappeared down the stairs. It thudded shut behind her.

There was a thought—an instinct—that I must leave here. I had plans. Salem Town. I started to the door. I did not mean to go to her. I wanted with all my soul to be away. And yet, as I passed the cellar door, I opened it. I stepped onto the stair; I let the door close behind me. She had taken the betty lamp; the stairs were in darkness. I saw the faint glow below, the disjointed bits of shadow. I took those stairs as one condemned, with slow and dreading steps and the knowledge that this was the end. After this, my soul would belong to Hell, and yet the Devil had me chained already. I could not stop.

When I reached the bottom, she looked up as if she were surprised. She had set the lamp on a barrel of salted pork. She had a pitcher in her hand, and she was bending to the barrel of small beer, but when she saw me, she straightened.

I wanted her to say something that would take this terrible responsibility from me. To beckon me on, or hold out her arms, or speak encouragement. I wanted to be able to say: *I could have turned away had she not done this, or said this. She was a temptress, a siren who bewitched me so I was not myself.* But she merely stood there as I came closer. She did not back away, or try to move past me. She did not give as I came so close to her that I felt the press of her skirts against my thighs. When I spread my hands over her hips and closed my fingers over her skirts and jerked her close, she only lifted her face to me.

I backed her against the barrel. I plunged my fingers into her hair, twisting until I saw her eyes water from the little pain, and then I took her mouth the way I had dreamed of taking her.

'Twas not a kiss . . . but more an assault, openmouthed, breathing her in, devouring her. I had never kissed Judith this way, nor in truth any woman, and yet I did not temper it. She opened her mouth to mine, and I tasted her tongue and the cider she'd drunk, the wintergreen she'd chewed, little bits of it still clinging to her tongue.

I heard the pitcher fall to the ground. I felt it rock into my heel. I kicked it away and pressed her back still again, jamming her hard into the barrel, easing away only far enough to reach the lacings of her bodice, which I yanked and tore until they gave, until it fell open beneath my hands. I wrenched the string of her chemise so it fell open and her breasts were freed. I pressed my palms to them, but the touch was not enough—I was like a demon even to myself.

I balled her skirts in my hands, drawing them up and up, petticoats, chemise, shoving them around her waist, gathering the pocket beneath her skirt with them so it turned upside down, and keys and thimbles and coins clattered to the floor. Her thighs were bare and warm. I lifted her, and she put her hands around my neck and helped me, crying out as her hip cracked against the keg, as the lid rocked. Then she was sitting on it, her legs spread, curved around my own hips, and I loosed my breeches and thrust inside her with such force that she cried out, though 'twas not a cry of pain, and I swallowed the sound. I braced my hands on the edges of the barrel and rocked her until the lid became unsettled and I felt the beer spilling over my fingers; I smelled the yeast and malt of it, filling the air along with her scent: lemons and musk and sex. She gripped her ankles to the small of my back and met my every thrust, and we battered each other in pleasure-pain and denial, in recognition.

I came in a surrender of my soul—a pleasure so intense 'twas as much a torment, and when she cried out, 'twas against my lips—a rush of breath, a sudden lax, and we were throbbing together. I heard our breaths, mingled, shallow. I felt the beating of her heart against my chest.

I closed my eyes, resting my cheek against her hair. I could not catch my breath, nor admit myself to the world again. 'Twas only when I heard the steady *drip drip* of small beer on the floor that I became aware. My hands were wet, the scent of beer heady, and I was afraid of myself.

"Forgive me," I whispered against her jaw, not knowing for whom I said the words—myself or her, or . . . God. "Forgive me."

"You take too much responsibility, Lucas," she said, stroking the hair from my face.

"Who else shall take it?"

"Me, for one," she said. "Or . . . fate. Or God. I cannot help but think . . . I would never have chosen this for myself. My sister's husband—"

"Your brother."

"No." She shook her head against mine. "No, I will not call you that any longer. You are not my brother. I will not accept that sin too."

"It does not matter what you accept. The truth is there. A sin cannot be something else simply because you wish it so."

"And you . . . believe this is a sin."

"What else could it be?" I cried. I pulled back from her, looking at the shadows of her eyes, her hair—wild now, falling over her shoulders, her bared breasts. 'Twas a mistake to look at her thus—the moments that had just passed filled my head again, along with a quick, relentless desire that filled me with despair. I could not fight this, not over and over this way. Having sinned once, I would sin again—now that I knew the feel of her, the taste.

She reached out for me. "I wish it were otherwise too. But I am . . . drawn to you. Do not mistake me—I did not want to be, and yet I cannot seem to help it. And I . . . I have been thinking . . . Perhaps this is what I came to Salem for. Perhaps 'tis what God wanted of us all this time."

I loosed myself from her grip, reaching for my breeches. "I cannot believe that."

"Because you won't allow yourself the pleasure," she accused. "Because you would rather be unhappy—"

"I am not unhappy."

"Ah, Lucas, look at yourself!" She gestured at me, and I glanced down, watching myself fumble with the fastenings of my breeches. "Already you lock yourself away from me. What just passed between us . . . 'tis so rare. Have you ever felt anything so powerful before now? Even with Judith?"

'Twas true, and yet my guilt over that was overwhelming. "Satan has read my heart; 'tis all. He presented me with a temptation he knew I could not resist."

"I am but Satan's minion, then," she said.

I could not restore my equilibrium. "I don't know what you are!" I was defeated. "I don't know what you are."

She said nothing. I did not move as she eased herself from the keg, and her skirts fell again to cover her. Her bodice was still unlaced; her breasts still bared, but she let it be. Her gaze lifted to mine. She whispered, "I have not been happy, either, Lucas. Not for a long time. This seems . . . 'Tis a gift. Would we not be wise to take it?"

I stepped away. Coldly I said, " 'Tis a lure set by the Devil to trap us. We cannot mistake it for anything else."

I turned my back on her and raced up the cellar stairs before she could call out to me.

Happiness . . . Ah, what was that but the greatest delusion of all?

Chapter 22

I came from the cellar, hurrying to the barn and harnessing the horse in a fever to be away. It wasn't until I was nearly a mile from the house before I realized I was trying to race Saul through the half-frozen mud and icy snow.

'Twas only the thought of Charity that brought any kind of settlement to my soul. 'Twas only the knowledge that I could not fail her—at least not more than I had already done.

When I finally arrived, breathless and freezing, at Daniel Poole's house in Salem Town, I was calm enough to speak. Though when he opened his door and looked at me with concerned eyes, I thought he must see my sin shining like a new-made raiment upon me. 'Twas all I could do to appear myself. When I told him over dinner of Charity, he said thoughtfully, "I had thought you seemed troubled, Lucas," and I was relieved and ashamed that he had not guessed more.

"She is only grieving," Daniel said to me as he downed a tankard of cider. "To lose a mother . . . 'tis a hard thing, especially one so good as Judith. Bring Charity to my house. She will heal—Alice and I will make sure of it, and she will be good for my children. Little Alice has longed for an older sister. Bring her a week from Saturday."

I agreed with relief. Daniel was a good man, his wife godly. There were no better hands in which to entrust my daughter.

'Twas dark when I arrived home. I put Saul in the barn and rubbed him down, lingering over the task, before I went to the house. As quickly and quietly as I could, I went into the parlor and closed the door. 'Twas a fire laid there for me.

I stood for a while at the window, until I heard the steps in the hall. Someone was awake; 'twas no doubt who it was. I left the window and lay upon the bed, staring up at the hanging herbs. I tried to remember Judith, but her face was fading already in my mind. Seventeen years together, and I was forgetting her so quickly. I rubbed my face with my hands as if the motion would bring her back, and when it did not, I simply lay there watching the coals of a fire I could not bring myself to tend.

I saw the light shafting through the door as it cracked open, and Susannah followed it. The candle lit her face with a soft glow, and that reminded me of the way the betty lamp had illuminated her in the cellar. But for the fact that her hair was pinned up, her bodice neatly laced, we could have been there again.

She closed the door behind her, and then she set the candle on the mantel above the hearth and came to the side of the bed.

"Francis came by," she said—such a mundane thing, as if 'twere a common occurrence for her to be here, at my bedside, as if she were my wife, and we were discussing the day's events. It startled me so, I answered her in kind.

"What did he say?"

"The preachers are coming to the village tomorrow. Parris has agreed to have you both at the meeting."

"Where?"

"The parsonage." She hesitated. "There's other news as well. Annie Putnam is having fits now too. And Elizabeth Hubbard."

I sat up fully. "Francis told you this?"

"Aye. Whatever this is, 'tis catching . . . Did you go into town?"

"Aye. Daniel Poole has agreed to have Charity. I'm to take her a week from Saturday."

We fell into silence.

"I'll wish you good night," she said finally, taking the candle, moving to the door. If I said nothing, she would go.

I said, "Come to my bed."

For a moment, I thought she would refuse, and I was not sure I could bear it if she did. "Is this truly what you want, Lucas?" she asked.

"Aye," I said.

She set the candle back on the mantel, where it flickered and smoldered.

"Take off your clothes," I told her.

She smiled. "Ah, so that's how you want it," she said, running her hand over her breasts, sliding it down her bodice.

Her fingers were long and graceful as she fumbled with her laces—they had been knotted back together, I noticed, and remembered how I had broken them in the cellar. I reached for my knife—I had not undressed; it was still belted at my hip. I slid it from its sheath. It glinted in the candlelight, and Susannah went still. Her gaze slid to mine as I moved to sit on the edge of the bed.

"Come," I said, and she stepped between my knees and raised her arms to allow me access. I slid the knife between the laces, slicing them easily, and then I sheathed the knife again and spread my hands beneath the lax camlet. I heard her breath, the little catch as I palmed her.

"I want you against my skin," she murmured, pulling away, stepping back. She no longer lingered; she slipped off the bodice and her skirts until she stood naked before me, her pale skin glowing in the near darkness.

She stepped over to me, again between my knees, and her scent came to me so strongly it rocked me back. I touched her knees, urged them apart, put my hands on her hips and made her straddle me. 'Twas like my dream, and yet not like it—she was there, and the scarlet bed rug glowed around us, coloring the half light. But this time, I was the one clothed, and she as naked as she'd been born.

She pulled at my shirt, her palms were warm on my chest, and then I was falling back on the bed, and her with me. The urge to take her, to possess her, was as strong as it had ever been. As I shed my clothes in a frenzy and pulled her down again to straddle me, I wondered if 'twould ever be different than this, or if we were destined, she and I, to need each other so fiercely each time, to never pause, as if every meeting were the last, as if we might lose each other in the moments after.

Her skin was not perfect after all. Her shoulders were speckled with freckles; she wore dark moles as beauty marks—one inside her elbow, one just above her navel—a tiny fleshy one at the curve of her neck and another just below her breast. There was a single scar on her back, a whip mark cut deep.

"He did not whip me so much," she told me as we lay, still coupled, in the cocoon made by green bed curtains. I had put the candle in the sconce above the headboard, and now it sputtered, ready to go out. "He preferred to use his hands. I think . . . He told me once that he did not want to mar the only thing he had of value. He planned for me to make a good marriage—to guarantee his future."

"But you ran away with the yeoman's son," I said.

"Aye. Though I did not run away with him, not exactly. 'Twas more as if I followed him." She shifted, twisting onto her back without untangling her legs from mine. "He had meant for me to come. He had asked me to, but I think . . . I think he was surprised when I showed up in London. He did not know what to do with me."

I traced her breast. I could not stop touching her. "What then?"

"I stayed with him a little while. Not long. A month . . . less than that. When he asked me to marry him, I left."

"Why?"

She gave me a bemused look. "How can you care about this, Lucas?"

"Because I am ridden by the desire to know you," I admitted. "Because you are in my head every moment, and I cannot understand why."

"And you think to learn the reason by knowing my history."

"No. Because . . ." I sighed, then closed my eyes, trying to think of the words. "Because when I am making a spinning wheel, I can tell by the fit of the wood in my hand what part it will be. People have never been that way for me. I am . . . mystified . . . by them. 'Tis not what I want now. Not for you. Not for . . ." *Us.* I could not say the word. I could not think of a future beyond this moment. I pulled her to me. "Tell me, why did you not marry your yeoman?"

"Because I did not love him. Because I ran away with him to punish my father. Because I was a girl from Lancashire and London is . . . London was . . . like no place I'd ever seen. I wanted to know every inch of it. To marry him would have been to fall into a trap. I was not ready for it."

"You were not ready when it came to Geoffrey, either? Or Robert?"

She smiled. "Will you list them all for me?"

I didn't smile back. "I cannot name them all."

"Oh, Lucas." She kissed my cheek. "You have already done so."

I looked up at the herbs hanging like shadowed nests in the corners. "You must know this," I said carefully. "When it comes to that trap you speak of, I—"

She finished my thoughts softly. "You cannot marry me. I have not asked it. I will not. I do not need marriage."

"The law is clear. You are my wife's sister. 'Tis the law—"

"I understand well enough. I am no fool, Lucas." Her hand came up to rest against my face. "It doesn't matter. I am glad to be here. I was . . . happy to leave London."

"Why was that?" I asked quietly, half afraid of the answer, of Susannah's revelations, which made me as uncomfortable as her secrets.

"Robert was dead," she said matter-of-factly. "His son did not want me there."

"London is a big city."

"Aye." She sighed. "But it seems I've the heart of a country lass. I could not get Lancashire out of my bones. And so I left, to find it elsewhere."

I laughed. "To find it here."

She smiled back at me. "I was not certain, when I left London, that I would stay here. I did not think beyond the next tide."

"And now?"

"And now . . . I will stay until you wish me gone."

"Just now, I cannot imagine that."

Her fingers trailed lingeringly through the hair on my chest, a light tease, though her expression went thoughtful. "Perhaps you do not know yourself as well as you think," she said. Then, as if to ease her words, she leaned down to kiss me. She whispered against my mouth, "Again, Lucas."

I put my arms around her and rolled her onto her back and obliged her, but even as I lost myself in the sensation of her body, I felt a soft doubt that fed the guilt I could not quite appease, a quiet fear.

Chapter 23

———⬩———

I WOKE TO A POUNDING ON THE DOOR. THE ROOM WAS HEAVY STILL with night. I pulled my nightshirt over my head and stumbled groggily through the cold room, wrenching open the parlor door to see Susannah coming down the stairs. She glanced at me in question, and I shook my head and went to the door while she stood back, wrapping a shawl about her.

"Who is it?" I called.

"'Tis Sam Nurse, Lucas."

My daze cleared—I was suddenly wide awake. I grabbed my flintlock and pulled the door open, squinting into darkness barely eased by the faint glow of the snow. "What is it? Has there been an attack?"

"God save us, no," he said hastily. "'Tis nothing like that. There's news. About the afflicted girls. Father's sent me for you."

I looked at him in confusion. "But . . . the meeting. 'Tis not until this afternoon."

"The ministers have already been praying with the girls. Then late last night—they've seen witches, Lucas—or at least, the specters of some."

I heard Susannah's gasp behind me. I stared at Sam. "They've seen what?"

"Get dressed," Sam said. "I'll explain on the way. We must hurry."

Quickly I went to the parlor and dressed. When I came out, he was saying to Susannah, ". . . when the Hubbard girl and Annie Putnam were afflicted, they grew afraid. John Indian told his master of it last night, and the girls began calling out."

"What is this?" I asked. "What happened?"

"The Indian woman made a witch cake," Sam said, turning to me.

"A witch cake?"

"Mary Sibley suggested it to her. She and her husband mixed rye with the girls' water and baked it to feed to the dog. 'Tis said such a thing will help discover witches."

"It seems to have worked," Susannah noted.

"Aye," Sam said grimly.

"Tom Putnam's there?"

"His daughter's one of the afflicted. He's there. And his brother Edward. Now we should go. Father has said 'tis too strange a sight. You'd best be prepared."

"It could not be stranger than what I've already seen."

"Let us hope that is true."

Sam and I nearly ran the distance to the parsonage. The ground was slippery and treacherous; 'twas a thin layer of mud beneath thawed and refrozen ice. When we arrived there, dawn came on full, breaking into a sky heavy with clouds. The parsonage door was opened by Parris himself.

"Come in, come in," he said in a high breathless voice. Behind him, in the hall, I heard voices, screams, Nicholas Noyes's precise voice saying once, and then again, "Who is it? Who afflicts you?"

Parris turned to go back to the hall, leaving us to follow after. I closed the door behind us, enclosing us in this place that sounded more like a madhouse than a parsonage.

In the hall, the four girls were in the throes of agony. The littlest child, nine-year-old Betsey Parris, cowered under the table, barking a sharp punctuation to the moans of Elizabeth Hubbard, the doctor's niece, who grabbed her plump arms and moaned as if someone pinched her mercilessly.

The prayers John Hale tried to say were drowned out by their cries. Sam and I went to stand beside Francis, who watched from the corner. Tom Putnam and his brother Edward were there, along with William Griggs and one or two other villagers. I saw the slave woman, Tituba, in the corner, though her man was nowhere to be seen.

"Who afflicts you?" Noyes asked again, leaning close to Abigail, who screamed in his face.

"She pinches me! Stop hurting me!" she screamed. Her voice was too high, hard to listen to. She grabbed her throat, her pale gray eyes bulging as she gasped for breath.

"Dear Lord, this is untenable!" Parris cried.

Beneath the table, Betsey barked and scratched upon the bench.

Parris spun on his heel. He took two steps before he stopped and put his hands to his head as if the noise made him mad, and then he glared at Tituba in the corner. She cowered the moment his gaze found her, bringing her arms up over her head in a way so familiar to me that I cringed.

But he did not hit her then—perhaps 'twas the presence of us all that kept him from it. Instead, he cast his fist at her ineffectually. "What hell have your evil ways wrought?"

"None, Master. None."

"You liar!" He spun away, as if too furious to look upon her another moment. "You stupid woman! You and Mary Sibley both!"

John Hale walked calmly over to her. "Tell us again what happened."

Slowly she raised her head. "I tell you all this already. There is no more to be said."

"It is still not clear to me." Hale touched her arm. "No one will hurt you. You have nothing to fear."

Her dark gaze shifted to the girls. No doubt she thought there was much to fear in this place.

"Two days ago, Goody Sibley says me and John should make a witch cake," she said. "So I get some of Betsey's water and mix it with the rye and bake it to give to the dog. Goody Sibley says if there be witches, the dog will show it."

"What happened when you did this?"

She hesitated. Her glance went to Parris and then slid back again. "The dog, he eat it some. Not all."

"Did he show signs of bewitchment?"

"I saw nothing strange in him."

"No," Parris interjected bitterly. "Instead, two other girls became bewitched. My own children are seeing specters where there were none before."

As if on cue, Abigail, his niece, howled louder and screamed, "No! No! I will not!"

Tituba shuddered. "I did not mean for this, Master. I did not know."

Hale sighed and turned away. "It seems you might be right, Samuel. The witch cake must have been responsible for revealing to them the specters."

"Can there be another cause?" Parris asked. "The foolish woman has invoked the Devil to reveal himself. Look at them! Can anyone doubt it?"

"I will not sign your evil book!" Abigail shouted.

Little Annie Putnam rose, her cap falling from her head, her nearly white hair falling over her shoulders. Her arm was so stiff as she pointed that the cords of her muscles defined her skin. "Nor I! I won't sign it! I won't!"

Noyes rushed closer, his dark eyes intent. "Who is it that asks you to sign? What book? What do you see?"

"A woman! The devil's book!" Annie screamed. Then she, too, put her hands to her throat. She stuck out her tongue. It snaked to her chin, an impossible length. We gasped in unison, aghast, horrified.

Tom rushed forward. "She is choking! Help her! Can you not help her?"

John Hale grabbed his arm, pulling him back. "Stay, man. You must not interfere."

" 'Tis not your daughter!"

"Stay!"

Noyes thundered, "Who afflicts you?"

Annie's eyes widened. 'Twas clear she was being prevented from speaking by some force we could not see. Behind her, Abigail gasped. "Look! Look who is there beside her!"

Noyes turned to her. "Who does this? Who hurts her?"

"I do not know. Oh . . . I cannot tell! 'Tis the Devil. . . . Oh! There is the dark man. . . ."

Beneath the table, Betsey screamed. Parris lunged for her, falling to his knees, cracking his shoulder on the edge of the table. The child scampered away like a disobedient dog trying to escape a master—dodging beneath the bench, snapping at her father's hands. He became like an animal himself, trying to grab her.

"Who afflicts you?" Noyes cried again.

"Tituba, get yourself here now and help me!" Parris snarled.

The little girl cried out, screaming, curling into a ball, her dark curls hiding her face. "Oh! Oh! Titibee!" she cried—'twas a most piteous sound, torturous. "Titibee!"

John Hale gasped. Parris went still, as did Noyes. "What is it?" Noyes asked. "What did she say?"

Suddenly Abigail screamed out, parroting her cousin. " 'Tis Tituba! Aye, 'tis her! Oh, leave me be! No! Oh, she is pinching Annie! Aye, I can see her now!"

"No!" Tituba's eyes went wide in disbelief. She shook her head. "No, 'tis not me. They be mistaken. Look at me. I stand right here. I do nothing to those girls."

Annie Putnam's own scream was bloodcurdling. Large red welts began to rise on her arms.

It was impossible to believe, yet I saw it with my own eyes. I was struck dumb at the power of it. I could not look away.

"Child, can you not tell us who afflicts you?" Noyes said to Annie Putnam, and the girl cried, "'Tis Tituba; 'tis her!"

The slave woman did not move, even as all eyes turned to her. She did not try to run when Edward Putnam broke from the rest of us and went to the back door, clearly meaning to prevent her escape. She did not stop shaking her head. Her words were like a chant. "'Tis not me. They be mistaken."

Elizabeth Hubbard had not ceased her convulsions on the floor. "Who is it tormenting Elizabeth?" Noyes asked Annie. "Is that Tituba's specter as well?"

Annie froze. She looked to Elizabeth and shook her head. "No. No, 'tis someone else."

"Who? A woman?"

"I . . . I do not . . ." She looked upset, confused. "I cannot tell."

"Is it a woman or a man?"

"A . . . a woman."

"An old woman?"

"Aye," Annie said uncertainly. "'Tis an old woman."

"'Tis Sarah Good!" Abigail called out.

Quick fear came into Annie's eyes. "It is. It is. Sarah Good. She is hurting Betty!"

Parris stood from where he'd been under the table, without his daughter, who still cowered and shook beneath the bench, moaning, "Titibee. Titibee."

"Are there others?" John Hale asked.

"Many others!" Abigail said, and those strange eyes of hers seemed to glow. "Oh, there are three. Three women. 'Tis Tituba and Goody Good and another! I can see them! They are dancing around Betty. Oh, stop! Stop! Leave her be! Oh, leave her!"

Three women. Those of us watching moved back as if all pulled by a single string. The evil in this room was in the very press of the air; 'twas nearly impossible to breathe. To think there were specters within inches of us . . . I did not want to believe it, but I didn't know what else to think. Judith had not trusted these girls, yet had she meant Betsey, who was a mere child of nine? Or Annie Putnam, who was twelve? Those were girls closer in age to Jude than to Charity—I had never seen Charity with either of them. Even so, I could not look at them and think they were in any way dissembling. The welts still shone on Annie's arms. I had seen with my own eyes her tongue stretch to a prodigious, unimaginable length. How could this be a lie? How could this be anything but Satan's torments?

I glanced to Sam and then to Francis, and I saw that they felt what I did, that whatever doubts we'd had were gone. The village had surely been chosen by the Devil. My own worry for my daughter grew until I could not stay a moment longer. I grabbed Sam's arm to get his attention, and whispered, "I must go. Do you need me still?"

He shook his head and whispered back, "We'll stay until they name the third."

It seemed evil itself followed me from that wretched house on the path toward home. The darkness of the woods was nerve-racking, but even the openness of the fallow cornfields held the sense of impending disaster, of an evil laid so thick on the air that the entire village must be breathing it. I knew for certain after today that we were all afflicted. *Witches in Salem Village. Tituba and Sarah Good, and one other.*

When I reached my own door, I was cold to my very marrow. I came inside, stamping the wet snow from my boots, my fingers clumsy as I fumbled with the fastening of my cloak. When I went into the hall, Susannah was at the fire. Jude looked up from sweeping the hearth. When Susannah saw me, she stopped short. "What is it?" she asked in a hushed voice. "Lucas, what has happened?"

"Where's Charity?"

"Upstairs. She went to fetch some dried cod."

I hurried up the stairs, nearly running into Charity as she came down. She looked distracted and ill, her hair lank, her nearly color-less blue eyes the only tint in her face. She carried two stiffened pieces of codfish, and when she saw me, she stopped short, nearly dropping them.

"Father, you're back," she said.

"Give the fish to your aunt and come with me into the parlor," I commanded her, and her expression went wary, which broke my heart, that my own daughter had somehow lost her trust in me. But she nodded and did as I asked.

I closed the parlor door gently behind us. I motioned for her to sit at my desk.

"These girls . . . These *friends* your mother and I forbade you to see . . . Who was among them?"

She churned the fabric of her skirt so hard I thought 'twould surely tear.

"Which girls?" I demanded again.

"M-Mary Walcott," she said slowly. "Betty Hubbard and Mercy Lewis and Mary Warren, who works over at the Proctors'. Lately there has been Susannah Sheldon."

Not Betsey Parris. Nor Annie Putnam. Not Abigail Williams. Of the four girls afflicted, she had named only one. But one could be enough. Slowly I asked, "Were there no others? When you met at the parsonage, were the pastor's children there as well?"

She frowned. "I hardly saw the girl and boy."

"What of Betsey? Or Abigail?"

Charity went quiet. Her eyes went blank, as if she had fallen in-ward. "Charity," I said softly, "did you meet with Betsey too? Or Abigail?"

Her gaze came back to me. "Oh, tell me they have not died."

"They are not dead."

She reached out her trembling hands across the table to me. "We must leave this place, Father—we must leave, you and me and Jude. We must take Faith and leave before he finds us too."

"Before who finds us?"

"He is looking," she said. "I feel him every day, searching my heart."

"Who do you speak of, child?"

"The Devil." Her voice lowered, her lips trembled as she spoke the word. She was clearly terrified.

"God protect us," I murmured.

Tearfully she whispered, "You are in danger, Father. We are all in danger."

I could not help myself. I gathered her into my arms, and she grabbed hold of me and held me close as if afraid that I would be whisked from her. "I will not let him touch you, Charity," I whispered to her, thinking of little Betsey Parris scrambling back from her father's hands, of Tom Putnam racing—too late—to keep his daughter safe. "I have been to town already to arrange for you to go to Daniel Poole's."

She pulled away, blinking, uncomprehending.

"'Tis best, I think, that you leave the village for a while. Goody Poole will be happy to have the help, and the children—"

"You are sending me out?"

I took a deep breath. "Aye. Now that your mother—"

"You cannot make me leave you. You cannot take me from my mother."

"You are leaving me only for a short time, and your mother has been taken from you already," I reminded her gently. "You are closer to her in her place in Heaven—"

"She is not in Heaven," Charity said.

"She is with God, child. She was too good not to go."

"She is not there, I tell you!" Her voice rose, high, shaking. "'Tis my fault she stays. Every day, I hear her voice! 'Tis my fault. 'Tis my sin that holds her." She was shaking badly now, her face gone so pale there was no color, her eyes wild.

"Charity—"

" 'Tis evil that's here now. I could not keep it from her. I will not let it take you. I can't leave you here alone."

"I am hardly alone. There is Jude, and Faith is just next door. Your aunt is here."

I thought Charity would swoon. I reached for her, but she grabbed the edge of my desk, steadying herself. " 'Tis how she wants it. To be alone with you. To corrupt you . . ."

"Child, I do not understand you."

"You cannot make me go!" She screamed the words. "I will not go!"

It took all my strength to say calmly, "You will pack your things, and be ready to go to town on Saturday next. I will hear no more about it."

"No. No, you don't understand. . . ."

"I understand well enough. You are my daughter. You will do as I say."

"But . . . But you need me. Father, you don't understand. There is . . . evil . . . here." She put her hands to her face and crumpled before me, sobbing.

"Charity," I said, softening my voice, "you must believe I am doing everything I can to keep Satan from you—"

She only shook her head and raised her tearstained face to mine. "I am already lost. 'Tis you who must be careful, Father. 'Tis you."

Chapter 24

———— ✥ ————

I HAD NOT SEEN SUCH PANIC IN THE VILLAGE SINCE THE FEAR OF THE recent Indian attacks. Goody Osborne had been named as the third witch. The old woman had long been the village scandal: She had lived in sin with her indentured servant before she finally married him.

There were those who saw Satan in every shadow; they told tales of how Goody Good had bewitched their cattle and how strange and terrible beasts followed Goody Osborne about, only to disappear upon closer examination. And Tituba . . . Was she not an Indian, too, if only one from the West Indies? They practiced wicked and horrible things there: spells to bring illness, to call up Satan, to tell the future.

I kept my family as far from the terror as I could. Charity did not leave the house, even to milk the cow. I kept her busy studying scripture, and it seemed that since I had told her I planned to send her out, she applied herself with fervor. She spoke no more of evil; she kept from the window. 'Twas as if she were my daughter again, and the frightened girl of the other night an impostor.

When Good and Tituba and Osborne were arrested, I was relieved, along with the other village folk, but it was not over so easily.

The children did not recover; they complained still of torments.

And now there were two others added to the afflicted, and these names frightened me more than the others: Mary Walcott and Mercy Lewis. Both of Thomas Putnam's house. Both friends of Charity's.

I did not tell my daughter this. I prayed for the week to hurry by so that I could send her away to Salem Town and peace. The Saturday Daniel Poole and I had agreed upon could not come quickly enough. The accused witches would be examined before they were committed to prison to await trial. If Charity were still here, I would not be able to keep her from rumors, which had a way of riding the very air. I hoped this questioning would wait a few days—at least until after I'd sent her away.

But I was too late. Monday afternoon, I came into the house to find Hannah Penney already there, a grim look on her face as she nursed little Faith. Susannah stood at the hearth, looking stunned, and Jude whimpered and tried to escape from Charity, who held her tight against her side.

"What is it?" I asked.

Susannah said, "Hannah has told us that the examinations are to take place tomorrow at Ingersoll's."

"Tomorrow?"

"Aye." Hannah nodded. "John Hathorne will come from town for it."

"Perhaps he can bring sense again to this confusion," I said.

Charity's fingers were frozen around Jude's little arm.

"Let your sister go," I told her.

Charity looked frightened. "She must sit here by me. Jude, be a good girl. Sit still."

Jude squirmed away. "I want Auntie."

"Come then." Susannah went over to the bench, and held out her arms, and Jude threw herself into them. Charity's hand went to her throat—a simple gesture, but in it I saw again the image of Annie Putnam standing in the hall at the parsonage, her hands wrapped around her own throat, horror in her eyes.

Charity looked to me. "Is it true, Father? Is it true what Goody Penney says?"

In irritation, I glanced at Hannah, who shrugged and said, " 'Tis true enough. Now that they've arrested those witches, I pray there'll be an end to the afflictions."

It struck me then, what she had told Charity. "Dear God," I said, "you cursed woman. Can you not keep your mouth shut?"

Hannah looked stunned. "I have only said the truth."

"It is true, then, Father?" Charity said. "Mercy? And—and Mary?"

"Aye, 'tis true," I said brusquely. I gestured to Hannah. "Get back to your own house. Gossip somewhere else."

"But I—"

"Go," I told her.

She was sputtering, but she gathered up my daughter and hastened to the door. When she was gone, I said to Susannah, "Until next week, keep Hannah away."

"I must see them," Charity said urgently. "I must see Mary."

"That is the last thing you shall do," I told her. "You shall stay here until Saturday, when you will go to town."

Susannah frowned when I said it, though she said not a word. She went to the fire and I felt her disapproval linger in the air and wondered why she censured me, when I was doing what she had asked me to do, when I was sending my daughter away. I felt besieged on all sides, and when Charity lapsed into silence, I was grateful. When she went to the window, I did not say a word. Four days, I thought. Four days until she was gone to town.

I went to the examinations alone. The frosty breaths and excited talk of fifty or more villagers filled the air while I—with some other members of the militia, and the constable's men—stood guard along the road from town. We waited for the magistrates, then fell into step beside them and held back the crowd as John Hathorne and

Jonathan Corwin rode to the doors of Ingersoll's, where Samuel Parris and Tom Putnam waited to greet them.

"We had not expected such a crowd," Tom said as we paused at the door. He looked harried and distracted, as if he had passed a bad night—no doubt he had. "There won't be room for everyone."

At this, the crowd began to murmur. There were angry shouts behind me.

"You can't keep us out, Putnam!"

"We've a right to see this!"

Parris stroked his chin. "Aye. 'Tis better if everyone has a chance to see."

"Is there a bigger building?" Hathorne asked as he dismounted. He was long-faced, with brown eyes, a serious mouth, and an air of efficiency that seemed to calm the crowd.

"A place not too far away," added Corwin. "I've ridden enough for one morning."

"There's the meetinghouse," Parris said. "We have held the entire village there."

'Twas an exaggeration—there had never been a time when the entire village had attended one of Parris's sermons—but no one argued it. Hathorne and Corwin agreed, and we moved to the meetinghouse. My neighbors filed inside, and we pushed back the pulpit to make room for a large table brought from Ingersoll's for the magistrates and the court reporter to sit at. I heard a roar from outside as the afflicted girls came—there were only the four—Annie Putnam and bosomy Elizabeth Hubbard, young Betsey Parris and her cousin Abigail Williams—as they were the ones who'd accused these women. The littlest Parris girl looked frightened, but the rest were calm and clear-eyed as they made their way through the crowd and sat where Hathorne directed them in the first row of pews.

The meetinghouse was more crowded than it had been on any Sunday or Thursday lecture. The benches were filled; people stood against the walls. The galleries creaked from the weight of so many witnesses. I stood beside Sam Nurse and Joseph Putnam, each of us holding a gun, militia-ready.

The crowd fell into abrupt, tense silence, and then a whisper set through the meetinghouse: "They're here. They're here." There was a commotion outside as the prisoners were brought up. Hathorne and Corwin took their seats at the table, and Ezekiel Cheever sat beside them to serve as court reporter.

"Bring in the first one," Hathorne said. He glanced down at the paper before him. "Sarah Good."

"The bar!" someone in the crowd cried. "Where is the bar?"

I glanced to the front—there was no bar of justice. Putnam rushed forward and put a chair opposite the magistrates' table, turning it around for the tall back to serve as the bar.

Hathorne said to the girls, "Turn away," and each of them did, lowering their eyes as Sarah Good was jerked down the aisle to the makeshift court. Goody Good was manacled, and the chains seemed too big and heavy on her wrists, though she was not a small woman. She was large-boned, but too thin, and obviously many months pregnant. Her gray-brown hair straggled into her eyes, and she was dirty and ill-kempt. 'Twas hard to know which was the dirt of the prison she'd spent the night in, and which her natural state. She was angry and sullen, muttering to herself as Constable Locker brought her before a crowd that had fallen into a hushed silence.

She should have been docile; 'twould have bought the crowd's sympathy, and mine, but she did not submit as they brought her to the bar and forcibly set her hands upon it. There was nothing but scorn in her eyes as she faced the magistrates. George Locker and his men stood at either side of her, wary and waiting.

John Hathorne rose slowly, clearing his throat, and pulled at his sleeve before he looked at her. From where I stood, near the front, I could see his gaze—as scornful as hers.

"Sarah Good," he began, raising his voice so it echoed throughout the eaves, deep and powerful. "Sarah Good, what evil spirit have you familiarity with?"

"None."

"Have you made no contract with the Devil?"

"No."

"Why do you hurt these children?"

She spat. "I do not hurt them. I scorn it."

The crowd was silent. I, too, leaned forward, impatient to hear.

Hathorne took a step closer. "Who do you employ, then, to do it?"

"I employ nobody." Her voice was harsh and strident. "I am falsely accused."

There was a murmuring in the crowd. I saw frustration in Hathorne's expression. With a flourish, he turned on his heel, toward the girls, who had obeyed him to a one in keeping their eyes from the woman.

"Children," he said slowly, "will you look at the accused? Tell us: Is she the one who torments you?"

Abigail Williams, Parris's niece, was the first to look. No sooner had she laid eyes on the woman than she screeched in a high whine. "Aye! Aye! 'Tis her! Oh, why do you torment me, Goody Good?"

At that, 'twas as if Hell itself emptied into the meetinghouse. Plump, pretty Elizabeth Hubbard fell to the floor in a fit; Annie Putnam pulled at her pale hair as if she would tear it out. Betsey Parris screamed that she was being pinched and bitten. Some watching rushed forward, trying to help the girls; others ran for the doors. Hathorne cried out vainly for silence. 'Twas nothing but screaming and crying and the rush of footsteps. The galleries shook and creaked, and I—along with Sam Nurse—grabbed my gun from my shoulder as if it were some sort of attack—though there was no one to shoot, nothing to do but stand there helplessly and watch the examinations fall apart around us. Even Sarah Good looked startled and afraid.

Parris yelled, "Turn her away! Turn her away!" Locker rushed forward and forcibly turned Goody Good's head from the children.

'Twas miraculous. . . . The girls quieted immediately. Elizabeth and Abigail were in a heap on the floor, and the moment the woman turned, they rose, breathing heavily, showing pink welts and teeth marks on their arms. Annie Putnam had been collapsed in Mary Sibley's arms, and now she stood. Little Betsey Parris was still weeping, but quietly, as one does after a fierce scare. The entire room seemed to freeze in chaos: benches upended, people halted midrise or in the act of fleeing through the door. My own heart was racing. At the girls' sudden peace, the room gradually returned to order, but 'twas a different feel to it now. The expectation had turned to horror.

Parris, who had seen such affliction for many days now, looked drained. At the table, Jonathan Corwin opened and closed his mouth like a gaping cod. John Hathorne seemed amazed. When he turned back to Good, 'twas with a vengeance.

"Sarah Good, why do you not tell us the truth? Why do you thus torment these poor children?"

"I do not torment them!"

"Who do you employ, then?"

"I employ nobody. I scorn it." The same words as before, but they had lost their power, and she her anger. She looked frightened now, and desperate.

"How came they thus tormented?"

"What do I know? Whoever you brought into the meetinghouse with you."

"We brought you into the meetinghouse."

"But you brought in two more."

"Who was it, then, that tormented the children?"

She looked puzzled. Then her expression cleared. "'Twas Osborne."

I closed my eyes briefly in horror. The murmurs of the crowd—appalled, disturbed, terrified—filled my ears. Hathorne was as one on to blood scent. He leaned close. "I have reports that you go muttering from people's houses when they displease you. What is it you say?"

She looked confused and afraid. "It is the Commandments. I may say my Commandments, I hope."

"What Commandment is it?"

She hesitated, her confusion more apparent than ever.

Hathorne said, "Who do you serve?"

"I serve God."

"What God do you serve?"

"He that made Heaven and the Earth," she said sharply.

"Here, sir," came a voice from the pews. I turned to see Sarah Good's husband rising. It had been so long since I had seen him, I had nearly forgotten his existence. He was thin and bowed, many of his teeth rotting or gone.

"Who are you?" Hathorne asked.

"William Good. That woman's husband, God save me."

"What have you to say? Is this woman a witch?"

"If she is not, she will be one very quickly," he said.

"Why would you say such a thing? Has she afflicted you? Have you seen anything to make you believe this of her?"

"No, not in this nature," Good said, gesturing to the children. "But she is a disobedient wife. She does not respect me or heed me. Indeed . . . I may say with tears that she is an enemy to all good."

Her own husband had turned upon her. . . . That, along with the spectral evidence of the girls, was impossible to deny, no matter how long or often Goody Good denounced the charges.

One could not witness these things and not believe the Devil was among us. When Goody Good was dismissed and Sarah Osborne brought in, weak and frail, supported on Locker's arm, I felt the air as a weight upon my shoulders. I could not take my eyes from the girls' fits when they were told to look upon her, and I saw Osborne's fear in the midst of it. I heard her shaken tales of how a shadow man had come to her—"A thing like an Indian, all black, which did pinch my neck . . . I am more bewitched than a witch!"—and felt a terrible certainty.

But all this was as nothing when they brought in the slave woman.

The moment Tituba entered, the girls fell into fits. Nothing could quiet them, not even Hathorne's direction that Tituba look away. He had to shout his questions over their screaming, over the chaos of those trying to comfort them. Tituba gripped the bar. Her dark eyes were large and frightened; one was blackened from a recent beating.

Hathorne yelled questions over and over again, and her voice grew fainter and fainter as she answered them, denials all. I did not doubt she was a witch, and I saw the same belief in my neighbors. How could I deny it given the evidence before us, writhing on the floor, crying out in pain? The questioning seemed to go on for hours, though it could not have been that. The din was impossible; my ears hurt straining to hear; my soul felt bombarded by the girls' sufferings.

Hathorne shouted, "Tell the truth. Who is it that hurts them?"

Tituba shook her head and swallowed nervously. "The Devil, for aught I know."

"How does he appear when he hurts them? With what shape?"

Abigail Williams cried out, "Why do you pinch me so, Tituba? Goody Good, why do you torment me?"

"With what appearance does he come?" Hathorne asked again. "When did he appear?"

Tituba seemed to sag. In a voice nearly too quiet to hear, she said, "Like a man. I think yesterday."

Hathorne went still. Someone asked, "What did she say?" and the whisper went around; the crowd went quiet. Miraculously, the fits stopped. The girls sagged, exhausted, listening.

My hands tightened on my gun—though why or how I should use it, I could not fathom.

Then 'twas as if the truth raced from Tituba, words so horrible 'twas hard to listen to them without terror. Sarah Good told her to hurt the children, and she was forced to do it. Good and the others

were so strong that they had forced Tituba to go to the Putnams'
with them; they had ridden on a long pole through the air. They
had forced her to attack young Annie with a knife—to which the
child wrung her loose white hair and called out, "'Tis true, 'tis true!
She tried to cut off my head!" Good prevented Tituba from listening to her master's prayers. The witch had a yellow bird that sucked
between her fingers, and a hairy creature like a dog or a wolf that
did her bidding.

"Who else was there?" Hathorne asked. "Did you see Goody
Osborne?"

"Aye," Tituba said. "There be a man too. And . . . others. There
be others."

There was an audible gasp. Hathorne looked stunned.

"Others?" he asked. "There are others? How many?"

"I . . . I don't know."

"Many? A few?"

"I . . ."

"More than three?"

Tituba swallowed. "Aye. More than three."

There was a terrified hush. *Others. There were others.*

The slave could not answer beyond that, though Hathorne was
relentless. After another hour, we knew nothing more—not who
those other witches were, nor how many. Finally the magistrate
seemed to run out of questions.

Tituba stood nervously, her hands gripping her skirt, wrists
bound by heavy iron manacles made for a man, so large they slipped
to the base of her hands. Her head was bowed, and she seemed exhausted. I was as anguished as the others in the room as Hathorne
called a halt to the proceedings.

"We shall take up again tomorrow," he said to Tituba. "For now,
you will go with the constable."

George Locker and his men came up beside her, and I saw how
they were reluctant to touch her, how they prodded her to move
with their flintlocks rather than their hands. The crowd was still as

they left, but the moment they went out the door, the meetinghouse burst into sound: arguments, fearful words, loud whispers. I glanced at Sam, who looked pale and stunned, and I knew I must look the same.

"Dear God," he murmured. "What has become of us?"

I could not answer him. The evil that had come into this house of God was unbearable, and terror stayed with me as I followed Sam from the meetinghouse into the dusk of early evening. I stood there a moment, watching my neighbors leave in close-knit groups, listening to the whispers. I saw the suspicion in their eyes as they regarded each other, and I thought back to what Francis had said days ago, about how no good could come of this. *Others. There were others.* How could we fight this? How had Satan gained such a foothold without our knowing?

But I knew the answer to that question already. It did not take much to give the Devil an open door. 'Twas as simple as a hungry heart, a soul that yearned. . . .

"Come," Sam said to me. "Let's to home. I'm weary of this place."

I nodded, and as he moved to the path, I started after him, stopping only when I dropped a glove. I turned to pick it up and saw from the corner of my eye a movement—a shadow hovering around the corner of the meetinghouse—and it caught me. There was a familiarity to the furtiveness. I straightened and turned fully to look, and 'twas then I realized who was hiding from me.

Charity.

Chapter 25

"Go on," I called to Sam. "I've left something in the meeting-house."

"I'll wait," he said.

"No. I won't keep you from your family. This might take some time."

He nodded, though reluctantly, and I waited until he'd turned and started to walk again before I hurried back to the meetinghouse. My daughter had disappeared, but I made my way to the darkened side of the building where I'd seen her. 'Twas cold, and the wind blew the shadows before me; the cold, icy stink of the swamp mud beyond was heavy here. Charity was not to be seen. I sped my step, nearly running around back, and I saw her huddled against the wall, as if she could hide by melting into the weathered clapboards.

She looked up and saw me, and then shrank into her cape and the shadow of her broad-brimmed hat, but she didn't try to move or run away. As I neared, I saw that 'twas not because she was meekly and submissively waiting for her punishment, but because she was paralyzed with fear. Her eyes were large and unseeing, her lips trembling, and I saw the constant movement of her hands beneath her cape.

"Ti-Tituba," she whispered as I came to her. "I heard h-her."

"You should not have come," I said gently. "I told you to stay home with Susannah."

Her gaze leaped to mine. She swallowed; it seemed to be difficult and painful. Her mouth worked as if she wanted to speak, but no words came.

I sighed and touched her arm. "Come with me, child. We'd best get home before it turns dark."

"Aye," she said unsteadily. "Aye."

I held out my arm, and she took it, stumbling along after me as I made my way around the corner of the meetinghouse, back toward the road. I was anxious to be gone; I felt still the evil of that room, and I pulled my daughter closer into my side.

She was shaking, her teeth chattering. The chilblains on her face had become scabbed from her constant rubbing. Saturday seemed too long to wait to send her to town. After what had happened today, I could not imagine letting her linger here, with Tituba's confessions tormenting her and her friends lapsing into fits. I resolved to take her to town tomorrow. No doubt Poole would understand, once I told him the affairs of the village—if he had not heard already.

"What possessed you to come?" I asked her finally.

Her glance was quick, horrified. "I . . . I had to know . . . what she would say."

Uncomfortably, I remembered the way Tituba's gaze had shifted to my daughter's face when we'd visited the parsonage together. I wanted to ask why that was, but I was afraid, and as if Charity read my mind, her shaking grew worse. I pulled her close, trying to still it with my strength.

"Wh-what will happen now?" she asked. "Wh-what will they do with her?"

I shrugged. "She will be urged to confess everything. Then there will be a trial."

"W-will she hang? Will those other wi-witches hang?"

"If they are guilty."

"And what of the De-devil, then?"

I tried to reassure her. "Satan will leave this village when he sees we will not tolerate him here."

She nodded against my shoulder, but I knew she did not quite believe me. 'Twas no surprise—I was not sure I believed myself.

"Father, you will not tolerate him, either, will you? You will help to fight him?"

"Aye," I reassured her. "I will help to fight him."

We were home quickly. The house smelled of stew and bread. Jude's innocent babble filled the air, along with Susannah's low replies.

I nearly had to push Charity inside. Jude quieted. Susannah turned from the fire.

Her glance went past me to Charity, and she straightened in surprised confusion. "Charity, I thought—"

"I snuck out," Charity said, bowing her head. She looked contrite, though I knew she was not. Neither was her "Forgive me" sincere, but this time I said nothing.

Susannah paused. " 'Twas no harm done, I suppose. I trust you ran into no trouble."

"Nothing but trouble," I said. "It seems the Devil has made a place for himself in Salem Village."

"The examination—"

"There was a confession," I said. "The slave woman confessed to being a witch."

Susannah went still. "She said that? She said she was a witch?"

"Aye. And that there were others. Good and Osborne among them."

"Others? More than just the three?"

I nodded grimly. Jude stared up at me with eyes as big as an owl's, and I said, "We'll pray tonight. Tomorrow I think we should fast. 'Twill be our own day of humiliation."

"We shall pray Satan away," Jude said.

"If it were only so easy," Charity murmured.

Susannah made a sound, and I glanced at her and saw her eyes were dark with worry. She searched my face, and I turned away and hoped she would take my silence as a sign that we would talk later.

She seemed to. Her voice was deceptively light as she said, "Well, if we are to fast tomorrow, we'd best eat well tonight."

As she laid the food before us and took her own seat, we fell into silence. Even my prayer of thanksgiving did not have staying power. Charity barely touched her supper, and my own stomach was churning, so I could not eat. Jude was the only one of us with any appetite, and it was too soon before we were done and the table cleared. I was sitting with my daughters at the fire, reading Psalm 78:49 for their lesson.

The candles had burned low when I finished and sent the girls to bed. I did not tell Charity of my plan to take her into town the next day, but let her go to bed protected by prayers. When she turned back to me as she took to the stairs, I saw again that plea in her eyes. *You will help to fight him?*

When they were gone, I said, "Tomorrow I'll take Charity to the Pooles'. I will not wait for Saturday."

" 'Twas that bad, then? The examinations?"

"Aye."

"Did the others confess?"

"They didn't need to. The girls' torments were obvious. And then . . . Tituba . . ."

"Is this something real, Lucas?" she asked quietly.

"Who would confess to this if it were not?"

"The girls are persuasive. 'Tis a shock to see them. But perhaps—"

"You think they dissemble?"

She hesitated. "Perhaps some of them. I have some experience with Mary Walcott."

"What experience?" I demanded. "What can you know of a seventeen-year-old?"

"I once was one," she said. She surveyed me steadily. "You are angry with me, Lucas."

I shook my head. "Not angry. But . . ."

"What?"

"This sin between us must end. I am more determined of it than ever. The Devil already has too much sway here."

She was quiet for a long moment. Then she said, "Oh, you foolish, foolish man." She knelt before me where I sat on the bench at the tableboard, her skirts billowing.

"Do not touch me," I said, holding up my hands to keep her away. "Keep your distance."

"Why?" she asked.

She was too close already. "You know the answer to that," I managed.

"I can no more help the fact that I share blood with my sister than you can change who you are." She took my hands, and I tried to pull away, but she grasped me hard, the balls of her fingers pressing tight into my palms. She leaned forward so that her breasts brushed my knees. "We could leave this place. 'Tis long past time, now that this . . . this Devil is in the air. We could take the children and go. There must be somewhere else in this godforsaken land. North? South?"

New York. The name flashed through my mind, shocking me, that this should be a temptation too. . . . "There is no place," I ground out. "Release me."

"I will not. You think you can make this terror go simply by ending what is between us, but you can't, Lucas. All you will do is make it worse. I won't let you do it."

"You have no choice. 'Tis my decision."

"No," she said. There was a force and determination in her voice that held me. She let go of me, but then she rose, so quickly that I did not know what she was about. She took my face between her hands and leaned close so that her lips were nearly on mine. "Tell me that you can resist this, Lucas, and I will leave you, I promise it. Tell me you do not want to kiss me, and I will go away."

She had given me the key. Such a simple thing. *I don't want you. I will not kiss you.* 'Twould be so easy.

I pulled her down to me, openmouthed, groaning, feeling the will for her eat away everything else: my vow to my daughter and myself, my fears. All were as nothing compared to this.

She answered me back, meeting me in primitiveness, and entangled we moved from the bench, stumbling together to the parlor.

I kicked the door closed. Together we found the bed and fell upon it, and there was no thought, only longing and the urge to fulfill it. I felt her legs about my hips; I heard her moans. My breeches were off. Her hands were on my skin, both soft and rough, urging and restrained. I rode her with an unconscious pleasure I had never felt, not ever. She was moaning beneath me. Lifting her hips. Calling out my name. "Lucas . . . Lucas . . ."

Someone screamed.

The sound penetrated my consciousness at the same moment I came. I felt Susannah jerk beneath me, and as if in a dream, I turned. I saw the open door, the light of a candle slanting across the floor, into my face, blinding me. I saw a figure, and then a face.

Charity. Charity standing at the open door, her eyes wide in wordless shock. She raised her hands, shaking, dropping the candle so it spattered wax onto the bed curtains, rolling still alight across the floor. She screamed again, a wretched, endless echo.

I jerked from Susannah, grabbing for my breeches and yanking them on. "Charity. My God, Charity."

I reached for my daughter, and she wrenched away, horrified. I grabbed her, trying to quiet her, but she only screamed into my chest and beat and scratched at me. I held on.

"Charity," Susannah said. "My dear, my dear—"

Charity was shaking so hard her teeth chattered together. She twisted from me, staring at Susannah, who held her skirt to her nakedness, before she fell to the floor, clutching her throat. She was no longer screaming, but her moan was otherworldly, a terrible sound, and she gasped as if choking. In a panic, I grabbed at her hands, trying to pry them loose, but she was stronger than I. Her eyes rolled in her head. She began convulsing on the floor, and I could do nothing but stare at her.

Convulsions. Like Elizabeth Hubbard and Abigail Williams.

I sank to my knees beside my daughter and put my head into my hands. 'Twas too late. Too late. The Devil had her.

And I had handed her to him.

Chapter 26

"LUCAS, YOU MUST GO," SUSANNAH SAID, YANKING ON HER SKIRTS. The room smelled of acrid smoke and scorched harrateen. Charity gulped air as if she were drowning, her stomach swelling beneath her chemise as if something were alive inside her. "You must get the doctor, and quickly."

I stared in helpless dismay at my daughter. "What can he do for her now?"

"There must be something. He's treated the others. Surely he must know—"

"He prays. 'Tis all he can do."

"Then we need him to pray. You must go to him, Lucas."

I reached for Charity, and she hissed at me like a cat.

"Don't touch me!" she screamed, lashing out. Her nails clawed my cheek; the sudden pain startled me and I jumped back. 'Twas what I deserved—this and so much more.

Numbly I rose. "I'll go for Griggs," I said, because I could think of nothing else to do. I hurried from the parlor, and Susannah stayed with Charity and did not follow me.

I grabbed my flintlock and my cloak and ran through the darkness to the barn, where I saddled and mounted Saul.

I was hardly aware of how I reached Griggs's house; only that suddenly I was slamming my fist upon his door, shouting out,

"William! William! Wake up!" until the door creaked open beneath my onslaught, and he peered through the crack. His gray hair was stiff and spiky with sleep; his fowling piece was in his hands until he realized who I was.

"Lucas," he said. "What has happened? What is it? Indians?"

"'Tis an attack of the Devil," I said to him, and the door opened farther. I saw the dark circles beneath his sagging eyes, his dawning understanding.

"Another afflicted girl," he said.

"Aye. My daughter. Charity."

"There's naught I can do—"

"You will come to see her, William," I told him. "There is no point in arguing. Whatever your protests, I will not hear them. I cannot leave without you."

He sighed. "Very well. One moment." The door closed, and when it opened again, he was ready, his gun in his hand. Beneath his open cloak, he still wore his nightshirt, rucked up and tucked loosely into his breeches so it bloused nearly to his knees.

I waited impatiently while he saddled his horse, and it seemed hours had passed since I'd left Charity writhing on the floor with Susannah standing over. We rode quickly back, leaving the horses in the yard.

Susannah was alone in the hall. "Where is Charity?" I asked. In alarm, I hurried to the parlor, tearing at the fastenings of my cloak. "Why are you not with her? Dear God, she could hurt herself—"

"She's asleep, Lucas." Susannah's voice was soft and quiet; the meaning of her words did not hit me until I was nearly to the parlor door, and then I stopped in surprise and looked over my shoulder at her.

"Asleep?" I asked. The notion was startling. I could not fathom it, that the Devil had left her so suddenly. . . .

"Aye. She fell unconscious just after you left."

Unconscious. 'Twas an odd word choice, as odd as what she offered as truth. "Did you give her something? Some potion?"

"A potion?" Susannah looked confused. "No. I simply held her hand, and she quieted."

I thought of how I'd tried to take my daughter into my arms and how she'd fought me; my cheek even now stung from her nails. I glanced at Griggs, who was watching Susannah with a strange look, as if he did not believe her explanation, either.

Slowly I turned back to the parlor. I did not know what I expected to see. But there was my daughter, in the bed that Susannah and I had lain upon only an hour before, tucked beneath the scarlet bed rug. My little girl who was no longer a little girl. In sleep, how peaceful she was. I gripped the door frame and filled my eyes with her; 'twas all I could do not to run to her side and grab her hand, to beg for her forgiveness. "'Tis a deep sleep," I whispered.

I heard Griggs come up behind me. "Aye. 'Tis not unusual. Between fits, they are seemingly well, with nothing to show for their torments but a few bite marks, perhaps."

"Is there nothing you can do for them?" Susannah asked.

"I have no power against the Devil," William said. "In my own house, I have seen to it that Betty does not harm herself, but more than that . . ." He sighed again and clapped his hand to my shoulder as he passed by me into the parlor. I watched as he went to Charity, as he leaned down over her, and the energy that had driven me single-mindedly to the doctor's house and home again dissipated as quickly as a single breath. I was suddenly exhausted.

After a few moments, Griggs turned to me. "Let her sleep. 'Tis best. Keep her as quiet as possible. Prayer seems to work for some of them. For others, it only agitates them further."

"Is that all I can do? " I asked, hearing the anguish in my voice. "Is there nothing I can give to her?"

"She is not fevered. This is nothing physical, Lucas; 'tis but a spiritual affliction. Whatever beings attack her cannot be swayed by any poultice. She will recover, or not. I cannot tell."

He moved away from the bed; his visit was over. I knew there was nothing I could do to keep him here. I followed him to the door. "Thank you for coming, William. Forgive me for rousing you from your bed."

"I wish I could do more," he said, putting on his hat.

"Shall I ride back with you? 'Tis a dark night."

"No. I've a flintlock on the saddle, and my horse is a fast one." Griggs went to the door, where he paused, his hand on the lever. Slowly he turned back, his expression troubled. "Has she called out, Lucas?"

"Called out?"

"Has she put a name to the specters tormenting her?"

"Dear God," I murmured.

"She hasn't said a name," Susannah said. I had grown used to her silence; the sound of her voice was painful to hear.

"She will," Griggs said. "They all do. Bring her to Ingersoll's tomorrow during the examinations. See if she is at all affected by the other girls."

"How could she not be?" Susannah asked. "I should think 'twould be better to keep her away from them. They cannot help but feed off each other."

Griggs said sharply, "If there are witches in the village, 'tis in our best interest to find them. There are others, Tituba said. We must use all our abilities to discover who they are."

"You surprise me, Doctor. I would have thought your first interest would be healing."

There was anger in his voice when he said, "Do not forget, my own niece is involved in this. I want only the best for her."

"Then perhaps you should send her to town, or to Boston."

"You would let witches roam freely? You would give the Devil such power?"

"He only has what power you give him," Susannah told him. "I would think young girls are hardly—"

"Enough," I said, angry that she would dare to dispute these things that she could not possibly understand. "You do neither us nor Charity any good, madam. Quiet yourself."

I did not care when she flinched. I wanted to punish her as I punished myself. I looked back at the doctor. "We'll bring her tomorrow. Godspeed, William."

Griggs looked at Susannah and then back to me, nodding. "Good night," he said as he went out, and the night swallowed him. The room felt still and heavy, as if there had never been a disturbance here, as if Susannah and I had held these postures for an eternity.

"I think it cannot be good to take Charity to Ingersoll's," Susannah said. "You planned to take her to town tomorrow. Tell me you will do that."

That she could go on as if nothing happened sickened me. I could not believe she would still think of sending Charity out now. I shook my head. "No."

"Lucas, you cannot mean to—"

"This is beyond me now," I said. "I cannot help her, and you have proven to be no use to her at all."

"I . . . I don't understand," she whispered. "This has been a strange night. Let us take comfort from each other."

I recoiled, staring at her in disbelief and horror. "Do you not understand? The comfort we've taken in each other is what led to this. How many more signs must God give us before we end this sin?"

"No, Lucas, I . . . I will not let you do this."

" 'Tis not your choice! I have had *enough* of this. Dear God, my daughter is tortured by the Devil, and we have let him in. How can you speak of taking comfort?"

"Please, Lucas. . . ."

'Twas as if she could not stop herself. She touched my hair, and when I made to jerk away, she came closer, letting her hand fall to my cheek. Impossibly, improbably, I felt desire. That she should have this power over me, that she could make me want her now . . .

I grabbed her hand, stopping her. "No. This must end."

There was desperation in her eyes. "I will not let it."

I saw the warmth in her gaze, and because of that, I wanted to hurt her. I gripped her wrist harder and said, "I suggest you go into town for your needs. There are dozens of sailors there eager to oblige."

I saw shock in her expression, and then pain, and I threw her from me and turned away, feeling a terrible satisfaction as I left her standing there. I went, without a backward glance, to the parlor, where I shut the door tightly behind me, closing her out, dismissing her.

I leaned against the door for a moment, then forced myself to look at my daughter, who slept painlessly and well. I went to her side, where I stayed the night through, praying for salvation.

Chapter 27

———— ❦ ————

CHARITY WOKE WITH THE LATE DAWN. SHE HAD SLEPT NEARLY motionless the night through, and I dared to hope that perhaps last night had been only a passing fit due to momentary shock. I waited anxiously for the moment she opened her eyes.

When she finally did, I was not even looking at her. I was staring blankly at the window. It wasn't until she said "Father" that I realized she was awake, and I jerked around to see her.

Her eyes were clear; there was no delusion there. I grabbed her hands and mumbled such a quick prayer to God that I barely knew the words I said, only that they were heartfelt. "Charity, you are yourself."

She frowned a little, and when the worry and fear came into her expression, my heart sank—I had been relieved too soon. I saw when the remembrance hit her. She glanced around, to the door, the bedcovers, and seemed to shrink inside herself. She pulled her hands from mine. They were trembling as she raised them to her face and moaned, "Oh, I am too late. I am too late. I saw what you did, and so did Mama. She said that you could . . . you could tell wickedness . . . that you could . . . fight it, but you cannot, can you?"

" 'Tis one thing to tell wickedness, Charity, and another to fight it. I am only a man—"

"You promised . . . to keep the Devil from this house. You promised to help me fight him. Only yesterday, you promised it."

"I know," I said. I felt the tears coming to my own eyes. "I know."

She was crying so hard she could hardly say the words. "Has God left you then, Father? As He has left me?"

"He has not left you."

" 'If Christ hath no possession of thee, thou art possessed by the Devil,' " she quoted softly.

I grabbed her hands and held them fast. "We will pray. We will go to meeting, we shall fast in humiliation. This . . . bewitchment . . . that has come over us—we will send it away. I promise you this. Charity, my dear, I promise it."

"You cannot keep your promises. The Devil has already corrupted you."

I wanted to deny her, but to deny would have been a lie, and I could not do that, either. I stared at her, wordless, undone. I rose and stepped away from her, turning from her accusing countenance.

"You will not even deny it," she said—such misery, such desperation.

I sighed, beaten. "Aye, I will not. There is weakness in every man, and the Devil has found mine. I would that you had not seen it."

I could not bear to see her reaction to my words. Instead, I stepped to the parlor door and went into the hall. Jude and Susannah were coming down the stairs, and I stopped short, caught—my weakness both before me and behind me. My daughters, Susannah . . .

"Lucas," Susannah said. "What has happened? Is Charity . . . ?"

"She's well enough. As soon as she's ready, we're off to Ingersoll's."

"Lucas, you can't—"

I glared at her. " 'Tis none of your concern."

"Aye, it is," she said, coming to me. When I stepped away, she said in a quick and desperate voice, "You are a fool if you do not hear this."

"No," I said. "I was a fool before. Look what your counsel has brought us. 'Tis time I listened to someone else."

"You've been quick enough to take the blame for this. I wonder that you do not want to affect the cure."

"And you have taken no blame at all," I pointed out. "Which of us is wrong? Dear God, my daughter is ailing; you have tormented me for weeks with your concern. I would think you would be anxious to see her well."

"I am. But this is not the way."

For a moment, I wavered. Then I heard Charity stirring in the room beyond, and I knew my answers must come from God alone.

I said, "I'm taking her to Ingersoll's."

"You cannot do this. Please, Lucas. Take her to town. The Pooles want her—"

"The village needs her more."

"There are others who can do that work. Would you sacrifice your daughter to this . . . this madness?"

"I will be with her. There's no need for further sacrifice."

Susannah hesitated. She glanced back at Jude, who had gone to the fire, and I closed my eyes in dismay, for in my distress I'd forgotten she was even there.

"Then I will come with you," Susannah said.

I did not argue with her. When Charity and I set out for Ingersoll's, Susannah and Jude followed.

The mud and ice of the ordinary green was overflowing with people, the tavern door left open. Villagers lingered in the doorway, talking in loud and animated voices while they waited for the examinations to start in the meetinghouse next door. The smell of beer and roasting meat hung heavy in the damp air. There was anticipation and anxiety too—for every neighbor who greeted me solemnly, there was another alight with excitement, as if this were some merry entertainment.

I hurried Charity through them, into the ordinary, thinking 'twas time to get this over with, though I could not say even in my mind what *this* was, or what I thought would happen, what I expected to see. I pushed through the crowd, letting Susannah follow with Jude behind. A short ways into the ordinary, Charity stopped suddenly, yanking on my arm, and I saw that she was staring straight ahead. I followed her gaze and felt a sinking in my stomach when I saw what she looked at. Her friends. The afflicted girls.

They sat together at a table, crowded around it the way they'd been the day of Faith's baptism—so long ago now that it seemed like another world. They were guarded over by Tom Putnam and his brother Edward and Samuel Parris, along with Doctor Griggs and Nicholas Noyes and John Hale. The magistrates were at a nearby table, eating heartily. The prisoners had not yet been brought from the jail, and just now the atmosphere was loud and drunken and cast with anticipation.

William Griggs glanced up just then and caught my eye, grimly gesturing for me to come forward.

At the table, one of the oldest girls—Mary Walcott—went suddenly still. She had been knitting; there was already a goodly length of green fabric trailing across the table. Now her needles stopped their relentless movement. She swiveled hard, staring into the crowd with narrowed eyes, staring at Charity. My daughter gasped and halted so quickly I nearly stumbled.

The crowd began to murmur—I thought for a moment 'twas because of Charity, but then I heard a shout from outside that grew in intensity and volume. "They're here! The prisoners're here!"

The crowd seemed to turn as one; a wave of noise passed from the door to where the girls sat. A dozen necks craned to see out the windows. But Charity did not take her eyes from her friends, and so neither did I. 'Twas as if the hand of God came down upon them in one swipe; in the same moment, the little Putnam girl went stiff and Abigail Williams began to shake and scream. Mercy Lewis pressed into a corner as if she were being attacked on all sides, swatting at the air.

Through the crowd, I heard a shout—"Lucas, you must take her from here!" Susannah's voice. In that moment, I realized that Charity was trembling as one with a fatal fever; her face had gone gray. She slipped from my hold, sagging to the floor with a moan like a wounded animal.

The crowd backed away, soft cries of alarm and concern mixing with the animal noises coming from my daughter's throat, the screams of the other girls. I fell to my knees beside her. "No, Charity, no," I whispered. She had gone boneless where before she'd been rigid, so I could not keep my hold on her. Desperately I shook her. "Charity. Charity, come back to me," but it was clear she no longer saw or heard me. When I looked into her eyes, I saw she was there, but not there, a strange contradiction, one I could not measure.

I heard another cry from beyond, and another. The magistrates leaped to their feet; tankards spilled, splashing through the din. Corwin shouted at the crowd to be silent—a useless order; he could barely be heard beyond a few feet. Parris began to pray loudly.

My own daughter fought me with every movement. She was making that terrible gurgling sound that reminded me of the first time I'd seen her thus, on the parlor floor, shaking at the horror she'd seen: her own father fornicating with his sister. . . .

"She . . . hurts . . . me," she moaned.

"Who hurts you?" I asked desperately. "Who does this to you?"

"She is pinching Charity!" the Putnam girl called out. "Oh, make her stop; please make her stop!"

Noyes frowned. "Who afflicts her? Is it Goody Good? Or Osborne? Is it Tituba?"

"No, no, someone else," said Annie. "Someone else."

"Who is it?" Parris asked.

"I do not know. Oh, I do not know."

Charity would not tolerate my hands. Desperately I cried, "Will someone not help me?" and saw how they backed away—except for one person. One person, who pushed through the crowd.

Susannah.

I had been looking for her, I realized, and this realization shocked me. My anger over what we'd done had not faded in any way, yet when I saw her, I was strangely relieved. Jude clung to her legs, her little cap askew, her light brown hair straggling into her face. Her hold was so tight that Susannah could barely move, but still she came toward me.

Then, suddenly, she stopped. Her gaze went past me, and I turned to follow it and saw that Charity had gone still. Charity was staring at her as if all the horrors of the world had lit upon Susannah's face. Then my daughter screamed and curled into a ball, throwing her arms over the back of her neck as if to protect herself.

Mary Walcott shouted, "Oh, be gone, you wretched spirit!" She stood now at the table, her eyes wide and dark. She pointed with a knitting needle into the air. "Leave Charity be! Stop hitting her! Oh, look at her prance around—'tis as if she's on the stage! 'Tis a red bodice she wears—oh, you vain creature!"

I went cold.

"Who is it?" Parris asked. "Who hits her? Who?"

Charity launched to her feet with such force the crowd swayed back. " 'Tis the black man standing beside her. He whispers to her! Oh, Father, make her stop! Stop!"

"Who is it, Charity?" I asked—I could hardly hear my own voice. "What are you saying?"

Her gaze cast through the crowd. With growing horror, I followed it. With a shaking hand, she pointed to Susannah.

Mary Walcott said, "Leave her alone, Susannah Morrow! Have you not punished her enough?"

The name landed with the force of thunder. I heard it ringing in my ears. I heard Charity's cry, "Aye, aye, 'tis her!" and the gasp of my neighbors, Jude's whimper of dismay. I could not even move. I could do nothing but stand in shock, even though I had known. . . .

I had known this would come. I had known. . . . Everything I'd questioned rushed back to me: Charity's fear of her aunt, Susannah's reluctance to bring her here, the way she'd quieted Faith. And most damning . . . most damning of all: my own inability to resist her.

I looked at her. She was staring at me as if to find strength from my face, but when I met her eyes, she went pale and shrank away as if she recognized my thoughts and had no defense against them.

The girls took up the cry: "Susannah Morrow, Susannah Morrow . . ." I saw her grasp Jude by the hand and step backward into the crowd. I made no move to stop her as she disappeared. My own confusion was too great; there was even a part of me that urged her to run.

"Where has she gone?" someone asked, and I realized they were looking for Susannah, and that Charity had taken her place at the table with the other girls. No longer my own daughter, but belonging now to this crowd, to these accusers, to Tom Putnam, who listened with a grim expression to her charges.

From the door of the ordinary, I heard the call, "The girls! We need the girls in the meetinghouse!" I turned to see Ezekiel Cheever pushing through the crowd, and beyond him, through the window, I saw the form of Susannah's blue cloak, and Jude beside her, hurrying down the path with Hannah Penney. I felt an uncomfortable and strange relief.

Ezekiel arrived red-faced to the table. He was breathing hard; his words came in gasps. "The prisoners are waiting, Your Honors. 'Twould be better if we could start soon. The crowds . . ."

Hathorne nodded. With an abrupt and authoritative gesture, he motioned to the crowd. "We'll adjourn to the meetinghouse."

'Twas like a river moving toward the door. Within moments, my neighbors were emptying from the ordinary, and the girls went suddenly calm again, as if soothed by God's giant hand. Edward Putnam and Tom began to lead them out, along with the ministers. I was the only one unmoving, and as they passed, I grabbed Charity's hand and pulled her from her friends.

Tom reached for her. "We need her testimony, Lucas."

"Not hers," I said. "Not for these women. Charity has said nothing of those accused now."

"She may—"

"No," I said firmly. "She will not go today."

"Release her, man," came John Hathorne's voice. He had stopped at the door, and he motioned impatiently for me to let my daughter go. "She is a witness now. We shall return her to you at the end of the examinations."

Tom took her arm, and I reluctantly released my hold on my daughter. She went with him as easily as a lamb, with only a final look back at me—her gaze troubled and dark, confused. Her arms were covered with welts that were beginning already to fade, as if she were recovering from some terrible disease.

But I knew better. She was not recovering; she was in the very midst of it, and I was afraid for her. I could not leave her.

Quickly I followed after.

The meetinghouse was as crowded today as it had been yesterday, more so, I thought, because those who had not heard the first day of examinations had rushed to listen now. I cared nothing for it, not at first. When Sarah Good was led in and questioned again, I watched Charity as she called out with the others. In my wretchedness, I could not even listen to the testimony. I heard nothing but her cries until Hathorne said, "Who among you is William Allen?"

William rose, twisting his hat in his hands. "I am he."

"Did you not testify that this woman came into your chamber one night and sat upon your feet?" Hathorne asked.

I thought of a cold winter night, of Susannah standing at the end of my bed, with scarlet all around. It had been a dream, I'd thought. Only a dream. Had it not been?

"'Tis true," said William. "She bore a strange light with her. When I . . . When I kicked at her, she went away."

"What say you to this, Goody Good?"

"I was never in that man's house," the woman replied. "He lies to spite me."

"Why do you not say the truth?"

"'Tis no truth I know."

I listened in growing dread. It had been a dream. Yet, I could not help but remember how real I'd found it, how I'd burst from my bed to follow a figment of my imagination, how the window had been opened when it had been closed before, how solid she'd felt.

I had thought only the afflicted saw the specters. Only the girls in their torments. But William Allen was a hardworking man not given to flights of fancy, and his experience was enough like my own that I could not discount it.

'Twas then the word came into my mind: bewitchment. And this time it had a power I could not ignore.

Chapter 28

WHEN THE EXAMINATIONS WERE OVER, AND THE PRISONERS WERE led from the meetinghouse, and then the afflicted girls, I hurried after them. Tom had already forgotten his promise to return Charity to me; he had a tight hold on her arm as he led her down the path. When I rushed to him and stopped him with a shout, he looked disconcerted and faintly guilty.

"I had come to find you," he said, though I did not think it was the truth. "Do you think it wise, Lucas, to take her back to your house now, given what has happened?"

I glanced at Charity, who was blank and exhausted. There was nothing in her eyes, not even recognition of me. She stood as one whose spirit had left her. "She is my daughter," I said. "Do you not trust me to know what's best for her?"

Tom looked flustered. "I have not questioned that. But this child called out on your wife's sister, who lives with you. Until we can inquire into this latest accusation, I cannot believe 'tis safe for her to be there."

"Where would you suggest?"

"There is room at my house—"

"No." I took Charity's other arm. "I will find a place for her myself."

"As you wish. But it would be good to keep her close to the village for now. We will need all those who see the specters." Tom stepped away, but before he had gone many feet, he stopped again and turned back to me. "What think you, Lucas?" he asked in a quiet voice. "We had all thought this would end after the first three were arrested. But there has been no relief. Mary Warren was afflicted today as well, and my own wife . . ." He paused, obviously pained. "My own wife has begun to see visions. If we are to believe Tituba, there are many more witches. Yet this time we are not talking of beggars or slaves. I think . . . we must tread carefully here. Shall we believe that your sister is one of them?"

I knew what he was asking me: whether or not I would deny my daughter, whether there should be a pursuit of the accusation against Susannah, if I would join them in it. I did not yet know how to answer him.

"Let me talk to Charity," I told him.

Tom hesitated, and I saw the suspicion cross his eyes and knew that he, too, wondered about my relationship with my wife's sister, that he believed I would try to influence my daughter to exonerate Susannah. Though I cared little for Tom, what I saw on his face wounded me. I found myself wanting to say to him, *Do not be so quick to judge me. I am so uncertain.*

I bit my tongue until he walked away. Then I looked again to my daughter, who stood listlessly beside me. "Shall we go home, Charity?"

She roused. The fear that came into her eyes was inescapable. "Home? Is she there?"

"Aye."

"I cannot go there."

I had meant to question her about Susannah, but with those words, there was no need.

The wind blew, cold and damp, and Charity shivered. There were few of my neighbors remaining; even Ingersoll's had emptied, and so I led her there, seating her on a bench at the end of a table and gesturing to Sarah Ingersoll for a pitcher of beer. When it came,

I poured some for myself and my daughter, but Charity pushed it away, saying that the smell nauseated her.

"Pray with me," I said.

Charity looked at me with clear pale eyes. "Aye. We should pray for truth, Father. Though I wonder . . . Will you know it when you see it?"

She had never spoken to me such, and I was stunned into silence.

"You said the Devil has found your weakness," she went on. "Do you really believe so, Father? I-I do not think I can fight him alone."

I took her hand; her skin was so icy cold 'twas strange to touch it. I gripped her fingers to warm them. "I am still myself, Charity. I will not leave you to fight alone."

Tears came quickly and suddenly to her eyes so they shone blankly, like the surface of a mirror. She drew her hand from mine and hugged herself tightly, withdrawing from me.

Sarah Ingersoll came over. "Will you be having something to eat, Lucas?"

"No," I said, and then as she made to step away, I stopped her. "Sarah . . ."

She glanced at Charity, who had put her head into the crook of her arms, obviously exhausted. "Whatever I can do, Lucas," Sarah said kindly. "You know that."

"Will you keep her here for me?"

Sarah hesitated only a moment. "Are you sure this is what you want?"

I did not pretend to misunderstand. There was no love lost between myself and the owner of the ordinary, Nathaniel Ingersoll, who was Sarah's father. He was a deacon in Parris's church, one of Tom Putnam's best friends. Keeping Charity here was akin to leaving her with Putnam, except that now Ann Putnam senior was having visions as well. Here, at least, was Sarah's cautious hand. She and I had been friends many years, in spite of the fact that her father and

I disagreed on village politics. I could trust Charity with her. I did not doubt it.

"Aye," I said. "If you would promise to care for her."

Sarah nodded somberly. "I'll care for her as if she were my own."

Together she and I took Charity upstairs. There was a small storage room at the back of the house, with a bed surrounded by casks of beer and kegs of Canary and Malaga. When Charity was settled onto the mattress, I stood staring at her for a moment after Sarah left. I pressed a kiss to her forehead, and she did not stir, not even when I whispered again, "I will not let you fight alone." Finally, I left her, quiet and spent in the dark little room.

Sarah waited for me outside the door. "I will see no harm comes to her," she assured me, and I smiled my thanks at her and left the ordinary.

The moment I was outside in the cold gray of dusk, my thoughts turned to the woman who no doubt awaited me at home. She *was* a witch—Mary Walcott had called out her name; no wonder Susannah hadn't wanted Charity to go to the questioning—she knew she would be named.

I hurried for home, running faster when I thought of Jude, alone in the house with Susannah, of what I must do. When I rushed through the door to find Susannah and Jude at the settle by the fire, a perfect picture of domestic harmony, I prayed I was not too late.

When Susannah saw me, she put down her mending and rose, coming toward me with an uncertain smile. Then she stopped, glancing past me as if she expected to see someone else. Her smile changed to a frown. "Where's Charity?"

"I've left her at Ingersoll's."

"Would she not be safer at home?"

I heard the insincerity now. The sound of her voice was as a scraping on my skin.

"Is Charity very sick, Father?" Jude asked from the settle.

"She is sick with the pain of true righteousness," I said, ignoring Susannah's gasp.

Jude looked confused. "She said Auntie was a witch, but she's no witch, Father; I know it."

I said nothing; I could not. The despair I felt at her affirmation was overwhelming. I saw the way my daughter turned to Susannah, the bewildered plea on her face.

"Tell him, Auntie. Tell him you are not a witch."

Susannah paused. To me, she said, "I am not a witch."

I moved past her, saying, " 'Tis late, Jude. I will see you to bed."

Jude glanced again at Susannah. I moved to block her view and said again, "Come."

She came to me then, but not without a reluctance that pained me. I took the bed warmer and filled it with coals, then led her upstairs, settling it between her sheets. I waited while she crawled into the trundle and together we said a prayer to God for strength and forbearance.

When I was leaving, I heard her voice again, small and quiet. "She is not a witch, Father."

I went downstairs. Susannah stood at the table. "What is it?" she asked. "Why do you look at me so?"

"How else should I look at you after what happened today?"

"Come, Lucas, surely you do not believe—"

"My own daughter?"

She said quietly, "I am not a witch."

"Nor are Goody Good or Goody Osborne by their own admission. If that is true, then what do those girls see? Why does Tituba confess?"

"Perhaps because your pastor beats her."

"What of the girls, then? Do you accuse them of dissembling?"

"Some of them. Mary Walcott, yes. The older Parris girl, probably."

"And what of Charity? What of her?"

She had the grace to hesitate. "Charity is . . . troubled."

"Aye. Troubled. As would any girl be who saw her father—"

She held up her hand to stop me. "Don't say it, Lucas. Do not torture yourself this way. You cannot blame yourself."

"Who else should I blame? You?"

She looked startled, as I had expected her to—how often was the Devil required to answer for his deeds?—and then she said, "Could it not be that no one is at fault? There are things that just happen, Lucas. Perhaps the stars lined up in just such a way, or the Fates—"

"I cannot attribute this to luck."

"Charity's troubles started long before last night. There is Sam—"

I heard the name and rage swept over me. "Do not dare impugn my daughter in my hearing again. This is none of Sam's doing, but yours. Charity's troubles began the day you set foot in this house."

"You cannot believe that."

"I cannot believe the other."

Her voice was careful, devoid of emotion. "Charity has deluded herself."

"The Devil would answer the same."

"What would you have me do to prove my innocence?" she asked desperately. There was fear in her eyes, an expression that reminded me somehow of Judith. "I am your lover, Lucas. You can deny it, but that does not make it less true. Think of what we are to each other. Please . . . do not let your guilt delude you too."

"That I should live with such sin—" I began.

"What is between us is no sin."

I snorted my contempt at her words. "What would you call it then? Bewitchment? Obsession? I know what you have done to me. I had thought 'twas only a dream, but 'twas your specter instead, putting a spell upon me—"

"I don't know what you mean."

"Of course you do," I said. "Did you not order your specter to climb onto me, to sit upon my hips in the dead of night, to hold me still so I couldn't breathe? Did you not order it to say that you would have me, whether I willed it or not?"

"No," she whispered. "No. I don't understand you, Lucas. I never did such a thing."

Her denial was fodder for the fire building in me. "I wondered why I saw no footprints in the snow outside my window when you left, but Tituba answered that for me. What long pole did you fly away on? Do you keep it in this house? Tell me, so I can burn the cursed thing."

She shook her head. "I never flew on a pole. I never went to your bed, Lucas, not without your wanting me there. It must have been a dream."

"What dreams have such real power? I could feel you. You were as real as you stand before me now."

"Perhaps 'twas a very real dream, then," she said, "but a dream, nonetheless. Things are not always what they seem, Lucas. You know that. When I first came here, I believed you beat your children and Judith."

She was adept at this, this switch in subject, the turning back of guilt, the Devil's trick.

"I cannot explain this by a misunderstanding," I said. "Nor can you."

"I have explained it. 'Twas a dream."

"William Allen was visited by Sarah Good's specter too. Do you know about that? Is it a trick all in the Devil's service must learn?"

"I cannot answer that."

"Cannot? Or will not? She did the same to him as you did to me. She sat upon him. She held him prisoner in his own bed for an hour."

Susannah glanced away. "Such nonsense. Is that what was said at the examinations today? Is that what you would use to condemn me?" She looked back to me again. "You cannot do this. I know what you think, Lucas—if I'm the Devil, meant to tempt you, 'twill appease your guilt; 'twill absolve your sins. But there is no sin here, and I am not a sacrifice to be made to your God. I love you—"

"What can you know of love? You could not even bring yourself to marry the men you lived with. When you tired of them, you left. What can you know of the kind of love that keeps a man and woman together for seventeen years? What can you know of sacrifice?"

I used my words like weapons, battering her, and she went white with hurt. I buried my remorse with savagery—the Devil would turn my own emotions against me, and I would not give him the chance. I turned on my heel, starting to the parlor, but then I remembered Jude upstairs, sleeping and vulnerable, in danger now that Charity had exposed Susannah.

"I want you in the parlor tonight," I said, "or in the cellar. I don't want you near Jude. I will sleep out here on the settle to make sure you stay away from her."

She stared at me in disbelief. "You cannot mean it."

"Aye, I do. What choice will you make? The parlor? Or the cellar?"

She paused, and then she said quietly, "The parlor." I stepped back from the door and motioned for her to go to it. She hesitated as she passed me. I held firm.

Chapter 29

I WOKE TO THE SOUND OF SUSANNAH TENDING THE FIRE. I SAT UP, sore from a night on the settle, disoriented.

There was a knock on the door.

Susannah jumped and spun around, spilling a handful of meal onto the hearth in her surprise. Clearly, she thought it was the warrant for her arrest, and I knew it could be. Wearily I made my way to the door.

I was not sure whom I expected to see. One of the constables, perhaps, or Tom Putnam. Even Samuel Parris would not have been a surprise. But when I opened it to find Nicholas Noyes standing on the doorstep, I was perplexed. "Parson. 'Tis an unexpected visit."

"Forgive me for coming at such an early hour, Lucas," Noyes said. "I've come to talk to your sister."

I ushered him in, saying, "Susannah—'tis Nicholas Noyes. The parson from town."

She stood stiffly, her hands clenched tightly before her. "Good morning, sir," she said. She let silence fall after, and 'twas loud and uncomfortable.

Noyes shuffled within it. "I-I've been asked to speak to you regarding our poor afflicted ones."

"I know already of their accusations," she said. "Have you come to arrest me?"

He shook his head and smiled wanly. "This needs care, as I'm sure you realize. There is no point in haste—no one wishes to make arrests in error. The whole village greatly admired your sister. Even in town, we knew of dear Judith's good works."

I understood then why he was here, what he hoped to gain. Susannah was no beggar, no scandalous woman, and no slave. My family was respectable, and she was a part of it. Despite their suspicions, and the girls' outright accusations, they were wary now of making a mistake.

I saw Susannah's puzzlement. "Are you saying . . . 'tis my sister's reputation alone that has saved me?"

"We would take care in this," Noyes said again. "And to that purpose . . . I've come to take you to Thomas Putnam's house."

"Why?"

"Three of the girls are there. Little Annie, of course, and her cousin Mary Walcott. Mercy Lewis as well. John Hale and I have been counseling caution. We believe 'twould be wise for you to talk to the girls."

"You want me to talk to them?" Susannah's eyes, her voice, radiated skepticism.

"We'd like to see if perhaps there has been . . . a mistake. You understand, we would be sure in this."

"Do I have a choice in this?" she asked.

Noyes looked at her. " 'Twould be best, I think, for you to talk to these girls."

"You did not answer my question. I asked you: Do I have a choice in this?"

"No. I'm sorry."

Susannah took a deep breath. Then she took off her apron. Her hands smoothed over her skirt, went to her hair—'twas as if she primped for company. I could do nothing but watch her, even as she turned to me one last time before she grabbed her cloak and went with Noyes out the door. Her expression was as blank as Charity's had been yesterday, and I felt the familiarity of that look as a chill that cut straight into my bowels.

I was too weak in this, and dangerously alone. I needed help. Guidance. Someone to give me the strength to keep my children safe. There was only one man I could trust with my deepest fears. Sam Nurse.

I took Jude to the Penneys' house, where I left her with Hannah and Faith. I instructed her not to return home until I fetched her. Then I went to find Sam.

I told him everything. My friend listened to the whole, sordid tale, and then he nodded in silent understanding, and I did not feel so alone. Together we went to the magistrates, and I told my tale again—without saying to Jonathan Corwin the one thing that mattered. That Susannah and I had been lovers was a sin I could not admit—to tell Sam was one thing; to write it down for my neighbors to gossip over . . . that I could not do.

Sam stood at the back of the room, silently supportive through the three hours I was there. After I'd told my story, Corwin sat silently, reading over my words as he rubbed his closely shaven beard. The red-gold hairs glinted in the candlelight.

Finally he put aside the paper I'd signed and looked up at me. "These words are true, as you know them?"

I nodded. "Aye. I've written no lies."

"When did your sister come to this place?"

"October twenty-second."

"You remember it well," Corwin said in surprise.

" 'Twas the night my youngest daughter was born," I told him bitterly. "The night my wife died in childbed. I'm not likely to forget it soon."

"She's your own family."

I closed my eyes briefly. "I'm afraid, with my wife's death, I was not so vigilant as I should have been. Satan found an open door— no one is more ashamed of that than I. I have prayed for forgiveness. I have done my best to strengthen my family against his onslaught. Had I been successful . . . there would be no need to come to you now."

Corwin watched me steadily. "Your own daughter is much besieged."

"Aye. My regret is that she warned me about Susannah, and I didn't listen. I could not believe—"

"'Twould have been difficult, I think," Corwin said, sitting up and handing the paper I'd dictated back to Ezekiel Cheever. "Judith was so good. To believe ill of her sister . . ."

I said nothing to this. I thought of all the stories my wife had told me, all the reasons I should have known what Susannah was from the beginning. The truth was, I had thought ill of her before I even knew her. 'Twas another thing I could not explain, because to explain it would reveal how driven I was by my passions, how Susannah had used such a terrible weakness—my carnal nature—against me.

"You are not the only one to speak out against her," Corwin said. "There has been other testimony since yesterday."

That surprised me. "Has there been? Who?"

Corwin shrugged. "There were many witnesses who saw her use magical chants to calm a child during a baptism. Another man has come forward with a spectral visitation similar to yours. A woman claimed her child went into convulsions and died soon after your sister passed by. There are other tales as well. I cannot afford to dismiss anything now, not with circumstances as they are. We wait only to see if the girls continue to call out against her."

"And then?"

Corwin met my gaze steadily. "If all continues as I expect, we will issue the arrest warrant tomorrow."

I rose, mumbling my thanks.

"Thank you for coming forward, Goodman Fowler," Corwin called after me. "We shall see that the Devil finds no reason to tarry in Salem Village."

Aye, 'twas what we were doing, I knew. Providing fallow ground for the Devil's seeds.

"You did the right thing," Sam assured me as we went outside. "You had no choice. If she is a witch, 'tis best to reveal her now, before she can do more damage."

I had no words as he left me. I thought I was heading toward home, but then I found myself going a different direction, deeper into the village, to Ingersoll's.

There were men there, sitting at tables and drinking beer. The smell of stew and fire smoke was deep and heavy. When Sarah saw me, she came hurrying over.

"Charity's been asking after you," she told me in a low voice. "I heard they've taken Susannah over to Putnam's today. She heard it as well; 'tis no keeping her from news here."

I nodded. "I did not expect to."

"Tom wanted Charity there, but I said he'd have to take it up with you."

"I'm grateful for that," I said, though it hardly seemed to matter now, not given where I'd just been, what I'd done. "Where is she?"

"Upstairs."

I hurried past her, up the stairs, back to the little storage room where I'd left Charity only yesterday—years ago now, it seemed. I knocked upon the closed door and heard the shuffling of her feet, and then she was peering at me through the crack, my blue-eyed, pallid daughter.

"Father," she said, and there was surprise in her voice—and relief, genuine pleasure. "Oh, Father."

She opened the door fully and came into my arms; I was so undone by her greeting and my own emptiness that I held her tight. "How do you, child?"

She pulled away, her expression miserable. "I am not well."

I took her shoulders and held her so she could not do otherwise than meet my eyes. "I went to the magistrates today. I testified against your aunt. Jonathan Corwin has told me they will issue an arrest warrant for her tomorrow. She will no longer torment you, Charity. She cannot hurt you again."

Tears came into her eyes, a pure and overwhelming relief. 'Twas then I realized why I was here, what I wanted from my daughter. I was looking for redemption, for forgiveness. 'Twas in her eyes now, a light that filled my heart, a supreme comfort. Whatever doubts I'd harbored fled; to see Charity's hope at my allegiance was as the greatest restorative.

She came again into my arms, throwing her hands around my neck, holding me close. I felt her joy and triumph—I had not seen those things in my daughter for so long that now the memory of how I loved them came sweetly back to me. I had not known how much I had missed them.

Then I heard her whisper against my ear, "Make sure they chain her, Father. Their specters can escape if they are not chained." And the sweetness of her joy fled in my sudden realization of what we'd done, of what it meant.

Susannah had not returned when I fetched Jude from Hannah's and came home. It had begun to sleet, and 'twas nearly dark before I heard the latch turn at the door. Susannah hurried inside, her blue cloak so wet 'twas nearly black, her skin pink from cold, her hands red when she peeled off her gloves. There was no sign of Noyes behind her, and I had heard no horse bring her up the path—nor did I hear one leave.

She was sober and quiet. I did not need to ask her what had happened; I knew by the look on her face what her visit to Putnam's had been like. She seemed shaken and fearful, and I, with my knowledge of what would likely happen on the morrow, could not stay in the room with her. Hastily I put Jude to bed and curled up myself on Charity's feather bed, which had lately held Susannah too. My dreams were dark and lingering, and I woke exhausted and anxious.

They came for Susannah in the late morning. Jude and I were at the table, while Susannah chopped soaked cod for dinner. Susannah had been preoccupied and silent all morning long, her movements hurried and short. At the sound of the knock, she dropped the knife. It clattered to the hearth, and she let it lie. She put her hands on the board and bent her head. I saw her expectation in the stiff set of her shoulders—she knew what this was.

I rose and went to the door, and though I had expected it to be the warrant for her arrest, when I saw George Locker—one of the constables—standing at the door, I was startled anyway.

"George," I said. "Good morning."

"Not so good, I'm afraid." He handed me the paper that held the order, and I read it quickly:

> *Whereas Messers. John Londer, Lucas Fowler, Thomas Putnam, and Samuel and Sarah Shattuck of Salem Village in the County of Essex, personally appeared before us and made complaint on behalf of Their Majesties against Susannah Morrow, for suspicion of witchcraft by her committed, and thereby much injury done by Mary Walcott, Charity Fowler, Abigail Williams, Ann Putnam, Jr., and Mercy Lewis, all of Salem Village, contrary to the peace of our Sovereign Lord and Lady William and Mary, King and Queen of England, etc.—You are therefore in Their Majesties' names hereby required to apprehend and bring before us the said Susannah Morrow about eleven of the clock to the meetinghouse in Salem Village, and there to be examined, and hereof you are not to fail at your peril.*

It was signed by John Hathorne and Jonathan Corwin. 'Twas exactly as I'd imagined it would be, except for the inclusion of my name, which startled me, so that George Locker said again, "I am sorry, Lucas, but I must insist—"

Dutifully I stood back. Susannah had turned, and she was pale, though she faced us with a quiet equanimity that made me feel my name on that paper as if it were burned there. George Locker pushed past me in a disconcerting jangling of metal.

"'Tis a warrant for my arrest, is it not?" Susannah asked.

I held out the paper. "I—everything seems in order. 'Tis naught I can do—"

"And naught you would do, in any case," she said, her voice low as a whisper. Her words settled on me uneasily, though I should not have cared. Her punishment was just; I had only followed God's orders in making sure 'twas carried out.

George pushed back his cloak and reached for something. Black iron, chains—'twas a moment before I realized they were manacles.

"My God," Susannah murmured. It seemed her knees buckled for a moment; then she gained composure.

"Father?" Jude asked from the table. Her voice was high and plaintive. "Father, what is happening?"

"'Tis nothing, Jude," I said.

Jude stood, frowning in worry. "Auntie—"

Susannah smiled, though it seemed an effort. "'Tis nothing to fear, Jude. I'll go with the constable. 'Twill only be a few days, you'll see."

"I'll explain it to you later," I told my daughter.

Jude would have none of me. Her face was pinched and white. She did not take her eyes from Susannah. "You said you would not leave me."

"And I shall not. I shall not."

Jude began to cry. I went to her and pulled her tight against me. When George put the chains on Susannah, Jude gasped, and I whispered a prayer in her ear. She did not mind me. She went still as George opened the door to take her aunt away.

George said, "You're needed at the meetinghouse now, Lucas."

Then they were gone.

"Where have they taken her?" Jude asked.

"We must pray 'tis to her redemption," I said.

Jude jerked from me. "She is not a witch," she said, and ran to the door before I could stop her, wrenching it open. There was only rain beyond, gray and cold; they had already disappeared down the path, though the rattle of Susannah's chains still echoed, a mournful, eerie sound.

Chapter 30

———— ✦ ————

I TOOK JUDE TO THE PENNEYS' AND RAN AS QUICKLY AS I COULD INTO the village. Already the crowd had gathered, with members of the village militia lined up before the door to guard the way. Susannah and Locker were not yet here, though I could not have beat them; I assumed they held her somewhere until the girls could be gathered, and just as I had the thought, I looked up to see them led over from Ingersoll's. I searched the group until I found my daughter, who looked calm and at peace. Though I stood at the doorway, she did not seem to see me as Thomas Putnam and his brother took them inside. I followed, pushing my way to the bench behind where they were seated. Charity turned as if she sensed my presence.

"Do not be afraid, child," I reassured her. "All will soon be well."

'Twas then I heard the whisper starting from the back, the unmistakable sound of the accused being brought to the meetinghouse, and Charity cried out, leaping from her bench and falling to her knees along with the other girls. I grabbed her, holding her still, while Thomas Putnam did the same for his daughter, and my neighbors came forward to help some of the others. Charity struggled mightily in my arms. 'Twas nothing but sound and chaos, and through it all, I saw the top of Susannah's head as Locker led her down the aisle; I heard the clank of those chains.

They brought her to the front, and she turned to look at the girls. Her gaze went from one to the other, finally lighting on Charity . . . then looking past her. To me.

She moved toward me, crying out, "Lucas—"

Locker yanked on the chain, and she stumbled back; whatever other words she'd meant to say died in her throat. The sound of my name lingered in my ears. Charity's fingers curled like claws around my arm.

"Turn her away from them!" Corwin shouted from the magistrates' table, and Locker obliged, roughly turning Susannah from the girls, pushing her to the makeshift bar of justice.

Joseph Herrick, one of the other constables, came rushing up to stand on her other side, penning her in. "Do not look at them!" he shouted at her when she tried to turn back again. "Keep your eyes away." He put her hands on the bar. She stood facing the judges, her eyes directly on them, never glancing to the chaos of the girls.

The girls did not cease their afflictions. The crowd was unruly and loud; Susannah was the stillest person in the room.

John Hathorne went to stand before her. The crowd hushed, and Susannah glanced up as if she'd just realized Hathorne was there.

The crowd gasped. Someone said, "Dear Lord, she smiled!" and I saw Susannah's confusion, the way she looked to us as if searching for her error. Hathorne, too, seemed shaken, but only for a moment. Then he stepped closer, and his words were loud and ringing, unaffected by the vibrant presence of her.

"Susannah Morrow, you here stand charged with sundry acts of witchcraft. The afflicted persons are even now dreadfully affected by you."

"I am innocent," Susannah said in a low voice. "I have done no witchcraft."

Hathorne turned to the girls. "Look upon this woman and see if she be the one who has been hurting you."

Mary Walcott shouted out, "Aye! 'Tis her! 'Tis her!"

Charity shoved against my arms. "Oh, Aunt, why do you torture me so!"

Hathorne said, "What do you say now that they charge you to your face?"

"I have never hurt them," Susannah told him. "I barely know them."

"You barely know them? You barely know your own niece? Your sister's child?"

"Oh, aye." She lifted her hand weakly, and the girls went suddenly still, each lifting a hand as well. 'Twas an affliction too horrifying to stand, as if they were mere puppets, controlled by Susannah's strings. The crowd quieted; every eye was on the girls as Susannah said, "Of course I know Charity. I love her as if she were my own. I have never hurt her."

" 'Tis not what she says."

" 'Tis her imagination then. I have never intended to hurt her."

"What contract have you made with the Devil?"

Susannah shook her head. As if pulled by a single string, each girl shook her head.

"Dear God!" someone called out. "What horror is this?"

Susannah paused. She tried to turn her head farther, to look at the girls, but Herrick stepped up closer, and she frowned and turned back to Hathorne.

"What contract have you made with Satan?" Hathorne pressed.

"None. I have made no contract with him."

"She lies!" young Annie Putnam called out. "She calls the Devil her God!"

Mary Walcott shouted, "She asked me to sign the Devil's book! She took my hand and said if I did not, she would cut it off!"

"It is not true," Susannah said, but the other voices drowned her out. She quieted, biting her lip.

"Look how she bites her lip!" Charity screamed. She jerked out her arm, which held the proof, a bite mark so pronounced that I was amazed. How had the specter done this, when I was holding her so tightly? "She is biting me! She bites me! Owww! Look at this! Look at this!"

"And me!" Elizabeth Hubbard, the doctor's niece, leaped up.

"And me!"

Hathorne turned away in concern, walking to where we stood. He motioned to me to release my daughter. When I did, Charity and Elizabeth Hubbard and Mary Walcott ran up to the magistrates' table, where they pushed in between Ezekiel Cheever, who wrote feverishly, and Jonathan Corwin. The crowd was silent as Corwin looked them over.

"There are bite marks," he said grimly to Hathorne. "These poor children have been bitten."

"No," Susannah said. At the desk, Charity and her friends fell into convulsions. Susannah lifted her hand as if to halt them, and they each lifted a hand, even from where they lay on the floor, as if forced to the movement.

"Dear God, stop her!" Tom Putnam called out in anguish. "Hold her still!"

Joseph Herrick grabbed Susannah's hand, and forced it again to the bar. Locker leaned over to whisper something in Hathorne's ear, and the magistrate nodded sternly and went over to Susannah again.

"How came it that when you passed the meetinghouse this hour a board fell?"

She looked confused. "I . . . I don't know. 'Twas loose, I think."

He waved to Locker, who stood smugly by. "This witness says 'twas solid."

"I have no power to affect buildings," she said.

"What power do you have?"

"None. I have no power."

Hathorne's voice rose. "What contract have you with the Devil?"

"I've made no contract with him."

"She lies!" Charity called out. She rose to her knees. "She

brought the Devil into our house! She bade me lie to my father—not once, but many times!"

The words she said brought such a misery into my soul I could hardly stand to hear them. The room now was charged with my failure, with the true horror of what I had allowed to happen to my family. Tom Putnam looked at me, a measuring glance that was at once pitying and satisfied, and I looked away, wishing this was over, wishing Susannah were gone. Locked far away, someplace where I might never see her.

"What say you to all this you are charged with?" Hathorne asked Susannah. "Can you not find it in your heart to tell the truth?"

"I do tell the truth."

Hathorne turned to look at my daughter. "What say you, Charity Fowler? What testimony do you make against your aunt? What is the truth?"

At the question, Susannah's fingers gripped the back of the chair so hard her knuckles stood out in clear relief.

Charity stood. She was calm, and her voice was even, almost a recitation, as if she had the words from another place. She did not look at me, or her aunt, but only at Hathorne. "She knows spells. She taught them to my sister, to make her sewing neat, to make the butter come. She has tormented me in visions. She bade me join the Devil. She followed me where I went and told me to lie to my father. I have seen her with the black man—there he is now, beside her! Oh, look how he whispers in her ear!"

"He strokes her cheek!" Mary Walcott called out. "He has given her a little bird to suckle!"

"A yellow bird!" another shouted.

"I have no bird," Susannah whispered.

From the back of the meetinghouse, a woman said, "Did you see the way she calmed that baby in meeting? Why, 'twas the Devil's song she whispered!"

"She wears the Devil's clothes! Such a worldly woman!"

"No," Susannah said—uselessly; the evidence was mounting before her. "These things are not true."

"How came you into my bedchamber one morning and held me down by my throat?"

For a moment, I thought I'd spoken. They were my words. I saw Susannah jerk around, searching the crowd for me; then, in confusion, she looked beyond me, to the man who'd spoken, to John Londer. The girls fell back as if her glance had pushed them. The constable grabbed her arm to hold her in place.

"'Tis a lie," she said roughly. "'Tis a lie."

Hathorne stepped before her, his eyes on fire. "If 'tis a lie, then why do others say the same? What do you say to the same accusation by your own brother?"

If John Londer's words had been a shock, Hathorne's were more so. I felt the stares of my neighbors, their speculation, their fears realized, and then I felt Susannah look upon me. I was a coward, a man who had just escaped the clutches of the Devil with his clothing still burning. I could not bring myself to look at her.

Hathorne pressed on. "What say you to this horrible act of witchcraft?"

"'Twas a dream he had. A dream only."

"A dream?" Hathorne asked with the full crush of sarcasm. "A dream, you say?" He swiveled on his heel. "Lucas Fowler, did you not say that this woman possessed you in your sleep? Did you not say that she held you down for nearly an hour with a strength so prodigious you could not move? Did you not say she disappeared through a window that was locked when you went to bed, but then it was opened?"

Slowly I looked up. I kept my gaze on Hathorne, though Susannah wavered like a wraith behind him. "Aye," I said quietly. Then, from the corner of my eye, I saw Charity standing there, waiting, and I said with a stronger voice, "Aye."

"Did you not say that she came back to your home one day,

after gathering flax, and though there had been a terrible rainstorm, she was not wet, not even her boots?"

I nodded. I remembered it well, though I'd attributed no power to it at the time, not until Corwin had said something during my deposition, and I suddenly remembered. "Aye. 'Tis true. She was not wet, though the horse was."

I saw Susannah's confusion, and then she glanced at Charity, who began to shake and pant as if her breath would not come, and I saw something come into Susannah's eyes, a memory quickly shielded, a lie, and I felt a strange hopelessness, a despair I could not name.

Charity clutched her throat. Her eyes rolled back in her head.

"Turn her away!" Corwin shouted.

"Not yet," Hathorne said. "Take the woman to the afflicted girl."

The constables each grabbed one of Susannah's arms, leading her from the bar over to Charity. Susannah did not resist when one of them pressed her hand down upon the linen cap covering Charity's hair.

The moment she touched my daughter, Charity quieted, as did every voice in that room. I stared at her in disbelief. There was a familiarity to her calm that I recognized. I remembered bringing William Griggs to the house only to find my daughter sound asleep, a blissful, strange, and even sleep. The realization of what Susannah must have done hit me. I looked up at her in horror.

"You made her sleep," I said, and she recoiled a little, as if stunned by what she saw in my face. "When I left for Griggs, 'twas you who made her sleep. What spell was that? What spell is this?"

"There was no spell," she said. "She was tired. Such fits tire her—"

"How know you this?" Hathorne boomed out.

I saw the panic in Susannah's eyes. William Griggs came forward from beneath the gallery and said, "She told me she cared nothing for how many witches there were in the village. She told me the Devil has only what power she gave him."

"I said nothing like that," she protested weakly. "You misheard. Lucas, tell him. Tell him the truth of what I said." She reached for me, but the constable's men dragged her back to the bar, and the girls cried out all around me, so I sat in the midst of a mad frenzy.

"Do you not see how they are tormented?" Hathorne shouted. "You are acting witchcraft before us. Why have you not a heart to tell us the truth?"

"I am innocent," Susannah cried. She struggled against the constable as if trying once more to see the girls.

"Turn her away!" someone called out.

"Have you not given consent that some evil spirit should do this in your likeness?"

She shook her head. The girls did the same. Elizabeth Hubbard's motion was so grotesque it seemed her head might twist off. With a cry, William Griggs pushed through the crowd to get to his niece.

Charity was unmoving now, cast under Susannah's spell, in a trance.

"No, no," Susannah said. She sounded desperate, caught. "I am innocent of this. I am no witch."

"They say 'tis your likeness that comes and torments them and tempts them to write in the book. What book is it that you tempted them with?"

"There is no book. I know nothing of it."

"Tell us the truth!" Hathorne thundered. He brought his fist down on a nearby table so hard Ezekiel Cheever jumped. "How came these persons to be so tormented? Why do they charge you with doing so?"

Susannah swayed, as if her strength had left her, as if she would have fallen without the constables holding her.

"She's going to swoon," Joseph Herrick said.

Hathorne said, "'Tis said you were an actor, on a stage. Is that where you met the Devil?"

"I am not a witch," she insisted. She sagged; one of the constables caught her against him.

"Take her away," Hathorne said finally. "We'll question her again later."

I stood there helpless, watching as they pulled her down the aisle so she stumbled and tilted, her hair loosened from her struggles, tumbling over her shoulders.

I should have been relieved. 'Twas over. I had done my duty; I had supported my daughter and rid the village of Susannah's wickedness. Though I had fallen to temptation, I had redeemed myself now. Surely God smiled upon me at last.

Yet I could not forget the expression on Susannah's face as I had said the words to condemn her. And I thought how odd it was that I had done this thing, this thing my daughter and my neighbors had wanted from me, this thing that should send the strength of righteousness bursting over me, and all I felt was a dull aching at my temples, an impatience over my daughter's screams, a sense . . . this terrible sense . . . that I had betrayed us all.

PART THREE

SUSANNAH

—Persuasion—

Men will fight for a superstition quite as quickly as
for a living truth—often more so, since a superstition
is so intangible you cannot get at it to refute it,
but truth is a point of view, and so is changeable.

—Hypatia of Alexandria

Chapter 31

———❦———

LOCKER AND HIS MEN LIFTED ME ONTO MY HORSE AND FASTENED the chains to the saddle. I still heard the screams of the girls in my head; Hathorne's face filled my vision yet, with his intense eyes and long jaw—a demon in the flesh. But the worst of it . . . Ah, the worst was Lucas.

Lucas, the man who had lain with me and held me and known me. Lucas, offering proof of my supposed covenant with Satan. . . . Dear God, I could not fathom it. I had suspected that Charity would speak against me, and her friends, but I had not expected it of Lucas, though I knew I should have. His torment had been too real, his despair over his daughter heartbreaking, and I knew. . . . He'd had no choice but to believe Charity.

Knowing this did not make my anguish more bearable; it only made me angry that I had not seen it before, that I had been so unprepared.

I had been afraid when they came to the house to arrest me. I had been afraid standing in that room, facing my accusers. But now I knew terror. I had told myself that the villagers were reasonable people, and if they were not, then certainly the magistrates would see the truth. But there were no reasonable people—the whole village was in the grip of this horror. I should have seen these things; I *had* seen these things. Last night, when Nicholas Noyes took me to Putnam's house and those girls had screamed that my specter was roasting a man over the fire—I had known what would happen. I should have run then from this town, and yet I had not wanted to be a coward. I had thought that together, Lucas and I could dissuade them. . . .

How foolish I had been. I had no friends here; I had depended on Lucas for everything; I had depended on his love for me. Now I could not help but remember the other night, when I'd longed for his comfort and he had told me bitterly to go into town to find a sailor. Those words came back to me, echoing of another time, of other words said nearly the same way. *You're better fit for a whore than a wife.* I saw again Geoffrey standing contemptuously at the door, watching as I packed my things to go to Robert, and now I wondered if perhaps 'twas true, what he'd said. What would I have seen had I dared to look deeper into Lucas's eyes—his love for me, or something else?

I sagged in the saddle. The horse stepped into a pothole and stumbled; the movement jarred me and I bit the side of my tongue. I cried out and Locker turned in his saddle to see, and then turned back again without a word.

We were going to town—I knew that. To jail.

But when we finally stopped, it was before a large, many-gabled house of dark wood. The constable dismounted and tied his horse.

"Where are we?" I asked in confusion. "Why have we stopped? Is this the jail?"

" 'Tis Judge Corwin's house," he told me.

Corwin's house. I had a sudden vision of the man, smaller than his counterpart, watching intently from the magistrates' table in the meetinghouse while Hathorne strode like an actor throughout the room. "Why?"

"More questioning," Locker said, coming back to unfasten the manacles from the saddle. This time, he took my arm to help me from the horse—if he had not, I would have rolled off the animal and lain helplessly in the street; I was so cold and exhausted I did not think I could make my legs work. The iron of the manacles froze the skin at my wrists. They were too large, so the rough edges balanced painfully against my bones, and so heavy 'twas an effort to lift my wrists, so I no longer tried.

He forced me up the puddled path to the house, and rapped sharply on the door. 'Twas answered by a young girl—a servant or a daughter.

"Constable Locker," he said.

She stepped back to allow us entry. "The judge said to meet him in his study."

She led us inside and turned sharply up a dark and narrow set of stairs. The constable pushed me ahead of him, propelling me up the stairs, because I could barely pick up my feet to move. The girl took us into a small room that held a desk and shelves of books and two chairs.

"They should be here shortly," she said, lighting a rack of candles. She went to the small window and drew the curtains, and I felt the sting of nerves, because the only reason for it, I could think, was to hide us from view.

I turned to Locker. "What else can they want from me? I answered all their questions."

He told the girl to fetch some beer and waited until she left, closing the door behind her, before he said to me, "They have only just begun."

I stared at him, dismayed, and he smiled. "We've taken more testimony against you than any of the others. There'll be questions yet."

"I cannot answer more questions," I told him.

'Twas then I heard the opening of the front door, and voices, the heavy clomp of boots and the low murmur of the servant girl. Corwin was here, along with someone else—perhaps even a few others, by the sound of it. I pressed back anxiously into my chair. The men were up the stairs in a moment, pushing into the small study: Jonathan Corwin and the preacher Nicholas Noyes.

Jonathan Corwin closed the door behind them, and the room became immediately dark and stuffy. No sooner had he closed it than the servant girl returned with the beer.

Corwin took it from her and poured beer into tankards and passed them around. I found myself leaning forward, my throat suddenly dry. I had not had a drink in several hours.

They did not pass one to me. I looked at Corwin. "Please," I said, "might I have a drink?"

Corwin paused in the midst of gulping from his tankard. He looked at me over the rim, and then set it down. "You're thirsty?"

"Aye. It has been a long time—"

"Did you hear her?" He looked at Noyes. "She's thirsty."

Locker and Noyes stood as if made of stone, studying me as if they feared I would turn into a demon before them. Corwin turned to me. "If you desire a drink, why do you not conjure one up? Surely the Devil would appease your thirst."

I closed my eyes briefly in quick exhaustion. Dully I said, "I have no covenant with the Devil."

"Why do you not tell the truth? We know that you do. We have testimony from several men who claim you visited them in their rooms in the night, that you were wearing a red bodice. Mary Walcott claimed that you bewitched Robert Proctor with that bodice. Your own brother—"

"They are wrong," I said quietly. "I have never visited with any of them. I did not bewitch Robert Proctor."

"There is an entire congregation that will say you used your demon spells to quiet a baby in meeting. Is that not true? What Devil has given you such spells?"

"'Tis not true. I know no demons."

"Your niece says you have used the demons of the air to find her and follow her."

"She is mistaken."

"Do you accuse her of lying? Do you accuse these other poor, afflicted girls of lying?"

I glared at him. "They would know best if they do. Why do you not ask them?"

He recoiled as if I'd struck him. Then he leaned close so I could smell the scent of beer on his breath, and my mouth went dry in want of it. "Lucas Fowler, your own sister's husband, has said you have bewitched him."

I turned away, determined to hide from them my hurt.

"What say you to that?"

When I didn't answer, he took a long draught of his tankard. Then he shoved that cursed beer close so I could smell it.

"Your spells made butter come. Samuel Shattuck says you walked by his son one day and the boy went into fits and has been ill ever after. What say you to this?"

"I do not know Samuel Shattuck and his son."

"What of Annie Putnam—do you know her?"

"I know of her. I have never spoken to the child."

"What of the day you were taken to her house, and she fell into fits and claimed you were roasting a man over the fire?"

I glanced to Nicholas Noyes, who stood silently watching by the door, his expression tight. I said, "I was nowhere near the fire."

"Can you deny 'twas your specter tormenting the girl?"

"I did not see what she saw." I gestured to Noyes. "Nor, I think, did the pastor."

Noyes's lips thinned. "I saw a child being dragged into the flames. I know it took two grown men to keep her from throwing herself upon them."

"I am not strong enough to drag Mercy Lewis into a fire," I retorted. "To drag two men as well would be impossible. I cannot imagine that my specter would find it any more likely."

"So you admit you have a specter."

I had been staring at Noyes. Corwin's words were so quick, I was flustered. "No . . . I mean—"

"How often does your specter meet with Satan?"

"I have never met—"

"How often does the Devil come to you?"

"I—"

"Why do you not tell us the truth? Why not confess?"

The smell of the beer tormented me—I was so thirsty 'twas hard to think. "There is nothing to confess."

"Can you deny you quieted the child in meeting?"

Wearily I said, "I cannot deny it."

"Do you deny urging your niece to lie?"

I tried to swallow; my throat was so dry I coughed.

Corwin's eyes bored into me. "Do you deny it? Do you deny that you do not listen to the prayers said in your own house, but disdain the word of God instead?"

The questions pounded me, another hour, two more. I stopped trying to answer. My head spun so, I thought I would swoon if I did not have a drink. Corwin kept that beer just out of my reach, close enough to see it. He refilled it twice, and smacked his lips noisily and greedily as he drank. The preacher stood back, watching, interjecting a question here and there. Locker said nothing, but went to the window, where he pulled back the curtain now and again to look out.

The world was fuzzy and gray before my eyes, Corwin's face distorted, when he finally stood in exasperation and gestured roughly to Locker.

"Take her to the jail. Fetch the surgeon and tell him I want a search done tomorrow with female witnesses."

Locker pulled me to my feet. I stumbled, falling into his chest, and he pushed me away more forcibly than he needed and yanked me from the room and down the steps again, out into the cold. 'Twas nearly dark now, the air freezing. This time, he did not bother to put me on the horse, but led me down the street, dragging me by my chains like a horse on a lead rope while I tripped and fell on the rough, muddied road.

When he finally stopped, I was filthy from feet to hips, and it was clammy, cold mud that cut through my cloak and my skirts and petticoats to my skin.

Before us was a building that looked too small to be a jail. 'Twas a single story only, with clapboards worn as gray and colorless as the sky. Just behind it was a narrow band of flat land and weedy hillocks and bog, the stinking wet mud and shallow water of a tidal river. "This cannot be the jail," I said.

"Aye, it is," the constable assured me. He jerked me to the door as if I were struggling against him, instead of merely stumbling over the icy mud of the street.

He went not to the main door, which was padlocked, but to a smaller one off a lean-to at the back. He did not bother to knock, but ushered me into a dark room barely lit by a single candle. I was assailed instantly with the stink of urine and filth. 'Twould have been bad enough on its own, but mixed in were odors of boiled cabbage and salt herring, and the stench of salt-washed mud and rot from the river.

"What's this?"

'Twas a man's voice, and as he spoke, I saw his shadow rise from a table, and without him blocking the hearth, the room became light enough to see. 'Twas a tiny place—a hearth, a large worktable, and kegs of what I took to be beer or cider lining the walls.

"Susannah Morrow," the constable said from beside me.

"Ah, yeah. We been expecting you, lady fair." The jailkeep smiled mockingly. He was tall and dark, dressed in filthy homespun, and his hair was spiky, as if he had not combed it in a goodly while. He wiped his arm across his face, and I saw the grease on his fingers, and looked beyond him to see the remains of a meal on the table. At his belt hung a ring of keys. "Come on, then," he said, motioning for us to follow.

I saw the door then, a door with a massive lock, and suddenly my knees would not bend; George Locker had to push me to make me move.

"Your friends were sent to Boston Jail yesterday," the jailkeep said.

"My friends?" I asked.

"Them other witches," he told me. "Lucky you, you'll have the cell to yourself for a piece. Not for long, though. I hear them girls are still calling names."

He unlocked the door and pulled it open, stopping for a moment to light a lantern before he stepped into darkness. The constable pushed me again, and I stumbled through, nearly falling, while the jailkeep laughed.

Here, the wet-rot smell of the river was stronger. 'Twas a room about twenty foot square, with three cells bearing a heavy door and a tiny barred window. Each was very small, and held two bunked beds with straw pallets, and a slop pail. There were windows along the hall, but they were small as well. It had not been warm in the outer room, though there had been a fire going, but 'twas a paradise compared to the cold here.

'Twas a horrible place, the most horrible I'd ever seen. But though I expected the jailkeep to open one of these barred doors, he continued on to another padlocked door half hidden in shadows. He gave me a lewd smile before he unlocked it as well, and pulled it open.

"Here's where you'll be. The witch dungeon." He laughed; 'twas an eerie sound that echoed in the darkness. The air turned dank, the kind of damp cold that creeps into bones. Before me were open slat stairs. The jailkeep took them as one familiar enough with a place that darkness was no barrier, and his lantern lit the way for the constable and me.

Again I balked—I could not walk past my dread. Locker pulled on the end of the chain binding my wrists, and I went. Down, down, and then into a room so cold and damp and foul I could not believe I was to stay here. It, too, was divided into cells, some too small even for a child. The stone floors were damp through my shoes, the low-ceilinged walls—made of brick and stone—dripped moisture that smelled of the mudflats. I heard a scurrying in the shadows, a squeak.

I began to tremble. There were no windows, only heavy iron sconces in the walls meant for lanterns or rushlights.

The jailkeep must have seen my horror. "Don't worry, lady fair. It ain't so bad. Sometimes them rats even sleep with you. They like to be warm too." He went to one of the larger cells. The key scraped and rattled in the lock; the door creaked as he pulled it open. He said to Locker, "You want to chain her to the wall?"

Locker shook his head. "There's no need."

The jailkeep shrugged. "As you wish." He turned to me. "But if you be trouble, I'll put 'em back on you right quick."

I looked at the constable. "You cannot leave me alone."

"You won't be alone," he said. "You've got Jem here to watch you."

Jem nodded. "I'll keep a good eye on you, lady fair. You bet I will."

That frightened me more than the rats and the dark, but I said nothing as George Locker closed the cell door and the lock clanged shut.

They left me then. Jem took the lantern. I watched that small bit of light grow fainter as they went up the stairs, and opened the door; then the light was gone, and I was in a darkness so deep I could not even see the denser shadow of myself within it.

I heard the steady drip of water down a wall, and the squeaking came again, a shuffle in the straw. Carefully I backed away, remembering where the bed was and moving in that direction, until I felt the rough wood of the bunk against my backside. I felt along it—just a straw pallet, without a blanket or a sheet. When I sat, I smelled dust and mildew—not even clean straw. Who knew how many other bodies had slept on it? Still, 'twas not on the ground, and I was grateful for that, though I knew how rats could climb.

In the lack of any other sound, my own breathing was loud and uneven. I pulled my cloak close about me, but the damp chill seeped steadily past it. I wished I had thought to bring a scarf, a blanket. I would have given much to have my fellow prisoners here, even such women as that, both for company and warmth.

I don't know how long I sat there, trying to keep warm, but finally I heard the scrape of a key in a lock, the creaking open of the door above the stairs. I saw the faint glow of light coming through the barred window, but then I saw 'twas only Jem, and the lantern only made plain what had disappeared in the darkness. In the end, I preferred not to see the hell I was in.

The jailkeep smiled again as he came to the cell. I saw he was carrying a bottle, a blackjack noggin, and a bucket that emitted some foul smell. "Thought you might be hungry," he said. "You hungry, lady fair?"

He didn't wait for me to answer. He shoved the pail inside, and then the noggin. "Your friends're gonna be sorry they missed this one."

Cautiously I came from the bed. "What is it?"

"Prison stew. Nothin' but the best scraps for witches, eh?"

I had been hungry, but when I took the pail and opened the lid, my appetite died. The smell was horrible, the same boiled cabbage I'd smelled upstairs, along with chunks of something else, pared away and dotted with maggot holes that I could see even in the dim light of the lantern. "I cannot eat this."

Jem shrugged. "You'll be hungry for it soon enough, I'll warrant."

I reached for the noggin. 'Twas beer at least; I knew it by the smell. In relief, I gulped it, and then choked at the salt and pickle taste of it. " 'Tis tainted," I gasped.

" 'Tis what the prisoners get," he said. "Drink up."

I pointed to the bottle. "What is that?"

" 'Tis mine," he said. He held it close to his chest. "This be fine Barbados rum—it won't be comin' close to your greedy hands. Drink your beer."

I was thirsty—even the beer was better than nothing, and so I drank. Yet it left a dry salt taste in my mouth; when I finished, I was nearly as thirsty as when I began.

I had barely emptied it when Jem pulled a stool I had not seen from the shadows. He settled it in the corner of my cell and sat down, leaning back against the wall, setting the lamp on the floor beside him. He uncorked the bottle and took a long great sip that made my own throat constrict in longing.

I wiped my mouth with the back of my hand. "What are you doing?"

"I been paid to watch you, and that's just what I'm going to do."

I gestured to the door. "I can hardly escape."

"You been accused of a witch. I hear you can send your spirit anywhere. And I got to watch for your familiar, case he makes a visit."

"I'm not a witch."

"They all say that," he told me. "But I'm guessin' the best liars be servants of the Devil."

I stepped back, leaving the foul stew and the empty noggin abandoned, and went to the bed, where I sat again in the shadows. I sat there for a few moments, listening to him gulp his rum while my thirst raged in my throat and my bladder grew heavy. I bore it until I could not any longer, and then I got up to use the slop pail in the corner.

"I need to relieve myself," I told Jem. "Turn away."

He only smiled and gestured with the bottle. "Go on," he said, and stared at me unabashedly, until I was forced to pull up my skirts and squat over that pail while he watched. I retreated again to the bed, humiliated and horrified. There was nothing to do but curl up on the pallet and try to sleep.

I did not allow myself to think of Lucas or Charity—such thoughts were too painful, too uncertain. Instead, I thought of Jude and Faith, soothing myself by thinking of the baby's soft, downy head, her solid weight. Only a few weeks ago, Hannah had come by and put Faith in my arms, and then sat at the table with Jude while

I taught them both a game I'd played as a little girl, one with sticks thrown into a pile and grabbed up one by one. Now I thought of that time, of Jude laughing and Faith falling asleep nuzzled against my breast, and the memory warmed me as no fire had ever done; I forgot my thirst. Finally I fell asleep.

I was in the midst of a dream where I was waiting on a great hill for Lucas to come, and through the fog I saw his shadow upon a horse. I heard him call my name. Then 'twas as if I were yanked back, falling, and I startled awake to find a man bending over me, his rummy breath in my face, his fingers gripped tight around my arm.

"Now, now," he whispered. "Wake up, dearie."

I was groggy, still sleep-fed. For a moment I was not sure where I was. I felt his weight against me, his hand at my hip. The straw of the pallet was hard and scratchy against my cheek. The man laughed in my ear, and I remembered suddenly: I was in jail, and this was Jem, the jailkeep, and his hands were all over me. I gagged and rolled, trying to get him off me, but he stuck like a tick, all hands. My rolling had only managed to put me on my back, and him on top of me. He laughed again and relaxed, holding my wrists, his body full on mine.

"Don't touch me," I said.

"Not so fast, not so fast," he said. "Just makin' sure you're awake is all. Nothin' more." But he wriggled his hips against me, and I felt the hard ridge of his cock between my legs.

He was stronger than I, even as thin and scrawny as he was. I closed my eyes and burrowed deep within myself, waiting for Jem to pull up my skirts and be done with it. But he only pressed himself against me, humping me through our clothes, and whispered, "Aye, you'd like that, wouldn't you? Well, I ain't bewitched by you like them others."

Still, he lay upon me until I felt him jerk and go still; then he rose, pulling at his breeches, and I heard him move to the stool again and settle upon it. Then I heard him laugh, and I felt the end of a long, sharp, pointed stick. "No sleep for you tonight, lady fair," he said, and his laughter echoed like a demon in my head. "Tell me, when does your familiar come?"

When Jem finally left, early in the morning, I fell into a shallow, restless sleep that could not have lasted more than an hour, perhaps two. When I heard the cell door opening, I dragged myself awake, expecting to see my tormentor. Instead, I saw a man I didn't recognize, who wore Jem's key ring at his waist. He was followed by two women and a greasy-haired man of middle years.

The man with the key ring was older than Jem, with graying, sandy brown hair and no front teeth. "This here's the one," he said to the other. "Make short work of it, will you? I've got things to do."

The other man and the women came inside. The women were matrons, dressed in homespun, with the caps upon their heads nearly hiding the color of their hair. The man was dressed in patched breeches and a vest so stained 'twas hard to see what the color had been—and in the dimness, impossible to tell in any case.

He stopped just inside the door and looked at me, and then a grin moved over his pock-marked face. "Now then, are you sure? I was led to believe 'twas an old woman."

Jem's replacement shook his head. "This is the witch."

"What is this?" I asked, bewildered by their talk. "Are there more accusations? Are you victims as well?"

The man laughed. The women looked faintly horrified. At the cell door, the man with the key ring snorted. "Didn't Jem tell you they'd be comin'?"

"No. Where is Jem?"

"Sleepin' like a babe," he said. He winked at me. "You wore 'im out last night, for sure."

I ignored that. I looked to the strangers in my cell. The man was carrying a leather bag, which he set aside, and I began to feel a sick foreboding. "Who are you then?"

"I'm a surgeon," he said. "These two women are my assistants. Please stand."

I drew back into the shadows of the bed. "Why?"

"We've been asked to search you."

"Search me? For what? I've nothing but my clothes."

"Stand," he said again. When I made no move, he glanced at the new jailkeep, who sighed and came reluctantly over.

"Come on, gel," he said, pushing past the still-silent women. He jerked me from the bed so hard I gasped and cried out. "Stand up for the man, or I'll hold you still for 'im."

I stood with as much dignity as I could muster—a dignity that lasted only as long as it took for the women to set upon me.

I could not understand what they were doing—testing my arms, I thought, running their hands over my hips, looking for something. Then I realized they were undressing me, unlacing my bodice, unfastening my skirt, and I began to struggle against their hands.

"Be still," one of the women said crossly, slapping me hard. The jailkeep held me so tightly I could not move. When the women slid off the sleeves of my bodice and chemise, I felt the heat of shame work its way over my face. They stripped me bare, so 'twas nothing but my skin against the cold dampness of the prison; I stood there before four strangers completely naked.

The surgeon came forward. "Lift your arms," he said, and made me raise them over my head, though I was weak and could not hold them that way without trembling. The women stepped forward then to hold them there, to hold me still while that man ran his hands over my body. He pinched my nipples, pulling them, twisting them. I heard his breathing go fast and coarse, and smelled the onion and smoke smell of him, the grease of his hair. I wanted to struggle against him, but the women and the jailkeep held me still, and I was too exhausted to do more than flinch when his hand lifted my breast and he bent so close I felt the heat of his breath on my nipple.

I had a mole there, a little fleshy thing. Now he pulled it, gently at first, then harder. He held out his hand, and one of the women dropped her hold on me to fish in her pocket. She pulled out a small packet of pins, which flashed in the lamplight, and held one out for him. He took it, and I gasped as he pierced the mole with it. He glanced up at me. "Does that hurt?"

I turned away from him. He wiggled the pin again, until the flesh went numb and I felt nothing, not even when he pulled it loose. "Looks to me like a teat," he said. "She don't feel a thing."

The women bent close. "Aye," one said breathlessly. "Look at how it seems it has been suckled upon."

"'Tis dry now," said the other. She glanced up at me. "When did your familiar last eat?"

I understood now, what they were looking for. Preternatural teats, used to nourish a witch's demon familiar. "I have no familiar," I said. "'Tis just a mole."

They ignored me. The surgeon rose and looked again at my breasts. "You see how fresh and full they are now? We shall check them again in the evening to see if they have changed."

"There is no need," I said. "They look as they ever do."

"Bend over," the surgeon said.

"I will not," I told him.

The jailkeep grabbed my breast, squeezing it so hard tears came to my eyes, and said, "Bend over for the doc, lest you want more o' the same."

I could not fight them, and as I bent and grasped hold of the edge of the bed, I lost the will to do so. I felt that surgeon at me, probing into my deepest parts until I was beyond humiliation or feeling. I barely knew when it was over, only that they were gone, and I was left alone in the darkness.

Chapter 32

———

'TWAS LATER THAT DAY, OR THE NEXT MORNING—I HAD NO NOTION of time in this dank and forgotten place—that they put the chains on me again. "The girls complain still of your specter pinching them," Jem told me. "They say 'tis because you're unchained that your spirit is free." He yanked the end of the chain to a place near the bed where there was one of many metal rings embedded in the stone, and chained me to it.

The chain was short; I had barely room to get to the bed, and when I was there, I could lie in only two positions comfortably. I was too exhausted to care. I was grateful to be alone, to finally rest. Sleep was all I could think of, all I wanted.

As the days passed, my hours were broken only by the jailkeeps bringing me food or poking me awake to watch for my familiar. I was not taken for another examination, though I had expected and dreaded it. I began to feel as if I were sinking into darkness—I was confused and disoriented. I thought often of the night I'd left Lancashire for good, the last time I'd seen my sister before our ill-fated meeting here. How I'd lain waiting until my parents fell asleep, until I heard the quiet, even rise and fall of Judith's breath, how quietly I rose from the straw pallet so that I would not wake her. Earlier I'd gathered my few belongings into a sack—a second bodice, an apron, two pairs of stockings—and hidden it away behind a barrel of salt meat. I'd made no noise as I retrieved it, but I heard Judith stir, and I froze until she whispered, "I will tell them you left early to see the parson. 'Twill be hours before they think to look for you."

In the darkness, I could see nothing of her expression. But I felt her goodwill, and though I hurt at the thought of leaving her, I did not think of staying, nor of urging her to come with me. "Thank you," I said.

"Send a letter to me in care of Parson Gibbs. 'Twill be safe with him. I would know where my sister is. I do not want to lose you."

"Judith, I—"

"You must go. Godspeed," she whispered, and as I gave her a quick embrace and turned to go, she said with soft bitterness, "Tell William . . . it should have been me."

'Twas what Judith did best, aiding me with kindness and sacrifice, and then, when I was lulled and vulnerable, stabbing me with her anger so that I should feel guilt for it forever. I had bought my life with her sacrifice, and she had never let me forget it. But she was my sister, and I loved her, and I'd always known she loved me.

Yet we had spent more time apart than together. Her letters came irregularly, one or two now and then, or a sudden bundle of them delivered to me by a sailor or a merchant who'd had them from a trading vessel. I'd envied her life. She had a husband, children, a new life, while all I had was a set of cluttered rooms and a faithless lover. When I finally left Geoffrey for Robert, I wrote her that I'd found the man I'd been waiting for, but the truth was that Robert had a grown son and wanted no other children, not even with the woman he said he loved, and it was not long before I found myself yearning again for Judith's life.

When she finally began to write of trouble, I knew it must be bad, because she could no longer contain it. Robert had died only a month before. I was free to go to her now, to help her—or so I told myself. Perhaps it was only that I'd hoped that Judith's family could fill the void I felt.

And it had. When Judith died, part of me went with her. But I was grateful, too, for the opportunity fate had given me. Once again, my sister's sacrifice had bought me a life. But I had been clumsy. I had trampled in where tenderness was required, and now, what had I but a niece who believed I was evil, and a lover who had made himself my enemy?

What can you know of love? 'Twas the question Lucas had asked me, and I knew it was a fair one, because in the years I'd been away from Lancashire, though I had never lacked for a lover, I had never truly been in love. I had wanted to be, but I chose badly each time, and my hope that someday I would find what I had been searching for dwindled with every year.

Did I believe what I'd told Lucas, that 'twas as if God had given us a gift—or was it merely that I'd been in the first flush of promise, when I believed that at last I had found what I yearned for?

I had no answers, and the questions swirled in the dank, stale air around me so that I thought I would go mad.

'Twas more than a week, or so Jem told me, before I realized why I'd been forsaken. It seemed Salem Village was concerned with its other witches, which multiplied like flies at a rotting carcass. Now they were brought into this dimness one by one—and with their coming, my own torments eased. I was left alone finally as the keeps and the surgeon turned to the other prisoners. I could sleep at last, and 'twas only then I found my madness abating, hour by hour, borne away by company and rest. I found my spirit returning, and with it a will to survive, a faith that soon, some honorable, rational person would call an end to this. But as I saw the hopelessness in the other prisoners, I began to wonder if there could be such a person in Salem.

Martha Corey came first, disoriented and angry, barely speaking to me as she bore the humiliations I'd borne alone. After her came a little girl—four-year-old Dorcas Good, whose mother had been removed to the Boston Jail. The child had confessed to being a witch. When she was given into our care, she cried and screamed curses, but after several hours of such terror, she climbed willingly into my arms to sleep, her chains clanking against mine. In her quietness, she reminded me of Jude, and the thought of that little girl made me keep little Dorcas close.

Then came elderly Rebecca Nurse—a woman whose hospitality I'd enjoyed during the Indian scare—and 'twas then I realized that the world had gone mad.

Perhaps because she was so elderly and so obviously frail, they did not chain her to the wall. They put her into the dungeon, and she stumbled in the darkness, obviously confused and bewildered.

"Rebecca," I managed finally. "How come you here?"

She stumbled to the pallet beside me, and put her head in her hands. "Susannah, 'tis a terrible thing. A terrible thing indeed."

"Who would call you a witch?" I asked her.

She frowned, and touched her finger to her ear, and I remembered she was going deaf. I said again, louder, "I cannot imagine why you are here."

"Those girls." Her voice softened to a whisper. "Those girls. And Ann Putnam too, now. She said I appeared to her in her fits."

"The child is—"

"Not the child," Rebecca said, shaking her head sadly. "The mother. 'Tis no love lost between Francis and Tom Putnam. I have told Francis not to argue with them. 'Tis too much power for a single family."

In the corner, Martha Corey had been sleeping, and now she woke. She stared in surprise at Rebecca. "You? They have accused you now? What wretched turn is this? Have they all gone mad?"

Rebecca seemed to sag. "I have wondered," she murmured, "what unrepented sin God has found in me that He should lay such an affliction upon me now, in my old age."

"Do not torment yourself," I said. "You have led a godly life."

She closed her eyes. "We must pray to God that we will be saved from this."

We spoke little more. The four of us sat as statues. When the cell door opened again, Rebecca started and rose, stumbling to it as if she expected there had been a pardon, a mistake.

I was surprised to see a man following Jem into the cell. He held a shadowed bundle. When Jem raised the lantern, I saw 'twas Sam Nurse, Rebecca's son, Lucas's friend.

I watched Rebecca's shoulders shake with tears as her son came toward her. Sam's arms were full of blankets and a heavy cape. They fell to the floor as Rebecca went to him. He held his mother like a babe, stroking her back, murmuring into her ear. When he looked up and saw me there, sitting in the shadows, I knew that this was not the same man who had turned away from me as I walked the aisle to my examination. This was a man railing at circumstance, a furious man. A man rallying to fight.

"Susannah," he said tightly, "forgive me for disbelieving you. 'Tis a . . . confusing time. Look at this! When my own poor mother can be accused of such a thing, a woman who was ever a lamb of God—"

"Aye. 'Tis unthinkable."

His expression was sad when he looked at me. "Jude talks of you," he said quietly. "'Tis clear the child mourns your absence."

"I miss her as well." I did not ask the question I longed to ask.

Sam must have known it. I had never thought him entirely unaware of what existed between Lucas and me. Now he said, "He is confused, Susannah. 'Tis his own daughter who is afflicted."

"I know," I said.

"What would you have him do? Denounce her?"

I did not answer that question. "Do you think the girls are bewitched?"

"They are . . . too biddable, some of them. I do not know what to think."

"I would not have Lucas do what he cannot. He loves his daughter. I think . . . I have no doubt Charity believes the things she says are true."

Sam hesitated. When he spoke, there was reluctance in his voice. "Are they true?"

"I have said before. I am no witch."

Samuel looked uncomfortable. "Why does she accuse you? Her own aunt?"

"Charity lost her mother the night I arrived. We have been at odds since."

He nodded thoughtfully, but said nothing more to me. I listened with half an ear as he described to Rebecca what we should expect now: There would be a trial, but he did not know when. Increase Mather was not returned to New England from London with the new charter; as yet, the Massachusetts General Council had no authority to act. Until the new governor arrived, we would wait here in prison.

Sam stayed but a little longer. He left reluctantly, and when he was gone, Rebecca took the blankets and cape and clean linen he'd brought her. She came to where I sat on the bed.

"We will not be here long," she said to me, the fervor of a prayer in her voice. "God will redeem us. God will set us free."

Such fortitude she had, such faith. I wished for just a little myself, but my God had left me long, long ago, on a day when I'd borne my father's first beating without flinching; in truth, I did not miss Him.

This time, when I heard the footsteps coming down into the dungeon, I thought nothing of it. I did not even look up until Jem said, "Here's one to see you, lady fair," and I glanced up to see Lucas standing at the door.

I stood, and the chains at my wrists clanked unbearably and rattled against the wall. I saw Lucas's gaze go to them. He was pale and thin; his face was hollowed and bruised from what looked to be exhaustion.

I said quietly, "Where have you been?"

He turned to Jem. "Take her out of the chains."

Jem shook his head. "Them girls—"

"My daughter is one of the girls. I say take her out."

The jailkeep hesitated. Then he came across the cell to me, unlocking the chain from the ring in the wall.

"Take them off her," Lucas said.

"I can't."

"Who would know? Ten minutes is all I ask."

Jem glanced at me, then at Lucas, and then he unlocked the manacles so they clanked on the floor. I had grown used to moving at the end of the chain, to measuring my movements. When the chains fell, I did not move, unable to lose the habit of constraint.

Lucas stood at the cell door, looking oddly lost. "Sam told me he'd seen you."

"Aye. When they brought his mother in." I sounded bitter. I saw Lucas wince and glance to the corner, where Rebecca stood.

"Do you need something?" he asked. "Blankets?"

"Aye. Blankets. And some clothing, if you would. It gets mightily cold here."

He nodded. His glance took in the cell, and I knew what he saw and saw too his horror in it. "This is not . . . what I expected."

"What did you expect? A gabled house? A fireplace? A servant? Try Judge Corwin's. I was questioned there late into the night once. I would rather this."

"Susannah—"

"Why have you come, Lucas?"

He came toward me quickly. When he was only a foot from me, it seemed he suddenly remembered where we were, who he was, and he stopped. "I cannot stop thinking of you. I cannot stand to see you this way."

"How did you think I would be?" I asked. I touched my hair. It fell lank around my shoulders, tangled with bits of straw. I knew I'd lost weight by the fit of my clothes; my stomach growled all the day through; I was thirsty constantly. "Why are you here, Lucas, when you have not come for so long? Why did you not warn me you would testify against me?"

"I cannot tell you that."

"Do I not deserve an honest answer?"

"I cannot tell you, because I don't know. My God, the world is in chaos. 'Tis nothing but fear everywhere, and suspicion. . . . I should have done as you asked. I should have sent Charity away, even when . . . Parris sent little Betsey to town. I have heard that already her fits have eased."

"Can you not do the same?" I asked him. "Surely 'tis not too late—"

"It is too late. Charity has grown worse, but I cannot tell. . . . Susannah, if witches are here in the village, if the Devil has truly come, I cannot take her from the authorities who need her."

"There are others to do that work."

He was quiet for a moment. Then he said, "She and some of the others called out on Elizabeth Proctor." The others in the cell gasped, and Lucas nodded his confirmation. "Aye. 'Tis true. And Rebecca—there is talk that your sister Sarah will be accused as well."

"You cannot mean it!"

"She walked out of Parris's sermon on Sunday. She took offense to his text. 'Twas from John: 'Have I not chosen you twelve and one of you is a devil?' So soon after your arrest, Rebecca, Sarah could not stand it. But she called attention to herself, and in these times, that cannot be good. I think there will be others accused as well. The girls are talking of a wizard now, a man who rules the witches—"

"Lucas," I said, "you must leave this place."

"They do not talk of me," he said impatiently. "Charity says so many things, and I . . . What shall I do? She is my daughter. How can I not believe her? I know her too well to think she lies."

"Why have you come then?" I asked. "What do you want of me?"

He laughed bitterly, then sagged onto my pallet, burying his face in his hands. "What do I want of you? What *don't* I want?"

I sat beside him on the pallet. "You know I did not do the things they accuse me of. Your dream was only a dream. My only sin was in not understanding well enough Charity's grief, or her guilt—"

He held up his hand to quiet me. His voice was rough when he said, "Why can you not confess?"

"Because I'm innocent," I cried. "You know this, Lucas. You *must* know it. 'Tis yourself you seek to save, not me. This absolution you want—'tis for your own soul."

He lurched to his feet then, hastening from me, and when he was gone, I closed my eyes and leaned back against the damp stone wall while the darkness of my future rose up once again.

Chapter 33

———— ❧ ————

A FEW DAYS LATER, JEM CALLED THAT I HAD ANOTHER VISITOR. I hoped it might be Lucas again, to bring me the blankets or clothes that I'd asked for. But then I saw 'twas Hannah Penney. Hannah, bearing a bag on her back and little Faith in her arms.

Jem had not put the manacles on me again after Lucas's visit, and for the last days, I'd hidden in the shadows, not moving farther than the limits of my chains to keep Jem from remembering that I did not wear them. But when I saw Faith, I forgot myself; I went running to Hannah.

"You've brought her," I said, reaching out for the babe. Hannah put the child in my arms, and in sudden realization I looked up to meet Jem's gaze, certain that he would chain me up again. I could not bear it, that I would have to relinquish little Faith in order to be manacled. The child was even now cooing at me, reaching for my loosened hair.

But Jem simply turned away, disappearing out the door.

"What is it?" Hannah asked. "What do you look at?"

"Nothing. 'Tis nothing." I smiled at her. "Hannah, I am so glad you've come. And to bring Faith . . ."

"She is more yours than mine," Hannah said, but she did not smile back at me. She reached for the bag slung over her back. "I've brought clothes. Lucas said you'd asked for some, and he did not know what to choose. I . . . went through your trunks."

"Leave them here," I said, leading her to my bed, where we both sat on the stinking straw. I played with Faith's fat little fingers. "How are things in the village?"

"Oh, 'tis terrible. Terrible." Hannah glanced to where Rebecca lay curled and sleeping, and then she said in a low voice, "They arrested Sarah Cloyce this morning, and Elizabeth Proctor too. It has gained a force now that even the government cannot deny. Today I heard that the exams are being moved to town so Deputy Governor Danforth can attend."

I bent close to Faith and breathed deep her scent. "Perhaps 'tis a good thing. This needs clearer heads."

"Aye." Hannah's tone was hesitant. I looked up to see her watching me closely, as if she expected at any moment that I might sprout wings and fly away.

"What is it, Hannah?" I asked.

She looked down at her hands, which she twisted in her lap. "I came here today to talk to you. I thought perhaps . . . We have been friends, have we not?"

"Aye."

"There have been things . . . I cannot explain them."

"I don't understand you."

She looked up at me. "I have not testified against you, Susannah, and I will not. There is already enough evidence, enough that the magistrates have bound you over—"

Suddenly I felt sick. "Hannah—"

"You have spent too many years in worldly pursuits; 'tis clear the Devil has had traffic with you. Who else but a demon could quiet a child so easily?"

I tightened my hold on Faith. "She likes to hear singing. 'Tis all it was."

"I put bay across the doorstop—do you not recall the day you would not come into the house, but bade me bring Faith out to you?"

I did remember it. 'Twas months before, when I'd traipsed over the field to the Penneys' to bring the clothes Judith had sewn for Faith. Clouts and belly bands and pilches, shapeless linen gowns drawn by bobbins, warmly wadded biggins—all so tenderly sewn it had nearly broken my heart to see them, to see the evidence of Judith's hopes. . . .

"There was mud on my boots," I said. "I had crossed the stream and slipped on the bank. Do you remember? The basket I carried the clothes in was streaked with mud. You were sweeping the house, and I . . . I did not want to track the dirt inside. . . ."

She shook her head sorrowfully, as if she recognized the lie and pitied my need to tell it. "You could not cross the bay—no witch can."

"It was the mud—"

"Oh, Susannah." Hannah leaned forward, her expression intent. "You have been found out already. The judges are learned men; they cannot be wrong. There is no cause to lie to me. I know you are a witch. I have suspected it for some time. I've come to beg you to confess. 'Tis time to cleanse your soul, to turn to God. Before you are hanged, you must absolve yourself."

"Hannah, I am not a witch."

"Please. For the sake of your own soul, confess the truth. Would you be hanged as a liar? Would you die unregenerate?"

I was stunned by her words. "I am not going to die. This is a mistake. I will be redeemed at my trial."

"You will not be redeemed unless you tell the truth. You must confess to your covenant with Satan. I'm begging you, Susannah, for the sake of your soul. . . ."

"How can you believe this? How can you put this babe in my arms and believe I am yet a disciple of evil?"

Hannah's eyes became bright with tears. "I am hoping the child will move you to do what you must. Lucas gave me leave to bring her. Do not leave this world unredeemed, Susannah. Cleanse your heart."

"Lucas . . . gave you leave? Does he know . . . why you've come here?"

Hannah sighed. "My dear Susannah, there is not a one of us who would have you end your life as a reprobate."

I could not believe Hannah could know me, and yet still believe . . . But this place, this town, how dark it was. How afraid they all were.

"Lucas is in a sad way," Hannah went on. "To testify against his own sister. . . . How much easier 'twould be for him if you admitted the truth."

I wished she would leave, but because I wanted Faith a bit longer, I suffered Hannah's presence until the babe fell asleep in my arms and I handed her back and watched the two of them go.

I felt Faith's warmth in my arms for a long while after. I opened the bag Hannah had brought: a blanket and another skirt of rich green, some clean linen. And there, at the bottom of the bag, lying in wait like some wretched viper, was the red paragon bodice.

The next day, Sarah Cloyce was brought to jail, along with Elizabeth Proctor and her husband, John, who had called the girls liars at his wife's examination and had been accused himself. They all spoke of how the moving of the examinations to town to accommodate Thomas Danforth and another man, Samuel Sewall, a judge from Boston, had turned what was already chaos into unimaginable horror. Danforth had taken over the questioning, Sarah told us, and the exams had become as talked about and well attended as a hanging—which, she said bitterly, there soon might be. My isolated days in prison were over. Now we were visited often. People had begun to come and stare at us through the door as if we were the poor wretches of Bedlam, or the mangy animals in the Tower of London's menageries.

I began to suffer from nightmares. Deep in the night, I would jerk awake to find Dorcas Good curled into my arms, her body tight against mine. I would hear the weary pleas of the latest residents, begging for sleep as Jem prodded them awake to question them, to watch for familiars that never came. In my head was the single word: *Confess. Confess.* I woke exhausted and undone. *Confess.* The word was a constant echo in my head.

'Twas soon after, that Rebecca and the Proctors and Sarah Cloyce were moved to the Boston Jail to make room for four others: Martha Corey's husband, Giles, among them, and someone else who surprised me, someone I had not expected ever to see held a prisoner in the dungeon. Charity's friend, mousy little Mary Warren, the Proctors' maidservant.

When the girl was brought in and saw me, she turned back to the door as if she might try to scratch her way free. But Jem closed the door in her face, and she sank to the floor and buried her face in her arms, sobbing piteously.

'Twas a mystery why she was here; she had been seeing specters only last week—Elizabeth Proctor among them, from what the talk in prison had been. There was a part of me that hoped . . . for what, I didn't know. That perhaps clearer heads had indeed prevailed. But with that thought came a fear. I had been afraid for Charity; now my worry grew stronger.

I approached Mary as if she were a wild animal I did not want to frighten away. Giles Corey said gruffly, "Leave the little bitch be. Let her suffer; 'tis what she deserves," and Abigail Hobbs, who'd been brought only the day before, loose-haired and wild-looking, chuckled and said incomprehensibly, "Aye. She knows, she does. She knows."

I ignored them both. I knelt beside Mary Warren. She jerked away from me in a jangling of chains. The shoulder of her bodice slipped and I saw the healing marks of a good thrashing.

"What happened?" I asked. "Why are you here?"

She steadfastly ignored me.

"Let her rot," Giles said again. "She's as much a liar as the rest of 'em. Proctor said he beat the Devil out of her and well he should."

Mary glanced at him with burning hatred in her eyes—a look so intent it transformed her mousiness into something almost strangely pretty.

"They claim she signed the Devil's book," Giles told me. "No doubt she's confessed to it too."

"Is it true, Mary?" I asked her. "Did you confess to being a witch?" When she said nothing, I whispered, "What of Charity?"

She looked back at me, expressionless. "What of her?" she asked. The contempt in her words took me aback. She turned away again, and though I longed to ask more questions, 'twas clear she wouldn't answer. Finally I did as Giles suggested; I left her alone.

It was not long before the magistrates came to the cell to take her out. They did not take her from the dungeon—I heard the opening of another cell door; here, everything echoed against the stone. I knew they'd put her into one of the other cells—I had seen them all, and I knew how small it was. 'Twas hardly room for Mary Warren and those men to stand one up against the other.

Their voices rang out, loud enough that we could hear as well as if they stood in this cell with us.

'Twas Hathorne's voice first, relentless from the start. "Abigail Williams has said that Goody Proctor made you sign the Devil's book. When did you do this?"

Her voice was soft, a whisper. I could not catch it.

Hathorne said, "You confessed to it."

"No, no, I did not. I was confused. I did not understand."

"When did you sign the book?"

"I did not sign. There was no Devil's book."

"You have said before there was: Which is true? Is there a book? Did you not say your mistress signed it?"

"I did. But . . . 'twas not true."

"Not true? She did not sign the book?"

There was silence. I heard Mary sobbing, such a quiet sound, so loud against these walls.

"'Tis a lie," she said finally. "'Tis all a lie."

At this, the others in the cell with me perked up.

"A lie?" 'Twas Jonathan Corwin. Well did I remember his cruelty. "What is a lie?"

"All of it. All of it." Mary was sobbing so hard now 'twas difficult to understand her. "They have dissembled. . . . I have dissembled. You might as well examine a madwoman and take notice of what she said, as take the word of any of the afflicted."

"Dear God," Martha whispered. "Did I hear . . . ?"

"Ssshhh," hissed her husband.

"A lie? Did she say a lie?" Abigail Hobbs went to the door, peering out as if she hoped to see something. "Why, 'tis not a lie, none of it. I have seen them witches dancing in the dark with the Devil. In the woods, off Parris's field. You can hear the spade-foot frogs there now, loud as you please, singing the Devil's song, them evil things. . . ."

"Quiet yourself, you crazy witch," Giles said, but I was as shocked by the woman's words as I had been by Mary's. When I turned to stare at her, she looked right at me with her dark eyes. She smiled as if she knew me.

"Aye, you too," she said. "I seen you there too, didn't I?"

I was shaken. Hannah's words—*Confess*—and then Mary's *They dissemble, all of them,* and now this madwoman staring at me with eyes that seemed to see beyond these dungeon walls. . . .

Hathorne said, "You testified against your master. Was this a lie?"

"I never accused him," Mary cried out. "I would not accuse him!"

"Tell us the truth, Mary," Corwin said. "What has afflicted you now so you cannot tell us the truth? Who has blinded you? Goody Proctor? Her husband?"

"No one. I tell you, no one! I am telling the truth. All are lies."

"Your fits were only deception? How can that be? Were you not
in fact fighting the Devil? Did he not attack you when you resisted?"

She burst into tears, piteous sobbing that did not let her speak,
and though they kept questioning her, Mary Warren did not answer
again, but only cried as if her heart would break. Finally the magistrates called Jem down and I heard their footsteps along the hall as
they left her; their shadows passed fleetingly by the door.

Martha Corey sighed and went back to her bed, and the madwoman began to pace the length of the cell. I went to my own pallet, turning away from them all. But Mary's words kept me staring
into the dark for a long while, and I wondered: What had happened
between those girls? What secrets did they hide? Why had they
banded together this way? What had caused it, what were they hoping for?

And worse . . . why had no one yet asked them?

I did not expect to see Lucas again; so when, a few days later, he
came again to the cell to see me, I stared at him in surprise. How
long had it been since his last visit? Two weeks? More? He looked
more haggard than before, his eyes red-rimmed. There was a
translucent fragility to his skin, deep shadows, hollows.

"Lucas," I whispered. "Dear God, what has happened to you?"

"I cannot live with this," he said in a strangled voice. "I cannot
do it."

Warily I said, "You cannot do what?"

He glanced to the others, who were paying us no attention, and
I took his arm and led him to my bed. When we sat, he said in a
voice heavy with tears, "When Charity accused Rebecca, I could
scarce believe it. Then . . . last night, Charity told me she saw Judith
come to her in a winding sheet. She says Judith's spirit accuses you
of murder—a small child whom you drowned in England; a crew
member of the *Sunfish* you stabbed with a meat knife and pushed
overboard; and another man, a stranger you met in Salem Town,
whom you strangled with your bare hands."

I stared at him. The charges were so absurd I had to resist an urge to laugh.

Lucas closed his eyes briefly. "I do not believe her. I know it cannot be true. 'Tis . . . madness." Tentatively he took my hand, and when I did not protest, he held it tight—something he had never done before. "This is all . . . madness. And yet . . . it has moved beyond me, Susannah. It has moved beyond us all. The ministers cannot stop it, no matter how they pray and fast. Last week, our old pastor, Deodat Lawson, came to pray for the girls, to try to stop this. Instead, there are seven more afflicted—not just girls, but four women now—and here Rebecca is accused, and her sister. And now I ask myself—if the things Charity says now are not true, if she is truly . . . deluded . . . then . . . can there be truth in anything else she's said?"

I did not know what to say.

"What happened between her and Sam?" he asked me.

I was surprised by the question, but I answered as well as I could. "I suspect Sam . . . seduced Charity, that she . . . did not resist him, perhaps she even fell in love with him. I believe Judith felt 'twas an unsuitable match, and she paid him five pounds to leave, and that he did so without a backward glance."

Lucas's face was grim. "Judith had said something to me, but I . . . I didn't heed it. I saw Charity as a child, and yet . . . she is no child. She is sixteen now. *Sixteen.*" His voice turned bitter. "The days have leaped by, and I did not mark their passing. I look at her and I wonder: Where have I been? 'Twas my task to keep the Devil from her, and yet here he is. How could I have failed her so completely?"

In the corner, Dorcas began to cry that the chains at her wrists were hurting. Martha went to soothe her. Lucas's glance went to her. He watched as the child went into Martha's lap and the woman pressed her hand against the child's hair and murmured some little comfort. When he looked back to me, it seemed that something had changed in his manner. I could not tell what, only that there was a change; there was sudden purpose in the way he squeezed my hand and released me, in the way he stood.

"I will not leave you here," he whispered, and then, before I could protest, he went to the door and demanded, "Jailkeep, open the door."

"Lucas," I called out, hurrying to him, but he was already outside the cell, and Jem closed the door in my face.

Lucas paused. I had curled my fingers around the bars of the window, and he touched my knuckle and smiled—such an astonishing thing. I had not seen anything like it on his face before—not bittersweet, not sad, but soft and sweet.

I watched until I could no longer see him, as he followed Jem up the stairs, out of the dungeon. The things Lucas had told me, his concerns about Charity, his struggles . . . There was nothing easy in them, nothing to hope for. But as I turned back to the others, I felt for the first time a strange and wonderful fullness in my heart.

Chapter 34

⟡

THE NEXT MORNING, LITTLE DORCAS GOOD WAS LED AWAY. SHE clung to me and cried as the other jailkeep, Richard, tried to pull her from the cell, until he commanded her to quiet, and said, "You're goin' to see your ma." She, too, was on her way to the Boston Jail, and I was lonely again when they took her, even in this cell full of people.

An hour later, Richard pushed his way through the gawkers at the door and shouted at them to leave. When they had gone, shouting and cursing and laughing every step of the way, he gestured to me with a leer and a wink. "Come on, you—the pretty one. Get on over here. You've been summoned."

I'd had my fill of being summoned. "Tell them I will not go."

"Aye, you will. Danforth hisself asked for ye."

"Why?"

"How should I know?" Richard unlocked the door and came inside; a pair of manacles dangled from his hand. "Come on now."

I did not make it easy for him. Richard jerked my arms from behind my back and forced the manacles on my wrists so roughly that the healing welts and sores burst open again to sting and burn. When I cried out, Richard ignored me. He pulled me to my feet, and led me out of the cell and up the stairs.

The thin light coming into the cells upstairs burned my eyes; so used was I to darkness. When Richard led me outside, the sun was unbearably bright. I had to close my eyes to keep them from hurting.

The air was brisk, but not freezing, not as it had been the last time I'd seen the sky. While I'd been in jail, the winter had gone; I felt spring already. I had grown used to the stale, rotting scent of my cell, and now the scents of the sea, of drying cod, salt mud, and the tannery, were so new to me that I was overwhelmed. I blinked and stared at the world through watering eyes. The sky was pale blue, with dozens of ship masts thrusting into it, so tall I could see them even past the houses. 'Twas as if the world had been newly tinted; trees were budding, green shoots pushing through where the sun shone warm. The snow and ice that had covered the ground when I'd last been outside were gone; there was only mud now, the unpaved roads nothing but a morass of deep carriage-wheel ruts and puddles.

It seemed impossible that there should be a change, that I should have been imprisoned for so long. 'Twas unfair that I had not been present to see the winter fade. The days passed as they always did—with me, or without me.

'Twas a thought that sat heavily upon me as I followed Richard. It turned out there was not far to go—a block or so, just past the Salem Town meetinghouse that sat across the street from the jail.

"What is this place?" I asked Richard.

"The courthouse," he said tersely.

I stopped in surprise and dismay. "'Tis my trial? I had not expected—"

He jerked my chains so I had to walk or fall. "Come now. I ain't got all day for this."

No one crowded the street; when we went inside, I saw the magistrates' desk and the bar of justice and the benches—all empty. The Proctors had said there were crowds watching the pretrial examinations; surely there would be as many for the trials themselves. Yet the room was empty.

Richard paused only a moment; then he turned, and I saw another door, which he knocked upon. "The prisoner's here," he announced to the wood.

I heard a step; then the door was opened by a man I had not seen before. He had thinning hair and an unsettling air of command about him. He glanced at me, then stepped back to allow us entry. In a deep voice, he said, "Bring her in."

'Twas a small room, with a desk and chairs that reminded me greatly of Jonathan Corwin's study. As if to make that memory brighter, I saw Judge Corwin standing at the desk along with John Hathorne, who had questioned me so brutally at the examination. I stopped short. Then I heard a voice, a quiet "There is nothing to fear, Susannah."

I turned to see Lucas standing there. Lucas, and behind him Thomas Putnam and Samuel Parris.

I grabbed the back of a nearby chair. My chains rattled and clanked against it. "What is this?" I whispered. "Why am I here?"

"I must confess, 'tis what I wonder as well," the man with the deep voice said. "What is it you wish to tell us, Goodman Fowler? What news have you?"

"Let her sit," Lucas said firmly, and when none of them protested, I did so gratefully. Then he looked to the man who'd opened the door. "Governor Danforth, you are a busy man, I know. I would not take up much of your time. You were not present when this woman was imprisoned, yet what I would say now requires your attendance."

Danforth nodded somberly. "Proceed."

"Susannah Morrow is my wife's sister. My wife died in late October, and since then, Susannah has lived in my house. Six weeks ago she was . . . accused of the terrible crime of witchcraft. I testified against her." Lucas did not look at me as he said these words. He gestured toward Hathorne and Corwin. "These men have my deposition on record, along with my signature."

"I have it here," said Corwin, motioning to a heavy record book on the desk.

Lucas said, "'Tis all laid out for you. What is not laid out for you is the truth. What I have not said is that I lusted for Susannah Morrow from the moment I first saw her. What I have not said is that I was bewitched by her. I could not resist the temptation of her—"

"My God, Lucas," I said, "I'm begging you. . . . Have you not said enough already?"

"Is that your testimony?" John Hathorne asked. "That she possessed you? That she led you into sin?"

Lucas shook his head. "I tried to lay the blame at her door. Believe me, I tried. But the truth is that Susannah did not lead me. I have been . . . obsessed by her, and I wanted to believe that obsession was not of my own making. I wanted to attribute it to the Devil, because I could not bear the thought that I could fall into such sin without Satan leading me there. I could not bear the thought that I could . . . want . . . so desperately. Susannah is my wife's sister. What is between us is a sin, and I know this. But 'tis not bewitchment. I have been deluded, as I believe my daughter has been as well. I wish to withdraw my testimony."

There was stunned silence, mine no less than the others'.

Then John Hathorne asked quietly, "Have you fornicated with this woman, Goodman Fowler?"

Lucas met Hathorne's gaze steadily. "Aye."

Samuel Parris said, "God forgive you, Lucas." Then they all began to talk over each other in horrified voices.

Tom Putnam stepped forward, his eyes wide in his pale face. "This cannot be true. You are led by your cock, Lucas. Admit at least that the only reason you recant this now is because you want her still."

Lucas laughed. "Aye, I want her still. Is there a man among you who does not?"

"She has deluded you."

"No. I was deluded before. Now my mind is my own."

"How can you recant this testimony, when so many are clearly afflicted?" Hathorne asked.

"There may be witches," Lucas said stubbornly. "Susannah is not one of them. I'd lay my life on it."

"Your own daughter is one of the afflicted," Tom insisted.

"She is misguided."

"How can you know this?" Samuel Parris asked. "How can you say there is another judgment when 'tis clear the girls are tormented by your sister's specter? They have called out her name. They have seen her. How do you explain this?"

"I cannot explain the others. Charity was close to her mother. She has been troubled since Judith died. I have not been . . . vigilant, and she has taken solace in delusion. 'Tis because of me she is so sorely afflicted."

"Because of you?" Hathorne burst out. "You are the cause of the child's fits?"

"Had I been more attentive, I believe she would not be one of the afflicted."

Corwin frowned. "Has this woman put a spell on you to make you say these things?"

"No. There is no spell. I come here of my own free will—"

"Your own daughter calls out upon this woman. How can it be that she is so afflicted, and you, who live in the same house, who has . . . fornicated . . . with this . . . this *witch*, is not so tormented?"

"I have explained it already. Her mother's death—"

"—has left her feeble-minded. Aye. But perhaps 'tis something else. You have said that you refused to acknowledge the truth of your feelings for this woman. Can it be that you are denying the truth of her role as Satan's minion as well?"

"These are lies," Lucas said impatiently. He turned to Danforth. "These are lies, sir. Susannah Morrow is no witch. I believe my daughter will admit the same when she is removed from the others."

"Are you claiming that the others lie?" Corwin asked.

Lucas shook his head. "I hardly know them. I have no way to judge."

"But you say your daughter will recant her testimony."

"Aye. I think she will."

Putnam asked, "Have you spoken with her, Lucas?"

"The last time I saw her, she told me of visions," he said, and I knew with dismay what he spoke of, the visit of her mother's spirit, the charge that I was a murderess. Charity had said nothing of recantation. She was worse than ever. Lucas spoke now from hope and determination, nothing more. 'Twas what he wished to be true, not what was.

Danforth was quiet for a moment, thoughtful, and I saw how the others deferred to him, and I grew cold.

"Where are the afflicted girls?" Danforth asked into the silence.

"Some stay in the ordinary here," Corwin replied. "Some in the village. There was scheduled to be an examination today, but there has been a delay. They have not all returned home."

"Where is your daughter, Goodman Fowler? Is she in the village or here?"

"I don't know," Lucas said, and I saw how it pained him to admit it. "She has not lived with me since her fits began."

Charity had not even been with him; she had been trapped with those girls, gathering power in delusion day after day.

When Danforth told the constable who stood behind me, "See if the Fowler girl is one of those at the ordinary. If she is, bring her back here," I knew what would happen. When I looked at Lucas, I saw with dismay that he knew it too.

Putnam turned slyly to Lucas. "Unless Lucas prefers she not come."

Lucas gave him a sharp look, but he said, "Bring her. She is sixteen now, no longer a child, and I have hidden too many things from her. I would not hide this."

The constable left. When the door had shut behind him, Hathorne said to Danforth, "What do you expect from this?"

"Why, corroboration," Danforth said with a small smile. "Proof that Goodman Fowler has not himself been bewitched into saying lies."

Lucas made a short, angry sound, and turned away, and Parris, who stood behind him, stepped back and murmured a small prayer. Lucas said bitterly, "The time for prayers is long past, Pastor," and Parris looked at the floor and grew quiet.

"I would ask for one thing," Lucas said. "I have not spoken to my daughter since I came to see the truth. She cannot yet know how I feel. I would ask that I be given a chance to talk to her alone."

"I cannot give you that," Danforth said. "You have said she will recant; I must be assured she does so of her own free will, without influence."

"She is influenced every day by those girls."

Danforth raised a brow. "But you are her father. You have directed her every day of her life. Surely she will know already how much faith to lend to your words."

The room was silent as we waited for Charity to be brought in.

At the knock on the door, Lucas jerked from the window; Putnam and Parris went still; Hathorne looked up from the record book. Danforth rose slowly from the bench and said, "Bring her in."

The door opened. I was sitting behind it, so 'twas impossible for Charity to see me at first, and I caught a glimpse of her as the constable brought her in. She looked far worse than when I'd seen her last; she was horribly thin, the knobby bones of her wrists and her shoulders stood out; her jaw and her cheekbones looked strangely sharp. The chilblains at her face were gone, but what remained was a reddish rash that she scratched at. Her skin was waxy pale, her hair lusterless. Yet what was the same was the way she stiffened at the sight of her father, the yearning for him that seemed to stretch her very skin, the way she leaned in his direction as if she waited hopelessly for a touch that never came.

Oh, see that, Lucas, I prayed wordlessly. *Hold her.*

Perhaps he would have. I had thought he would. But then

Hathorne rose from the desk and distracted Charity's attention, and when she turned, she saw me sitting there. The blood left her face; her eyes went wild. She pointed a shaking finger at me, and screamed, "Oh, there she is! There is the murderess! Where are the bodies you have buried, Susannah Morrow? How they cry for you!"

She stumbled back; she would have fallen had not the constable been there to catch her. But she struggled so in his arms that Locker had no choice but to lay her down upon the floor.

The other men stood back. Lucas ran to her. "Charity," he said, kneeling beside her, trying to pull her into his arms—'twas a scene so like the first time, when I'd stood naked beside him.

"Charity," Lucas whispered to her, holding her wrists away from his face so she could not claw him. He was intent; the desperate love in his face was painful to see—he was a man wrestling for possession of his daughter's soul, and losing. "Listen to me. Listen to me. You must stop this now. Stop it! There is no Devil in this room!"

Charity's gaze went past her father. "There is a man in a winding sheet! He says she stabbed him! Oh, how white he is! 'Murderer!' he calls her. 'Murderer!'"

Lucas gave her a little shake. "This is not true, Charity. I have already told these men that Susannah is no witch. I have told them the truth of things."

She was trembling now, gooseflesh rising on her skin. "She has bewitched you. The Devil has you! I see Satan speaking in your ear!"

"'Tis nonsense," Lucas said.

"She has swallowed you! I knew it! I saw it! She has swallowed your soul! Oh, Father, how can it be so? How can you have let her in?"

"No, Charity—"

"Oh, here she comes! Keep her away from me!" She jerked from him, putting up her hands to ward off an invisible attacker.

"She sits there on the chair," he said. "Charity, this is delusion—"

"I have seen enough," Danforth said, coming forward. He grabbed Lucas's arm. "Release her."

"I will not!" Lucas wrenched from the deputy governor's grasp. "Charity, listen to me. If you would listen to me, you would see the truth."

Danforth gave a nod. Tom Putnam and John Hathorne rushed forward to grab Lucas's arms. He tried to shake them off, to cling to his daughter. Desperately he said, "Charity, 'tis your father. My God. My God, I love you. Do not do this—"

She leaned over and vomited. 'Twas bile only, but shining within it were two pins.

Tom Putnam released his hold on Lucas. "Oh, dear God, look at this!"

Lucas escaped them. He grasped Charity hard, pulling her to his chest. She was stiff and unwilling, but he held her tight, caressing her hair. "Believe me, Charity. Believe me. Susannah is no witch. How could I love a witch?"

Love. The echo of it cracked in the room. Charity twisted from Lucas's arms with forcible strength at the same moment that Tom Putnam and John Hathorne finally pulled him loose. Lucas went stumbling back, held tightly by those men. Charity screamed. The pins in that little pool of yellow bile glinted.

I saw the way Danforth looked at Charity, that horrible, repulsed pity. Then he glanced up at Lucas, and I saw something else, something calculated. Suspicion and fear were dark in this room. I thought suddenly of John Proctor, who'd come to his wife's examination an innocent man and left a prisoner.

"Let me touch her," I said to Danforth. "Let me touch her."

The deputy governor paused. He glanced at Hathorne, who nodded, before Danforth assented. I rose in a clattering of chains and went to my niece. I laid hands upon her the way I had been made to do at my examination.

She calmed, as I had known she would, as she had done before. When she settled, I pulled her to me as best I could with these wretched chains about my wrists. Like a baby, without will or protest, she came, and I knew what it looked like: as if I had bewitched her. I held her as I had dreamed of doing during the long sea voyage to Salem. I held her as if I were the mother she had lost, the mother I would never be. She went limp and fell asleep in my arms, staying there until I felt George Locker pulling me away, while Samuel Parris lifted Charity and took her from the room.

I looked up then, into Lucas's face, and I saw a quiet faith there, a faith in me. I knew what he felt; I knew the power of it, how he'd fought it, and so this victory was the most precious gift I'd ever been given. He loved me enough to trust me against all reason, to make this sacrifice, to put his own life in peril to choose me.

I could yet do the same.

I turned to Thomas Danforth. "The things she's said are true," I told him quietly. "I have bewitched him."

"No," Lucas said forcefully. "Dear God, Susannah, do not do this."

I ignored him. "I would like to confess. Who will hear it?"

"No! No!"

"Quiet him," Danforth said, and I felt a moment of terror as he motioned to George Locker. The constable went immediately to help Tom Putnam and John Hathorne take Lucas from the room.

He struggled; they had to drag him to the door. Even then, he grabbed the door frame and looked back at me, and there was fury and dismay in his eyes. "I will not let you do this, Susannah." Then they yanked him away, and the door shut behind them.

Chapter 35

———— ❦ ————

I WAS ALONE WITH THOMAS DANFORTH AND JONATHAN CORWIN, and I was terrified. I had wanted only to save Lucas; I had not thought beyond that.

"You are confessing to being a witch?" Danforth asked.

I nodded. "Aye."

Corwin said, "We must bring her before the bar. We should examine her as we have examined the others."

Danforth nodded. "Get the afflicted girls, the Fowler girl as well." He turned to me as Corwin left. "You understand what you are confessing to? You understand witchcraft is a capital offense?"

I tried to suppress my fear. "I understand."

He looked at me thoughtfully, and then he took me into the courtroom, to the bar of justice, where I was made to stand and wait. It did not take long before the girls were brought from an ordinary nearby, along with a crowd of people anxious to see. I recognized Charity's friends as they were brought in: Annie Putnam, Mary Walcott, and Elizabeth Hubbard were among them, along with two I did not recognize. And then, brought in last, though she had suffered the morning worse than any, was Charity.

She and the girls performed on cue—how cynical I was, that I expected such. Charity screamed louder than the others, though just a half hour before, she'd lain quietly in my arms. I wondered if she even remembered it. I wondered if she'd felt the peace we'd shared for just a few moments together.

Hathorne returned, along with Thomas Putnam and George Locker, who came quickly to stand beside me. I craned my neck for a view of Lucas, but I saw him nowhere.

"Susannah Morrow," Danforth began, "you have today confessed to being a witch, have you not?"

The girls went eerily silent. The courtroom talk died immediately. I had the strangest thought—'twas as if I were on a stage, and the people gathered in the benches were not witnesses in the courtroom but a paying audience looking for a good entertainment. Geoffrey's words came to me: *You give them what they want, is all. They like exaggeration, my love. They want to be horrified; they want to laugh. . . . 'Tis easy enough. Throw in a trick dog, and they'll be in the palm of your hand.*

I understood him then, as I had never quite before. 'Twas the first time since I'd come to Salem that I felt in control of anything. They were ready to hang on my every word, captivated already, bewitched. And suddenly I knew what I must do.

"How long have you been a witch?" Danforth asked me.

"A century," I said.

Danforth looked surprised. "A century? How can that be, when you are barely above thirty years?"

"My spirit is very old."

"You would have us believe that your spirit has lingered for seventy years beyond your age?"

"Evil is timeless, is it not?"

There was a gasp from the audience. Charity stared at me with unblinking eyes.

"What demon are you, that you can exist for so long?"

"No demon. Only a servant of the Devil, as you have all called me."

Danforth looked smugly satisfied. "How often do you visit with the Devil? How does he come to you?"

"Nightly," I said. "He comes as a man."

There was furor in the front row. Mary Walcott had been knitting. Now she looked up and shouted out, "She is the mistress of the Devil!"

"Quiet, quiet!" Danforth held up his hand. He turned back to me. "And what of Goodman Fowler? Did the Devil command you to bewitch him?"

"Aye."

"How have you bewitched him? What spells have you used?"

I paused and looked out at those faces, those people who were enraptured by my words, by their worst fears made flesh, their most rampant curiosities. I understood then what they needed from me. Their horror went deeper than a simple obsession with the Devil. 'Twas a fear of God, of fate. They wanted explanations of why things happened, reasons they could understand and believe: If Indians attack your village and kill your mothers and fathers, 'tis the Devil who has led them here, because you have done something wrong. If little John dies of a strange fever, 'tis because I have looked at him as I passed, and not because of a curative failure. What blame there was in this blameless world they wanted mounted. They wanted assurances: *Prayers work; I am one of God's chosen; my destiny is not Hell, but Heaven. . . .*

Yet I had spent these last eighteen years in London, and I knew . . . nothing was assured, and prayers were only prayers, and I knew in that moment that I would be hanged for my inability to give them relief, to provide them with solace.

Danforth said again, "What spells did you use to bewitch your sister's husband?"

I stared at him, and then I laughed. "With my hands," I said, and when he turned red, I laughed again. I saw Mary Walcott sitting there, knitting away, and said, "With a red bodice and a will to have him, with my hands and my mouth—aye, I bewitched him. I took him against his will as often as I could."

Mary stopped her knitting and looked up. "The black man is whispering in her ear even now. Look at him there!"

Charity hugged herself hard. She was shaking uncontrollably.

"Have you seen this woman with a black man before today?" Danforth asked Mary Walcott.

"At her examination," she said. "He whispered often in her ear."

"He stood beside a white man," Charity offered.

Danforth went still. "A white man?"

"Aye," she said quietly. "He made the black man tremble. He has made all the witches tremble in fear."

"What of your aunt?" Danforth asked. "Did he make her tremble?"

"She trembles at nothing. Even God does not frighten her."

Danforth turned to me. "Is this true? Are you so evil that God cannot frighten you?"

I met his gaze. "The Devil has promised me solace and eternal life. I have no fear of God."

"Which others have you consorted with? Who else here is a witch?"

"I am new to this place. I don't know their names."

"Abigail Hobbs has said there are witches' Sabbats, whereupon you gather to drink red wine and eat red bread. She says there is a wizard there who performs the sacrament in a terrible parody of Christ. She has seen you there. She says you sing so they can dance. That you sing the Devil's songs."

"Aye, she does!" Charity called out. "She does sing the Devil's songs!"

"Tell us," Danforth urged, coming closer. "Do you sing the Devil's songs?"

"Aye. I . . . have sung."

"At these Sabbats?"

"I have sung at places you would not approve of."

"What else happens at these meetings?"

I hesitated. Every eye was turned toward me. "There are huge fires built, bodies swung over them to burn, and then there is music and dancing; there is feasting while the flames rise and flicker. We eat meat that looks red in the firelight, and there is much laughing and singing."

"And this . . . This is the witches' Sabbat?" Danforth asked.

"This is Guy Fawkes Day," I said.

The courtroom erupted in chaos, but for Mary Walcott, who kept knitting. I caught her gaze, and I saw how it burned with hatred, and all I could feel for her was pity. Horrible pity, that she should be so trapped here, that she should be so desperate—

"Enough!" Danforth shouted. "You toy with us, madam, as the Devil bids you."

I was allowed to say nothing more. Danforth gestured to the constable, who dragged me back hard from the bar of justice; the crowd was rising and shouting. In this chaos I was taken away.

They pulled me out into the street, where the people shouted at me and pushed. Someone threw an apple, which hit me on my cheek so hard tears came to my eyes. Another threw a half-rotten cabbage that exploded where it hit my hip in slimy leaves and the smell of corruption. Locker did not handle me gently. I tripped and stumbled, and my hair fell into my face—'twas tangled and dull, with a foul smell, but I could not move it from my eyes; he would not let me stop, and he held the end of the chains so I could not lift my arms.

But in spite of this, I felt victorious. I had saved Lucas from arrest. I had managed to manipulate them well enough to save my lover's life.

Jem took my chains from Locker and led me down into the dungeon again. When he twisted the key in the lock, he began to chuckle, and I stared at him in confusion as he pushed open the door and shoved me inside.

And then I saw what had caused his amusement.

Lucas waited for me with the others.

He was in chains.

Jem closed the door behind me, and I heard the lock. I fell to my knees. "Lucas," I whispered. "My God. Oh, my God."

I felt his hands on my shoulders as he knelt before me, and then he lifted his arms over my head so he could hold me close.

"Why are you here?" I asked desperately. "I cannot believe . . . Why are you here?"

"They've accused me of being a witch," he whispered.

"But 'tis not possible. I told them I'd bewitched you. I told them—"

" 'Twas over from the moment I withdrew my testimony. Before you even confessed. 'Twas nothing you could say to change it."

"It cannot be. I will not let them do this."

He gave me a bitter smile. "You knew it too, Susannah. You saw the way they looked at me. I had thought . . . I had hoped my reputation would save me, but I should have realized. . . . If even Rebecca Nurse could be arrested, what chance did I have?"

I wanted to cry. "I cannot believe this. Surely this will end. Surely someone will see. There must be clearer heads—"

"What clearer heads, Susannah?" he asked fiercely. "Where shall they be found? The preachers believe. Magistrates believe. Did they tell you they arrested nine others? Including Mary Easty, Rebecca's other sister?"

I stared at him in dumb surprise.

"A week ago, they confiscated Proctor's property. They left his maidservant with the care of Proctor's five children and not even a pot to cook in. George Corwin took it all, sold the cattle at half price, killed some."

"George Corwin?" I asked.

"Nephew to the magistrate," Lucas said wryly. "He was made high sheriff a few days ago. There's no love lost between Proctor and the rest of the village. They say he'll hang as a convicted witch—'tis only a matter of time before his property belongs to the crown, and 'tis certain enough that they'll take it now. Is this the work of clearer heads? Is this what I have to look forward to? Do you know the maid they gave Proctor's children to?"

I hated to ask the question. "Who?"

"Mary Warren. Charity's friend. One of the girls who accused Elizabeth Proctor of witchcraft."

"Mary Warren?" I frowned at him in confusion. "But . . . but she is here. I heard her two nights ago. She's been accused of being a witch."

"Aye. When she protested the accusation of John Proctor, the girls turned on her as well. 'Tis said he has been a father to her. She cannot have liked to see him arrested."

"But . . . they questioned her here. Last night. I heard it all. She says she is not a witch, that the girls lie."

"Who knows the truth anymore? The world's gone mad, Susannah. Do not forget this. Nothing is as it should be."

"What of Jude and Faith?" I asked. "What of Charity? What will become of them?"

"Faith is still at Hannah Penney's. Tom Putnam has promised to see Jude there as well. No harm will come to them. And Charity . . . Today was the first time I'd seen her since she told me of her vision with Judith. She stays still at Ingersoll's. They have made my daughter . . . a stranger to me."

He rested his forehead against mine, and I felt something wet drop onto my cheek. He was crying. "You should not have done it," he whispered to me. "I would not have asked it of you. I did not want it."

" 'Tis too late now. 'Tis done."

"They will not let you rest until you reveal others; you realize this? If you do not reveal others, they will hang you. How long can you toy with them, Susannah? They are not foolish men."

"Until I can think of a way to save us both," I said.

Lucas sighed. " 'Tis in God's hands now."

" 'Tis in our own hands," I corrected him. "It always was."

Chapter 36

———⚜———

THAT NIGHT, THEY BROUGHT THE NINE OTHERS IN, SO NOW THERE were fifteen in a cell meant for four. There was not enough bedding; Jem and Richard brought in straw and spread it around, wadding it to serve as beds. Lucas shared my pallet. In the midst of so many other people, we were as an island, alone.

The next morning, Sam Nurse came to deliver blankets and scowled at me in contempt. He'd no doubt heard of my confession.

I watched as Lucas went with Sam to a corner, where they huddled together, talking. I heard a rustling on the pallet above me, and Giles Corey came down to use the slop pail. When he came back, I expected him to climb to his pallet again, to join his wife, but he stopped before me. "So you've confessed," he said. The force of his contempt was formidable. "Who've you dragged down with you, witch-bitch?"

I gave him no response, and felt a guilty satisfaction as Giles Corey shrank away.

In the corner, Sam rose, and Lucas with him. They clapped each other on the shoulder, and then Sam called for Jem and the door opened and he was gone without a look in my direction. Lucas turned to me, dismay and sorrow hard upon his face.

"What is it?" I asked him. "What news did Sam bring? Are the girls . . . Oh, tell me 'tis not bad."

Lucas sank onto the pallet. "'Tis Charity. When she heard they arrested me, she had such fits they could not stop her." His voice went toneless, a dull recitation, a listing. "She tried to throw herself into the fire, not once, but many times; she hurt her wrist in trying. She also vomited pins and a key, and bit her tongue so her mouth was full of blood. She stares now into space and will not see or speak to any living thing. Sam said"—here Lucas's voice broke—"she is insensible. Her mind is . . ."

"You cannot leave her to them. Lucas, you must tell Sam to take her away. Surely the Pooles will care for her until you can bring her home again—"

"You have more faith than I," he said. "Shall any of us ever leave this place except by dying?"

"Aye, we shall. There must be someone, Lucas, who will hear what we have to say—"

Lucas laughed; 'twas a terrible sound. "You have not been in the village for months, Susannah. You cannot imagine what 'tis like there. Suspicion everywhere; 'tis like a terrible tide that cannot be turned. There will be no quick end to this, I promise you. It only grows. Sam said Locker confiscated my land. The animals, my tools . . . 'Twas all taken and destroyed or sold. He took everything in the cellar and storage room. He poured the cider and the beer into the yard. The property I have poured my sweat into for the last sixteen years is forfeited to the crown."

"How can that be? You have not been convicted."

"Since when does that matter? 'Tis what happened to Proctor. I was not . . . quiet. After Charity told me her vision of the murders . . . I was more outspoken than I should have been. I should have known, but . . . but I have lived in this village for too long; I believed in rational men. I had forgotten my part. I forgot who I was, the enemies I'd made." His expression was grim. "'Tis almost certain I will be convicted, Susannah. You should know this. Convicted and hanged."

I stared at him in disbelief. "'Tis because you were on the Village Committee—is that your meaning? You believe this is deliberate? That the girls are naming their enemies?"

"If it didn't start that way, it may end so. You heard Mary Warren's confession. And Sam said people are beginning to talk; 'tis a feeling about that perhaps the girls are being led. They don't even know some of these people they're accusing. Bridget Bishop, for one, never laid eyes on them. And George Burroughs."

"Who is he?"

"One of the first ministers of the village," Lucas said. "He and Putnam were long at odds. He's in Maine now. They will have to go a long way to find him. But they may. 'Tis said . . . The girls say he's the leader of the witches. The wizard. Sam says that even Joseph Putnam is afraid. He told Tom that if a single member of his family was accused, he would come after him. But still he keeps a horse saddled and ready, and a loaded gun."

"Then there is hope. As long as there are doubters—"

"Susannah, don't hope for that. There are too many who believe. The deputy governor believes. At first, even I did not doubt the truth of the things these girls say."

"They would leave your children orphans?"

"If I am a witch, 'tis better I do not raise them."

"But you are not a witch, Lucas."

"Aye." He sighed. "There is evil here. There are none who deny that. And I have already contributed to it. My daughter is an accuser. You are here because of me."

"Don't say that. I did not take care to understand this world of yours."

"This was the life I chose for myself," Lucas said, "yet, when I think of it . . . Do you know that I have never heard my children laugh?"

"'Tis the village—"

"No." He shook his head. "No. Sam's children laugh. I have heard Daniel Andrew's sons roar with pleasure. 'Tis me. I have been afraid, and I have taught my daughters to be the same. 'Tis too late to change things, I know, but I wish—"

"'Tis not too late," I told him, and those words became my promise to him.

An hour later, Richard came to get me, and I was questioned once more in a still-empty jail cell on the upper floor—not by the magistrates this time, but by the preachers instead. They were gathering information to implicate others; I knew that, and I gave it to them the best I could. They were most interested in the details: The Devil's Sabbat especially fascinated them. I told them the story of the last supper, fashioning it as I went in shades of red and black, giving them the Devil.

I did all this, and thought only of how to help Lucas, what to do. I was driven by it. As the days passed, he returned from his own examinations, weary and bloodless, without even a sight of his daughter to ease him; his worries were transparent beneath his skin. I burned to free him, and when they arrested four others amidst hailstorms that rocked the end of April like God's icy tears, and New England received the news that Increase Mather was nearly arrived with a new charter and a new governor—the Indian fighter, William Phips—I knew I had not much time left. With a new charter and a new government, the trials could be set.

But worse than that was the news of Charity. Sam Nurse came as often as he could, and told us that Charity had lapsed into blank-eyed silence. She refused to take anything but broth. She was already nothing but bones. Now she was dying. I watched Lucas change with the news. I watched the desperation and the horror in his eyes; I watched the pounds drop from him. Though I begged him to eat, 'twas impossible to swallow the prison food: black cabbages, sweet potatoes crawling with maggots, corn rotten with borers. On Sundays, we were given a treat: a heavily salted soup made of a single ox bone boiled in water with dried apples.

'Twas summer in New England, yet in this prison, there was still winter dark and barrenness. The days passed; Increase Mather arrived in Boston, along with the new governor. By then, George Burroughs, the minister Lucas had talked of, had been arrested, along with several others. Mary Warren had recanted once again, no doubt desperate to regain her status as one of the afflicted after three weeks in prison chains. She was one of Burroughs's chief accusers now. I had heard there was a total of thirty-six imprisoned, but the number changed daily, and showed no signs of slowing. The others in the cell with us talked in hushed trepidation about when the trials would begin, what would happen once the governor learned of what had passed here in Salem, but I did not let myself worry over such things. I was a confessed witch; I would hang soon enough. I had grown accustomed to the thought.

But I could not let Lucas die.

'Twas two days after Increase Mather returned that I finally determined how to save him.

I had been lingering by the cell door while Lucas slept, when I heard a rustle in the hallway, and a giggle and a groan that were not of suffering but of pleasure.

I glanced out the barred window, wondering who satisfied themselves in the hallway instead of seeking privacy elsewhere. Soon I saw the edge of a skirt come into view, and I leaned closer to see out. 'Twas a pretty, buxom girl with her cap askew and her bodice laces loosened. She giggled again as whoever she was with pressed her against the wall. Jem, I saw. 'Twas Jem, with his sweetheart.

I was immediately annoyed, and then I saw how she pushed him away, still hesitant as he pulled at the laces of her chemise, and I saw then the color of the skirt she wore—a bright leaf green, a color too bright and vain for this place, and the idea came so fast into my head 'twas as if I'd been struck with it. Quickly I went to the bag Hannah had brought me all those weeks ago and rifled through it until I found what I was looking for. The cursed red bodice.

I took it with me back to the cell door and slapped my hand against the bars. "Jem! Jem, come here!"

He buried his face in the girl's neck.

"Jem!"

She pushed at him a little. "Shouldn't you see to them?" she asked.

"I've other things to tend to now," he said, leering at her.

I slapped the bars again and kicked the door. "Jem!"

The girl pushed him again, and Jem sighed and stood back, jerking at his breeches as he came to the cell door. "What the hell do you want? I ain't your servant boy."

"I'm in need of help," I said.

The jailkeep cursed, then unlocked the door with a fierce twist. He turned to the girl and said, "You want to see the witches up close, Pru?"

She hesitated, but I saw in her eyes that vulgar curiosity, as if we might change before her eyes. Jem held open the door, and she slipped inside, keeping back against the wall, gasping a little when she saw the people inside, lying as they were in nearly every foot of space.

"They're like animals," she whispered in a wondering voice.

I could not help myself. "Aye," I said, raising my hand at her like a claw. "And if you get too close, we'll eat you up."

She gasped again, pressing hard to the wall. Jem only laughed. "What d'you want?" he asked me.

"I've spilled something on my dress. I need you to unchain me so I can change," I told him. Then I held out the scarlet bodice, holding it as best I could, angling it so the girl could see.

Pru made a little sound, like a mew; with relief and satisfaction, I saw how she stared at that bodice, with pure longing, with something like reverence. I had seen the same look in Mary Walcott's eyes. Jem had bent to go through the keys on his ring, but when he heard her sound, he looked up.

I held out the bodice. "Would you like to touch it?" I asked Pru. "The material is exceedingly fine."

She glanced at Jem. She did not want to come near me, I saw

that, but neither could she resist the lure. Carefully she stepped forward, touching the sleeve of the bodice, just barely, and then she touched again, lingering this time.

"'Tis paragon," I said. "From London. Made by Madame Bertrice. Do you know her?"

Pru shook her head. "I've never seen London."

"She has a fine shop. This was made for me, but I have lost so much weight. . . ." I sighed. "'Twas once quite lovely."

"'Tis lovely still," she said in a hushed voice.

I glanced at Jem, at the way he was looking at her, the way he looked to me. I held out my hands again and gave a little shake of my chains. He jerked his head at Pru to tell her to go. She slipped out, and when he bent close to unlock the manacles, I said, "What do you think she'd give you, Jem, for a bodice like this?"

Jem went still.

"Jemmy, can you hurry?" Pru whined from the hall.

"Quiet," he said over his shoulder. "Be quiet a moment, will you?" He turned back to me. "What're you saying?"

"Think how pretty she'd look in it. She's more buxom than I, but 'twould fit her well, I think. Imagine how she'd look in nothing but this—"

"Enough," he said. His voice was rough, his breathing rougher. "Give it to me."

I yanked it away again. "No, no. 'Tis not yours for nothing, Jem, my boy."

"Jemmie?" came the voice in the hall.

Impatiently he said, "All right, then. What d'you want for it? A bottle? Fresh beer?"

I met his gaze. "I want to ransom Lucas Fowler."

Jem glanced to where Lucas slept on the bed.

Quietly I said, "How hard would it be, to turn your back some day, to let him just . . . slip out? You won't find a bodice like this in all of New England. And think what your pretty Pru would do for you, how appreciative she would be."

"'Tis a risk for me," he said uncertainly.

"What risk? You're the jailkeep. How can the council expect you to keep prisoners for free?"

"Oh, I'll be paid."

"With what? By whom? Lucas has three children, none of them adults, two but infants. There's no other family, no one to pay his jail fees if he is convicted. They've already taken his property for the crown. I'm a confessed witch—I will surely hang, and no one here cares enough where my body lies to redeem it. If he was to hang too—'twould be a loss, then, for both of us. Every day he stays costs you money. Why not take what you can now?"

He hesitated.

I looked down at the fabric. "'Tis a beautiful color. 'Twill add pink to Pru's fairness. And she wants it, Jem. Did you see how she looked at it? I think she would give anything to feel it against her own skin."

He swallowed tightly. "Aye," he said quickly, as if afraid he would change his mind. "Very well. 'Tis an even trade."

"You'll let Lucas escape?"

"Tomorrow," he whispered. "In the evening, when the crowds are gone."

"The chains?"

"Have him feign illness. I'll unchain him and take him upstairs to tend to him. Once we're there, I'll turn my back, and he can . . . do as he will."

"The bodice for his freedom, then," I said.

"Jemmy, will you hurry?" Pru cried.

"Give it to me," he said.

"When 'tis done," I told him; though I saw he wanted to protest, Pru called again, and he was gone.

I went back to where Lucas slept. "'Tis your last night here, my love," I whispered. I watched him sleep for a long time.

Chapter 37

I LISTENED TO THE MOANS OF THE OTHER PRISONERS, THE CONstant talk, the sound of crying from another cell. This place was never quiet; 'twas like a living tomb, bodies buried alive. I didn't dare think beyond tomorrow night, when I would be here alone again.

I watched as Lucas and Giles Corey spoke quietly in the corner, and then I saw them laugh together before Lucas made his way back to the pallet and settled in beside me. 'Twas all I could do to keep from telling him outright what I'd done.

"What were you talking about?" I asked him.

"Ah . . . nothing," he said, leaning his head back against the wall. "A time several months ago, when we were hunting together. 'Tis of no account."

"You like Giles."

He shrugged. "'Tis a small village. 'Tis better to like than not."

I asked, "Have you been happy here, Lucas? In this village? Has your life been what you hoped it would be?"

He looked at me oddly. "Such a question. . . . You have been in a strange temper this evening."

"Thoughtful, more like," I said.

His thumb moved over mine, a soft caress. "Have I been happy here?"

"You loved Judith," I said. Before he could answer, I said quickly, "No, do not tell me. There is not an answer you could give to that question that would make me glad."

He was quiet. His eyes, when he looked at me, were such a burning blue I saw their color clearly in the shadows. "What of you, Susannah? Were you happy in London?"

"I have ever been a wanderer," I told him honestly. "If not by journeying, then at least in my own heart. Satisfaction has always . . . eluded me."

"And this . . . between us . . . Is this another journey?"

"It has felt to me as if we have always belonged to each other. I would not have wished it so, and yet . . . I cannot deny it. And I can promise you: I have never felt such a way before."

He squeezed my fingers. His expression went bleak. "Aye."

I spoke in measured tones. "There is no future here. Not in the village."

"The village may not exist when this is over."

"But if it did, if all was resolved; if you had the chance to leave it—"

"Judith is buried here, and our children," he said slowly. "But 'tis time, I think, to find a different world."

"You would leave then."

"Aye. If we ever escape this place."

"Lucas, you must promise me that you will go. If you have the chance, you will take the girls and go as far from the village as you can."

He made a puzzled frown. "Why do you speak so? They've not even set the trial date—"

"But if . . . if they find you innocent, do not wait for me. You must promise me that you will go."

"And leave you to a hanging?"

"Aye, if it comes to that."

"I would do what I could to convince them otherwise. I would not leave you to face death alone."

"You must," I said. " 'Tis not me who matters, Lucas, but your daughters."

I had chosen the best argument, I knew. He loved his daughters. In the end, he would do what was best for them.

"I'll promise it," he said finally, "if you promise me something in return."

"What is it?"

"If there comes a way out of this, you will take it as well. You are no witch; don't let them hang you for it. If I promise to leave you, then you must promise the same."

"Aye. I promise it."

He leaned back again, satisfied. " 'Twill be over soon. It must be over soon."

I nodded, and laid my head upon his shoulder. "What will you do with your future, Lucas?"

"I have thought lately of New York. I can find work there, I think. There is the war to consider—'tis not as safe as Boston, but 'tis not New England, either. We would be safe enough, and I have thought . . . for us . . . There are places where laws do not bind us."

"And your own heart, Lucas, how does it reconcile what we are to each other?"

"I would not lose happiness," he said simply. "I have lived without it too long."

The next morning, I berated myself for trusting Jem—he was but a jailkeep; how had I dared to trust him? When 'twas Richard who brought us breakfast, I could not eat for the curses that filled my soul. I was short-tempered and distracted.

"What ails you?" Lucas asked me several times, and I could only shake my head and move away.

As the hours passed, I was increasingly apprehensive. When I finally heard the turn of the key, and Jem calling out that he'd brought our supper, I nearly fell to the floor.

Jem did not meet my eyes as he came inside bearing a large pail stinking of soup. He handed out the shallow, cracked wooden bowls—only six; the rest of us would wait until those bowls were empty, and Jem could use them again. He stood back to wait. Then he glanced up at me and inclined his head to Lucas; I knew 'twas time. I went to Lucas, who sat on the edge of our pallet, waiting his turn. In a low voice, I said, "You must feign illness. Now."

He frowned at me. "What?"

"You must feign illness. Jem will take off your chains and bring you upstairs. When he turns his back, you must go out the door. As quickly as you can. 'Twill be unlocked. Then you must flee, Lucas. Take the girls however you can, and leave this place. You talked of New York last night. You must lose yourself there. Do not let them find you."

He was staring at me.

"I have bought your escape," I said urgently, quietly. I felt the tears come to my eyes, and did not try to stop them. " 'Tis your chance for a better life."

"You've bought escape," he said in bewilderment. "How?"

" 'Tis of no matter." I glanced at Jem, who waited impatiently. "You must go, Lucas. Quickly."

"I will not go without you. It must be the both of us, or not at all."

"It cannot be the both of us." I looked over my shoulder at Jem, who was frowning; I grabbed Lucas's hand and called out, "Oh, Lucas, what is wrong?"

Lucas wrenched away. "Not without you."

"Don't be a fool," I whispered. "There is Charity to consider, and Jude. There is Faith. Think of what we spoke of yesterday. There is one chance. You must take it."

He hesitated, and I bent closer. "You promised me, Lucas. Last night, you promised you would go if the chance came—"

"I thought we were talking of improbabilities," he accused. "You knew of this then. I did not."

"What goes on over there?" Jem called out.

I raised my voice. "He's ill! Jailkeep, I think he's ill. Can you not do something?" I turned back to Lucas and murmured, "You must groan. Do something."

"I cannot in good conscience—"

I leaped to my feet. "Jailkeep, please!" I called out, and Jem came rushing over. Lucas looked up at me. I was crying—cursed tears.

"I will not—" he began.

"He's got a fever, I'm sure of it. 'Tis this wretched place. You must fetch a doctor." Then, for Lucas's ears alone, I whispered, "The children, Lucas. The *children.*"

He hesitated, and then he doubled over, groaning. Jem unlocked the manacles, and they fell clanking to the ground. He grabbed Lucas's arm, pulling him to his feet.

Lucas grabbed my wrist hard, his grip so tight that I had no choice but to stumble behind him. Jem said, "Not her," and pried Lucas's fingers loose.

Lucas twisted back to me. "Susannah—"

"You'll be fine, my love," I called to him. "Jem will see to it."

His face was anguished as Jem pushed him out into the hallway, and then the door shut again, and I sagged onto the pallet, still warm from Lucas's heat. Alone, in darkness, with my fellow cellmates scurrying around the pail of rancid soup like insects, and Giles Corey's eyes too dark and knowing where he sat watching on the bed above mine.

I waited for Jem to bring him back, to see Lucas stumble into the cell again, his chains clanking as the jailkeep sneered at me in contempt. When that did not happen, I waited for them to catch him. At every moment in the hall, every sound, every flicker of light, I sat up on my pallet, waiting to see him again. I did not sleep that night—no more than an hour. The cries of the suffering woke me, as they had not done in weeks and weeks. Each time, I woke expecting to see him lying beside me, and I was disoriented until I remembered that he was gone.

They did not bring him back that night, nor did they the next day. Giles Corey said to me suspiciously, "How ill Lucas must be, that they do not return him here," and I nodded and looked worried. 'Twas not hard to do; my mind was in constant turmoil about his escape. By the third day, no one asked questions of me, though I sometimes saw Martha and Giles talking low and urgently among themselves—talk that stopped when I turned. I kept my ears open, but heard no gossip except that Goody Osborne had died in the Boston Jail, her already frail constitution mortally weakened by her imprisonment. After I gave Jem the bodice, he assiduously avoided my gaze whenever he came to the cell, at least for the first week, and then he was as he always was, and I knew he'd forgotten Lucas.

The prison seemed even more like the very bowels of Hell—even the upper cells were filled now, and the sound was as one low, long swell that never eased. I heard nothing of Lucas, or of Charity, not until ten days had passed, not until the day that Richard announced to us all that the Massachusetts General Council had met and instituted a Court of Oyer and Terminer—a temporary court meant for extreme and unusual circumstances—to try us.

These last days, I had thought so much on Lucas that I had not had time to think of myself, or what I had confessed to. I had no hope that my life would last the summer. They would keep me alive long enough to condemn others—I knew this—but then 'twould be my turn, and I would hang.

'Twas in this mood that, an hour later, I looked up to see Jem unlock the door for Hannah Penney.

At first, I did not realize it was her. I saw her pause inside the door, and then she caught my eye and I knew her. She was not carrying baby Faith.

"Hannah!" I called. My chains banged against my legs as I moved; her eyes went to them, and I remembered—the last time I'd seen her, I had not been wearing them.

"Dear God," she murmured, and I saw her lips move in a quick prayer before she said to me, "The Lord has truly seen fit to punish you here."

I knew she was not talking about the cell itself, but of me. In these last weeks, I had formed an interest in my bones. For the first time in my life, I could see them in my skin, and they were fascinating to me, their knobs and valleys, their ridged definition. The ones at my wrists were so sharp that the manacles had rubbed the skin raw over them, sores that never healed; I almost expected the bones to come bursting through. I could feel hard edges in my face now—my jaw, my cheeks—there was no softness over them for my fingers to press into. Yet this was not frightening to me; here in this cell, we were all the same. In constant view of each other, we turned into skeletal horrors slowly and easily; there was none of the suddenness that must shock Hannah now.

I did not try to reassure her. "Have you news of Lucas?" I whispered.

Her gaze came back to me. "Aye," she said reluctantly. "'Tis why I've come."

"Is he gone? Please, tell me he is gone."

"Aye. Days ago now. I would have been here sooner, but there is such madness—"

I gripped her arm hard, shaking her a little so my chains rattled. "Tell me," I demanded, pulling her as far as I could from listening ears. "Tell me everything."

"He came one night to take Jude and Faith. I warned him the babe was not yet weaned. . . . He will have trouble with her, I'll warrant. I told him my sister once fed a child on cow's milk and sugar, though who knows—"

"Aye, aye. What else? What of Charity?"

Hannah glanced past me to the others, and then lowered her voice. "She was staying at Ingersoll's. You know she was sick. Wasting away, I heard, though I did not see her. She'd been abed, poor thing. Couldn't even speak her name, they said. Then, one morning, when they went to bring her breakfast, she was not there. No one found a trace of her. 'Twas as if she disappeared into the air. But if I had to guess—Lucas and Sarah Ingersoll were friends, and Charity was gone the morning after Lucas came to get the others from me. Sam Nurse has been tight-lipped about it as well. He knows something, I'm guessing, but he won't say a word."

"You've not said a word to anyone, have you? Have you told them you think 'tis Lucas who took her?"

She looked at me as if I were a fool. "Susannah, what should I say? 'Tis well known that he escaped, and Jude and Faith are gone from me when everyone knows they were put in my care. I've said nothing, but everyone suspects I saw him."

"Will they follow him, do you think?"

"Follow him where? No one knows where he's gone, except perhaps . . . you."

"Me?"

"Aye. Lucas bade me tell you: He's gone to the place you talked about. Those were his words."

The place we talked about. *New York.* "Have you told anyone this?"

"Not even George, though he's asked. 'Twas a message for you alone; I see no reason for me to tell."

"Thank you."

Hannah sighed. "They are not happy about his escape, I'll tell you. Perhaps they will try to find him, but my guess is 'twill not be for some time. There are so many others. You yourself confessed there were twenty or more. With so many witches, how can they risk the village to find only one? What is a single man in light of such evil?"

"I thank you for bringing me his message. It cannot have been easy for you."

"I welcomed the task," she said simply. "I have been praying for your soul, Susannah. I had wanted the chance to pray with you. I am relieved at your confession—such repentance can only help ease your way toward God's forgiveness. How tormented you must have been. When a soul longs so for Christ's salvation, 'tis an easy mark for Satan."

"Aye," I said, turning from her.

She clasped my arm tightly. "But the Devil can be conquered. Surrender to Christ is the only way."

I looked around to her again, to her pleading gaze, and I said, "I have surrendered already to too many things, Hannah."

"Pray with me."

I hesitated and looked down at this woman who had been my friend. If praying with her would give her peace, then I would oblige.

"Very well," I said.

She smiled and clasped my hands. "Those chains are not what keep you prisoner. Let us find God's grace together."

She prayed, and I closed my eyes and listened to her words. Yet 'twas not of God I was thinking, but of Lucas, of three girls bent close together in joy and fear as their father led them from Salem Village, slipping onto an empty road, where shadows were sharp against a bright spring moon.

PART FOUR

LUCAS

—Redemption—

Long is the way
And hard, that out of Hell leads up to light.

—John Milton
Paradise Lost

Chapter 38

———— ❦ ————

I DID AS SUSANNAH BADE ME, THOUGH 'TWAS WITH A WRETCHED heaviness in my soul that I crept out the door while Jem's back was turned and slipped into the night. I sensed that I would not see her again; the feeling added an urgency to my flight that made me run more quickly, though to run from her was the last thing I wanted to do.

The back door of the prison led to the muddy banks of the river. The tide was out now; the fetid mud of the river flats filled my nostrils; it seemed forever since my lungs had filled with anything but the stench of jail. The night was soft and warm; I heard the sounds from a nearby tavern, the creak of the ships on the harbor, the gentle tug of wind through their riggings.

I stayed hidden in shadows, a fugitive in my own town—the irony of it was not lost on me as I raced as surreptitiously and quickly as I could to the road leading to the village. At every sound of hoofbeats, I hid myself in the reeds and grass. Once, my efforts roused heath hens that flew squawking and frightened into the road. They so startled the rider that the man cursed and pulled up his horse, his breathing broken and anxious as he searched the fields for signs of Indians or thieves.

I had little time; 'twould be soon enough that the magistrates were told of my escape, and they would be searching for me. 'Twas very dark when I finally reached the outskirts of the village, only a short distance from my home, and I resisted the urge to go there, to see what damage they'd done to the land where I'd spent sixteen years sowing my sweat into the soil along with seed. Instead, I took the path I knew well enough to tread even in deepest darkness. I made my way to the Penneys'.

'Twas not without nervousness I did so. I had trusted Hannah with my children, but George Penney was still a toady to Hannah's father, and he to Nathaniel Putnam—their sympathies would lie with Parris and his supporters and the relentless search for witches. By now, the story of my recantation would be well known. They could not help but realize where I stood.

Yet my fears for my children had been a singular darkness the weeks I'd spent in that foul prison. I would not leave without them.

As I came closer, I saw the dim glow of light from within, and when I went to the door, I stopped, hearing a child's cry, a baby. Faith or Hannah's boy? I hesitated, suddenly frightened, and then I pounded the door with all my strength.

"Hold, hold!" came a voice from inside. George. I heard the creak of his footsteps, the pull of the latch, and then the pause. "Who is it? Who comes now?"

"'Tis your neighbor," I said, my voice rough from exertion. I did not sound myself, and I prayed he would not recognize me and bar the door. "I've news."

The door opened. "Wha—"

George's eyes opened wide; he gulped like a drowning fish, and then he was pushing the door closed again. Before he could, I shoved my foot inside. "Let me in," I said, pushing past him into the small house, which was loud with the sounds of children. From the hearth, Hannah looked up in fear as she bounced a child feverishly on her knee. It squalled louder.

"Oh, dear God," she exclaimed, rising, holding the child tight. 'Twas not my babe, but her own. "Lucas. My God, what have you done? What spell have you used to—"

"Where are my children?"

George stepped between me and his wife. He frowned, his corpulent face breaking into a dozen wrinkles. "Have they released you? We've heard nothing of it."

"No doubt the news will come tomorrow," I told him, and saw his skepticism as he scrutinized me. I had been in jail for several weeks; I could smell the foulness of it on my skin. "Where are my children?"

Just then, I heard running footsteps down the stairs; I saw a rush of white, and then there was a slam against me that nearly stole my breath, little arms going round my waist, a child pressing herself to me as if she could not hold me tight enough. "Father," Jude said. "Oh, Father, you've come!"

"Aye, I've come," I told her. "Get yourself dressed, child, and show me to your sister. We must go."

"Shall we go home, then?" she asked me, and I was held mute by the fullness of my love for her.

Finally I found my tongue. "We've a new home to go to. Hurry now, we've not much time."

"You cannot mean to take them," Hannah said. "They'll find you, Lucas, and then what? What will happen to them then?"

" 'Tis my job to worry over that," I said.

George nodded. He said to Hannah, "Fetch the babe and their clothes." When she hesitated, he said curtly, "Quickly now."

Hannah looked ready to protest. Her hold on her own child grew tighter, but then she pressed her lips together and hurried up the stairs.

"Thank you," I told George.

He looked grim. "I'll say nothing of this for as long as I can. But I will tell them eventually that you were here. You know I must."

"All I ask is that you give me a few days."

"If I can." He jerked his head toward the door. "Is she with you?"

The thought of Susannah brought a sudden despair. "No. I'm alone."

"Where will you go?"

"Come, George, you know I cannot tell you that."

Hannah came into the room again. This time, her child was gone; in her arms was Faith, newly awakened, still sleepy. Jude was behind them. She carried a canvas bag that bulged with what was left of her clothes and Faith's.

"She's not yet weaned," Hannah said worriedly. "You will have trouble with her."

"There are goats along the way," I said.

"She's not used to it—"

"I will not let her starve, Hannah."

I saw she did not want to put the babe into my arms, but then George nudged her, and she did it. Faith gazed up at me for a moment, and I felt her little sigh, the settling of her contentment; she closed her eyes again, drifting into sleep.

I looked at Hannah. "You visited Susannah once before."

She looked wary. "Aye. We were friends."

"I would ask you to do one thing, if you would."

"She cannot, Lucas," George said. "You have already put us at great risk. If they knew we had seen you, helped you—"

"Aye, of course." I motioned to Jude. "Let's go, child. Are you ready to walk?"

"Aye, Father."

"Then say good-bye." To Hannah, I said, "I have never thanked you for caring for Faith. I'll say it now. I appreciate all you've done."

George went to the door, impatient for us to leave, and I turned to go. Hannah grabbed my arm. "Let me say good-bye to the child," and as she leaned close to kiss Faith's downy forehead, Hannah whispered to me, "I'll go see her."

I whispered back, "Tell her I've gone to the place we talked of."

She looked puzzled, but she nodded.

George said, "You'd best hurry."

I shuffled Faith into one arm and reached my other hand for Jude, who took it—such a simple act of faith, and one I hardly deserved. Together we hurried into the darkness. The door closed firmly behind us, and she crept close to me and said, "I will not be afraid, Father."

"We've not far to go tonight, Jude," I reassured her, hoping it was true. I had one more task, and 'twas a job I would need help for. The village had changed so much, I could not be sure of anyone, and I tried to hide my apprehension from Jude as I pulled her with me to Sam Nurse's home.

We stumbled through the rows of Sam's cornfields, dark, leafy shadows, the rasp of sharp-edged leaves against our shins. The plants were stunted; already the summer looked to be a droughty one. When we reached the end of the field, the front door opened as if he'd expected us. I stopped so quickly that Jude ran into me, and I motioned for her to be quiet, and then saw Sam in the square of light. Slowly I came out of the shadows.

His gun was in his hand; at my approach, he lifted it. "Who goes there? Who is it?"

"'Tis Lucas," I answered quietly.

"Lucas?"

"Aye."

"But you were—"

"No longer," I said, staying my distance, keeping Jude behind me for safety. "I would know, Sam, are you friend or foe?"

A profound disgust crossed his face, and he lowered his gun and said, "Friend. Friend, of course. How can you ask otherwise?"

"I take nothing for granted any longer."

"No. No, you should not. But you are welcome here. More than welcome. I would shoot anyone who came to get you, so tired am I of this brutal business."

I came forward, bringing my daughters with me. "I would not have endangered you this way if I did not need to."

"There are worse kinds of danger. I would rather be shot for defending a friend than be safe and witness innocent people die. Dear God, what Hell is this?" He motioned for us to come in, and then he shut the door tightly behind us and called out, "Mary! Come quickly."

Sam's wife hurried down the stairs. When she saw us, she paused; her hand went to her cap in surprise. "Oh . . . Lucas . . . thank the dear Lord; have they released you, then?"

"Susannah bought my escape," I told her.

Mary took Faith. "Let me put the babe to bed. Come as well, Jude. You look exhausted, poor dear."

Jude gave me a questioning look, and I nodded. "Get some sleep, child. Go on with Mary."

"Will you be gone when I wake?" she asked me fearfully. What this town had done to my children—what *I* had done. . . .

"I'm going nowhere without you and Faith," I told her.

"Promise?"

"Aye. 'Tis a promise."

"And Charity too?"

I glanced up at Sam, who watched me carefully, and said, "I intend so."

Jude went willingly with Mary after that, and when they were gone, Sam said, "What are your plans?"

"We cannot stay here, not longer than tonight," I told him. "They'll come looking for me. Perhaps they are already looking; I have no way of knowing."

"Mary and I will watch the children until you can send for them, if you wish."

"No. I won't leave them again. I have already been remiss in my duty to them."

"It could be dangerous to take them."

"Any more dangerous than it would be to let them stay?"

Sam was somber. "I wish I could say aye, but we both know that what you say is true. Dorcas Good is four years old. My sainted mother—" His voice broke, and he paused a moment to right it. "There is no safe place in this village."

"I hate to do it, but I must ask one more thing of you, my friend."

He met my gaze. "Charity."

"Aye. I cannot leave without her."

" 'Twill not be easy to fetch her from Ingersoll's without anyone knowing."

"And I must not be seen. I would not ask this of you, but there is no one else I trust, and I will not leave her here to be destroyed."

He looked at me sorrowfully. "It may be too late for that, you understand. She has not eaten more than broth for days. She does not speak, but only stares—"

I closed my eyes against my sorrow and regret. "Aye. But if she dies, she will be with me, and not these other men who care for her only to use her in their war against the town."

Sam nodded. "We should go, then, before Sarah Ingersoll is abed."

Our plan was a simple one. We would take Sam's horse and mule, but no cart to slow us or make noise on the path. When we arrived, I would hide around the back, near the swamp and the stables, while Sam talked with Sarah and the two of them decided how best to spirit Charity away from the tavern.

"You had best be prepared to ride without her, if you must," Sam counseled me as we rode into the village. "If you do not keep safe, we have no hope of ever rescuing her."

I agreed to that, though I did not think I would be able to leave her.

'Twas growing late, and there were still lights glowing from the windows at Ingersoll's. Most men of the village had gone to bed. In times past, those wanting a game of shovel board or cards would have gone to Bishop's Tavern on the Ipswich Road, which dealt in such things, but I doubted 'twould be so now. Already the village felt different to me, not home, not any longer. Now I wanted only to take my daughters and go far away, to leave behind Judith's grave, and the graves of all those small souls she'd borne. I had been in mourning for most of my life, I realized suddenly, and this village was as a graveyard, my own charnel house, and I longed for a breath not scented with dust and bones.

There was a movement beyond the windows, and Sam jerked his head at me and whispered, "Go now. Quickly."

I led the mule around back. The smell of the swamp mud and skunk cabbage was strong, and newborn mosquitoes swarmed in helpless clouds around our heads. I could see nothing from here, so I listened, but the hum of insects and song of peepers mating in the waters beyond filled my ears. I glanced to the darkened windows on the second floor, to the one I thought was Charity's.

When I heard rapid footsteps, I drew the mule back farther into the shadows.

"Lucas?" came Sam's whisper.

I dismounted quickly, and stepped around the corner. Sam came hurrying to me.

"William Allen would not leave," he explained. "Sarah finally shooed him out. Hannah's abed, and Nathaniel's at Tom's. Sarah has no idea when he'll be back, but it should be shortly. We've very little time."

Together we raced to the front door. Sarah had blown out all but one lamp, and she waited for us uneasily. When she saw me, she smiled—but 'twas not a greeting, more a sympathetic motion.

"Oh, Lucas, 'tis glad I am to see you," she said. "I'm so sorry, what happened to her—"

"We've no time for this now," I said. "I know you've done your best."

"Aye. She's nothing but skin and bones—" She cut herself off and shook her head, handing Sam the lamp. "You know where she is. Mama's a light sleeper, so you must be quiet. I'll keep watch at the door."

Sam took the stairs quietly and quickly. I was right behind him. He paused at the top, and I went past, leading the way to my daughter's door, pushing it open. I rushed to her, falling to my knees at her bedside, listening for her breath. When I heard it, soft and too shallow, I closed my eyes in relief.

"Come," Sam said, looking back at the open door. "Wake her and let's away."

I shook her gently. "Charity. Charity, 'tis your father. Wake up."

She did not move, but lay as one drugged with sleep. I shook her again, more urgently this time, because Sam filled the space with tension, and I could not help but listen for Nathaniel's step inside the front door.

I whispered again, "Charity, you must wake."

Still, she did not move. I wondered if this was part of her catatonia, and finally I lifted her, blanket and all, into my arms. Sarah was right; she was a bundle of bones, nothing but sharp joints and limbs too lanky to hold well. She would have been hard to carry in any case; she was sixteen, not a child to cuddle in my lap.

She woke then. Her eyes went wide; I heard her intake of breath, and I clamped my hand over her mouth and said, "Charity, 'tis nothing to fear. I am your father."

She arched against me, trying to escape—and I felt a desperate fear that my words had not calmed her. But there was no time to waste. Sam turned and went down the stairs, and I followed him, while Charity pushed and fought me. Sarah hurried over with the lamp.

"Quiet, child," she murmured. "All is well. You are safe."

My daughter reached out for Sarah, who said again, "You are safe, my dear," before urging us to hurry. "Go now. 'Twould be best to be far from here."

Sam and I rushed out the door and to the back of the ordinary, where I'd left the mule. I put Charity onto the saddle, and she tried to jump off the other side. She would have managed it too, had I not mounted quickly after and taken her tightly into my arms.

"You must be quiet," I said into her ear. "If we are caught, 'twill be worse for all of us." Again I put my hand across her mouth, holding her tight as I dug my heels into the mule. I heard the hooves of

Sam's horse pounding behind me as we fled the green, back to the road, riding without pause back to the house. Charity did not fight me as we rode, or if she did, I could not feel her above the jarring of the mule. I had hoped perhaps that she would know me then, that 'twas only that we'd awakened her so suddenly that she was afraid, but the moment the mule halted, Charity wrenched from my arms and threw herself from the saddle.

I was stunned at how quick she was. Once she was on the ground, she ran, only a pale white shadow in the darkness. I leaped off the mule, racing after her, not daring to call out. I overtook her within yards, grabbing her so she stumbled and went down; I went down with her, pulling her to my chest and rolling while she beat upon me with her fists. She cried out, "Release me, spirit! Release me! Avoid! Avoid!"

I grabbed one of her fists with my free hand, holding it still. "I am no spirit, Charity, I am your father."

"My father is dead!"

"I am not dead."

"I know he is! Mama told me he is dead!"

"Your mother is with God." I rolled until she was beneath me, and pinned her with my legs, holding her still, and then I stared into her face, which was wet with tears I could see even in the darkness. "I am no spirit, Charity, but your own father, come to take you away from here."

She spat into my face. "Liar! You are the Devil come to me with my father's face."

I did not bother to wipe the spittle from my cheek. " 'Tis an elaborate ruse for the Devil. A horse, Sam Nurse, Sarah Ingersoll . . . Are they all spirits, then?"

She hesitated. I felt her gaze hard upon my face, and then she said, "Father. Father, is it . . . you?"

'Twas a question, but she did not seem to require an answer. I saw the distress come into her eyes before she said wonderingly, "I did not kill you. I did not kill you. . . ." She began to sob.

I rolled off her, and gingerly I gathered her into my arms, expecting that she would bolt at my touch. She collapsed against me, and I held her there until she crawled into my lap like the little child she had once been, putting her arms around my neck to hold me close. I felt the warm wetness of her tears on my skin and cried myself for all the years I'd lost, for the child who had slipped away from me to journey alone into madness . . . and the man who had let her go.

Chapter 39

SAM GAVE US THE USE OF HIS CART AND THE MULE, THOUGH I HAD no money to give him, and no certainty about when they would be returned. He provisioned us for several days' journey, and gave me a flintlock and powder, and some coin. When I protested, he said bleakly, "I would that I could help the others so falsely accused," and I knew he was thinking of his mother. I accepted his generosity with humility.

"I will send word when I arrive."

"'Tis best if you do not, Lucas. Who knows if they will choose to pursue you—'twould be better if I know nothing. But then, when this is all over"—he smiled weakly—"then I may apply to you for a new cupboard."

I clapped him on the back and said my most heartfelt good-byes to the man who had been such a good friend to me.

I left as soon as we could, afraid that my lingering would bring trouble to his family. 'Twas near twilight—the roads were emptiest now, though night was the most dangerous time to travel. I had no other choice, not given my travel companions: an infant, a six-year-old, and a girl so haunted and frail she seemed transparent beyond the sharpness of her bones.

The way was difficult, the girls sleepless and irritable; Charity constantly watched the road beyond us, the trees, the fields, as if she saw demons in every shadow. Perhaps she did. She barely ate, and twice she broke into fits where she called out to her mother, and I was only able to still her by holding her so tightly in my arms she could not move.

I had planned to go to New York, where I suspected there would be no pursuit, but in the end, I could not abandon Susannah so completely, in spite of how dangerous it was to be close. I told myself I would go there someday, with her beside me. We would find a haven there, where the influence of the rationalist Dutch was strong. They did not put so much credence into the fact of witchcraft—only a short time ago, such disbelief would have been abhorrent to me; now 'twas my salvation.

Yet if I could not go to New York, neither could I stay in Massachusetts. I must stay hidden—if not for myself, then for Charity, who still suffered her afflictions, who would have been obvious and suspicious to anyone. So I went deep into Connecticut, where the three of us found lodging in a boardinghouse in a town at the end of a narrow bay, where I thought to stay until I found work enough to take a small house of our own.

Our room was mean and dirty, with a single small window. The furniture consisted of a rickety table and a bench, and two straw pallets covered with blankets that I rented from the landlord. I put Charity and Jude on one, while Faith and I shared the other; she whimpered and fussed while we all tried to find exhausted sleep. Faith had turned colicky with travel and the change to goat's milk and cow's milk—whatever I could afford to buy on the route. If she was not thriving, she was not languishing, either. Jude did well; she accepted things so easily, and this new place was a delight to her.

I grew more and more worried about Charity. I took a job at a nearby sawmill, but I had never made friends easily, and now I did not know who to turn to—anyone here I might tell would be immediately suspicious. The talk of Salem was the greatest bit of gossip in the town, enough so that I called myself by my stepfather's name to disguise myself. I could not go to a preacher and confess that my daughter was afflicted; they would assume the witchcraft plague had come to Connecticut. I did my best; as the days passed into a warm June, I prayed with them every night, and not the way I had done—I took care not to speak of the Devil at all, or of sin.

I cared for Charity as if she were a babe. I talked to my daughters at the table as if they were my neighbors, and interested in the goings-on in town, though they knew few of the people. Faith was eight months old now, and could sit up by herself. I would sit her on a burlap bag beside me on the floor and lean down to tease her or chuck her chin, and say to her things like, "Do you think this weather will hold, Faith?" The child gurgled back to me as if she understood my words. Jude would laugh, but Charity would not even smile. Her thoughts were her own, her eyes steadfastly silent.

Until a hot day in mid-June.

I spent that morning close to the saw, blocking out the sound the best I could with rags tied around my ears, concentrating on feeding the wood into the blade, watching my hands—dangerous work, work that required focus. Yet as I always did, I thought of Susannah. I wondered about her; I dreamed about her as I'd seen her last: too thin, the hollows beneath her collarbones deep, the ridges of her ribs a map beneath my hands.

I told myself I would know if she died, and I prayed it was so, though I did not truly believe it. God had proven fickle to me these last years, and I was bitter enough that I believed he might punish me by taking what I'd loved too much. My children. Judith. Charity. And now . . . Susannah. I listened greedily whenever the talk in town turned to Salem and the trials, and I knew that Governor Phips had been more concerned with the French and Indian War than with witches, and had left Salem to William Stoughton, his lieutenant governor. While the government had set up a court of Oyer and Terminer to try the accused, the girls still called out, filling the prisons with witches, though no one here seemed to know their names. I could not reveal the reason for my interest. All I could do was pray that my friends would escape this scourge, that Susannah would survive it. I prayed that those sitting judgment would prove more farsighted than the villagers.

That hot summer day, I was thinking of those things when I walked from the mill into the barely cooler evening air. I was covered with sawdust and sweat; my hair was plastered to my head. The rasping of the saw, the sluice of water, still rang painfully loud in my ears, so I did not at first hear the cries of the man who ran after me. 'Twas only because I paused to take off my gloves and shake the dust from them, that I even saw him there at all. It was Edmund Ames, who worked with me at the mill.

"Have you heard? Have you heard?" he bellowed. "They've hanged one of 'em!"

I should not have known what he spoke of. He had provided no context for it. Yet I understood immediately. Ames frowned and looked at me more closely. "You should take yourself home, man."

"Which of them?" I asked him. "Which one of them did they hang?"

"Some woman." He shrugged. "I didn't catch her name. Does it matter? One witch gone, a hundred more to follow."

He went past me, leaving me there on the street. The urge to ride back to Salem as fast as I could rushed over me; I began to run. I was halfway to the room I shared with my daughters when I realized in dull desperation that I could not return to Salem; even if they had hanged her, I could not attend to her body. I would be thrown back into prison the moment I set foot where I was recognized; I was in danger even here.

I stood there blindly in the street, the curses of a man whose cart and horse had to careen to miss me sounding only as a faraway echo. Gradually I became aware of the world around me again—the women pausing to gossip with their neighbors, gathering before a nearby shop, their voices alive with the story of the hanging in Salem. What Edmund Ames did not know, these women would, I realized. 'Twas their business to know.

An old woman moved from the others, hobbling with her full

basket to her door. I hurried over, slowing as I reached her, pretending to be only a passing neighbor with a healthy interest in local gossip, nothing more.

"Who was it?" I asked her. "Who did they hang?"

She eyed me and gave a crooked grin. "Some woman who owned a tavern. I think the name was Beckett. Or . . . Blister. Somethin' like that."

I felt a rush of relief that made me put a hand to the wall for support. A tavern owner with the name of Beckett or Blister. Bridget Bishop. It did not surprise me that she'd been the first to be tried. She had been suspected of witchcraft once before, many years ago. There would have been more evidence against her than the others.

I listened with half an ear while the woman told me the rest of the story, obviously delighting in having an audience to herself. As I left her and made my way home, the tale gathered full-blown in my head, as if I had witnessed it.

'Twas a frenzy, the old woman told me, as if she'd seen it herself, though I doubted she had set foot in Salem in her life. Even as Bridget Bishop choked and struggled in death, the afflicted girls kept up their mocking; they were not silent until the condemned was pronounced dead. Goody Bishop was cut down without ceremony, her body dumped in a crevice in the rocks. They began to cover her with dirt, but the digging was too hard, and so they left her there for the crows and wolves to find, her leg and arm sticking out like some bizarre plant. They walked away without even a prayer.

That image stayed with me. I found myself remembering Bridget as she had been in life—pretty and energetic, ornamented always with bits of lace, with a voice so low and raucous it marked her forever as a tavernkeep.

I was saddened and troubled as I walked slowly to the boardinghouse, barely greeting our landlord before I went up the rickety, dark, and narrow steps to the room where my daughters waited. As I approached the door, I heard sounds—the same ones I heard daily: Faith's fitful crying and Jude's tuneless singing as she tried to comfort her. I paused, wondering what I would tell them about the hanging, what would be Charity's reaction. I opened the door and stepped inside.

The room was hot and close—though the tiny window was open to let in whatever breeze would come, the room was under the roof, where the sun beat all day. Charity stood there, motionless, still listless, staring out unseeingly. She did not turn when I came inside, though Jude stood from where she bent on the floor next to Faith. She smiled at me, and Faith's whimpering burst into a full-blown cry when she saw me; she lifted her arms as if I were her savior, as if she could not bear another moment without me. I crossed the room and took her up, overwhelmed and humbled once more at how great was this child's affection for me. She calmed, clinging to me with her little legs, as happy now as she had been miserable a moment before. So changeable, so easily mended—a lack of complexity I envied.

"May we go out, Father?" Jude asked me eagerly.

I shook my head, watching her face fall in quick disappointment. "Not tonight. 'Tis too much gossip about today. 'Twill be better to stay in."

Charity turned slowly from the window. "Gossip," she said, her voice devoid of emotion or inflection. "I have watched them running about all day, chased by demons—"

"There are no demons here," I told her sharply.

"Aye, there are demons everywhere. Have you not told me—"

"I have not always been as wise as I should be."

She looked surprised, and then she frowned. "'Tis not your fault, Father. Have you not always said that the Devil could lead even the best of us astray?"

They were the wrong words for today, the wrong words given that I'd just come from hearing of Bridget Bishop's death. I was tired of fearing evil; I had had my fill of Satan and his minions, of grasping superstition that walked the streets like a young man searching for love, promiscuous and needy.

Suddenly I could no longer stand the thought of Charity staring out that window, seeing demons in every shadow. I could not bear the weight of terror that sat daily on her shoulders.

" 'Tis enough," I said, and then, without meaning it, my voice rose. " 'Tis enough!"

Charity's eyes went wide.

I handed Faith to Jude and said tersely, "Go downstairs. See if Goody Rich has a cake for her." Then when Jude paused, looking hesitantly at Charity, I said, "Go. I've things to discuss with your sister."

She went quickly, and I waited until the door closed behind her. I heard her steps down the stairs, and then I turned to Charity, who was watching me in pale fear, gripping the windowsill.

"I want the truth from you," I said to her.

"The—truth?"

"Aye. I'm surprised I never thought to ask it before now."

"I-I don't understand you, Father. I-I have ever told the . . . truth."

"Have you?" I took a step toward her, and she flattened herself against the window. "Is it the truth that sent Goody Bishop to the hangman two days ago, accused of witchcraft?"

Charity's face went white. "Goody Bishop?"

"Aye. They hanged her on Friday, leaving her husband a widower and her sons without a mother."

"She was a witch."

"Was she? I wonder."

"Aye, she was, Father; she was." Charity started toward me, her hands outstretched, a plea in her voice. "We saw her specter—"

"You have never met Bridget Bishop. For if you had, I would have punished you for going to her tavern."

She stopped midpace.

"Did you know her, Charity?"

"I-I knew of her."

"Had you ever seen her?"

Slowly she shook her head.

"Then how did you know this specter who afflicted you was her?"

"They—they told me it was." Her voice broke when she said it. She began to shake.

"Who told you?" I demanded.

"Annie," she said. "Annie Putnam. She said her . . . She said her father knew Goody Bishop."

"Did Annie see Goody Nurse as well? Who recognized her specter?"

Charity's shaking grew worse. She grabbed her skirt.

"Who recognized her specter?" I asked again.

"Did they . . . hang her?" she asked, in a voice so quiet I could barely hear her.

I did not answer. Once more, I said, "Who recognized Goody Nurse?"

"Annie did. Annie . . . did."

"And what of Susannah?"

Charity's eyes filled quickly with tears; her shaking grew so she could not hold herself still—this affliction I recognized. I knew its stages the way I knew each corner of this room, and so I expected it when she backed away from me, holding up her hands. She gasped, "Do not touch me. Leave me!"

I advanced on her. "Who do you see, Charity?"

" 'Tis her! 'Tis Susannah!"

"It cannot be Susannah. She is in prison. In chains. Her specter cannot get to you here."

She looked at me wildly, and then her gaze leaped to the fireplace. "Mama!"

"Your mother is with God," I said. "She is no servant of the Devil. She is with God."

Charity fell to her knees. Her eyes were wide and black; her mouth was a silent hollow of a scream.

I felt the familiar helplessness, the pull of compassion that made me want to go to her, to hold her. Yet I knew how she would push me away; I knew the strength of that unseen force. I could not fight it. And so I did the only other thing I could do, the one thing I had not yet tried. I went to the bench and sat down, and I said, "There is no Devil holding you, Charity. Your mother is dead, gone to God. There is no evil in this room but what you make."

She shuddered. "Leave me! Oh, do not hurt me so!"

"I have not left you," I said quietly, evenly. "Your mother's spirit is only a blessed one. There is no black man beside you, Charity. There is only me."

I did not know if I imagined that whatever force held her prisoner loosened its hold. I could not say for sure if the tension I read in her body eased even a little. But I felt I saw some answer in her eyes, and I said, "I have not left you, Charity, and I will not, no matter what has happened. You are my daughter. I have loved you since you were born. That will never change."

Then I rose and went to the window, leaving her to her labors on the floor while I stared out at the darkness growing below, the soft summer twilight. I listened to the sound of children, laughter, the creak of a well's rope, and the silence behind me. Then I realized—'twas no longer silent in the room, but there was the hushed sound of crying instead. I turned to see my daughter curled on the floor, her shoulders shaking in sobs, her face in her hands—just a young woman crying out her heart, all demons gone, the air quiet and soft.

Carefully I went to her and put my hand on her shoulder, and her sobbing became greater. "I am such a sinner," she hiccuped. "How can God love me now?"

"What happened, Charity? Tell me what happened."

She looked up slowly from her hands, staring at me through watery, red-rimmed eyes. Then, as if her words had been lodged in her throat and I had set them free, she said, "I did not mean for you to be accused. I did not mean it, I swear to you! When I thought you would die, I was ready to die myself. . . . I would have died, had they hanged you. 'Twas not what I intended. Not what any of us intended."

"What did you intend?"

"I meant only to save you. I was . . . I was so afraid. I have been so afraid. . . ."

I sat there, listening while she told me how my apprentice had seduced her and she had fallen in love with him. How Judith had been horrified at her sin and sent the boy away with five pounds and did not tell me what had happened between my daughter and Sam. Judith had strictly bade Charity to keep it silent as well. Charity had lived in terror that I would find out, and when Judith died, she lived in fear her mother's protection would cost Judith her rightful place with God. She feared that her sin, and the lie about it, kept her mother's spirit here on earth, in league with Satan. Charity believed Susannah had come at the black man's urging, and Susannah, with her London ways and bold honesty, had only made plain that fear.

She had looked for solace with her friends, and they had told fortunes with simple tricks that were in themselves a terrible sin, and that sin upon all her others cast her into an icy barrenness so great she could not see for the blackness of it. She had watched me fall, too, into the Devil's spell, even as she had fought to save me. And now she could no longer see her mother's spirit, and she was terrified as she had never been.

"I cannot see the end of it, Father," she said finally, burying her face once more in her hands. "I cannot see the end."

I could not bear to see her this way, nor to think of what Judith and I had done to this sensitive girl. I touched her hands, and when they fell away from her face, I told her, "God cannot punish you for feeling His torments so deeply, my dear. You are not bound for Hell. This will all end, and not in some eternal flame, I promise you."

"'Tis not a flame, Father," she said simply. "'Tis ice, and dark. 'Tis a great cold shadow over my heart."

"'Yea,'" I quoted softly, "'though I walk through the valley of the shadow of death, I will fear no evil, for Thou art with me.'"

She glanced away. "When I accused those in Salem, was I doing His work? Or the Devil's?"

I let out my breath in a long, slow hush. "I don't know. I ask you again: What did you intend when you called out those names, Charity? Was it the truth you said? Or was it all lies?"

She looked at the floor and went quiet—for so long, I thought she would not speak. Then, finally, she looked at me, and there was a bleak sadness in her eyes. "I don't know," she whispered. "I cannot say."

'Twas a truth I understood, though she could not have known it—she was still so young. What we believed, what we wished to believe, the uncertainty of experience . . . We were never far enough from our own minds to see things as they really were. What was dream, what was truth, and what was only rationalization . . .

'Twas sometimes safer left unknown.

Chapter 40

I MISSED THE TIDES OF SALEM. HERE, THERE WERE TIDES, YET . . . IN this town, those tides did not belong to me. I had grown with the rhythms of Salem. In my mind, I haunted its streets. I was a free man here, freer than I had ever been in Salem, and yet I felt as if my life was half undone, as if it had always been so, even before Judith had died, even when I had owned my own farm and made my living turning pieces to fit together for spinning wheels. There had ever been a hollowness I had tried to fill with God. 'Twas my sin that He would never be enough, that I was a man with flesh-and-blood desires who needed a partner for this journey. Would He condemn me for that when my hours on this earth were over? Or was this God I'd been taught to revere not the same God who'd laid out my life, who knew already the beginning and the end, and every path in between?

I needed devotion and time for those questions; I was too busy to do more than ask them now. My days were caught up in working at the mill, in caring for my daughters, who were the singular joy in my life. I had begun purchasing wood from the mill, and I borrowed what tools I could and bought others. In the middle of our lodging-house room, I began again to work the trade I loved. In the late evenings, I would sit by the light of a candle while I listened to the soft breathing of my daughters, and work the wood until it was smooth and shining. I fashioned a cupboard for our clothes, another chair, and then a piece to sell. As the summer went on, and the news of Salem drifted in through the open window, I worked my worries and my fears into pine and oak and thought of Susannah. I wondered if she was still alive, if she had died already—who knew what news tomorrow might bring? When I'd heard that they had convicted and hanged poor Rebecca Nurse, I was afraid; when a month later came the news that George Burroughs and John Proctor had been hanged as well, I began to dread the sunrise. Surely soon, they would turn to the confessed witches. But I heard nothing of those who had confessed; it seemed they had disappeared into the stone and mud of the prison. There was only word of more and more accusations, stretching to Andover and Topsfield, even to Boston, where incredibly, Captain John Alden, the son of our founder, was accused. I heard of farms neglected as relatives spent long hours visiting those in jail. Despair settled over all of New England; my own sent me often to the window, as Charity had gone before, staring out beyond the narrow roads and roofs of this town, out to sea, as if I could see through the miles.

"You are not well, Father," Charity told me one morning in late September, when she woke to find me sitting exhausted at the table, turning a spinning-wheel rod over and over in my hand. Even the sight of her, at peace now—as the stretch of days had made her—did not cheer me. On the pallet, little Faith roused and murmured, and Charity scooped her up and carried her to me.

"You do not sleep," she said. "You hardly eat. You put me in mind . . ."

Of myself. I heard the words she did not say, and I looked up and put aside the rod, taking Faith into my arms. "There is nothing to fear," I reassured her. "I am well enough."

Charity said nothing more, but went to slice bread for breakfast. She called to Jude to rouse herself—the sun was up, and she must go and fetch some water. Faith wiggled in my arms, and absently I set her down upon the floor to play with a ball of knotted string.

I heard Jude leave, and then her footsteps again, the splash of water on the stairs as she struggled with the bucket. She came inside breathlessly, saying, "They've hanged eight more. Goody Harrison told me at the well. They hanged Mary Easty too. And they pressed Goodman Corey to death because he would not plea."

"What of the confessed witches? Is there word of—" I paused, caught by the way Charity turned and stared at me. "What is it? Why do you look at me so?"

Her hand went to her mouth. "I did not understand before. . . . Oh, forgive me—"

"Forgive you for what?" I asked impatiently. "You speak in riddles."

" 'Tis . . . Susannah you ask after, isn't it, Father? The reason you are not truly with us is because . . . you wish to be with her."

I was startled to silence. Then I said, " 'Tis not so simple, Charity."

"Tell me, Father—do you love her?"

At the door, Jude went still. Faith chirped on, oblivious and innocent. I half expected Charity to fall into a fit, although she had not done such a thing for months now. I had kept from mentioning Susannah to her deliberately. She had been too fragile at first, and afterward, I grew accustomed to not saying Susannah's name, and as a habit grows worse the longer 'tis unchecked, the more I'd grown adept at avoiding the subject of her. Yet now I saw an understanding in Charity's eyes that I hadn't expected, and I realized— she would be leaving me soon, though she did not know it. Soon she would look up and see a boy standing in the sunlight, and he would take her breath, and she would go with him. She would become the wife of a fisherman, or a cobbler, or a shopkeeper. There were so few hours left now that belonged to me, and the truth was that when they had been mine alone, I had not been watching and so had let them slip away.

And now, 'twas a woman who watched me, and not a little girl, and I owed her the truth, however she might dislike it. "Aye," I said carefully. "I love her."

From where she stood, Jude gasped in delight. I could not take my eyes from my eldest daughter.

Slowly Charity sat upon the bench, folding her hands on the table before her. She bowed her head as if in prayer, and when she looked up at me again, I saw wisdom in her eyes—wisdom wrest from darkness.

"Then you must go to Salem, Father. Bring her back to us."

I did not go immediately; I could not. The terror that had all of New England in its grip was not yet faded—to go back meant my own death, in a town where death had become a daily affair, and I could not leave my girls to be certain orphans. I had no choice but to wait, past Michaelmas and into October, when the summer heat faded slowly, leaving behind colored leaves and morning chill.

Then one night, I woke to see the moon shining in through the little window, undulating like the reflection of sunlight on water, dappling the blankets that lay across myself and little Faith, who had curled into my side to sleep, her gentle breathing an easy counterpoint to my own. I heard the soft click of the door, and turned my head to see it open, strangely unafraid, unanxious, simply waiting.

'Twas a shadow that slipped into the room and then closed the door. And I knew, without knowing, who it was. I watched as she came into the moonlight, and I saw her—not as I'd last seen her, in a stained bodice and dun skirt that hung loose on her bony slenderness—wearing a bodice of blue with silver lace, cut in the fashion she liked, with slashes in the sleeves and a neckline cut to show her full breasts. She was laughing as she stepped into the room.

I sat up, the blankets pooling around my waist while the babe beside me slept on undisturbed. I reached out, and she came to me, and settled onto my lap, and I felt the warmth of her skin, her solidness. I felt the soft strands of her hair, which fell loose over her shoulders.

"There are days I hear the tides still," she said to me. "They seem to beat in my heart, and all I can do is think of you. Will there be tides where we are going?"

"There will be tides," I told her. "There are tides in New York." She laughed and answered, "Oh, Lucas, how happy we shall be there. Come for me now; I am anxious to see you. Come for me."

Then she was gone.

I woke, disoriented, distressed, reaching for her, crying out with a longing so sharp 'twas a pain. There was no moonlight playing across the blankets, only the darkness of a heavy-clouded night, but in the shadows I heard the tides she spoke of, Salem Harbor, the river snaking past the prison that came and went as regularly as the hours. I smelled the sea on the air, though the window was closed against it now that the weather had turned; I smelled the start of a storm.

'Twas time, I knew. Time to go for her.

When morning came, and with it the wind and the first lashing rain of the season, I kissed my daughters and gave them most of the money I'd saved, counseling them to be frugal, to mind Charity, to wait for me. They each of them laughed with joy when I kissed them good-bye and gave me their blessing and their love. I held those things with me like a shield against the rain as I went to fetch the stabled mule that Sam Nurse had loaned me. 'Twas there I heard the news: There had been a decision to try the confessed witches, but before trials had been scheduled, Increase Mather had spoken to a convocation of ministers in Boston and condemned the trials and the spectral evidence used against the accused. An anonymous letter had been circulating in Boston and Salem decrying the proceedings, raising skepticism and protest. The governor had ordered the trials postponed and no one else imprisoned.

The tide had turned.

I stood listening, thinking of my dream, of how Susannah had come to me, of her call. I heard again her words from long ago—*It has felt as if we have always belonged to each other.*

A year ago, I had set out in another storm, riding for this very woman through rain that lashed at me and wind that pushed at my back. These laws that God abided by, the ones He had created, did they include such a thing as destiny? Had there been a reason for my finding her, for every moment since, a plan laid down by God for my happiness, for a life fulfilled? Or had it merely been accidental, happenstance, a trick of fate—one road taken, another abandoned? Who had I been fighting all this time? The Devil, as I'd thought? Or God?

The answer lay with wiser men than I.

I turned the mule into the rain, and chose the road that led toward Massachusetts, and Salem Town, and called out for the animal to hurry, to hurry. I had lingered too long already.

She would be waiting.

Author's Note

Except for the Fowler family, and their neighbors the Penneys, most of the characters in this novel are real. Because this is a work of fiction, their dialogue and their reactions to the incidents in the novel are imagined, based on my readings of seventeenth-century transcripts and other material.

Susannah Morrow's experiences as an accused witch are based on the experiences of several real-life accused witches, including Martha Corey, Susannah Martin, and Bridget Bishop. In reality, Martha Corey was the fourth witch to be accused. She was tested at the Putnam household, as Susannah is in the novel, and examined and arrested a week later.

By October 1692, nineteen men and women had been hanged as witches, one man pressed to death, and hundreds more imprisoned and/or accused. Estates had been seized by the crown upon the arrest of many of the accused in anticipation of a guilty verdict; children were left behind to fend for themselves or be cared for by neighbors; property was destroyed. By the time the panic ended, the social and economic fabric of Salem Village and its environs had been shredded. Those who had been imprisoned were ordered released in May of 1693, but only after they had paid the bills they'd incurred in prison for food and lodging. For many, this was an impossible debt to repay. Their farms had been left fallow for a year, their children were beggars, and their relatives were already drained financially from attempts to free them. Though many families immediately began petitioning for restitution, it was not until 1710 that the General Court passed an act reversing the convictions (but only for those whose families had specifically petitioned the court), and not until December of 1711 that it granted some restitution to petitioning families.

Samuel Parris remained the pastor of Salem Village. In 1694, he read a statement in meeting where he admitted giving too much weight to spectral evidence. He was ousted from the village in 1697 and replaced by Joseph Green, who did much to mend the rifts caused by his predecessor.

In 1697, Samuel Sewall publicly confessed his guilt over his part as a judge in the trials of the accused—one of the only expressions of guilt or error made by any of those involved in the trials.

The girls of Salem Village, for the most part, disappeared from public records, and little is known of what happened to them.

In 1706, Ann Putnam Jr. apologized publicly for her actions.

She was the only one of the girls to do so.